MEET ME AGAIN ONE DAY

MEET ME
BOOK 2

VERONICA WYNNE

Copyright © 2024 by Veronica Wynne

Published by Anxiety Brain, LLC

Edited by My Brother's Editor

Cover design by Forever Star Cover Design (formerly Kylah Cover Designs) and Amber Thoma

Chapter images by Rebekah Sinclair

All rights reserved.

This book is a work of fiction. Names, characters, places, and incidents are the products of the author's anxiety-riddled brain or are used fictitiously. Any resemblance to actual persons, living or dead, businesses, companies, events or locales is entirely coincidental.

No part of this book may be reproduced in any form or by any electronic or mechanical means, including information storage and retrieval systems, without written permission from the author, except for the use of brief quotations in a book review.

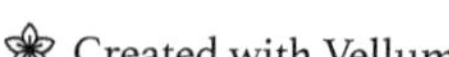 Created with Vellum

For all the women who've been told that they'd change their mind one day... when they met the right person, or they fell in love, or they captured a unicorn under a fucking rainbow just after a summer rain.

It's okay to be who you are. Someone will love you for it.

Everyone who doesn't... well, they can find less.

CONTENTS

AUTHOR'S NOTE

This is primarily a note to my real-life family. I am so grateful to you for supporting me—and I also think there's something you should know before you read this one.

This book is steamier than the first one. I'm not sorry about that...just so we're clear. But if you're uncomfortable with that, skip or skim the following sections:

- Chapter 7 after they leave the restaurant
- Chapter 12 after the page break
- Chapter 15 after they leave the party
- Chapter 32...in its entirety
- Chapter 36 after their conversation
- Most of Chapter 37

TRIGGER WARNINGS

Dear reader, I am a fan of trigger warnings—mostly because I have some triggers, myself. This one may not be as "triggery" as *Meet Me at Home*, but who am I to say what's triggering for you and what isn't. If you don't need to know the potential triggers, you can ignore this page, but I want them to be here for those who do.

Meet Me Again One Day is a contemporary romance that discusses heavy topics, including the death of a family member (off page), a life-threatening medical event, and complex familial relationships. Please take care of yourselves.

PLAYLIST

Galway Girl - Ed Sheeran
Someone You Loved - Lewis Capaldi
champagne problems - Taylor Swift
Not The Sun - Morgan St. Jean
Last Night - Morgan Wallen
exile - Taylor Swift feat. Bon Iver
'tis the damn season - Taylor Swift
With Or Without You - U2
Atlantis - Seafret
Is it Just Me? - Emily Burns and JP Cooper
Fine - Kyle Hume
A Little Bit Yours - JP Saxe
Please Don't Be - Hazlett
you broke me first - Tate McRae
Penthouse (Healed Version) - Live - Kelsea Ballerini
The Alcott (feat. Taylor Swift) - The National, Taylor Swift
Wouldn't Come Back - Trousdale
I Loved You Then (And I Love You Still) - Woodlock
Locksmith - Sadie Jean
marjorie - Taylor Swift

The Last Time (feat. Gary Lightbody of Snow Patrol)
(Taylor's Version) by Taylor Swift, Gary Lightbody
Just Yet - BIZZY
White Flag - Dido
I'd Run to You - CJ Starnes
Dancing In The Dark - biz colletti
mine - Kelly Clarkson
Northern Attitude (with Hozier) - Noah Kahan, Hozier
The View Between Villages - Extended - Noah Kahan
this is me trying - Taylor Swift
Somewhere Only We Know - Keane
Intrusive Thoughts - Natalie Jane
Handle - Emily Hackett
Please Forgive Me - David Gray
Lego House - Ed Sheeran
Everlong (Acoustic) - Foo Fighters
Men On The Moon - Chelsea Cutler
Skin and Bones - David Kushner
Stand Inside Your Love - Smashing Pumpkins

You can listen to the playlist on Spotify by scanning the QR
code with your smartphone's camera.

CHAPTER 1
GAS STATION BRO
MAGGIE

Galway Girl - Ed Sheeran
June, Five Years Prior

"Excuse me, miss..." A voice I don't recognize reaches me, but I ignore it because I'm not in the habit of talking to men I don't know. Especially if they feel so entitled to speak to me that they're interrupting me.

The actual audacity.

"Miss?" he calls again.

I sigh and straighten, resigned to the fact that he is actually talking to me and not someone else.

When I look to my left, I find a man who's probably in his midtwenties, maybe six feet tall, wearing a ball cap (backward, for anyone wondering), watching me with curious milk chocolate eyes.

Eyeing him skeptically, I place an agitated hand on my hip, knowing damn well that type of body language won't leave room for the *damsel in distress* vibe. I allow my eyes to skim up and down his body.

If I were a man—this dude, perhaps—I'd think that a person looking at me like this was checking me out. But I'm not a man. I'm a woman. And if you're a woman, you know that I'm not checking him out (although, to be fair...he *is* attractive).

No, if you're a woman, you know that I'm memorizing his notable features and what he's wearing.

Plain black T-shirt. Blue jeans. Black Chucks. Gray ball cap with the Major League Baseball logo on the back. The fitted kind —not adjustable. Brown eyes. Brown hair peeking out of the bottom of the cap. Athletic build, but not jacked.

You know...just in case.

I can't see the team logo since the cap is backward, but I'm willing to bet it's the local team. The colors look like they work.

Perhaps because I still haven't said anything, and now I'm just staring at him, he speaks again.

"Are you all right? Do you need help?"

I blink at him. "What makes you think I need help?"

He blinks back. "Well, you're standing in front of a car with the hood up and jumper cables on the ground...it looks like you might need a jump, and I was wondering if you'd like help with that."

I narrow my eyes at him. I can't argue with his logic, even if he's incorrect.

I hum through pursed lips before I respond. "Well, I think that's a fair assessment, but you're wrong."

I turn back to the car and release the hood, letting it fall closed with a heavy thud. Using the classic blue paper towel that every single gas station keeps by the pumps, I wipe the dirt and grime off my hands. I'm not going to pick up the cables off the ground just yet. Bending over would put me in a more vulnerable position. Instead, I lean against the car and fold my arms over my chest.

Now, under normal circumstances, I'd expect a man to check out my rack. I'm fully aware that I have great tits, and this person is a red-blooded man. Assuming he's interested in women, he'd have to be made of stone to not notice the way my arms push my breasts up in this position.

If I'm being honest, I'm doing it on purpose. It's something I do to test a man's intentions. Sometimes, it's exactly what I'm looking for—an attractive man's attention. Other times, that attention is exactly what I'm *not* looking for. Either way, this tells me what my next steps should be.

And also, I like my tits, and I'm not afraid of cleavage. Most of my wardrobe shows it off at least a little bit.

Like I said, under normal circumstances, a dude checks out my rack real quick.

But this dude? His gaze doesn't dip. His eyes stay steady on mine, except for one single second when they flick to the jumper cables on the ground and the closed hood of the car behind me.

"Okay. That's fine. So you're good?" he asks, eyes jumping back up to mine again, completely skipping over my tits.

I'm considering my response when a familiar voice cuts in.

"She's good."

My favorite brother, Nick, comes to stand next to me, two bottles of Diet Coke and a can of Pringles in his hands.

I love my brother more than almost anything in this world. He's a good dude. Solid to his core.

He's always been there for me. My whole entire life.

He's the only one in our family who seems to accept me

for who I am. The only one who doesn't try to change me to fit their mold—their Catholic, getting married early, and popping out babies mold.

I'm more of a free spirit. One who will work hard, travel the world, and never, *ever* get married. And no, I won't change my mind. I just don't want to be married. And Nick is the only one who accepts this about me.

We have a bunch of siblings, but this one...he's the best. I don't know what I'd do without him.

And right now, he's asserting some male dominance over this random dude who I'm sure he perceives as bothering his baby sister.

He eyes the Hot Stranger, same green eyes as mine flicking over his person before returning to mine. "You okay?"

I nod once and smile. "Sure am."

"Good."

He hands me the Diet Coke bottles and the Pringles can, then goes to the front of the car and picks up the jumper cables, coiling them back up, popping the trunk, and placing them back where they belong.

"We were actually helping someone else who needed a jump. And then I checked the fluid levels," I tell Hot Stranger.

His brown eyes had wandered to my brother as he worked, but when I start speaking, they snap back to me.

And yes...they return to my face. Not my tits.

Fascinating.

My head tilts with curiosity as I assess him, but he's not giving anything away.

And his eyes remain on mine.

Curiouser and curiouser.

Just an innocent person trying to be helpful. What a concept.

"Kind of you to check in," I concede. "But I'm good."

He seems to think about that for a moment before nodding. "Good."

With one last glance toward Nick, who is now taking one of the Diet Coke bottles from my hands and swiping the Pringles can as an afterthought, he takes a step backward.

"Have a good night."

"You, too." I nod.

And then Hot Stranger turns around. I watch him walk back to his car—a dark gray Honda Civic hatchback—slide into the driver's seat, and maneuver out of the gas station parking lot. I was right about the ball cap. He roots for the home team.

"You flirting with random gas station bros now?" Nick teases me.

"Awwww, he wasn't so bad. Just checking to see if I was okay." I laugh, moving away from the passenger side of the car so Nick can get in. I get my keys out of my jacket pocket and climb into the driver's seat. "His assessment was reasonable. A person standing alone by their car, hood up, jumper cables on the ground."

Nick's eyes slide over to me, skepticism clear on his face.

"Stop it," I say with an eye roll. "He wasn't creepy. He didn't even stare at my chest."

Nick groans, squeezing his eyes shut. "Gross."

I can't help but laugh. This dude...so in love with his girlfriend that he's going to propose to her soon, and I'm sure they're fucking like rabbits, but he can't stomach the thought of a stranger noticing my (awesome) rack.

Goddamn patriarchy.

I also can't help but poke the bear.

"If you got it, flaunt it, you know?"

He groans again, dragging his hands down his face.

I hide my laughter by turning the key in the ignition, the engine roaring to life. I have a gorgeous Mustang that my uncle helped me restore. My mom's older brother is a mechanic and was more than happy to offer his assistance when I wanted a car at age sixteen but could only afford this beaten-up old junker.

I'm not a mechanic, and I certainly don't pretend to be, but I've always been fascinated by the way things are put together. While that experience didn't make me want to work on cars for a living, it did throw me deeper into my obsession with building things, which is how I became an architect.

Actually, that's why I'm hanging out with Nick tonight. He wanted to take me out to celebrate the fact that I'm an official architect now. I finished my architectural experience program with the firm I've been with for the past three years and just today got word that I passed all my exams. No more internships for me. I'm the real deal.

Nick and I didn't do anything particularly special—we don't have to. He took me to our favorite Irish pub for pints and boxty. It's where he and I go to celebrate things.

"What are you doing this weekend?" he asks, looking up at me from his phone. I have no doubts he was texting Kate to let her know he's on his way home.

"Going out with the girls tomorrow night to celebrate."

I only have a handful of female friends. Given my chosen field and growing up with so many brothers, it was only natural for me to end up with a lot of guy friends. But they're not who I want to go out with for a night of dancing.

Nick's brow furrows. "Who are *the girls*?"

I pull out of the parking lot with a smirk on my face.

"Mae, Jen, and Kelsie."

Architecture is still pretty male-dominated, but the ladies are coming in hot. There were about five women in my class, and we mostly stuck together—less of a friendship circle and more like an alliance. We were a united front against misogyny and bullshit. We always had each other's backs, even if we weren't spending time together outside of coursework.

But over time, I grew pretty close to a couple of them, and those two are my ride-or-dies. They came into town specifically so we could go out to celebrate. They'll crash at my place and head back out the next day.

We're going out with a friend from work, Kelsie, who's been an architect at the firm for a couple of years now. We're alumni of the same university, though we didn't know each other when we were there.

"You're going to be careful?"

I roll my eyes and glare at him from the corner of my eye.

"As careful as we can be, yes. We'll watch our drinks and make sure we all leave together, but instead of telling me to be careful, you should really be telling men not to assault women."

His head falls back onto the headrest, eyes closed, hands in the air. "Maggie, I don't need a feminist rant right now. I'm aware of the position modern society puts women in. That doesn't mean I'm going to be less worried about my baby sister, nor does it mean I won't teach my own son how to treat women. Both can be true—I can be worried about you and also promise to do better with the next generation."

I glance at him and see him lift his head. His arms fall to his legs and his shoulders droop.

"Maggie, I'm only asking because I love you. I'm not trying to be patronizing."

I take a deep breath and consider his words. I know he's coming from a good place. I'm just so sick of being told to "be careful" when there's not a hell of a lot I can do about this kind of stuff.

While he might sound annoying right now (trust me, he is), he says it with love.

"You know damn well I'll be careful," I concede quietly.

He seems to sigh a breath of relief and I choose to let it go.

But I also make a mental note to tell Kate so she gives him hell.

∼

Mae and Jen got here a couple of hours ago. We've been drinking champagne at my place while getting ready to go out. The music is happy. The smiles are massive. The dresses are skimpy.

Jen zips my dress up and swats at my ass. "You look gorgeous, babe."

I wink at her in the mirror. She expertly applied a smokey eye for me. I'm more minimalist in my makeup approach, but Jen is all about getting dolled up. I could watch YouTube tutorials for days and still not make my face look like this. She also tamed my curls into something resembling "controlled," and they look pretty good, I think. I'm feelin' good. Like it will be a good night.

Mae looks up at us from her spot on my bed. She's bent over, slipping her heels on.

"*Daaaaaamn*, girl. You look like you just landed your dream job."

I primp my hair and shimmy my shoulders to a sound-track of whoops and hollers from my ladies.

"All right, babes, I'm ordering the Uber."

I slip on my favorite black heels with the bow on the back and grab my clutch. When I stand to my fashion-enhanced full height, I top off at five-foot-seven. I'm as tall as Jen flat-footed. Mae is wearing slightly shorter heels, so we're about the same height.

"Where to first?" Mae asks.

"Dinner. We're too old to be drinking on an empty stomach," Jen replies.

"We're not old," I protest.

Jen rolls her eyes. "We're not in college anymore, ladies. Let's put something in our bellies."

As much as I hate to admit it, Jen is right. Dinner is a good idea. We meet Kelsie at my favorite pizza place and split a large between the four of us. After, we head to a club downtown that has become a regular stop when they visit. We dance and laugh and sing (badly) at the top of our lungs.

We're all getting sweaty, and I suddenly can't remember the last time I had a glass of water, so I volunteer as tribute.

I make my way through the crowd to the bar and shout my need for water to the bartender at the first opportunity. While she's filling the plastic cups and shoving straws into them, I feel someone lean against the bar next to me. I ignore them, grabbing a coaster and fanning my flushed face with it.

"Excuse me, miss..."

I freeze immediately. That voice sounds awfully familiar. And recently familiar. I can feel his gaze on me—and if I'm right about the source of the voice, assessing brown eyes like a weight on the side of my face.

"Miss?" I can hear the smile in his voice as he begins this

conversation the same way the one from yesterday began. I find it endearing, but I don't want him to know that, so I force my mouth into a straight line and lift my chin.

Slowly, I turn to face him.

Hot Stranger is standing right next to me.

I was right about the smile. It's soft—more in his eyes than on his mouth.

Snark is my default, and it certainly won't fail me now.

"So, what? You stalking me now?"

He huffs a laugh, making his smile wider, and pairs it with a good-natured eye roll.

"I can't stalk you if I don't even know your name."

"Seems to me a dedicated stalker would have figured it out," I shoot back, wanting to see what he comes back with. He's cute, and he seems to be game for joking around with me.

"Well, you've got me there. As it turns out, I'm not actually stalking you." His head tilts as his eyes roam over my face, pausing for just a second on my mouth before meeting my gaze again. "But I saw you again...I couldn't not come over and say hi."

I hum noncommittally.

"Can I buy you a drink, stranger?"

Of course, that's the moment the bartender sets four plastic cups of cold water in front of me. I smile at her in thanks before she turns her head to Hot Stranger and tips her chin up in question.

He holds up his index finger and points to my water. The bartender pulls another plastic cup out and starts filling it for him.

It's my turn to tilt my head in assessment. "Didn't you just offer to buy me a drink, and now you're not getting one for yourself?"

"Yeah, but I'm driving tonight. I had two. It's water for me from now on."

"How responsible."

I shouldn't really be impressed by his decision to not drive drunk. That should be the norm, right? We should expect people to make the right decision there.

This just goes to show you that the bar is on the floor and the exact reason I'm happy to be single.

The bartender slides the cup across the bar, and he digs his hand into his back pocket to get his wallet. Despite the fact that he ordered free water, he still leaves a tip.

Fascinating.

I watch him bring the cup to his mouth, and the clear liquid slip through his parted lips, and for whatever fucking reason, it makes me think dirty things. It doesn't help matters when he swallows and licks his lips.

I return to my task of fanning my face with the coaster, hoping he doesn't know I've been ogling him like a creeper.

"You want to get some air?" he asks. "There's a patio upstairs."

I look back to the dance floor to look for my ladies. Mae and Jen are dancing with a couple of guys, and it looks like Kelsie found a smokin' hot femme to dance with, but I'm not going to disappear without telling them what's going on.

"Sure...but I need to deliver these waters. I'll be right back."

"You gonna disappear on me?" His eyes are dancing with amusement, but it's a genuine question.

I smirk. "I guess you'll have to wait around and find out."

I saunter away from him, dodging dancing bodies and flailing arms, making my way to our group. When I reach them, they take their waters from my hands carefully, so we don't spill anything.

"I'm gonna go get some air," I shout over the music into Mae's ear, stopping her from turning back to the dude she's dancing with.

She looks at me with concern.

"I'm fine. Just hot."

Her eyes narrow, but she slides the straw between her teeth and drinks.

I roll my own eyes in response. "I'll be with the guy standing at the bar wearing a dark T-shirt and jeans."

She glances over my shoulder and tilts her head, eyes assessing. They travel up and down, like they're memorizing his appearance before flicking back to me.

"If I don't see you back here within the hour, I'll look for you." She lifts her wrist and sets an alarm on her smartwatch. "Never go to a second location," she advises.

"Yes, ma'am."

Her lips purse in irritation, but I wink at her and spin back around to make my way back to Hot Stranger.

Holy shit, I still don't know his name.

Nick's voice is irate in my mind.

I march back up to Hot Stranger and look up into his beautiful brown eyes.

"I'm not in the habit of going to second locations with strangers."

He smiles. It's arresting. I feel my facial muscles relax as I stare at it.

"Well, my name is Ethan." He offers his right hand for a shake. "And I feel inclined to point out that the patio upstairs is still the same location. Just a different floor."

I need to speak words. His hand is suspended between our bodies. Something about him is giving me a feeling in the pit of my stomach. Like this moment is powerful. Like it could change my life.

And the adventurous side of me is *just* interested enough to dive in headfirst.

"I'm Maggie." I place my right hand against his, which engulfs mine, and I swear something shoots up my arm.

His eyes soften with a smile. "Maggie," he repeats, his voice filled with something like reverence. "The pleasure is all mine."

CHAPTER 2
NOT SURE WHAT GAVE YOU THAT IDEA
MAGGIE

Someone You Loved - Lewis Capaldi
June, Present Day

City lights are one of my favorite things in the world. I know a lot of people prefer a starry sky, the lack of industry and human intervention—it provides a lot of quiet. It gives them a sense of peace for a while. But me? I love the lights.

I think it has something to do with knowing that people are out there trying to make their dreams come true.

That office building with the lights still on is full of people working hard to try and get a promotion. Or cleaning crews working to put food on the table. Or maybe someone working late because they're working through grief.

Not that I'd know anything about that.

It's people doing things with their lives. Good things. Probably also some bad things. But I prefer to look at the good things.

My brother Nick taught me to focus on the good things.

That's really what I'm doing right now, while I stand in front of this giant window, whiskey in hand, staring at the glowing city, surrounded by a pre-dusk, colorful sky. The pinks and blues fade together like a painting. All around me, coworkers are schmoozing with one another, kissing executive ass, and generally attempting to brown-nose their way into promotions and special projects.

I don't like many of them, if I'm being honest.

Being one of the few women in architecture means I'm constantly clenching my jaw to keep it from dropping during meetings when they don't even try to hide their false praise of our boss's bosses.

Sucking up to people is a waste of time. I'm all for being professional and polite (to a degree), but at *no* point will I be sinking to the levels these jackals are willing to lower themselves to. Jesus, have some pride.

Of course, this kind of attitude means that sometimes, people think I'm a bitch. Occasionally, they even say it to my face.

Frankly, I feel sorry for them. Feeling threatened by a curly-haired, five-foot-three woman who's younger than them has to be tough on their already-fragile ego. And that's a *them* problem. Not a *me* problem.

The thing is, I've been the odd woman out my whole life. I'm the black sheep of my family, the least traditional one in my friend group, and the nerdy girl in school from start to finish. I've always been different. Work is just another place where I'm different. I don't let it bother me, but *they* bother me.

One of the particularly obnoxious ones laughs far too loudly, cutting into the serene moment I'm sharing with the city lights. I turn my head in a manner that I don't even care is inconspicuous or obvious and stare at him. Some C-level executive is beaming at this twatwaffle, happy to have told a joke someone is laughing at.

I down the rest of my whiskey, allowing for an eye roll as I turn back to look at the city lights one more time, then make my way over to the bar for a refill.

Setting my glass on the bar with a kind smile, the bartender—a blonde in her twenties who, I'm positive, has been hit on by every single asshole at this party—takes it from me. She sets a clean glass on the bar and grabs a bottle. She knows what I'm drinking. I've already chatted with her tonight.

Knowing the level of bullshit she's likely put up with from these people, I slide some cash across the bar as she slides the whiskey toward me.

"Thank you," I tell her.

"Thank *you*," she reciprocates, inconspicuously taking the bills and shoving them in her pocket.

"Let me know if you need anything." I dart my eyes toward the obnoxious assholes swarming the executives.

She doesn't let her eyes follow mine, but I see understanding in her expression.

"Thanks," she says with a smirk.

I wink before I turn to leave, intending to find some appetizers to graze on, but my eyes land on a man in his late fifties walking toward me. It's true that I can't stand many of my coworkers, but this one...this one, I adore.

Marvin James is the only reason I'm still at this firm. He hired me for an apprenticeship and then a real job once I was finished with that. He's been a fierce advocate for me over the past few years. He's tough, but compassionate. Demanding, but kind. Talented in a way that turns many people into arrogant pricks—but not Marv. He's still humble, even nearing retirement, and he's more than willing to share his experience and expertise with those who show promise.

I admire the hell out of him.

"Maggie," he greets me as he gets close enough for me to hear. "Come here, I want to show you something." His head jerks toward his office.

I'm happy to follow him, especially if it means I can get away from the kiss-asses across the room.

We walk down the hallway toward his office, farther away from the noise of the party.

Marv's office is smaller than you might expect from someone in his position. For all the times he's been promoted at this firm, he wanted to keep the same office. It's not flashy, but it has a large window overlooking the city and is big enough for a desk, a couple of cushy chairs, and cabinets full of thousands of drawings and prints he's made over the course of his career.

I love his office. It feels like a second home to me. I've spent hours in here talking to Marv in one of these comfy chairs, listening to funny stories about previous clients and ridiculous requests. He's never been shy about his work—he's often let me sit on the floor, pouring over renderings from all over the world. He's worked on so many projects, he can always find an example of something useful for research. At the start of new projects, it's not unheard of for him to go to a meeting and find me in the same spot on the floor with a sketchbook full of notes and his designs spread out in front of me.

Marv feels like an uncle in some ways but like a mentor in all professional ways.

"Shut that door behind you, will ya? And have a seat," he says, motioning to the chairs in front of his desk.

I do as I'm told, shutting the door and taking a seat in my favorite of the two chairs.

"Ahh. Here we go." He turns some drawings around toward me. "Look at this."

I peer across the desk at plans for a large building, but which large building, I'm unsure. "What am I looking at?"

"*These* are the preliminary drawings for the building in Paris." He raises his eyebrows as if he's clueing me in on a secret.

I blink twice. "It looks like a great start."

"It is," he confirms. "And *you* would be great on this project."

I blink again.

"You *are* putting your name in the hat...aren't you?"

"I was thinking about it," I hedge.

The truth is, I've been thinking about it *a lot*. Like, all the time. I want to be on that project. But it also involves being an ocean away from my family—my life—for months. Maybe a year.

I absolutely want the opportunity. But my life isn't *only* mine at this point. I have to think about other people. So I haven't actually decided to submit my name yet.

"Maggie, there's really nothing to think about," Marv continues. "This is the opportunity of a lifetime. You could put your name on the Paris cityscape."

I roll my eyes and smirk. "Marv, it wouldn't be my name."

"It might not be at the top of the list," he concedes. "But it *would* be on the list." His eyes are practically glittering with excitement.

Marv is being overly generous with this description. Since our firm will be considered managing architects on this project, we'll be at the bottom of the list. The French firm will provide the architects of record, and we'll be part of their team.

I give him a pointed look, which he returns with an unamused expression.

I lean back in the chair I could pick out blindfolded by the feel alone. It hugs my back, cutting off around my shoulder blades. The well-worn leather is cool beneath my legs. I take a sip of my drink before I respond.

"It's a fantastic opportunity."

"...that you will take, yes?" He nods pointedly.

I smile. "I would like to take it. I need to talk to Ethan about it."

"You don't really need your husband's permission here, do you? This isn't 1950."

"He's not my husband," I clarify. "And no, I don't need his permission, but we're in a committed relationship, and I think it's fair to discuss it with him before agreeing to throw myself in the ring."

Marv studies me for a moment, eyes clear and assessing. "Fair enough," he finally responds. "But if he says no, call me, and I'll talk some sense into him."

I can't help the chuckle that escapes my mouth. "That won't be necessary."

"You just let me know."

He's only half-joking.

I meet his gaze for a brief moment before looking back at the drawings. "Thanks, Marv."

Marv talks to me for a few more minutes about the Paris plans before someone knocks on his door, beckoning him back to the party to make a toast.

We walk back together, him muttering under his breath about bureaucratic bullshit while I try to keep my laughter inside.

He gives his toast and charms the crap out of the room. I'm listening, I swear, but I'm also counting down the minutes until I can finally go home to Ethan.

Our fifth anniversary passed this week rather unceremoniously. We acknowledged it, of course, but it was the middle of the week, and we were both rather busy with work. It made more sense to wait for the weekend to celebrate—and that's what we're doing tonight. Ethan picked up champagne, and we're ordering carryout from our favorite place. We're both at a place in our lives where we'd rather be at home in comfortable clothes than dressed to the nines in a restaurant paying fifteen dollars for cocktails.

You might say we're old, and I don't fucking care. I can make a cocktail cheaper at home and do it in leggings with my hair in a messy bun *after* my face has been scrubbed clean and refreshed with my favorite moisturizer.

So we'll hang out together. Maybe watch a movie. Maybe skip everything and rip each other's clothes off before we even make it to our bed. Never know. We'll see.

I just have to make it to seven o'clock.

WHEN I FINALLY GET HOME, it's seven-thirty. As I approach the door, my feet are aching in my heels, but the soft music I hear coming from our apartment revives me a bit.

Ethan is...Ethan.

It's hard to even describe how much he means to me at this point. Over these five years together, Ethan has seen me through some of the darkest times of my life. He's helped me get through the sudden death of my brother, professional setbacks, and untenable expectations from my family.

He's kind and funny and so very sweet. (Except when I don't want him to be, if you catch my drift.)

He's the love of my life.

And while I know my views on life and relationships aren't traditional, he accepts me for who I am and loves me regardless.

And maybe I'll also get the opportunity of a lifetime in Paris soon. I can't wait to talk to Ethan about it. I know he'll be supportive. I'm sure he'll be sad I'll be gone for a few months, but I'm confident we'll survive. That we'll get through it and be stronger in the end.

I have faith in our relationship and in my ambition—and I'm certain Ethan feels the same way.

My life is very nearly perfect, and I feel grateful. My sisters would say they're *blessed*. I can't help but smirk at finding something in common between us—such different people somehow born into the same family.

I unlock the apartment door and push it open. The music gets louder but still acceptably low for conversation. Dropping my keys on the tiny table by the door, I call out to Ethan to let him know I'm home.

"Hi!" I hear him call from a different room.

I set my bag down against the wall and check my hair in the mirror. It's not great, but my wild curls are still mostly tamed.

Maggie: 1

Humidity: 0

When I turn the corner, a beautiful bouquet of roses is waiting for me on the table next to champagne in an ice bucket, and my Ethan, wearing a dark-blue button-down shirt, charcoal pants, and a massive smile.

"Look how sweet you are..." I croon, wrapping my arms around his neck.

"Happy anniversary, baby," he says, pulling me flush against his body and kissing me.

I feel all the tension melt from my body. The annoyance of my coworkers is gone. My mind is completely focused on Ethan.

"Happy anniversary," I whisper as he pulls back.

He smirks and kisses me one more time before reaching for the champagne.

"I already got the food. Picked it up on my way home. And this should be chilled by now." He picks up the bottle and begins ripping off the foil to open it. "How was the party?"

I groan. "It was fine. You know I hate hanging out with those dudes. But it wasn't all bad." I want to tell him about putting my name in the hat for Paris, but I'll do it later tonight. I don't want it to overshadow whatever he apparently has planned.

"I'm glad it wasn't terrible." He gets the cork out with a pop and pours glasses for both of us.

When he hands me one of the flutes, I can see mischief in his eyes.

"What's going on with you?" I ask in a teasing tone.

He looks at the ground, and I swear his face looks a little flushed. "Nothing, I'm just..." He huffs a laugh before meeting my gaze again. "I'm just happy."

"Me too." I smile, leaning in to kiss him again.

Ethan takes a deep breath and raises his glass in the narrow space between our bodies. "To you," he toasts.

"To us, babe."

We tap our glasses and sip our champagne with goofy grins on our faces. The bubbles are delicious. And I'm deliriously happy with this man.

"Hmm..." he hums as he swallows, looking up toward the source of the music. "Do you remember this song?"

"Of course I do. I love this song."

He takes my glass and sets both of them on the table, then takes my hand and pulls me toward the music.

Wrapping one arm around my waist and taking my other hand in his, he starts slow dancing with me.

"But do you remember where we heard it the first time?"

I smile. "Of course I do."

We were on the rooftop deck at the club the first night we hung out. The vibe was more chill up there. The club music wasn't being pumped through those speakers. It was meant to be a place to take a break from the loud thumping music, so they were playing regular pop stuff at a reasonable volume. We'd talked for a while until Mae came barging through the door looking for me, Jen hot on her heels. When they found me, I was laughing my ass off with Ethan. I had no idea a full hour had passed, and they were worried.

Upon finding out I was okay, they both narrowed their eyes at Ethan and then headed to the rooftop bar for more water.

I see his eyes glimmer with unmistakable love, and I know he's remembering that night, too.

"I never would have thought that night that we'd end up here...five years later," he says.

"Me either. You were just some gas station bro."

He laughs. "Gas station bro?"

"That's what Nick called you when we got in the car. He asked me if I was flirting with gas station bros now."

My chest squeezes with the familiar pain I've grown accustomed to whenever I think about my brother. I miss him all the time. The gaping hole his death left in my chest and in my life will never be filled.

Ethan pulls me closer and kisses my forehead, like he knows what I'm thinking. And he probably does after five years.

"I'm glad you agreed to give this gas station bro a chance."

"Me, too."

Some expression passes over his face, but he looks down, and I can't decipher it.

"These past five years have been the best of my life, Maggie."

He seems like he has something to say and is nervous for whatever reason, so I pull our linked hands to my mouth and kiss his fingers to keep from the feeling that I need to say something.

I can't exactly return the sentiment. They really haven't been a great five years, but they would have been far worse if I didn't have him. So I just wait patiently for him to continue. When he does, he meets my eyes again, and I can see the nerves. It's confusing, to be honest. What could he possibly be nervous about around me?

"I can't really pinpoint the moment I knew I loved you. It just happened...it was gradual. Just one day, I couldn't imagine my life without you. And then I realized what this... warm feeling was that I had in my chest all the time. I was so nervous to tell you, but when I did, I realized I had no reason to be because you loved me, too."

I smile at the memory. At the way his hands shook. At the way his eyes were so open and hopeful.

"I love you more today than I did back then, Mags. I love how sarcastic you are. How funny. How you know how to diffuse any uncomfortable situation. How you support me. How you always have my back. You're the greatest thing that's ever happened to me."

"Ethan…" I whisper through a throat thick with emotion. Tears are blurring my vision, and I'm already sniffing.

He takes my hand from the nape of his neck and lets go of my right hand, which I promptly use to dab at my face.

When my vision is cleared enough to see him again, he's kneeling in front of me.

On just *one* knee.

The tears stop immediately, and my chest seizes.

"Ethan…"

"Maggie, I'm in love with you. I've been in love with you for five years, and I'm going to love you for the rest of my life. I want you by my side through anything and everything —thick and thin, sickness and health, and all that."

All the breath has left my body, and I'm sure I'm staring at him with wide eyes and a gaping mouth as he lifts his left hand to hold up a ring.

"Margaret Helen Rafferty, will you marry me?"

I blink at him.

Holy shit, what is happening?

I blink some more. Then swallow.

I look from the ring to his right hand holding my left, then to his knee on the floor and then up to his eyes— earnest and beautiful and hopeful—and I feel my chest crack a little.

"No."

CHAPTER 3
WHAT THE ACTUAL FUCK
MAGGIE

champagne problems - Taylor Swift

Ethan is blinking repeatedly as he stares up at me. He shakes his head, like he's trying to shake out the cobwebs. "No?"

My eyes cut involuntarily back to the gorgeous diamond ring, but I force them back to his face. "No..." I repeat.

He's quiet for a moment, still blinking, a frown forming on his face. "That...isn't really the answer one expects in this situation."

What the actual fuck is happening right now?

"W-what are you doing?" I stammer. "Why-*why* would you propose to me?"

His eyes widen. "What kind of question is that?"

"What kind of question was *that*?" I shoot back, gesturing up and down his still-kneeling form. That fucking ring keeps catching my eye—so perfectly round and sparkly. "For fuck's sake, can you please put that away?"

It's at that point I realize he's still holding my left hand, so I rip it from his grasp and pace away from him. I need space. I feel like my chest is caving in.

He frowns severely, but stands up and slips the ring back into his pocket. "What the fuck is going on here?"

My jaw comes close to hitting the floor, a laugh trying to escape my throat. "Yes, exactly, what the fuck *is* going on here?"

Ethan stares at me, aghast. "Well, I thought I was going to propose marriage to the love of my life and that she'd probably say yes because she loves me, too. But that is *not* what has happened tonight. Instead, she seems pretty pissed at me for something that would have gotten every other man in this situation a tearful hug and some celebratory sex."

I wish I could say my anger outweighed every other emotion in this moment, but the hurt is easily winning against the rage. My eyes burn immediately, and I have to turn away from him, looking up in an effort to keep the tears from falling down my face.

The reality of this situation is sinking in faster than I want it to. He fully expected me to marry him, which means that after five years together, he still doesn't know a goddamn thing about me.

"So that's what you expected tonight?" I ask, still avoiding his gaze. "An ecstatic Maggie who would throw her arms around you and happily slide that ring onto her finger for the rest of her life?"

"Basically, yes."

The anger in his voice is borne from embarrassment and surprise. I know it to be true, but I can't bring myself to care.

My head shakes on its own volition in what I'm sure is shock, but also the anger is seeping back in, and I'm welcoming it because anger is easier. Anger feels actionable. Despair does not.

"Well, I'm not sure what gave you that impression, Ethan." I turn, finally meeting his gaze. "I have always been transparent about this. I have said it over and over and *over* again: I don't want to get married. To anyone. Ever."

His shoulders slump as a truly *sad* expression takes over his face.

"Why not?"

I close my eyes with a sigh. I've fielded this question so many times over the years. Time and time again. But I never expected Ethan to ask. We've been together for *so long*, and after the very first time (which I felt was understandable and quite important), he'd never asked me again.

"I have told you this before, and I know you've heard me say it to other people," I start, my voice low. "I don't believe in it."

"How can you possibly say that?" His voice is growing stronger, more insistent. His anger is taking over, too. "Your parents have been married for over forty years, and they're *intolerably* happy together. Why in the *world* would you not 'believe' in it?"

His use of air quotes on the word *believe* turns my blood to ice. Somehow, he's not done, though.

"It's not like you came from a broken home, Maggie. Your family is fucking perfect."

My teeth grind together automatically in an effort to prevent myself from screaming at him. My family is wonderful. I know that. They're kind people with good intentions, and I love them dearly.

But I'm not *them*. I never have been. I'm very much the black sheep of my family, and he *knows* that. He has to. And he *definitely* knows how much it bothers me that I don't feel like I can relate to any of them anymore.

"It's fine for them. It clearly worked for them. But it's not for me, Ethan. I don't want it."

His eyes harden, and I see the muscle in his cheek jump. His turn to grind his teeth together, I suppose.

"So, what? What have you been doing here? You assumed we wouldn't get married and we'd just live together for the rest of our lives? This is it? Nothing more? That was your plan?"

"Yes." I stare into his eyes when I say it. "And until a few minutes ago, given that you've never *one time* brought this up after our initial conversation, I thought you were on board with that plan."

"Well, I'm not!"

It's not quite a yell, but it's louder than he's been speaking.

I swallow hard before responding. "Yes, that's clear now."

Ethan lets out a frustrated groan and turns away from me, pulling at his hair.

I can't believe this is how this evening has turned out. I expected champagne and a relaxing evening followed by hot sex, and instead, we're borderline yelling at each other. I can't remember the last time we had a fight.

Is this a fight?

The deep recesses of my brain know this is more than a fight, but I can't think about that right now.

In all fairness, I'm sure Ethan is also wondering how this evening has gone so far off the rails. In fact, that's one of the only truths that is keeping me grounded.

But I won't allow an antiquated societal convention to

make me believe my feelings are invalid or wrong or stupid. This is how I feel.

"Ethan, tell me something," I say, making my voice as patient and gentle as I can manage, burying the anger and pain deep in my belly while I speak. "Why do you want to get married?"

He turns toward me with stark sadness in his eyes and when he speaks, his voice is softer. Sweeter. "I just told you all the reasons I want to marry you."

My chest cracks a little bit more because I know that if I were a different woman, I would have melted like butter.

All the reasons I want to marry you.

It's every woman's dream...right?

Unfortunately for Ethan, I am not one of those women.

"I'm not asking why you want to marry *me*, specifically. I'm asking why you want to get married *at all*."

He watches me carefully while he takes a moment to consider his answer. "Because when two people love each other as much as we do, they get married and promise to love each other forever."

"It's what *many* people who love each other do...but it's not what they *have* to do."

"But that's how they show their commitment to each other," he argues. "They stand in front of all their friends and family, and they agree to be together for the rest of their lives."

"We can do that without getting married."

"It's not the same!" His voice rises again, his hands returning to his hair to pull at it.

I force my voice to remain even and calm, regardless of the storm I feel raging in my blood. "Why not?"

"It's just not! You wouldn't have a ring on your finger. You wouldn't have my name. We wouldn't be a family."

I press my lips together to keep from saying the thing that's on the tip of my tongue—that I'm trying to make a name for myself professionally. That even if I were to marry him, I wouldn't take his name. This particular moment doesn't seem like a great moment to tell him. It's irrelevant anyway. Saying it would only serve to further hurt him, and that's not my goal.

The room is silent for a long moment. When he speaks again, his voice is heavy, but calmer.

"I want a lifetime commitment, Maggie. I want to know you're *in* this...every single day for the rest of your life. I want that. I *need* it."

His words have me closing the distance between us with cautious hope. I take his hands in mine and place them against my chest, directly over my heart.

"Ethan...you have it. You already have it."

His brow furrows in confusion.

"You already have a lifetime commitment from me. You have for years," I clarify.

He rests his forehead against mine with a sigh, our clasped hands trapped between us. "Then marry me. Marry me, Maggie." His voice is pleading, and it serves no purpose except to slice me open that much further.

I swallow the giant lump in my throat as my eyes burn with fresh tears. "I'm sorry..."

He pulls back to look at me. "Why?" he asks, not out of anger, but out of something much deeper. He sounds tortured.

I shake my head and close my eyes, letting our hands drop from my chest, but not letting his go. They fall heavy, but I hold them tightly.

"Maggie, I want us to be a family. I want us to have our own family."

"Ethan..."

"Don't you want that, too?"

"Of course I do."

"Then *why*, Maggie? Why won't you marry me?"

"It's not about *you*, Ethan..."

He huffs a breath, letting my hands go and turning away from me. He palms the back of his neck, his head falling back.

"Ethan, listen to me."

He stops a few paces away, slowly facing me again, sadness swimming in his eyes.

"I love you. I want to be with you for the rest of my life," I assure him. Hopefully. "But I don't need a ring to be committed to you. I don't need to stand in front of our friends and family to profess my love for you to count you as family. I have loved you and been committed to you each and every day for the past five years. You *are* my family."

I finally lose the battle with my tears. They escape my eyes, burning paths down my cheeks and leaving room for my voice to waver.

He quietly watches me while I try to get control of myself, averting my eyes because I just can't look at him without feeling sharp pain in my chest.

"Apparently, you don't feel the same way," I add quietly.

"Oh come on, Maggie..." He doesn't sound angry at this point. More frustrated. Defeated. "You can't be mad at me for wanting to marry you."

"I'm not mad at you for wanting to marry me. I'm not even really mad at you. I'm..." I pause, trying to define what exactly it is that I'm feeling. To some extent, I am mad at him, but definitely not because he wants to marry me. I'm mad because he didn't listen to me. I'm hurt that he disregarded my expressed views on the topic. "I'm sad, I suppose," I finally say.

"The fact that you're sad I proposed to you is baffling to me." He shakes his head, and I can see the anger rising back into his eyes. "That's not a normal reaction."

I take a deep breath in an attempt to curb my own anger flaring to life at the sign of his.

"Ethan, I'm not mad at you for wanting to marry me or sad that you feel that way. I'm sad that after *five years* you still don't know who I am. Have you just not been listening when I talk?"

"Of course I listen when you talk, but honestly, the fact that you don't want to marry me is kinda fucked up. For five years, I have loved and supported you, and you can't do this *one* thing for me?"

I rear back, shocked to my core. I feel like he punched me in the gut. Once the initial jolt wears off, I manage to whisper, "That's not fair."

"Well, excuse me for not playing fair, but I've had kind of a rough night. My girlfriend of five years turned down my marriage proposal."

The words slice at me, leaving a thousand tiny cuts all over my body. "I'm sorry your girlfriend turned you down tonight," I respond, eyes burning, throat tightening. "If it's any consolation, I just learned my boyfriend hasn't listened to anything I've said on the subject of marriage for the past five years. And that feels pretty devastating, too."

He somehow finds the audacity to roll his eyes—a choice that manages to incinerate the remaining sadness in my heart and allow complete fucking rage to rise from the ashes.

"Don't. Don't you dare try to turn this around on me by making it seem like my feelings on the topic are ridiculous."

"They *are* ridiculous!" he yells. "Have you even thought this through? You want to have kids, Maggie! You would intentionally have children out of wedlock in your super Catholic family?"

"Yes!" I yell back. This is a hill I will literally die on. "And don't act all self-righteous here. You're not religious at all. You barely believe in God, so don't bring up this 'out of wedlock' bullshit."

The thing about fighting with someone who knows you so well—or at least...who you *think* knows you so well—is that they know how to really hurt you. They know what will dig into your subconscious. They know what will either leave a lasting impression after you're gone or manipulate you into staying. Either way, the end result is that you're miserable.

Every time you argue with someone you love, this is a choice you make. To either address the issue at hand and try to solve it...or let it spiral into something toxic and damaging.

Unfortunately, Ethan seems to be choosing the latter.

"Your family would flip their collective shit, and you know it," he spits.

"Who cares? They'd get over it because the most important thing when a child enters the world is that they're loved and cared for. Kids don't care if their parents are married. They only know what's normal to *them*."

"So it's okay for kids to believe parents don't have to get married? What kind of lesson does that teach them? That it's okay to get women pregnant and not stick around for them?"

"Come on, Ethan, that isn't even an issue here. There's no way in hell you'd leave your own child."

"Of course I wouldn't because I believe kids should have

two parents who are present in their lives. Two *married, committed* parents."

I narrow my eyes. The underlying message in what he's saying is equal parts patriarchal bullshit and flat out infuriating.

"Are you saying babies are a good reason to get married?"

"Well, it's not the worst reason."

My jaw drops open, and I turn away from him. "Holy shit, Ethan," I mutter as I begin to pace. "The divorce rate is over fifty percent. What kind of lesson does *that* teach children?"

"That's different!"

"How?" I demand. "How is it different?"

"Because those parents are committed to each other!"

"What? How can you even say that? They're clearly not committed to each other anymore since fifty percent of them are divorced, and their kids are stuck in the middle. Marriage does not guarantee you'll be with that person for the rest of your life. There are *no* guarantees in relationships, Ethan. Not even in marriage."

"Obviously." He looks at me pointedly.

"Obviously," I return.

He runs his hands through his hair, sighing, trying to calm himself down. "You have to admit it's more complicated when parents aren't married."

I resolve to calm down as well, to match his volume back down where we began.

"So what if it is? *Life* is complicated. Having parents who are committed to each other, but aren't married is no more complicated than having two parents who *hate* each other and are embroiled in a vicious divorce."

"Why are we even talking about divorce?"

"Because it's relevant."

"I'm not divorcing you! I would never."

We're borderline yelling again, so I stop myself before I respond, letting the room fill with silence. I close my eyes and rub my temples, trying to stave off a headache. When I open my eyes, I find him watching me.

"Do you think anyone actually gets married assuming they'll get divorced?" I asked, my voice mercifully calm and steady.

He breaks eye contact and shakes his head. "I don't understand why you won't even consider marrying me."

He's changing the subject because he has no argument against that point. I know it, but I let it go because clinging to it won't help matters.

"I told you," I respond. "It's not about you."

"It's a *little* about me," he says, incredulous.

"No, it's not," I assure him. "I love you, Ethan, and not wanting to get married doesn't change that."

I take a deep breath before I push forward to the part about this argument that's bothering me the most.

"I have always been transparent about my feelings on this topic. I told you when we first started dating that I didn't want to get married. I was adamant about it."

"Yes, but that was *years* ago."

My breath catches in my throat. I freeze, not blinking or breathing or twitching. I'm completely still as I process that sentence and all the derivations it comes alongside.

You'll change your mind when you meet the right person.

You'll change your mind when you're older.

You'll change your mind when you're ready to have a family —it will be different then.

You'll change your mind when you feel your biological clock ticking—and by then it might be too late.

I've heard it all before. A million times. From my sisters. Aunts. Uncles. Random old people at family weddings.

But *never* from Ethan.

My feelings on this subject were never different. They never changed. Being in love with Ethan didn't make me suddenly believe something different, and I'm certainly not going to change my tune now, when he's angry and hurt because I'm not accepting his proposal.

"Ethan, I have been very clear about this. I don't want to get married. If you thought I'd eventually change my mind..." I trail off because there's no good way to end that sentence.

...you were kidding yourself.

...you're delusional.

...you're secretly a manipulative asshole.

See? None of it is nice. And I'm not choosing the path where I hurt him intentionally. He's choosing it. But I'm not going to. This entire situation sucks enough.

"It's not that I look down on people who want to get married—there are plenty of beautiful reasons for wanting to be married to another person, as you fully understand. I can be committed to you, and love you, and bear your children, and be your partner in all things until the day I die... but I don't want to get married. And that doesn't make me broken, or misguided, or confused, or traumatized. I don't need to be *fixed* because I'm not *broken*. I just don't want to get married."

I take a few breaths before I continue because I know what I need to say next, and I don't want to.

"But if you do...if being with me without a ring on my finger is not enough for you...then this will never work."

The look on Ethan's face is one of complete shock with

hints of panic. He shakes his head and closes his eyes. "No, Maggie, stop it. It's not funny."

The anger melts from my system, replaced with weary sadness. Tears sting my eyes as I watch him, head bent, avoiding my gaze. Finally, I force the words out. "Ethan, if I can't give you what you want..." My voice cuts out as my throat tries to close. I swallow hard and keep going. "...and you can't give me what I want—"

His head snaps up, eyes flying open in alarm. "Maggie, don't—"

"—then I think—"

"Please don't say it, Maggie," he pleads, eyes wide and terrified.

I could stop. I could not say it. But the bottom line is that it's not fair to either of us to continue a relationship that will not progress the way either of us wants it to. This might be the first time we're having the argument, but I'm certain it won't be the last.

"I think this is over," I whisper, heart breaking, nausea swirling in my stomach.

Ethan's jaw drops ever so slightly, but his eyes are swimming. "Maggie..." he breathes.

Tears fall freely down my cheeks. There's no way to stop them at this point. My brain can't cognate what has happened here, and he's staring at me, silently.

"It's not fair to either of us to have to make such a significant sacrifice. This will never work. You would resent me for not marrying you. And I would resent you for wanting me to do something I was so adamantly opposed to."

He collapses into the chair behind him, his head dropping into his hands. After a moment, he scrubs his hands down his face and looks at me, a million questions in his beautiful brown eyes.

How could you do this?

Why won't you marry me?

Why don't you want to get married at all?

Don't you love me?

How did this evening end up like this?

Looking into his eyes is too painful, so I look down to the floor.

"Maggie, you..." He exhales sharply, still in disbelief. "You can't possibly be ending this."

It's suddenly all too much for me to handle, and I turn away from him entirely, trying—and failing—to stifle the sob from escaping my throat. He's in front of me so fast, I didn't even hear him get up. His hands are on my shoulders as he tries to meet my gaze, pleading with me.

"Maggie, please don't do this. We can figure it out. Come on, we're so good together. Don't throw this away. Don't throw *us* away." He cups my face in his capable hands and kisses me. "Maggie, I love you. Don't leave me, please. I love you..." he murmurs in between desperate kisses.

The feeling of his lips on mine—once familiar and comforting—is completely different now. It's like someone else kissing me. That sensation shocks me to my core, and I find myself pulling him tighter against me, kissing him more fervently, desperately seeking anything I can recognize as the man I wanted to spend the rest of my life with.

But I don't find it. I don't find *him*.

I don't find anything.

I feel like I'm flailing around in pitch blackness, desperate to grab something solid to hang on to.

Fresh tears sting my eyes and fall through my closed lashes, the reality of the situation settling into my bones.

There's no coming back from something like this.

Between my tears and his mouth, I can't get enough air. I

pull back, gasping, and when I manage to say his name, it's only a whimper.

He tries to pull me back to kiss me again, but I step back and out of his reach. "Stop..." I sob. "Please, stop."

Alarm flashes through his eyes, and before I even know what's happening, he's on both knees in front of me, arms around my hips, head against my stomach, quietly begging.

It brings a fresh stab of pain to my heart to see him like this, but I still know it's the right thing to do. As much as I want to cave, to join him on the floor and take it all back, I just can't. I can't stay in this relationship when we both want different things. Even the act of proposing to me shows he doesn't understand me well enough for me to stay. Not after all this time.

I can't give in. Everything is different now.

Everything.

I take a few breaths to calm down, but there's no stopping the tears. Even as I say his name to get his attention, they're falling down my cheeks.

"Ethan, stand up," I say, pushing on his arms.

When he stands, I take two big steps back and see his face fall, all the hope draining from his eyes.

"I'll pack a few things and come back for the rest later."

His lips part, a million objections plain on his face, but I hold up a hand.

"Please don't say anymore."

You've said enough.

I look around the living room, a space we shared for years. At an apartment we made into a home together. I glance at the familiar furniture, the decorations we picked out, the mementos of our relationship.

In the blink of an eye, it's no longer my home.

I look back to him one more time, my breath shallow, my stomach clenching.

An entire conversation seems to pass in the silence between us, standing feet apart on a Friday night that neither of us saw coming.

Please don't go.

It's over.

How can that be?

You know it won't work.

But I love you.

I know.

Stay.

Slowly, I shake my head. *I can't.*

He takes a step forward, but I take a step back, maintaining the distance.

Before he can say another word, I walk swiftly into the bedroom to pack my things.

CHAPTER 4
STILL A SPITEFUL HAG

MAGGIE

Not The Sun - Morgan St. Jean

I trudge up the front steps of a beautiful home I'm very familiar with. I've been here countless times. Have decorated it for the holidays. Slept in the guest bedroom. Spent many evenings drinking wine on the back patio, listening to the sound of waves breaking on the shore. Listening to my brother talking about anything and everything.

As I reach the top step, the door swings open to reveal a gorgeous brunette wearing leggings and a thin, long-sleeved shirt. Her wavy brown hair is gathered into a messy bun at the crown of her head. Her cheeks are flushed, as if she'd been working out and paused to open the door, which was probably exactly right. She stands there, watching me as I take the final steps toward the door.

"Hi, Kate," I grouse. A duffel bag, stuffed with enough clothes and toiletries to get me through a few days until I could get the rest of my belongings, is weighing down my right shoulder. My purse and a couple of tote bags balance me out on the left.

"Hey, Mags." She reaches out to take the tote bags from me. "Come on in. I'll get the bourbon."

The best I can offer is a sad smile as I step over the threshold into the giant house Nick bought for Kate years ago. For a while after Nick's death, we didn't talk much—not on purpose. We were both just wallowing separately in our grief.

I was lying in bed at the apartment while Ethan hovered, trying to find ways to help and being mostly unsuccessful because there was no possible way to make me feel better.

Kate, on the other hand, offered a widower a room to rent while he looked for something more permanent following the death of his wife and subsequent move back to his hometown.

While it probably started off as a business transaction, it turned into something else. They ended up falling for each other pretty hard, which surprised them both, I think. Liam was on an assignment out of state for a while, but when he returned, they got together for real. That was about a year and a half ago. He lives here, but I don't see any signs of him now.

I drop my duffel bag on the floor next to the staircase alongside the tote bags Kate carried in and wander over to the couch, plopping down with a bounce. A glance to my left reveals a photo of Nick in a walnut frame, looking off into the distance with a serene smile on his face. I pick it up, studying the curve of his smile, which so closely resembles my own and feel that familiar pang of sadness.

Sometimes, I swear I can see him looking back at me in the mirror, especially when my curly hair is pulled back into a ponytail. It's then that I can see the shape of his face most clearly, the mischievous green eyes we both inherited shining a bit brighter.

The couch dips when Kate sits down next to me, setting two tumblers and a bottle of Blanton's on the coffee table. She glances up and sees me holding the picture of Nick, which she gives a soulful smile before uncorking the bottle and pouring us drinks. When she holds a tumbler out to me, I set the frame back on the console table behind the couch.

"So..." Kate begins, drawing a leg up onto the couch so she can angle her body toward mine. "What happened?"

With a huge sigh and a shake of my head, I fess up. "Ethan proposed to me."

Kate's eyes widen with surprise before blinking rapidly a few times and huffing out a breath. "Bad move, Ethan."

"Right? It's like he doesn't know me at all. Not even a little bit."

"I assume you said no."

"Of course."

"And what did he say to that?"

I fortify myself with a gulp of bourbon. "That he wanted to be a family. I told him we already were." Another sip of bourbon. "Apparently, he doesn't feel the same way."

"But, surely you discussed this before..." Kate begins slowly. "It's not like you've pretended you wanted to get married."

"Yes, we have discussed it. Of course we have."

"Do you think he thought you'd just...come around or something?"

"Apparently so." Confirming it out loud makes my stomach churn, but I douse it with some more bourbon and tell it to shut up. "He seemed genuinely shocked when I reiterated my feelings on the topic *yet again*. I truly think he believed I'd change my mind. 'When you meet the right person' and all that bullshit. Some people just don't want to get married. I don't see what the big deal is."

It's silent for a moment, save for the sound of me fidgeting with my glass.

"So, it's over then?" Kate asks gently.

"Yeah," I whisper.

"I'm sorry, Mags."

I wave a dismissive hand toward her and down some more bourbon. "I'm mostly just...disappointed. I thought we were on the same page, ya know?"

"I do. But it still sucks to break things off with someone you care about. Even when it's the right thing to do."

Kate knows a thing or two about that. She broke things off with Liam when she realized he was in love with her, and she wasn't ready for it. It was only a year after Nick died. Kate left out a lot of the details, but I know enough to know it was extraordinarily painful for both of them.

I look back to the picture of Nick, reaching out to touch the tip of his nose the way he used to do to me as a child.

"He would know what to say."

"He would," Kate confirms.

"I miss him," I squeak, tears brimming in my eyes again.

Kate takes my hand and holds it in her lap. "Me, too."

A tear slides down my cheek, but Kate reaches for a tissue and blots at it.

"He'd be so proud of you for standing up for yourself."

I scoff. "He'd be trying to tell me how awesome marriage is."

Kate's responding smile is wistful. "He would, yes. But he would also support you in your decision to not marry. And he'd be disappointed if you got married only because someone else wanted to."

I shoot her a skeptical look. I'm not sure I buy that.

"Your brother loved you like his own child. You kind of were, in a way. He helped raise you. He didn't think you were weird for not wanting to get married. He just wanted you to be happy."

She squeezes my hand once and then lets it go, grabbing the tissues and placing them between us.

"Thanks for letting me stay the night," I say as I wipe my face and nose with tissues.

She pulls a little trash can out from under the side table behind her and puts it on the floor by my feet.

"You're welcome here any time, Mags."

"I thought about going to Mom's but..." I glance up at Kate, who nods thoughtfully.

Kate knows I'm the black sheep of my family. I'm not like the rest of them. I don't go to church—on Sunday or other-wise—and I don't want to get married or be a stay-at-home mom. I know my mom wants to see me happy (preferably, settled down and married), but I just don't want to talk to her about this yet. She's going to ask why we broke up, and I know she won't understand why I didn't just accept Ethan's proposal.

Nick was the one who always accepted me for whoever and whatever I was. Now that he's gone, Kate is the next best thing.

"I get it. You can stay as long as you want. But I will say..." she says cautiously. "...when I told your mom some things I was *sure* would upset her, she was really kind about it. She said she wanted me to be happy and didn't press me about anything."

I huff a laugh. "You're not her spawn though."

"That's true, I'm not. But I was married to one of them." Kate smirks. "I'm only saying she might surprise you. You can do whatever you want and make whatever decision feels right for you, but I think she'd be happy if you shared this with her."

I groan a non-committal response.

The thought of talking to my mother about this raises a tiny voice in the back of my mind that has been plaguing me since I left the apartment.

"Kate, do you..." The words catch in my throat.

Kate frowns and tilts her head, waiting for the rest of the question.

"Do you think there's something wrong with me?"

"Oh, Maggie. Of course not." Her empathetic tone quickly turns to something harsher as she continues. "You know, if you were a man, you wouldn't be asking yourself that question. You'd think you were hot shit. You're only asking that question because you're a woman, and you've been implicitly trained to believe women have to be married to be worth anything. That there's something wrong with you if you want anything different."

She pauses long enough to meet my eye and fix me with a withering look.

"It's bullshit, Maggie, and I never want to hear you ask that question again. There is *nothing* wrong with you. You don't want to get married. So what? You don't have to. And you deserve a man who loves you for that choice. If Ethan can't accept this part of you, then fuck him. You deserve better. And if you legitimately change your mind at some point—if you *truly* find someone you want to marry—then that's one thing. But if you give in to men telling you you're broken because you don't want to get married, I'll kick your ass, Margaret. There's nothing further from the truth."

I can feel my eyes are wide in their sockets as I watch her

get more and more worked up as she talks. "All right, Gloria Steinem, I got it."

Kate takes a sip of her bourbon, seemingly satisfied with her contribution to feminism for the day.

"Nick wouldn't have been so boisterous about it, but fine," I mumble into my tumbler.

Kate sputters out a laugh. "He would have been nicer about it, that's true," she agrees. "But then again...Nick always was a nicer person than me."

I look up at her and find her gazing at his picture with a sad look of love in her eyes.

There's not a doubt in my mind she will always love my brother, but that she also loves Liam. That her heart expanded to let Liam's love in.

Just as I think about Liam, I hear the kitchen door open, followed by the sound of scampering paws on the vinyl flooring. Beaker rounds the corner behind the couch and sprints toward the kitchen.

"Hey, bud!"

Kate chuckles quietly beside me while footsteps grow closer. Liam comes around the fireplace wall, holding Beaker against his chest, a contented smile on his face.

"Hi, Maggie."

I manage to muster a smile for the man who very possibly saved my sister-in-law from unaliving herself. "Hey, Liam."

He walks over to Kate. Leans down and kisses her, whispering a hello before straightening and jutting his chin toward their bedroom. "I was helping Joe move some stuff around, and I'm gross. I'm gonna go shower."

"Here, I'll take him." Kate reaches up and takes Beaker from his arms.

I've never questioned the way I love Ethan, but watching

the way the two of them are looking at each other right now, I wonder if he ever loved me like that.

Doesn't really matter now, I suppose.

"Good to see you, Maggie," Liam nods to me.

"Good to see you, too." My smile is more genuine this time, albeit sadder.

I want what they have.

I thought I had it.

I stare at the unlit fireplace while I listen to Liam walk up the stairs and into their bedroom.

I'm approaching my midthirties, and I'm starting over.

For the past five years, I've been in what I thought was a loving, committed relationship with a good man, and now I'm not. All the comfort I felt in that knowledge has evaporated into the summer air, and I'm not really sure what to do with that.

"You can stay here as long as you want."

Kate's words interrupt my spiraling thoughts.

"Not such an evil shrew anymore, are you?" I take a sip of bourbon to cover my smile.

She doesn't laugh, but I can see her answering smile out of the corner of my eye. "Well, you're not much of a spiteful hag right now, are you?"

I huff a laugh, wishing I could be. Wishing I could have thrown insults and undercutting comments the way Ethan did.

But then again, that's not really who I am.

I didn't think it was who Ethan was either.

"I feel like I don't know anything anymore," I murmur, more to myself than anyone else.

"I know what that feels like," she answers quietly.

All at once, I'm exhausted by the events of the evening. I

down the rest of my bourbon and announce I'm going to bed.

She bids me good night. Tells me she'll leave a key on the kitchen island. Makes sure I have the Wi-Fi passcode and remember where she keeps the booze.

Later, I'm lying in the guest bedroom, staring at the ceiling when I make a decision.

Monday morning, I'm going to walk into Marv's office and put my name in for Paris.

And come hell or high water, I'm getting that spot.

CHAPTER 5
OH, FUCK...THE WHISKEY
ETHAN

Last Night - Morgan Wallen

Before I even open my eyes, I know I'm in for a hell of a day.

My head feels like someone put it in a vice. My mouth feels like cotton.

I groan at the sensation and immediately regret it when my head throbs harder.

I guess that's it then. I'm just not getting out of bed today. It's Saturday (right?) so it's not like we need to be anywhere. A lazy day sounds perfect.

With careful movements, I roll onto my side and reach for Maggie. If I feel this bad, she can't be doing much better.

I frown carefully when my hand touches cold sheets next to me.

Where is she?

She can't possibly be awake and moving around. Was I the only one that got hammered after—

The events of last night slam back into my brain all at

once. My proposal gone horribly wrong. The yelling. The tears. The begging.

The whiskey.

Oh, fuck the whiskey.

Before I even know what I'm doing, I bolt upright in bed, eyes wide and searching for her.

"No no no no no no..." I chant, ignoring the nausea as I clammer out of bed.

Throwing open the bedroom door, I call out for her, which makes my vision blur with pain. But still, I try again.

"Maggie?"

Even I—in my severely hungover state—can hear the fear and desperation in my voice. It's unmistakable.

I search the bathroom and the guest bedroom that doubles as a home office. When I get to the living room, I find my best friend Miles half sitting, half laying on the couch. I stare at him, and what I see in his eyes confirms every horrible, nauseating memory currently assaulting my frontal lobe.

"Hey," he says quietly.

"No..." My voice is basically a whimper.

He shakes his head. "I'm so sorry, man."

"No..." My vision blurs again, but this time, it's with tears.

Miles gets to his feet and tentatively takes a step toward me.

Flashes of our conversation—our *fight*—that ultimately led to our *breakup* add insult to injury.

The way I yelled at her.

I fucking *yelled* at her.

The way she tried so hard to not yell in return, only giving in a couple of times.

How she tried to explain her views on marriage, and I shot her down.

Now, in the extremely harsh light of day, I'm remembering every single time she ever talked about not wanting to get married. I remember our conversation, sure...the one we had years ago. But I'm also remembering the little comments that weren't necessarily directed at me. Bits and pieces of conversations I was a part of or overheard.

I don't think people need to get married.

Marriage is an antiquated system that benefits men, primarily.

*Women don't **need** to get married anymore...we can have bank accounts and own property and have jobs.*

I don't look down on people who get married...I just don't want to do it.

Fuck, I feel like the worst boyfriend on the planet right now.

But the worst memory...the one that's absolutely gutting me, is how utterly broken she sounded when she finally said the words.

I think this is over.

A sharp pain shoots through my abdomen, the force of it making me reach out for the nearest wall to steady myself. "Fuck..."

"Hey, you never know, man...maybe you can work it out."

I shake my head slowly as the tears break free. I can't even be embarrassed to be crying. I've known Miles for years. Besides...this situation—the one where I proposed marriage to the love of my life, who rejected me and then broke up with me—calls for some fucking tears.

"You two are solid. You'll figure it out."

But I know he's wrong. He didn't see her face last night.

He didn't see the pain in her gorgeous green eyes or feel the anger rolling off her body in waves. They're coworkers. He doesn't know her like I do.

I ruined it.

I ruined the best thing that's ever happened to me because I didn't fucking listen to her. I know she won't come back. Maggie isn't the type of person who sticks around, hoping things will work out. Maggie is a *doer*. Ambitious to a fault. She goes after what she wants, and it sure as fuck doesn't seem like I'm the thing she wants anymore.

I know she's gone for good.

And with that crushing thought, my stomach churns violently, making me bolt for the bathroom, where I throw up all the whiskey I drank last night.

"Drink this. Take these."

I force my eyes to refocus, tearing them away from the wall I've been staring blankly at for the past...I don't know. Maybe twenty minutes. I'm not sure.

A bottle of Gatorade is in front of my face, along with two pills in Miles' golden bronze hand.

"I ordered greasy food to soak up the rest of that alcohol," he says as I take his offerings.

The pills are difficult to get down my throat, but I manage it.

"Drink that whole thing," Miles instructs me. "We're not in our twenties anymore. Hangovers are harder to recover from. You gotta hydrate, man."

If Maggie were here, she'd want bangers and mash. Maybe boxty. My chest aches as I think of her, wondering where she is, who she's with, if she feels as wretched as I do this morning.

After my digestive system reversed itself, I began frantically searching for my phone, only to find out Miles had confiscated it so I didn't drunk dial Maggie. Apparently I'd become quite belligerent over that scenario.

Not that I remember any of that.

No, my memory gets fuzzy not long after I called Miles.

I remember calling him, but not him showing up. Or anything after that, really. I remember drinking whiskey straight from the bottle and crying.

"Eat."

Containers filled with pancakes, bacon, hash browns, and toast are splayed out on the coffee table.

I start off slow, eating a pancake until I'm sure I can keep it down, and then I dig into the bacon and hash browns. Miles turns on the television and immediately finds a bloody movie to keep my mind off things.

It's not possible, but I appreciate the effort.

By the time I finish eating, I'm feeling moderately more human.

"What did I say last night?"

"To me? Or to Maggie?"

I press the heels of my hands tightly against my eyelids. "I remember every word Maggie and I exchanged. What did I tell *you*?"

He doesn't answer me right away, choosing instead to dig something out of his pocket. He sets the engagement ring on the coffee table in front of us.

"You told me she said no."

I can't help but stare at the shiny diamond. I'd felt so sure when I picked it out. So certain she'd love it. A little voice in the back of my mind tries to rationalize that she might have liked it...she kept staring at it and asked me to put it away...like she couldn't *stop* staring and knew she needed to.

She just didn't like the thought of getting married. Or marrying *me*.

I tear my eyes away from the diamond and scrub my hands down my face.

"Yeah...she said no."

"You also said she didn't want to get married." He paused. For dramatic effect, perhaps? "Ever."

I groan. "Yep. She said that, too."

Miles is silent, but I can feel his eyes on me. I can practically hear his thoughts, they're so loud.

"Just say it, man."

"Did you seriously not realize she never wanted to get married? Surely you've talked about this. You've been together for a half-decade."

"Fuck, dude," I grouse.

"It's a valid question," he grumbles in return.

I know it's a valid question. I just don't want to talk about it. Because if everything Maggie said last night is true, I fucked up. I fucked up so severely I don't even deserve to be forgiven.

If everything Maggie said is true, I've been a selfish, inattentive prick for the past five years, and that's something I'm just not sure I can come to terms with yet.

"We...we talked about it early on," I admit. "But it never came up again. We moved in together...talked about our future. Talked about kids. I just..." I can't bring myself to say it.

"It felt like a natural next step," Miles fills in for me.

"Yes." I nod, grateful to him for understanding even a tiny bit.

He sighs. "It's not like Maggie and I ever talked about this, so I don't have any additional insight, man. I'm sorry this happened."

I finally pick up the ring. *Her* ring.

What the fuck am I supposed to do with it now?

I need to talk to her, so I ask Miles for my phone.

He looks at me out of the corner of his eye quickly before returning his attention to the television.

"Give her some time, man."

I lean back on the couch with an exasperated sigh. "Miles, she's—" I stop abruptly, trying to keep the emotion from climbing back up my throat. I have to swallow a couple of times before I can trust my voice again. "She's the love of my life. She's *mine*. I can't let her go without a fight."

He turns his head to look at me, but his face doesn't give anything away. His brow is furrowed. He's blinking normally, and I can tell he's thinking carefully about what he's going to say—not that I can tell what he's mulling over.

Finally, he looks back to the television before dropping a bomb on me.

"Did she talk to you about Paris?"

Maggie and Miles started working at the same firm after Maggie and I had been together for a couple of years. Miles is also an architect but ended up in Seattle working for a bit. He wasn't particularly happy with his firm and was looking for a change, so Maggie suggested he apply for an open position at her firm. Three years later, the two of them are just as good of friends as he and I are—and we grew up together.

"Uhh..." I will my sluggish, hungover brain to recall the random conversations I had with Maggie about her company working on a new building in Paris. That's all I can remember. "Your firm is working on a building."

He nods slowly. "Yes. We are."

And then silence hangs between us.

"Miles? What does that have to do with anything?"

He scratches his jaw with a sigh. "Ethan, I'm sorry to be the one to break this to you...but I think she's going to put her name in the running for the project."

I frown. Swallow hard. Blink slowly. "You sure?"

"I know Marvin has been encouraging her to put in for it."

Fuck.

Marvin is Maggie's mentor. If he recommends it, she'll do it.

People who don't know Maggie know that her putting her name into the hat for this project doesn't mean she'll get it.

But I know Maggie.

She'll get it. And fuck, she deserves it.

So...she'll be off to Paris.

I mutter a curse under my breath, rubbing my eyes while I try to find a way to dig myself out of a prison of my own creation. Another wave of nausea rolls through me, so I keep my eyes closed until it passes.

But it doesn't pass at all.

I know I'm the one that messed this entire thing up. This situation—my misery—is entirely my doing. But I'll be damned if I'm going to give up on Maggie Rafferty.

CHAPTER 6
FUCKING AMERICANS
MAGGIE

A ding, followed by crackly speech wakes me up. My head is lolled to the side, the only thing stopping my head from hitting the window being the neck pillow Kate gave me as a going-away present.

"Ladies and gentlemen, this is your captain speaking. We've begun our initial descent into Charles De Gaulle airport. Local time is six-thirty a.m. Current temp is sixteen degrees, with a perfect high of twenty-four today."

It takes my brain a moment to remember the pilot is using Celsius—not Fahrenheit—to communicate the temperature.

Phew.

"If Paris is your final destination today," he continues, "we hope you have a wonderful time in the city. If you're catching a connecting flight, the crew will direct you toward your connecting gate shortly. Once again, thank you for flying with us, and we hope to see you again soon."

As the pilot begins his announcements in French, I right my head—so grateful for the pillow because my neck *doesn't* feel like there's a metal pole in it—arching my back to stretch my shoulders as well as I can while still confined to my seat.

Kelsie is doing the same in the seat next to me, stretching and trying to wake up before we deplane and head to our rental. There are four of us on this team—two men, two women—and they've booked two Airbnbs for us in the city. The firm we're partnering with just renovated this building and were able to get us a decent rate apparently.

It's not like I'm paying for it. This is just what Marv told me.

Kelsie and I will share one apartment, and our male coworkers (Isaac and Wesley) will share the other. Both apartments are two bedrooms. I've seen photos and the improvements they made look gorgeous. There's even a tiny terrace with a little table.

The view though…that's what I'm looking forward to the most. It overlooks the city, and we can see the Eiffel Tower.

Or at least, the listing photos show a view of the Eiffel Tower from one of their apartments. It's entirely possible we won't be able to see it from ours. In fact, that will probably be the case, so I try to lower my expectations accordingly.

My personal life might be in complete shambles, but I'm about to spend six—maybe eight—months in Paris for work, and a win is a win in my book. Aside from throwing myself into this project (which I will absolutely do), I plan to pick up the pieces and just move on. It's not like I can do a damn thing about Ethan being Ethan.

After my brother died, I was pretty depressed, and I started having anxiety attacks, which had never happened to me before. When I finally confided in Kate, she encouraged me to see her therapist (a mindblowing sentence, if I've ever heard one), so I did, and I have to admit that Gwen helped me a lot. I've been seeing her for a few months now and when my relationship imploded, I was very grateful to have her because I needed her badly.

Gwen helped me feel less like I was flailing out of control. She helped me find some focus, so that's what I'm doing. I'm focusing on things I can control and doing my best to tune out the rest.

I can't control Ethan or how he feels.

I can't control what choices he makes.

I can't control what he wants out of his life or his relationships.

I can't even really control my own feelings.

But Gwen told me that thoughts become feelings, and I can reframe my thoughts to something healthier if I choose to do so.

So that's what I've chosen to do.

I'm choosing to reframe my thoughts and refocus my energy on things I can control.

What I can control are my actions and my choices.

Of course, that's why I put my name in the running for the Paris project. I couldn't control whether or not I got it, but I did get it in the end. So here I am, on a plane currently descending into Parisian airspace, and I don't have a single regret.

In a moment of weakness, I could probably admit to you that I'm sad. It's still my first instinct to take a million pictures and text them to Ethan. He was my person for five entire years, and now he's just...gone.

The implosion of my relationship—the one I thought was forever—is creating a shadow over the once in a lifetime opportunity I've earned. Like Marv said, I get to work on a building that will shape the Paris cityscape. My name won't be on it directly, but I'll know. I'll know I was there, and one day, I'll take my kids there and show them that mommy worked on that building once upon a time.

So yes, I'm sad. I'm sad that Ethan isn't celebrating this opportunity with me.

I'm sad that the theoretical kids I used to picture were *ours*—Ethan's and mine—and now they're not.

I'm sad that I'm basically fleeing the country, and I don't even have a home to return to. I moved all my shit out of our apartment before I left. Most of it is at Kate's house. She has the space.

I'm sad that my life has taken an unexpected turn.

But I'm excited about one very specific part of the direction the turn is taking me. The *Paris* part. The once in a lifetime opportunity part.

"Did you get some sleep?" Kelsie asks.

"Yeah, I did." I look over to find her relatively bright-eyed. I watched her take a CBD gummy partway through the flight. I've never tried one, but if she's this chipper after plane sleep, I might have to bum one from her tonight.

"Good. We'll get today to rest, but tomorrow, we hit the ground running."

I smile. I can't believe I get to do this.

The *Paris cityscape* and a building I get to work on.

"I'm ready," I tell Kelsie.

She gives me a knowing smirk and winds her earbuds up to put them away before we land.

As the city comes into view out the window, my thoughts turn to my brother. I'm always sad when I think about Nick, but under these circumstances, I can't help but think he's grinning ear to ear wherever he is. He knows how much this means to me. He'd be so proud.

We get our luggage from baggage claim and Uber our way to our apartment building, which does not disappoint. Our units are next to each other, and we're all just staring out our windows, then calling out to each other from our terraces, definitely annoying the hell out of the building's other residents. There's no possible way they don't already hate us.

I swear I hear one of them yell, "Putain d'amérlocs," which I have to Google in order to realize someone is calling us *fucking Americans.*

He's not wrong, but what does he expect? Has *he* seen this view?

We *can* see the Eiffel Tower, though we have to stand all the way to the right and press our heads against the divider. I'm still calling it a win.

We unpack a bit and then hit the city. We get coffee and pastries down the street from our building, sitting at a tiny bistro table outside while planning our day and creating a list of things we want to do during our contract.

It's a gorgeous day, so we opt for walking whenever possible and attempting to speak French to anyone we encounter. We've all been taking French language courses even though we know people will be able to tell we're not native speakers. It just feels respectful—like we should try while we're here. More often than not, they immediately start speaking to us in English, which consistently feels like we've failed at our task, though they're never particularly rude about it. Honestly, it just makes us want to try harder. We're all quite competitive.

We finish the day at a restaurant near our building, drinking fabulous wine and probably laughing loudly enough to easily identify us as *putain d'amérlocs*. Our server is very sweet though, so we end up leaving a tip, knowing it's not necessary or expected, but he was so nice to us. He rolls his eyes at us, but thanks us, nonetheless.

When we get back to our apartment, I change into pajamas, wash my face, brush my teeth, say good night to Kelsie (who is already changing her location to Paris on her LGBTQ dating apps), and lie down in my bed. Staring out the window, I take in the city lights and promise myself that I'll make the most of this experience. That I won't let Ethan follow me around like a stormcloud. That I'll live these months to their fullest.

CHAPTER 7
LA PETITE MORT
MAGGIE

'tis the damn season - Taylor Swift

"**D**on't drink that Italian swill," Vivienne tells me.

"I wasn't going to, I swear!" I promise. I truly wasn't. Even if I were thinking about it, I wouldn't dare in France.

Viv eyes me like she's trying to rip down a curtain to find the lie hidden behind it.

"I could never commit such an atrocity," I proclaim dramatically. "And in the city of lights, of all places!" I gesture toward the city like a freshman musical theater major while they laugh at me. I'm their dramatic American friend, and they're fine with it.

Thankfully.

The American team is out to dinner with our French counterparts, Vivienne, Dominique, Dax, and Henri. We've been working together for a couple of weeks now, and we decided it was time for us to get to know each other a bit better. They're pretty fun to hang out with thus far, and they're not giving us weird looks for sticking out like sore, American thumbs.

In fact, they're being rather kind about teaching us French things—customs, idiosyncrasies, and the stuff you can't read on tourist websites. They brought us to a restaurant today that wouldn't make it on any "must see" site unless it was specifically catered toward tourists who wanted to be off the beaten path.

It's glorious.

"I'll order for you," Viv offers.

The waiter is on his way over to our table. He goes straight to the French, knowing damn well the Americans won't be of much help. I'd say I'm offended, but he's not actually wrong.

Viv eloquently orders a couple of bottles of wine for the table and some starters.

"Is this what it looks like when we order in the US?" Kelsie leans over and asks me quietly.

"What do you mean?"

"Well, they're talking so fast...is that what we sound like?"

I shrug. "Probably."

Kelsie is definitely looking at Viv's mouth more than I'd consider "normal" for casual interest in the language. She hums, and I feel like I need to distract her somehow.

"Although we probably don't sound quite so intelligent with our midwestern accents and whatnot."

Kelsie isn't paying attention to me.

"I'm thinking of joining the circus while we're here."

Viv laughs at something the waiter says, and Kelsie's eyes twinkle a little bit.

"Maybe I'll fall madly in love with the bearded lady."

Nothing.

"Maybe I can find an elephant with oversized ears to lavish attention on."

It's like talking to a brick wall.

"Kels, just ask her out."

"What?" Kelsie looks away from Viv for just a second to give me a questioning glance.

It's then that the waiter nods to Viv and walks away from the table. As if she feels someone's eyes on her, she looks up and meets Kelsie's gaze. Heat sparks in both their eyes, and I'm fully aware I should remove myself from the vicinity so the two of them can talk.

Or whatever.

I get up and move to an open seat next to Dominique. She turns to me with her gorgeous smile, and not for the first time since I arrived, I wonder how the hell French women take care of their skin. Why do they always look like they're glowing? I resolve to learn all their secrets while I'm here.

"Are you all right?" she asks.

"Yeah, of course." I wave her off. "I just wanted to give Kelsie and Viv some time," I say, tilting my head discreetly toward the two women.

Her eyes follow the indicated direction, and she smirks. "Viv has always had a thing for taller women."

"Well, they certainly make a striking pair."

Vivienne with her auburn hair, hourglass frame, and full lips stands in contrast to Kelsie's outdoorsy, athletic build—narrow hips, strong legs, and small boobs.

"That they do," Dom agrees. "Oh good!"

I look back to her, frowning, to find her waving toward the door.

A tall man nods to Dom in acknowledgment and begins making his way over to our table. He's...beautiful is the only word I can think to accurately describe him. Brown hair that seems to have some sort of curl to it—maybe soft waves. Well-trimmed beard. Straight, Greek nose. Confidence flowing from him like a second skin.

He arrives at our table and kisses Dom on the cheek, touching her shoulder softly. I'm keenly aware of their body language. Are they together? That shoulder touch seemed pretty innocent—no heat or possession to it.

They exchange a few words in easy French, but I'm so distracted by him, I barely catch it. Something about his day and how long he'd be able to stay tonight.

Wait, stay the night...with her?

"Oh, Julien, I want you to meet my colleague, Maggie."

I snap out of my stupor at my name, plastering a polite smile on my face...and then this striking man's gaze is concentrated on me.

"Maggie, this is my brother, Julien."

Oooooooooh, her brother. Phew.

I was thinking far too many inappropriate thoughts for this to be Dom's boyfriend.

"Hi, Julien, it's nice to meet you." I hold out my hand out of habit, expecting him to shake it, but instead, he takes my hand, turns my palm down, and brings our joined hands up to his lips, leaving a kiss on the back of my hand so soft I'd think I imagined it if I didn't watch it happen.

Even so, I'm still questioning it.

His hazel eyes stay on mine the entire time, and I'm *certain* my mouth is hanging open.

"Tout le plaisir est pour moi."*

I think he just said the pleasure is his.

---

* The pleasure is mine.

My knees are jelly, but I won't let him catch me stunned any longer.

Maggie, get it together. Fast.

"My goodness, it's true what they say about the French," I tease.

His eyebrows lift, but it's Dom who asks, "What do they say about the French?"

"That you're all charmers," I start. "With good taste," I finish with a wink.

I withdraw my hand from his, and I don't miss the smirk on his face or the way his eyes dip to my chest.

There it is.

I can work with this.

"Maggie, *ma chérie*," Viv croons to my left, handing me a glass of the wine she ordered.

"Merci," I respond, trying not to cringe at my shitty American accent or the way I still struggle to pronounce my *R*s.

She smiles and goes back to Kelsie.

When I turn back to Dom and Julien, they're exchanging a look I try to ignore because I clearly wasn't invited to the silent conversation.

"So, Maggie, tell me," Julien begins—in what is the sexiest French accent I've heard thus far—"what's your story?"

I make sure to keep my mask of general interest and not let the pain enter my eyes when I think about my actual story. I don what I hope is an easy smile and deflect. "I don't have a story."

"Is that so?" Julien's head tilts to the left as he studies me, his eyes taking a journey around my face.

"Yep."

He's quiet for a moment, eyeing me like he's trying to

solve a puzzle. It makes me fidget, and I'm certain my cheeks are flushing based on the heat I'm feeling in them. I take a sip of my wine to hide my face, but it doesn't seem to do anything to divert the effects of his hazel gaze on me.

"Forgive me, but I find that hard to believe," he finally says.

A smug smile pulling at my lips, I turn the tables on him. "What's your story, Julien?"

He hums, eyes shining with amusement. "Touché, mademoiselle."

Like recognizes like, and I can tell this man doesn't want to talk about his past any more than I do. After all, I'm here to live my life, not mourn a death.

I've done that enough in recent years.

Food is brought to the tables while Julien and I chat. We carefully avoid topics that might be sensitive and instead talk about work (he's a stonemason), life in France versus America (politics, but in an educational, non-contentious way—we share viewpoints, regardless), and our favorite sports (football on both sides, but different kinds, obviously).

He makes sure I try a lot of different food, and I make sure to demonstrate my burning desire to speak the language. He doesn't make fun of my accent or poor *Rs*— instead, he helps me with pronunciation.

Julien is *kind*. He's gentle.

Though he's giving me heated looks tonight that make me hope he's not *always* gentle.

After the check has been delivered, and we've Venmo'd the appropriate person, the crew decides to hit up a club, but Julien and I decide to go for a walk.

To my apartment.

Right on cue, Nick's voice flits through my head.

You're going to show this dude where you live?

Chill out. I work with his sister.

Yeah, like that matters. A lot of women are assaulted by people they know. Or people their friends know.

Well, it's a good thing I'll be a willing participant then.

Gross.

Julien walks me all the way to my apartment door, making sure I arrive safely, and when we stop, he gently brushes a curl off my face before taking my head in his hand and kissing me.

His lips are soft, pillowy. His movements are sure, confident.

One hand is holding my keys, but with my free one, I gently touch his waist so he knows I'm all right to keep going.

His tongue teases my bottom lip, coaxing me to open up, so I do. And holy shit.

Have you ever been French kissed by a French man? I recommend it. I recommend it times infinity.

His other hand slips around my waist, pulling me closer, and that's the invitation I didn't know I needed to wrap my own arms around him.

He's tall and imposing without being intimidating. He's commanding without being aggressive. He's perfect right now.

The kiss quickly goes from sweet and sexy to four-alarm fire. We're both on the same page here. We know where we're going, and neither of us is trying to act coy about it.

After several moments, he kisses across my jaw, leaving me breathless and panting, then speaks low in my ear.

"Do you want to go inside?"

I fist my hand in his shirt to keep my knees from buckling. He's holding me, though, so I probably wouldn't fall.

"Yes," I breathe.

He pulls back just enough to spin me around by the waist, not letting go of me as I unlock the door.

His hands never leave me as we cross the threshold. Even when I close the door and lock the deadbolt, his lips are dragging down the side of my neck, stopping at my collarbone. His strong arm is wound around my belly, his hand sliding low but not all the way down. Just low enough to show me where he plans to go but letting me know he'll tease me, work me up before he lets me crash.

I hear my keys hit the floor as my hands start searching for him behind me. One hand winds around the nape of his neck and the other goes to his hand, still on my abdomen.

Silky smooth French spills from his mouth, causing my whole body to shudder. Why, oh *why* is that so hot? Not that it matters, but I think I understand parts of what he's saying. Something about wanting me. Something about need. Something about eating...?

Oh.

This time, my knees *do* buckle, but he catches me with that strong hand on my belly.

A soft chuckle escapes his lips before that same strong hand reaches farther around my body to my hip and spins me around to face him again. His mouth captures mine as his arms slide all the way across my back, enveloping me, pulling me in, pressing me against the bulge in his pants. His hands squeeze and caress and make me forget for a few moments that I'm here in part because I needed to get *away*.

The thought of Ethan trying to claw its way into my brain makes me break the kiss so I can look at *Julien's* face. Concentrate on *Julien's* hands. Watch *Julien's* mouth on my skin.

It grounds me. Keeps me in the moment.

We walk—me gently pushing him backward—still plastered together as we head toward my bedroom. Before I even know what's happening, he's sinking to his knees in front of me, and I'm completely mesmerized. I thread my fingers into his dark hair as he teases my belly with his tongue, unbuttons my jeans with deft fingers. Before he pulls them over my hips, he looks up, his hazel eyes meeting mine, making sure I'm still on board.

"May I? S'il te plaît?"*

I suck in a haggard breath. Did he seriously just ask permission? To do...what? Honestly, it doesn't matter. He can do whatever he wants. I think I'm going to die, regardless.

"Yes." The word is more breath than sound, but he hears it all the same because he's moving immediately after. He slides my jeans down my legs, then gently pulls up on each calf to get me to lift my feet so he can pull them off completely.

The way he inches back up my body is nothing short of torturous. His lips trace my skin as he rises, his fingers grasping the hem of my top as he stands, lifting it until I have to raise my arms so he can get it over my head. It lands on the floor somewhere.

"Tu es magnifique," He murmurs against my mouth. "Tu m'excites trop."†

I understood those.

I'm definitely going to die.

Cause of death: too turned on by a French man.

"Je vais te démonter."‡

---

* Please?
† You are beautiful. You excite me too much.
‡ I am going to rip you open.

I have no idea what that means. It doesn't matter. My vagina doesn't care.

He trails tonguing kisses down my neck, calloused hands moving to my hips, gently easing me backward toward the bed.

"Goûte chaque centimètre de ta peau."*

My hands grip his shirt, which makes me realize he's still *wearing* a shirt, and that is completely unacceptable at this point. I pull at the bottom, dragging it up his torso so I can see more of him. He obliges me, letting go of my hips so he can pull his shirt over his head and throw it somewhere.

And his body?

Fuck me.

Julien doesn't have a gym rat's body. No, this man lifts heavy shit at work everyday and uses his body to make works of art. He's not jacked like a bodybuilder, but he *is* defined. He has pecs and abs and veins and a trail of coarse dark hair leading down into his pants.

He's strong and confident, and he's watching me intently.

"You think my body is gorgeous? Have you seen yours?" I manage to squeak out.

He chuckles again, drawing me in for another kiss as he lays me down on the bed.

"Je n'ai pas besoin de toute ton histoire pour que tu te sentes bien."†

Too many words. Only caught a few of them.

He moves down my body, caressing my breasts along the way, squeezing my hips, then dragging my body into the position he wants me in.

---

* Taste every inch of your skin.
† I don't need your whole story to make you feel good.

"Amusons-nous ce soir, ma belle."*

I squirm as Julien leaves languid kisses along my inner thighs. He didn't take my underwear off, which I appreciate more than I anticipated. It's a flimsy barrier, but it gives my brain an extra second to catch up to my lust-addled body.

He makes eye contact with me as he licks up my center, and I swear to everything holy in this world, my heart stops. He teases me like that for a few seconds while I writhe, my hips moving on their own and fists grasping at the duvet.

The fabric separating his tongue and my body needs to go away immediately. My brain has caught up and is currently melting. Fortunately, he's on the same page.

His fingers hook into the strips near my hip bones and pull them down. Once they're finally gone, he returns his attention to the apex of my thighs and conducts an absolute master class in female pleasure.

He's using his tongue and his fingers and is basically making my mind glitch out. When I look down at him, I find him looking up at me with molten heat in his eyes.

I never decided what my epitaph would be. I'm sure someone will figure something out. Whatever, it doesn't matter. I want to be cremated, anyway.

"You taste so good," Julien says against my sensitive flesh. I barely notice he speaks in English, but I figure he did it on purpose so I could understand what he meant.

I lace my fingers through his hair and let my hips move. He's not pinning them down or telling me I shouldn't be an active participant, so here we go.

Every hill on this rollercoaster is one hundred percent worth it. It's anticipation and thrill and endorphins all crashing together in my brain.

---

* Let's have fun tonight, my dear.

My whole body erupts with goose bumps when he finally lets me come, and I don't want to know what kinds of sounds I'm making at this point. Whatever they are, they only seem to spur him on, so I'll just assume it's all right.

As I lay there, panting and somehow not sated, I hear the rasp of a zipper, the crinkle of a condom wrapper, and the hiss of his breath as he rolls it on.

He crawls on top of me, pulling me further up the bed with him. How? I have no idea. I'm deadweight. I died—*la petite mort*—but a death nonetheless.[*]

When he sinks into me, he looks directly into my eyes, watching for every reaction, every thought misfiring through my brain.

"Parfaite..." he breathes onto my lips before crushing his mouth to mine.[†]

From there, you'll just have to call my time of death. I'm nothing but a ball of nerve endings that is low on oxygen because I can't get a deep breath.

Julien is everything I need right now. He's attentive and gentle, but rough when I need him to be. He's encouraging and kind, but I'm certain every word he says to me is filthy as hell.

He takes care when putting me in a new position. He checks in with me to make sure I'm still enjoying myself. He kisses me anywhere his mouth can reach, no matter what shape we've formed. He's wonderful.

When we're finally both finished (me, three times and him, once), we lay lifeless on the bed together while we contemplate all our life choices. Or maybe that's just me.

We chat for a bit after he discards the condom, laying

---

[*]   The little death—the French term for an orgasm.
[†]   Perfect...

under the sheets, basking in a haze that neither of us seems to want to end. But eventually, I get a text from Kelsie that she's on her way back to our apartment, so Julien gets up and dresses. We're both fully clothed by the time Kelsie waltzes through the door.

"Oh, Julien, it's good to see you again."

"It's only been a couple of hours," he teases.

"Yes, well, I've been drinking. Time is meaningless."

I laugh at her as she bows dramatically, giggling when she stands back up.

"All right, off to bed with you, Kels." I gently nudge her toward her bedroom and then walk Julien to the door.

"Can I call you tomorrow?"

I think about it for a moment—not because I'm not sure if I want to see him (all of him) again, but because I know my head is a mess. So I decide to level with him.

"Yes..."

He must sense there's more to that sentence, because he tilts his head and threads his fingers into the hair at the base of my skull before he asks the question. "But?"

I smile. I'm not nervous to tell him, which I'm a little surprised by. I feel surprisingly comfortable around him.

"I just got out of a...long-term relationship. I'm not really in good shape for anything serious."

He smiles in return. "That's okay with me." And then he pulls me in with that hand still in my hair and kisses me. When he breaks the kiss, he slides his phone into my hands. I dutifully enter my number and, with one more kiss, he's gone.

CHAPTER 8
THIS FEELS LIKE A LOOPHOLE

ETHAN

With Or Without You - U2

"I'm sorry...I'm just still having trouble understanding," my eldest sister says, her eyes boring holes into my head through our phone screens.

Running a hand down my face, I sigh.

"I'm not sure what you don't understand, Rach. I've told you what you need to know."

I can practically hear her frown even though I'm purposefully averting my eyes.

"Ethan."

All the anger, frustration, heartbreak, and self-loathing from the past two months is crawling up my throat. I pinch the bridge of my nose in an attempt to squash the tears that want out.

"*Ethan.*"

I grind my teeth together and force out a single word. "What?"

The breath she takes in is audible through FaceTime.

I'm in for it. I just know it. She's silent for just a couple of seconds too long.

"Ethan Bennett Sawyer, look at me right now."

Fuck, she full-named me.

With a fortifying deep breath, I look up to the screen to find Rachel watching me with a mixture of concern and anger on her face. Her lips purse together in the way they do when she's made a decision.

And I'm scared. I won't lie.

I see her phone being jostled as she does something with it and all of a sudden, the windows are rearranging to allow space for my other sister.

"Goddammit, Rachel," I grumble.

"What do you expect, Ethan?"

"What's going on?" Abby asks.

My only response is a groan as I fall back against the couch.

"Our darling brother has been hiding shit from us," Rachel snipes.

"What? What do you mean?"

"Jesus," I mumble.

"Tell her, Ethan."

"You tell her, Rachel. You're the one who called her."

"Tell me what?" Abby asks. "What's going on with Ethan?"

I take a teeny, tiny bit of comfort in the concern I hear in her voice.

When I don't say anything, Rachel speaks up.

"Maggie and Ethan broke up."

Abby's gasp is obnoxious, but she quickly goes into maternal care mode. "*What?* Oh, Ethan, what happened?"

"Holy shit, Rachel, what did I ever do to you?"

"You were born, quite frankly, but I looped Abby in because she might be able to help."

"No one can help," I say, rolling my eyes.

"Maybe I can," Abby chimes in. "Wes and I broke up once. And then we got back together, and we've been married for ten years now. We have three gorgeous kids, if I do say so myself."

I didn't really think I could hate myself any more than I already did, but I'm realizing now that it's totally possible. I *absolutely* hate myself more than I did before Rachel called me a few minutes ago.

"Guys, you can't help."

"How do you know—"

"That's bullshit—"

"—if you told us what actually happened—"

"—we're very helpful—"

"—we could offer the female perspective—"

"—we're happily married women, you know—"

They're tripping over each other to tell me why they can help and why they're qualified, but I can't listen to it.

"Oh my god, please stop," I beg. "You cannot help. I fucked everything up, and now she won't talk to me, *and* she left for Paris a couple of weeks ago. Trust me, there's nothing you can do."

My sisters are silent for a blissful five seconds before Abby speaks.

"Oh, Ethan...sweetheart, I'm so sorry."

I take a stuttering breath, trying to get my shit together at Abby's sweet, supportive voice.

"What did you do?" Rachel asks.

"Fuck, Rachel," I groan.

"Come on, Rach, he's clearly upset. Cut him some slack." Abby tries her best to support me.

"Ethan, what happened? You still haven't told us." Rachel's tone is only slightly softened.

I swallow against a dry throat and admit the truth.

I tell them everything. About how I proposed. How she refused. How we had a massive fight. How she moved out. How we haven't spoken, and no matter how many times I reach out to her...she won't return my messages.

When I'm finished talking, I glance at the screen to find both of my sisters watching me with big, round, *devastated* brown eyes.

"Oh, Ethan, I'm so sorry..." Abby manages.

Rachel—who was so hard-nosed just moments ago—is suddenly silent.

"That's what happened. And you can't help. So just fucking drop it."

Neither of them say anything for another minute, and I decide it's late enough in the day to crack open a beer.

I FaceTime with my sisters at least once per month on a Saturday, and I've been dodging them recently. This is the best time to talk to them because it's nap time for the little ones and mandated quiet time for the older ones. Under normal circumstances, I'd talk to the kids when the adults are done, but I'm not in the mood today.

Quick math tells me what time it is in Paris.

It's past five o'clock for Maggie. Fuck it.

And then I wonder what she's doing and who she's doing it with. I rip the cap off the bottle with more force than necessary and chuck it into the recycling bin.

I can hear at least one of my sisters take a breath, like they're going to say something about the fact that I'm drinking at three in the afternoon. I cut a sharp look at the phone, and both of their mouths snap shut.

It gives me more satisfaction than it should.

Trudging back to the couch, I do my best to not look at anything around me. This entire apartment still feels like mine and Maggie's. She took her stuff, but not any of the framed photos that still hang on the walls or rest on the shelves. I oscillate between having them displayed so I can see her gorgeous face and taking them down because seeing her is too painful.

I don't want to be here these days, so I find myself looking for excuses to meet Miles for a drink after work, but I hate being around people, too.

And also, Miles knows Maggie. It's a double-edged sword.

He never brings her up, and I only allow myself to ask about her once per outing.

Collapsing onto the couch, I glare at my sisters again. "Can we agree to be done discussing this?"

Rachel frowns severely, but Abby's head tilts to the right, her sad eyes fixed on me.

"Ethan, we can't just—" Rachel starts, but I cut her off.

"You can. You can just fucking drop it."

"But...are *you* dropping it?" Abby asks tentatively.

I take a pull from my beer bottle while I think about my answer.

Of course, I'm not dropping it. But I don't know what to do if she won't pick up the phone when I call or return a single text message. I've even emailed her.

I *emailed* my girlfriend of five years just to try to get her to talk to me.

"I'm not giving up," I admit. "But I can't make her talk to me."

"Okay, well..." Abby's face changes into something more determined. "That's a start. You're not giving up. And you shouldn't. You two are so good together."

"You are," Rachel adds quietly, but I know she's not done. "You know what question I want to ask."

Honestly, I want to smash this beer bottle over my head.

"Yes, I know what question you want to ask, and I'm begging you not to ask it," I snap. "I can't right now. Like I said, I'm fully aware this is my fault, okay? I'm fucking trying."

They adopt identical expressions—lips pressed into thin lines, eyes bright like they have a million comments they're keeping to themselves.

I take the moment of silence to take a big gulp of beer.

Rachel blows out a breath and nods once. "Okay. It makes sense that there needs to be a cooling off period...let her calm down and get some space. But we need to be ready when the time comes."

I blink.

"You're right," Abby chimes in. "Let's brainstorm. How can you get messages to her?"

I blink again.

Neither of them says anything for a minute while I stare at them.

"Why do you look like a deer caught in the headlights?" Rachel snaps.

I shake my head quickly, trying to clear it. "I'm sorry, are you two trying to help me win Maggie back?"

"*YES,*" both of them yell at the same time.

I'm too surprised to say anything, but I feel my eyes get really wide.

"We already told you we could help, Ethan," Rachel says, rolling her eyes.

"We might be your sisters, but we're still women," Abby says. "Of course, we can help you."

"This isn't one of your romance novels, Abbs."

Her face goes stone hard before she points a finger into the camera. "Don't you dare make fun of my reading preferences. I'm the one who covered for you in high school when Dad nearly caught you sneaking out of the house to meet up with that Tammy girl who wore too much makeup."

"Whoa, calm down," I say, holding up my beer in place of my hand. "I'm not making fun of you, I'm simply reminding you that this is real life."

Rachel whistles low and shakes her head while Abby's eyes narrow.

"First of all, never tell a woman to 'calm down,' and second, saying this is *real life* diminishes the value of the entire genre..."

Abby keeps going, but I'm trying to figure out what I can say to calm her down without telling her to calm down again. I should have known better. It was a dumb thing to say. I'm tired and irritable.

"All right, separate corners," Rachel calls over Abby. "The reason we're having this discussion is to figure out how Ethan can get Maggie back. All other bullshit can be set aside for now."

On Rachel's end of the call, I hear a giggle, followed by a snicker. Her eyes dart to her left.

"You said a bad word." I hear my nine-year-old niece, Leah, speaking off camera.

"You owe a dollar to the jar," my eleven-year-old nephew, Aiden, says.

"That makes five dollars just today," Leah says.

"We're going to get that trampoline in no time at all," Aiden says, and then I hear what is unmistakably a high five.

Rachel grinds her teeth together.

"Don't you two have homework to finish?"

I can't help but snicker a little bit, which I try to cover up with a sip of beer. Abby is also trying—and failing—to keep a straight face.

Rach has always been a hard ass with sass. Growing up, we were the ones who took the brunt of her attitude, and it's never not funny to see her taking shit from her kids.

"I'll put the money in the jar. Just go do your homework and let me finish my conversation with your aunt and uncle. You can talk to them when I'm done."

Abby clears her throat, still trying to stifle her laughter.

"Where were we?"

"I think you're at five dollars. Because I'm not present in your home and therefore, not playing the game, I owe no dollars. Abby rarely swears, so she's in the clear for now."

"Smartass," Rachel mutters.

"What was that?" I ask, turning my ear toward the screen. "Was that another dollar?"

"Enough," she snipes. "Focus on your own problems, Ethan."

She manages to pull a genuine smile from me and even a small laugh.

"Okay, yes. Back to Ethan's problems," Abby says.

"So, she's not responding to any of your messages," Rachel begins.

I nod a confirmation.

"And she won't answer the phone?"

I shake my head. "Nope."

Abby frowns. "Do you think she blocked your number?"

That thought sends nausea rolling through me.

Could she have blocked my number?

I never even considered that to be a possibility, but I have called and texted her so many times that I could see her getting annoyed and just...making it stop in the only way she knew would actually work.

And then suddenly things click into place, and I just know.

Maggie moves on.

Maggie moves forward.

She wouldn't have looked back at someone who'd hurt her.

And I hurt her so badly.

With a sigh, I run my fingers through my hair and pull at the strands.

"Yeah..."

I have to clear my throat before I can say anything else.

"I'll bet she did."

Both of my sisters' faces fall.

"Fuck," I mutter.

"Swear jar, Uncle Ethan!" Leah yells from the background.

"Leah Marie, I asked for privacy," Rachel scolds. "Go do your homework, and I'll find you when I'm done."

I hear a door close, and then Rachel faces me again.

"Sorry, Ethan. You don't owe us a dollar."

Truthfully, I'll throw five or ten bucks in the jar the next time I go to their house, but I don't say anything because I'm still so devastated by this new information.

"Okay, okay..." Abby starts. "If she really did block his number, how can he get messages to her?"

"If she blocked my number, she doesn't want to hear from me, and I feel torn on trying to find ways around it."

"What?" Abby all but shrieks. "You can't give up on her."

"She's right, Ethan. You can't stop trying."

I tug on my hair again. "You two are so fucking confusing. My whole life you've been preaching consent and teaching me to respect women...to take them at their word *the first time* they say it, and now you're telling me to ignore everything you've ever taught me and bulldoze past her wishes?"

I'm met with two sheepish looks before Rachel manages to find a loophole in her own logic.

"She never actually told you she didn't want to talk to you, did she?"

I think back to our last conversation.

Please don't say any more.

That was the last thing she said to me. When she came back to get the rest of her things, I made myself scarce. She didn't even leave me a note. Her stuff was just...gone when I got home.

"No..." I say, tapping on my now-empty beer bottle, thinking. "No, she never explicitly told me she didn't want to talk to me."

Abby's eyes light up. "Okay, so let's operate under the assumption that she's blocked your number and find a workaround."

"Yes, if she's not getting texts or voicemails, let's primarily try emailing her," Rachel says as if she'll *also* be emailing my ex-girlfriend. "You can still text or call occa-sionally, just to see if anything's changed, but she'll never get those messages if she actually blocked you. They don't come in a deluge if someone unblocks the number. *However*, if someone blocks your email address, it usually just goes to their spam folder. So it's still accessible...it just requires more effort."

I think about that for a moment. It feels like less of an invasion. It still feels like a loophole, but the possessiveness I feel for Maggie is winning out. I can't give up on her.

I won't.

"All right. That's the plan, then."

CHAPTER 9
JUST HERE FOR A
GOOD TIME

MAGGIE

Atlantis - Seafret
October

My coworkers are talking a mile a minute, and I'm not catching any of it. My French has certainly improved over the past month—I'm picking up more words, and I'm able to be more conversational, but damn. I'm realizing that they actually slow down for me when I'm included in the conversation.

But right now, I'm just trying to keep my head down and focus on the task at hand—figuring out what stone would work best on the façade of the building.

I've narrowed it down to several options that would complement the surrounding structures. None of them will match perfectly, considering how old those buildings are and how new ours will be, but it will still be better than anything we'd be doing back home.

People in Europe care more about making it *right* versus making it *cheap* and *fast* so you can move on to the next project. I can't say that my firm really pushes us to turn projects over so quickly that we're increasing liability, but we're no different from any other American business.

Take the project, regardless of how much it will overtax your employees.

Execute the project as quickly as possible.

Save as much money as possible while working on the project to maximize profits.

Take on a new project.

Lather. Rinse. Repeat.

I'm not going to go so far as to say other capitalist countries aren't following the same game plan, but Europe seems to collectively care more about the quality of the work, rather than the quantity.

I realize that's a bold claim. And very generalized. But when it comes to building stuff...they just don't cut corners the way Americans tend to. They care more about the history of the space and the quality of the structure. And how could they not? They're so much older than us.

Some of the buildings in Europe are *thousands* of years old, whereas buildings in the US aren't more than three hundred years old. Any structures that existed at the time of —let's face it: robbery—aren't still standing, and the Industrial Revolution introduced new ways to do basically everything, including architecture and construction.

But Europe has survived hundreds of wars. France and England have fought wars against each other countless times, and that's in addition to the two world wars they fought as allies. Their cities were obliterated by bombs, but they painstakingly rebuilt with more modern technology while trying to honor the memory of the former structure.

As an architect, of course I wanted to work in Europe for a bit. It was a no-brainer.

The building we're working on is a new build. We'd

looked into the possibilities of refurbishing the old structure, but it cost so much more to fix all the problems it had than to just start over. The news wasn't *unexpected*, though it was unwelcome. Our team had collectively wanted the challenge of restoring the building to its former glory. Instead, we'll be doing our best to create a new structure that pays homage to the old one while offering better functionality.

"Maggie, what do you think of visiting the stonemasons tomorrow?" Vivienne appears on my left, and I have to blink a few times while my eyes adjust from my laptop screen to her in all her glory.

The stonemasons.

Julien.

Because of Dominique's connection to her brother's business, he's (apparently) often called upon for stone-related requests.

Going for nonchalance, I sit back in my chair, resting my elbows on the armrests and intertwining my fingers over my belly. "That sounds like a good plan. I'll be ready. I'm nearly finished. I can send a list of feasible options to the team."

"Très bien!"* Viv claps her hands together with a gleeful smile. "I'll let Julien and Gabriel know." She whips her phone out of her dress pocket (a dress pocket!) and starts tapping away, resting one hip against my desk.

Julien and I have continued to see each other on a semi-regular basis. We both know what's going on here—we've discussed it extensively. There's no long-term potential. I'm not staying in Paris, and he's not moving to the States. I'm not ready for a relationship, and he's not looking for one. We have an expiration date, and that's okay.

---

* All right / Very good!

I'm pretty sure everyone in the office knows what's going on with us. Or at least that *something* is going on with us. I did briefly discuss the topic with Dominique since he's her brother, and I didn't want to cause drama.

She literally laughed at me.

Folding over with laughter, she gripped my wrist, attempting to speak through wheezing breaths, I caught her squeaking out words I think meant *prude Americans*. When she calmed herself, she told me that she didn't care in the slightest and Julien was an adult who could take care of himself. Then, she kissed my cheek and said something that basically sounded like the equivalent of the Southern, *bless your heart.*

So while people might have an idea of what's going on, I'm not advertising it. Julien and I keep our hands to ourselves in public—for the most part. We don't go on dates, but we do see each other out at clubs or at dinner. Usually, the evening ends at one of our apartments, depending on where we are in the city.

Always, the evening ends in orgasms. Julien is...generous.

"D'accord,"* Vivienne says. "We're all set for tomorrow. We'll meet before lunch, and then we can all grab a bite together."

"Parfait,"† I offer with a smile.

Viv responds with a wink and a knowing smile, which I roll my eyes at.

Again, I'm not *not* excited to see Julien in the middle of my workday. I'm always up for seeing Julien. But I don't

---

* All right / Okay.

† Perfect.

need my coworkers getting all involved and trying to convince us there's some happily-ever-after for us.

There isn't.

I'm not sure there's a happily-ever-after for me at all.

EVERYONE IS SPEAKING in English for my and Kelsie's benefit. Their English is better than our French. I'd say it's because French is a difficult language, but let's face it, so is English, and they're doing just fine.

Regardless, the stonemasons say the list I made them is totally possible. We've narrowed down the choices based on the group's collective opinions and creative eyes, ruling out the selections that will cost an ungodly amount of money. Gabriel and Julien said the supply chain issues as of late will mean increased costs for a couple of the more elaborate options on the list.

I'd taken care to include mostly cost-effective options as well as some that were more aspirational, knowing we'd need to narrow them down. So I'm not offended or annoyed. I knew where we'd end up.

Mostly, I'm pleased I was on the right track. Glad I found options that work with the aging façades of the surrounding buildings. I'm excited to have the opportunity to contribute to this historic block in a historic city.

I feel someone watching me as I'm studying the samples the stonemasons got out to show us. When I look up, I see it's Julien. Of course.

My smile is instant, doing my best to keep my air of professionalism, but the look in Julien's eyes is anything but. There's heat there, and as his eyes slide down my body, they only burn hotter.

I can feel my cheeks heat, but when his eyes return to my face, I shake my head subtly, admonishing him for being so blatant in public.

He bites his bottom lip before winking at me and mouthing the English word "later."

Forget my cheeks—the rest of my body simmers. Jesus.

I avert my eyes out of sheer self-preservation and focus again on my colleagues' conversation about stone.

And not in a sexual innuendo way.

"D'accord," Dominique finally says. "Déjeuner.* Time for lunch. I'm starving."

"Me, too," Julien chimes in.

Although my heart skips a beat and my knees weaken enough to force me into placing a hand on the table, I refuse to look at him. I can feel his playful eyes on me, satisfied that he made me blush.

He sits next to me at lunch, subtly brushing his knee against mine every now and then. Leaning in to whisper in my ear when no one is paying attention to us. It's all fore-play, and if it were anyone else—if *I* were anyone else—I'd be concerned about boundaries and the slippery slope of falling in love because our chemistry is off the *charts,* and Julien is a genuinely good person.

With a French accent.

I *should* fall in love with him.

I *should* want to grab Julien up and keep him forever.

We get along. We have a great time together. He's atten-tive and kind and absolutely the type of person I could see building a life with long-term.

But as it happens, I *am* me, and I know myself well enough to know that I'm in no danger of falling for Julien.

---

* Okay. Lunch.

Tony Bennett may have left his heart in San Francisco, but mine is in my hometown with a pair of milk chocolate eyes and five years worth of memories I'd rather forget right now.

I'm not capable of falling in love with anyone at the moment, and I get a similar impression about Julien. As the saying goes: we're here for a good time, not for a long time.

~

December

"Allons-y,"* Julien calls. Grabbing my hand, he pulls me toward the market square so we can pick up some goodies for tonight—people from work are getting together at Dominique's place as a final party before people begin to split off for the holidays.

Julien and I met up after I was done with work. We had a quick dinner and then walked over to this market so I could check out the decorations before the holidays. By the time I return from my break home, it will be disassembled and returned to pre-holiday normalcy.

Time is flying. It's almost Christmas, and I am woefully unprepared.

Unprepared to go home and face my family.

To start planning for my return to the States...to my real life.

To be within four thousand miles of Ethan.

I'm not ready for any of it, though I know it's necessary. I'm not going to stay in Paris forever, and I need to be able to

---

* Let's go.

return to *something*. And as it currently stands, I have nothing in the US that's actually *mine*.

I moved out of the apartment I shared with Ethan when we broke up, and I stayed with Kate until I left for Paris. My stuff is mostly at Kate's, although some random things were taken to my childhood bedroom at my parents' house. When I return home after this project is over, I'll essentially be homeless. I'll have to stay with friends, with Kate, or—if I'm truly desperate—with my parents.

I'd rather not do any of that. I'm a person who enjoys her own space. I certainly don't mind sharing it when I have to —like living with Kate for a bit and Kelsie in Paris, or Ethan when we were still together. But right now? I just need space to build a new life all on my own.

So I'm enlisting Kate's help to look for apartments for me. She sends me what she finds that would suit my needs —all one-bedroom, one-bath's worth of my needs—and I send her my feedback. She's hoping to have apartments for me to look at when I get home for my two-week break. Depending on what's available when, I may be technically moving in before I have anything to *actually* move in. I'll have to sign a lease, and then she can collect my keys later on if I'm still not back yet.

"Ahh. Here we are," Julien says as we round one final corner and a scene directly out of a Hallmark Christmas movie unfolds before me.

Pop-up shops line the perimeter of the square, selling little trinkets, stocking stuffers, ornaments, and in some cases, pastries. Everyone is decked out with holiday cheer, wearing festive colors, wrapped up in hats and scarves and megawatt smiles. And right in the middle stands a massive Christmas tree, trimmed and decorated to perfection, shining bright, lighting the entire square.

"Wow..." I whisper. "It's gorgeous."

"I'm glad you like it," Julien says.

When I look over at him, he's smiling, just like I am, taking in the vendor stalls and festivities. He meets my eyes, and his smile gets wider. His nose and cheeks are red from the cold, but his gaze is warm and inviting.

I huff out a laugh at my own stupid luck for liking him, but not being able to fall in love with him. My breath is a white cloud between us, and of course, he notices.

"Let's get you something to drink to warm up."

He leads me to a vendor selling vin chaud* and gets us each a cup. It's warm in my hands, and the very first sip begins to thaw my bones.

"Merci," † he says to the vendor, dropping cash in her hand and turning to wrap one arm around my shoulders.

"She has the best vin chaud. I've tried others, but there's something about her recipe that makes it better than all the rest."

"Well, I don't have anything to compare it to, but it's quite delightful."

He smiles down at me. Kisses my head.

"Let's keep moving. We have things to do, people to see," he says, guiding me toward the first section of vendor stalls.

We meander along the perimeter, stopping when we see things we like, picking up food for the party. I buy some ornaments for my giant family and even a couple of things for myself. I won't have a tree this year, but I will in the future, and I want the souvenirs.

My mom always told us that Christmas trees should tell the story of our lives, from childhood to adulthood. Of

---

* Mulled/hot wine.
† Thank you.

course, she told me this for the first time after I complained that our ornaments didn't match. I'm partial to matching glass ornaments in a cohesive color scheme, but Mom always put up all the awful ornaments we made in school on the tree, even when they were falling apart. She said they reminded her of our childhoods, and that we were the best part of her adult life, so of course she wanted them on the tree.

With the formidable Helen Rafferty on my mind, I pick up one final ornament before we head over to Dominique's place.

CHAPTER 10
HAPPY FUCKING HOLIDAYS
ETHAN

Is it Just Me? - Emily Burns and JP Cooper

The view outside this window is boring. A lot like every other apartment I've looked at since Maggie moved out. Bland, dull, cold, lonely. If a view from the sixth floor of a building set on top of a hill can be any of those things.

The lease on the apartment I shared with Maggie is set to end on January 31. I already put in my notice with the management company that I'm not renewing the lease. It's a gorgeous apartment, and I love the location, but I can't be there anymore.

Everything about that place reminds me of Maggie. We found it together. We moved into it together. Celebrated the milestone in every room of it. Most of the time, I find myself staring at the television. It's on, but I'm not watching it. Instead, I'm thinking about Maggie.

What she's doing.

Who she's doing it with.

How long it's been since I've seen her.

How I'm still head over heels in love with her.

What it will take to get her back.

I realize that might make me sound pathetic, but if you were me, you'd feel the same way.

While some guys in this situation are out swiping on whatever app is currently most popular, I just...don't want to. I'm not interested in random women because I only want *one* woman. I want that *one* woman to come back from Paris and talk to me so we can figure out if there's a way for us to be together. I want that *one* woman to look me in the eye and tell me she doesn't feel anything for me anymore.

She has a tell when she's lying. I'll know if she's telling the truth.

So if she can do that, then—and only then—will I give up.

"What do you think, man?" Miles' voice cuts into my thoughts.

I turn to find him looking in the closet by the door. He turns on a light using a string that hangs from the ceiling and a cedar-lined space comes into view.

"Holy shit. They kept the cedar closets."

I nod, unsure of what to say.

He turns the light off and closes the closet door. "So, what do you think? You gonna take it?"

I look around one more time. It's barren. The carpets have been recently shampooed, the walls freshly painted that same eggshell white every apartment complex uses, and the space smells like it was cleaned in the last week. It's...fine.

"Yeah..." I nod again. "Yeah, I think so."

Miles watches me in silence as I walk into the kitchen and turn on the tap. Wait for the water to heat up.

This place has all the essentials—hot water, heat and air

conditioning, a place to sleep, and somewhere to plug in a TV. The only thing missing is the one thing I fucked up.

But there's nothing I can do about that right now. She's in Paris. I'm here. She's still not responding to my messages, and I have no indication that she's getting my emails. I assume they're sitting in her spam folder.

So I'll let her have some space.

For a little while, anyway.

"She's supposed to be back here for a couple of weeks… for the holidays," Miles says. His voice echoes off the bare walls of the living room.

I did text her to ask if she'd be home for Christmas, but surprise, surprise…she didn't respond.

"Yeah?" I turn to look at him over the small peninsula that separates the two rooms.

He nods. "Should be early next week."

"You talked to her?"

He doesn't answer right away. Like he's trying to decide what he should tell me, as someone who is friends with both of us.

Finally, he takes a deep breath and averts his eyes.

He's holding something back.

I know it before he even says the first word.

"Yeah, I've talked to her a few times. Not since last week. There's not much overlap on our current projects, so I'm not a consistent point of contact for her right now."

I don't look away from him. Maybe to make him squirm a little bit. Maybe just to let him know I know there's something else. But he's under no obligation to tell me what he knows. He gave an answer, and I'll have to accept it.

So, I nod. "I'm glad she's coming back to see her family for Christmas. It's been hard on them since Nick passed."

Miles never met Nick, but I obviously did. That first

night at the gas station, followed by countless family functions and celebrations. Births, deaths, holidays, family vaca-
tions. I was there for all of it, right by Maggie's side. He
eventually stopped calling me Hatchback—for the Honda I
had at the time. I understood it was just a minor form of
hazing, and it didn't really bother me. It always reminded
me of that first night when I asked the beautiful woman
with the wild hair if she needed help.

I remember being extremely conscious that I didn't want
to make her feel uncomfortable. I have two older sisters who
have schooled the hell out of me about what it means to be
a woman walking around in this world today, and I was not
about to make this woman fear for her life because I felt the
need to make sure she was all right.

I stayed several feet away from her—far enough that she
wouldn't be afraid I'd reach out and grab her. I kept my eyes
firmly locked on her face unless I was looking at her obvi-
ously-overprotective brother, or the car, or the jumper
cables on the ground in front of it.

When she crossed her arms over her chest, it took a
Herculean effort not to let my gaze dip to what I could only
assume at the time was fantastic cleavage, but I did it. I
resisted because I didn't want to seem like a pervert,
checking out the *not*-damsel-in-distress.

She was stunning. Gorgeous, witty, sassy, and I knew it
wouldn't be classified as anything other than creepy if I
asked for her number or to join me for dinner or even for
her name. I accepted that she was just a woman at a gas
station I would never see again.

And then the following night, I was headed toward the
bar at a club I didn't even want to be at when I saw that mass
of curly hair. Less wild, but still present. My relationship
with a higher power has always been shaky at best, but that

night after the gas station, I definitely threw up a prayer or a good thought or juju or whatever, asking the universe to put me in a position where I could meet the Gas Station Girl again.

And damn if the universe didn't deliver.

There she was in a skin-tight black dress that left nothing about her figure to the imagination, and thank fuck for that because all the blood in my body was draining away from my brain. When I finished my trek to the bar and finally got to see her profile—the same view I'd first encountered the night before—I couldn't help the massive smile that split my face in half.

The moment I spoke, I knew she recognized my voice. Her body went completely still, but the small smile on her face melted off, and her eyes widened.

It was when she turned to look at me that I knew I needed to somehow get her to talk to me—*actually* talk to me. None of this quick conversation bullshit where I don't learn anything about her. I wanted to take her somewhere quiet and figure out who she was. What she liked. What made her tick.

She took plastic cups full of water to her friends on the dance floor, and when she returned, I finally got her name.

Maggie.

A name I'd worship for the next five years. One I'd still worship if she'd let me.

We spent the rest of the night talking on the rooftop terrace. It was the greatest night of my life, except for every night thereafter with that curly-haired woman from the gas station. She told me she and her friends were out celebrating her official entry into the architecture world. We talked about our favorite foods, movies, music, and what we do with our free time.

At one point, her friends came bursting through the doors leading down to the club, eyes wild and frantic, looking for her. She called their names, and they stalked over to us with purposeful strides and murder in their eyes.

What I didn't know was that they told her they'd come looking for her if she didn't return within a certain period of time. And obviously, she didn't return. Because she was with me. On the rooftop. Losing track of time.

Maggie's friends calmed down once they saw she was fine and that I wasn't being creepy—we'd stuck to water, though our cups were both empty. So they went to the bar to get more drinks, dropping water off for Maggie and me, and then plopped themselves down on nearby chairs to cool off.

She and I stayed right where we were, talking and laughing.

By the time we parted ways, I had her phone number, she had mine, and I was well on my way to falling in love with her.

To this day, Maggie Rafferty is the best thing that ever happened to me.

And I fucked it all up.

"Are you two finished in here? Or do you have some additional questions?"

The building representative is standing in the doorway, looking back and forth between Miles and me. I have no idea how long she's been there or how long I've been staring into space and ignoring Miles. Or if he's even said anything else.

"We're finished," I tell her. "I'll take it."

IT'S the week before Christmas and—like a stereotypical man—I'm trying to wrap up my holiday shopping. My nieces and nephews deserve an uncle who has his shit together more than I do, but you don't get to choose your family, and I'm in the process of moving. I can only do so much right now.

I stop at a children's store in the outdoor mall to pick up some toys I hope won't annoy the shit out of my sisters (maybe just annoy them a *little*). Which is essentially what I tell the worker who comes by to ask if I need any help, at which point, she laughs in a way that is absolutely over-the-top. I might be a little funny, but I don't think that comment was particularly earth-shattering.

Is she flirting with me?

She's a few inches shorter than me. Blond hair in loose curls and blue eyes framed tastefully with eyeliner and something glittery on her lids. There's a small clip with a red velvet bow on it holding a portion of her hair out of her face, and she's wearing a green sweater with skinny jeans and black leather boots. She looks festive. Like she waits for the holidays all year-round. Her name tag says HOLLY in large bold letters.

Jesus, even her name screams Christmas.

She holds my gaze for a moment before turning shy... looking down, clearing her throat, and putting a lock of hair behind her ear. Her cheeks turn pink when she looks back up at me.

"I'm happy to show you around..." Her voice trails off at the end of the sentence, lilting up, turning it into a question, and it takes at least two seconds longer than it should for me to realize she's waiting for me to fill in my name.

"Ethan," I finish for her.

"Ethan..." she says through her smile.

I'm pretty out of practice with this, but I'm very certain this woman is trying to flirt with me.

"What kinds of toys do they like?"

I clear my throat and shake my head a little bit. *Get it together, Ethan.*

"My sister likes to get some toys that will actually keep them busy for a while...so maybe something educational but still fun."

"And how old are they?"

"Uhh..." I do some quick mental math, starting with the eldest. "Eleven, nine, eight, six, and four."

"Oh my, your sister has her hands full," she says, blue eyes wide and pink lips parted.

"No, no, I have two sisters."

"Oh, phew." She lightly wipes a hand across her forehead as if the thought of all those children seems terrifying. And maybe she's right. That's a lot of kids, and the youngest two are still feral. "All right, let's start over here with the younger kids stuff because it's easier. It's harder for the older ones."

"Is it?" I ask. I find that hard to believe.

"Oh, yeah." She glances over her shoulder as she walks away. "There's so much educational stuff, and there are still so many skills to develop when they're little like that. But the older kids have preferences and favorite movie characters. You can't get a kid who loves *Moana* a toy from *Cinderella.*"

I suppose she has a point. "I hadn't thought of it that way," I say, eyeing the displays we pass as we walk through the aisles. I nearly walk right into her when she stops, thanks to my lack of attention, but I catch myself just in time, putting a hand up and catching her shoulder.

Her smile widens, which frankly alarms me, so I pull my hand back as quickly as I can without it seeming weird.

"Here are some of the toys and games we recommend for kids ages five and six. Sight words, books that help kids learn how to read, little dry-erase booklets that help them learn how to write and practice their letters, and workbooks, of course." She turns to face the other side of the aisle and gestures toward packages that have buttons begging customers to *try me!* I immediately start pressing buttons to test the volume.

"And of course, here are the electronics-based toys that they can interact with. Some are basically little computers, and others have extra accessories so you can have expansion packs as they grow bored with the ones they have."

"Do they all have volume control on them?" I ask.

"Some do, some don't."

I make a mental note to only get ones with volume control.

"But some parents have a trick to help with the ones that don't have volume control...you can put a piece of tape over the speaker to muffle the sound."

That idea has me looking up at her with raised eyebrows. "No kidding?"

"No kidding. It works."

"Hmm. Well, I think that opens up my options a little." I press another button on a toy that makes a horrid amount of noise and even causes my sales associate companion to wince. "Oh, that's awful."

"Yeah...if it were up to me, I'd trash all of those."

"Noted. I'll skip that one."

"I got this one for my nephew for his sixth birthday," she says, picking up a toy that looks like a drawing tablet, but it has a fake pen attached by a string. "There are prompts that teach them how to write letters and spell words. It also has games to make it a bit more fun and engaging. He seems to like it. And my sister doesn't complain about the noise level."

I can't help but smile. She's amusing. And helpful. So I nod and take the toy from her.

"Sounds good to me."

"Great," she says, her smile growing even larger. "Okay let's move on to the six-year-old."

As we wander through the store looking for toys for the remaining hellions in my family, I find myself wondering what Holly wants out of life. Does she want to get married? Does she want two-point-five kids and a dog in a cute little house with a garden and white picket fence?

These things seemed so simple before. I consider myself a feminist and pretty open-minded individual, but sometimes I still have a hard time wrapping my mind around the fact that Maggie doesn't want to get married.

Doesn't everyone want to find their one special person?

Don't they want to make a commitment to that person?

I suppose I've never been too much of a fuck boy. I've slept with my fair share of women, but I'm not one to jump from one to another without much thought. I've never hooked up with more than one woman in a weekend or kicked one out before another could catch me.

I like being in a relationship. I like the comfort of it. The stability. Maybe it was from watching my own parents' marriage fall apart and the way it tossed all sense of normalcy out the window for us kids. I'm sure a therapist would have a field day with this mess.

Holly tells me about her holiday plans as she rings out my order. I'm only half paying attention, thanks to my existential crisis. I tap my card on the card reader to complete the transaction and begin picking up my bags.

"I enjoyed helping you today, Ethan," Holly says, stapling my receipt to other pieces of paper. "I included gift receipts for you, in addition to some coupons."

"Oh, thanks. I appreciate your help today," I say, taking my receipt from her.

"I hope to see you again soon," she says. There's a coy look in her eye as she waves goodbye.

I smile and nod politely before wishing her a happy holiday and getting the fuck out of the store. I'm hot and starting to sweat, and I just want to be outside in the frigid cold.

When I reach the sidewalk, I suck crisp air into my lungs and take a look around. It's starting to get dark, but there's still a little bit of daylight left. I decide to stop in one of the restaurants to order takeout, since the idea of cooking tonight feels daunting.

As I round the corner of the Chinese place, I catch a glimpse of wild curly hair and hear a laugh that haunts me in my sleep. Eyes laser-focused, I whip my head around to find her in the crowd again. She's walking quickly, and before I can even get my feet to work properly, she turns right, and I lose her.

"Fuck."

I see the white cloud of my breath, obscuring my vision for only a second before it dissipates. And then I'm running.

I take off in the direction she went, catching another glimpse of her as I make the right into the main square of the mall. Santa is sitting in a big chair, and a long line of red-cheeked children and their parents wraps around the building on the other side of the square.

Maggie is walking toward the other side—diagonal from

where I'm currently standing. Dodging people who are meandering at an infuriatingly slow pace, I make my way across the dormant grass. She takes a left and disappears behind the building.

"Goddammit," I mutter.

"Hey, watch your mouth. There are kids present."

I don't even bother to look for the source of the voice reprimanding me. I just keep going. But I do apologize to the person I bump into when I turn left the way Maggie did.

"Shit, Maggie..." I can't find her. I don't know where she went, and there are plenty of ways she could have gone. Stores she could have ducked into. The parking lot is right next to us, with others up ahead.

I start scanning the lot, but I don't see her, so instead, I walk by the stores, trying to search through the windows in a way I hope doesn't look like I'm completely unhinged.

Although honestly, maybe I am at this point. I probably look like someone who should be monitored—at least overnight.

After three, four, five stores, I hear her voice again. It's coming from the parking lot, but I still can't find her.

"Where are you, Mags?" I whisper out loud.

I'm tall, so I can see over people's heads, but I still wish I could get higher to see better. I remember there being a flight of stairs that leads to offices or something up ahead, so I run forward a few more stores until I reach the thruway. Standing on the third step up, I peer through the throngs of people and into the parking lot, searching for that familiar mass of hair.

But I don't see it. I can't find it anywhere. And what's worse is that I can't hear her anymore either.

I'm not sure how long I stand there, stubbornly searching even though there are no signs that she's still in the area. The sun finishes setting, and the temperature drops a noticeable amount. Eventually, I descend the stairs and slowly amble toward my parked car. I barely remember getting there, but I somehow do because the next thing I know, I'm unlocking my car and opening the back door to set down the kids' presents.

I open one of the bags to tuck the receipt inside, which is when I realize that Holly stapled her business card to the top of the pile.

Her phone number is written on it.

CHAPTER 11
EVERYTHING IS FINE. I'M FINE.

MAGGIE

"What do you think?"

Kate and I are looking at apartments. This is the fourth one I've seen today, and I'm more than ready to be done. I'm crabby and hungry, and I want to finish my Christmas shopping.

We have some other viewings lined up for tomorrow afternoon, and I'm not looking forward to a single one of them.

I open one of the bedroom closets—yes, there are two—and take a peek around. There's plenty of room to hang clothes and built-in shelves above the racks.

This apartment isn't half-bad, and I'm considering just taking it for the sake of not having to look at any of the ones lined up for tomorrow.

"The closets are pretty great," I say.

I can feel Kate's eyes burning a hole in my back. When I turn, she doesn't even bother to change her facial expression.

"What a ringing endorsement," she chides.

"Hey, closets are important."

"I know they are. I love my closet, and it's difficult to find good closets in apartments, but this one is certainly an exception," she admits. "But you don't seem to have a strong feeling about any of the places we've seen today."

I turn off the light in the closet and shut the door behind me.

"I just...I'm having a hard time with this," I admit.

Kate doesn't respond right away. I check out the second closet and then move to the window to check out the view.

"Does this have something to do with Ethan?" she asks gently.

I cut a look at her.

Of course it has to do with Ethan. How could it not?

I'm back home for about three weeks. I'm working out of our regular office and spending time with my family. While I'm here, Kate is determined to secure an apartment for me.

When I moved out of our apartment, I made sure automatic payments for my half of the rent were set up to go straight to the management company. Mostly, I did this so I wouldn't have to talk to Ethan. But I also didn't want to leave him stranded with rent on a two-bedroom apartment. That place was gorgeous and cost more than one of us could have comfortably afforded. I wasn't trying to screw him over.

So technically, I'm paying for that apartment through January, but after that, I'll have more cash to get my own place. I have enough savings that I can put a deposit on a place and "move in" on the first of February.

In reality, Kate will pick up my keys. I'll still be in Paris.

Searching for a new apartment makes this entire thing feel so...final.

I know I'm the one who left. I moved out and then moved to *Paris,* and I'm having a fling with a hot Frenchman in the meantime, but all of that is just...avoiding the problem.

Finding a new apartment is—for whatever reason—the thing that is dredging it all up for me.

"This just isn't what I thought I'd be doing at this point in my life."

She nods. "I know that feeling quite well."

And she definitely does.

My poor sister-in-law.

"But this place is nice," I say, changing the subject. I meander out of the bedroom and into the living room. There's a bathroom at the end of the hall and a linen closet in the hallway. It opens to an open-concept living room and kitchen with a little peninsula to separate the two spaces.

There's a decent amount of storage and a cozy living room. The whole place overlooks a cute street that is being developed. There's an old bakery, but a new bookstore. A pharmacy that's been there for decades and a new post office.

It's becoming its own little neighborhood and I...I kind of like it.

I can see myself getting takeout from the bakery on the weekends and sketching in the sun by these windows.

"What's the rent, again?"

Kate rattles off the numbers. It's...fine.

And I'm done thinking about this.

"I'll take it."

Her eyebrows shoot up. "Just like that?"

I take one more look around the apartment. It's empty

and sad right now, but no one is living in it. I'll make it mine soon enough.

"Just like that."

"All right. I'll get it handled for you."

"Thank you," I say with a firm nod. "Now let's get some food before I get any hangrier."

~

"THOSE WERE the best egg rolls I've ever had," Kate tells me as we walk out of the restaurant.

"They really were."

We had what would be considered a very late lunch or a very early dinner, depending on how you look at it. We still have some daylight hours, and we want to take advantage of them.

It's fucking cold outside, but I like this outdoor mall, and it has some stores I need to finish up my shopping. My nieces and nephews are all getting into sports, so I want to pick up some stuff at the sporting goods store. They also have one of those color-coded stores with a million purses and accessories, where I plan to get some stuff for my tween nieces.

"Do you need any other presents?" I ask Kate.

"I need stocking stuffers for Liam, and then I'm debating what to do for all the kids."

She's talking about my nieces and nephews. Technically, they're also her nieces and nephews, but since Nick died, it's...strange sometimes.

"Don't feel obligated. Just do what you want to."

"Yeah, but Nick would have wanted to get something for them, and money isn't as tight as it once was."

For a while after Nick died, Kate was (apparently)

freaked out about finances. He had a life insurance policy, but dying isn't cheap. So it didn't last as long as she needed it to.

And really, the house he bought was too much house for her to handle alone.

A few months after he passed, she found out that he left her a larger life insurance policy. So it ended up being okay—she has what she needs. And she can afford to buy the kids presents. But she also didn't attend family functions much for a while. Now that she's returning to the fold, I see her desire to make up for lost time.

"Let's hit up that store with the purses. That might be a good place to knock things out."

"Oooh yeah, we can coordinate colors for the girls."

"Excellent idea. I knew I liked you for a reason."

"Evil shrew," I mutter—quiet enough to make it sound like I was trying to say it quietly, but definitely loud enough for her to hear.

"Spiteful hag," she returns without hesitation.

It makes me smirk.

Kate is the twin I never had. I'm so grateful we reconnected. I missed her so much.

We collaborate on gifts for our tween nieces. We get too many sporting goods for the rest of them.

By the time we head to the car, we're laughing and loopy. The sun hasn't quite set, but it's pretty close. We move as quickly as we can, trying to generate our own body heat.

"You want to hang out for dinner?" Kate asks. "Liam is making something. I have no idea what."

Kate is a horrible cook. It's a running joke.

"We ate lunch at like, two in the afternoon. I'm not really hungry yet."

"Well, then hang out and have a drink while he cooks."

"Can't argue with that logic."

We weave our way through the crowds, splitting through the line of parents and children waiting to see Santa, who is sitting in a huge chair, listening to children's Christmas wishes and taking photos.

In the meantime, Kate regales me with stories from work—mainly about her dad and his inability to slow down and finally retire.

When we finally get to the car, Kate blasts the heat and drives us back to her house.

Liam is already making dinner when we get there. It's caprese chicken with brown rice, and I happily eat what I can stomach so soon after eating lunch. He's a great cook.

I sign a blank check so she can handle the deposit with the management company for the apartment. She tells me she plans to steal all my money and head to Turks and Caicos.

By the time I head back to my parents' house—yes, I'm staying with them over the holidays—I'm feeling marginally better than I was when we were apartment hunting.

It's probably just additional avoidance, but I'll take it for now.

"Wait your turn, Bradley Joseph," my sister-in-law, Trish, calls to my six-year-old nephew.

Kate snickers to my right, and I roll my lips between my teeth to keep from laughing. I don't know why it's so funny to hear them getting scolded, but it is. Maybe because it was usually me being scolded.

"Gracie, it's your turn." This comes from a different sister-in-law, McKayla.

The unwrapping portion of the Rafferty family Christmas has commenced and the kids are (predictably) feral. The Rafferty Christmas is always insanity, but it seems to be a bit extra this year. The first couple of Christmases after Nick died were more somber...understandably so. It's possible that we're finding a new normal. And also, Kate is back this year.

She didn't bring Liam, and when I asked why, she hedged a bit, saying something about easing back into things. It's her life. Her decision. But she did tell me that Helen made it *very* clear she was welcome to bring Liam by any time she wanted.

Gracie screams with excitement, and McKayla elbows her, prompting a hasty "Thank you, Grandma and Grandpa!" to fly out of her adorable face.

"All right, that means you're up next, guys," McKayla says.

The rule in the Rafferty house is that the person who gave the gift that was just opened gets to open one next. We make sure the kids get in there at least after each adult. There are just so freaking many of us.

"Oh, this one is from Maggie," my mom says, holding up the box I wrapped in pretty red and gold paper last week. I smile and nod my head before averting my eyes and taking a sip of bourbon.

I can hear her ripping the paper, and I'm just waiting for the moment she opens the box. I'm worried she'll cry. In fact, I think she *will* cry. I'm just hoping it doesn't bring the mood down.

Fuck, I should have given this to her separately.

I open my mouth to tell her to wait, but it's too late. She's already opening the box and pulling out the tissue paper. And then she's silently staring at the object in the box. The kids are paying her no mind, absorbed in their own presents, but all the adults are watching her.

Oh my god, what was I thinking?

My face heats, and I can feel nausea crawling up my throat. I open my mouth again, trying to say something. *Anything.*

"What is it, Mom?" Matthew asks, and I want to punch him in the face.

She takes a breath in just as my dad lifts his head, his gaze finding me on the couch.

His eyes are glassy, but he doesn't look upset. He looks happy, which makes some of my panic subside.

"It's..." my mom starts, her voice wobbly. She reaches into the bed of tissue paper and pulls out the ornament I got her at that market square in Paris. Slowly, the glass ornament comes into view as she holds it up for people to see.

About four inches tall, a figure with long white hair and a beard down to his belly hangs from a little gold string. He wears a white alb with a red stoll. His red coat has gold edges and matches his biretta. A gold sack is slung over his shoulder. He carries a gold staff.

"It's Saint Nicholas," my mom finally says, a tear falling down her cheek.

Kate puts her hand on my knee and squeezes, but I can't take my eyes off my mother.

Fuck, I made her cry.

I swallow hard. "I'm sorry, Mom..."

Her eyes snap to mine. "Sorry? Why? It's beautiful." And then suddenly, she's getting out of her chair and moving toward me. She reaches for my hand and pulls me up. "Come help me find a place on the tree."

I have no choice but to follow her as she drags me through Raffertys and presents and discarded trash on the floor. When we make it to the Christmas tree, she doesn't let go of my hand. She just starts searching for the perfect spot while I stare at her.

She's still so fucking beautiful. She has silent tears falling down her cheeks as her eyes dart around for an open space. Seven children and thirty years of teaching somehow only made her more gorgeous.

When she finds a place, she pulls me over to the right and carefully hangs Saint Nicholas on a branch just above eye level. And then she places her hand over her heart, smiling wistfully at the ornament.

But I just keep watching her.

Finally, she dabs at her cheeks and looks over at me. Her face falls just a tiny bit at whatever she sees on mine. With a glance at my nearly-empty glass, she starts tugging me back to her chair, where she picks up her own glass (empty) and then pulls me to the liquor cabinet.

"Did I ever tell you why Nick had a name that doesn't start with an M like the rest of you?"

"Um...you said he was named after someone," I say, frowning.

She nods as she tops off our glasses. "He was. Before Nick, I had two miscarriages."

I feel my eyes widen. I had no idea that had happened, and she's saying it so nonchalantly. Just...*yes, this was a thing that happened decades ago, and I can totally talk about it without sobbing.*

Gwen would call it healing or something.

"I was worried I'd never have another baby at that rate, and we wanted more children. Well then on Christmas Eve, I wasn't feeling well. Certain foods and scents were turning my stomach —things I'd eaten my whole life. Your dad was worried and suggested I take a pregnancy test." She leans a hip against the liquor cabinet while she continues, her eyes drifting up. "I was so shocked when it was positive, but cautiously optimistic. And then things...went well. The pregnancy was relatively smooth, aside from the usual frustrations of pregnancy, and then when we got to the hospital, the doctor assigned to us was named... Nicholas." She finishes with a smile. "It felt like it was meant to be. Our little Christmas miracle."

"I had no idea..." I say, shaking my head.

She shrugs. "That doesn't surprise me much. We talked about it so much after Nick was born, and then by the time we had the twins, we were so occupied with them that we didn't tell the story much anymore."

I nod and look down into my bourbon, feeling uncomfortable. Helen and I aren't alone very much.

"Have you ever told Kate that story?"

"Oh, yes. She's heard it," she says, with a self-deprecating laugh. "She probably heard it the first time we met her. Or maybe Nick told her before she even met us."

I feel a pang of guilt at my general absence from the family. I was always...out. I didn't want to hang around the house with my parents after all my siblings had moved out. And even when the twins were still at home, they had their own special kind of bond, so I felt left out then, too.

I've always been a loner. I think it's just the nature of being the youngest in a big family—especially when they're all so much older than you.

"Maggie! We skipped your last turn. Get back in here," Matthew calls from the other room.

"Let's head back, dear." My mom jerks her head toward

the living room and takes off ahead of me. I'm only a couple of steps behind her.

Something in the back of my mind tries to pull at me, but I'm so preoccupied with the guilt plaguing me that I don't let myself think too hard about whatever it is. I just make myself keep moving forward.

CHAPTER 12
BLISSFULLY DEVOID OF THOUGHTS

A Little Bit Yours - JP Saxe
January

I sleep through most of the return flight to Paris after the holiday. I'm exhausted from spending two entire weeks with my family. I love them, but holy shit are they a lot to deal with.

I will admit that staying with my parents was actually...nice.

My dad made sure to let me have space when I needed it. My mom made tea for two in the afternoons, and we'd eat homemade scones together while watching Christmas movies. Her favorite is *What a Wonderful Life*, while mine is *Home Alone*. We watched both, in addition to a slew of others, including cheesy Hallmark-style movies that gave me a stomach ache.

I had dinner with Kate at her house and drank enough of her wine to require a sleepover. I stayed in the guest bedroom and dutifully texted my mother to let her know where I was.

I went holiday shopping with friends. Spent more money than I planned on gifts for my nieces and nephews. Stayed up too late catching up with people.

I visited all of my siblings' houses and spent time with their kids, giving them candy, riling them up, chasing them around in the snow.

Cool Aunt Maggie may have swooped in gracefully, but she's hobbling back out.

On top of all that family time and togetherness, I was acutely aware of the person missing from the festivities.

Nick, yes. But Nick has been gone for a while now. This is our third Christmas without him. While his absence is still painful and depressing, it isn't "new" anymore.

No, the person missing is Ethan.

If I'm being super honest, I can admit that I tried to stay busy for the specific purpose of keeping my mind off him. I knew it would be difficult being back home. I worried about running into him or mutual friends and the awkwardness that would ensue. Especially if I ran into mutuals because they'd have questions...*what happened* from those less in-the-know, and from the ones we were closer to, *why did you break up with him* and *couldn't you have made it work* and *why won't you just marry him* and a million other opinions thinly veiled through their careful words.

But mostly, I was worried I'd see Ethan's face—his kind, handsome face and those chocolate brown eyes that sucked me in all those years ago—and just fall apart.

The truth of the matter is that I miss him terribly. I might be putting on a brave (or indifferent) face at work and with my family and friends, but inside, I'm...sad. I'm so sad.

Spending the holidays without Ethan was painful on a

level I was not expecting. People might think that because I was the one who chose to end the relationship, I wouldn't be so emotional about it. That I'd be content to move on, settled with the knowledge that I didn't lower my standards or cave and do something I didn't feel comfortable doing.

On some level, I think I expected myself to be less... devastated. And I do see how people might have less sympathy for me. It's a choice *I* made. Not one that Ethan made. I could see how people would have a wealth of sympathy for the man scorned—the loving, caring man who proposed to his long-term girlfriend and got shot down.

In this scenario, I'm the villain, and I get it.

But that doesn't mean I'm not struggling, too.

All that being said, I don't know where Ethan's head is. He could hate me. He could wish he'd never met me.

Let's say I did run into him, and I did fall all the way apart, begging him to give me another chance. (Not that I think that's a good idea. I think it's a terrible idea that would cause a similar ending down the road.)

The bottom line is that I don't even know if he'd have been receptive to giving me a second chance. We didn't exactly leave each other on a high note.

So I had a drink while we were halfway over the Atlantic and fell asleep. When I woke up, I was looking down at the Normandy countryside.

I look over toward Kelsie to find her still asleep. The rest of the passengers are mostly sleeping as well, but some are waking up and gathering their things so they're prepared when we land. According to the flight plan, we have less than an hour to go. And whether it's a good idea or not, I know who my first phone call will be.

WE DON'T HAVE to be in the office today. They're not re-opening until tomorrow after the holiday, so we have the day to readjust to the time zone shift and get settled.

Isaac and Wesley immediately call up the boys they'd been hanging out with before the holidays. They'd gotten into a regular boys night routine with some guys from the office and their friends. Kelsie calls up her latest fling.

And me?

"Salut ma belle..."*

Julien's arm grabs me by the waist and pulls me into his hard body. He smells like soap, his hair still a little bit damp from his shower. I waste no time at all tilting my head up to fuse my mouth to his.

And then we're moving. He shifts us to the side so he can close the door with this foot—or at least that's what I assume, because his hands never leave my body.

There's an urgency in the way he's touching me that I feel just as deeply. It's less about an emotional connection with him and more about needing to forget that I have feel-ings and emotions at all. I only want to feel one emotion right now, and it needs to be euphoria.

I think he senses it.

He shoves my coat off my shoulders, my purse falling to the floor with it. I slide my hands up his torso, dragging his shirt with me. With an impatient growl, he pulls away from my mouth and rips the shirt over his head, then pauses to divest me of my own before kissing me again.

We keep moving toward his bedroom as we continue to strip clothing off our bodies. By the time we reach his bed, we're only in our underwear.

---

* Hi, beautiful...

"Tu es trop bonne..."* he murmurs as he kisses his way down my throat, to my collarbones, unhooking my bra and letting it fall between us. My brain glitches out when his mouth seals around my nipple, making the French he whispers every time he moves to a new place on my body completely incomprehensible. I'm sure some of it is sweet and some of it is dirty, but all of it is hot.

Julien puts one knee on the bed behind me, wedging his thigh between my legs, providing delicious pressure before laying me down.

"Ta peau est si douce," † he says as he kisses a path toward my underwear, pausing to flick his tongue over the soft skin just above the waistband. It's torture, but worth it because I know what comes next.

(Ha. It's me. I'm coming next.)

His calloused fingers pull on my panties, dragging them down my legs and discarding them somewhere. Instead of jumping right back into his task, he places my ankle on his shoulder and looks down at me with eyes I could only describe as smoldering. He's devouring me with his gaze, taking in every inch of my body, so I take the opportunity to do the same.

I start at his gorgeous face, then move down to the tendons in his neck straining as he drags air into his lungs. Which, of course, draws my attention to his chest, with hard pecs above toned abs. His erection strains against his dark boxer briefs, his hips rolling forward slightly, like he isn't even consciously doing it.

With one leg up on his shoulder and the other wrapped around his waist, it's quite an erotic sight.

---

*   You are too good...
†   Your skin is so soft.

While I'm looking my fill, Julien's hands roam the parts of my body he can reach—mostly my legs and hips—squeezing, caressing, pulling me tighter around him.

"Fuck, Julien, please," I finally beg. He's killing me.

"Patience, chérie."* His beautiful mouth tilts into a smug smile. This asshole knows perfectly well that he's torturing me, and he doesn't care in the slightest.

"*Julien...*" I whine.

The smile is wiped off his face when he kisses the inside of my calf and finally, *finally* moves to where I want him. His hands slide under my thighs, and I watch his biceps flex as he pulls me closer. Holding my hips in place, he puts that talented tongue to good use, and I get my wish.

All my thoughts finally dissipate. My mind is blissfully devoid of a single thought that doesn't center around Julien's mouth, body, hands. I'm a jumble of nerve endings and want. I couldn't conduct simple math if someone asked me right now, and if architects know anything, it's math.

"Ça fait trop longtemps," he mumbles against my thigh. "Tu as si bon goût."†

If my math brain isn't working, my French translator brain sure as hell isn't.

"I...I have n-no idea what you just s-said."

That swirling thing he does with his tongue, combined with the way his fingers are curling inside me sends my back arching off the bed, a garbled sound bubbling in my throat.

"I said..." his deep voice comes out with a chuckle. "...that you taste good. And that it's been a long time. Far too long."

And after that, I lose what little gift of speech I had left. I

---

*   Dear.
†   It's been too long. You taste so good.

don't know who taught him how to do this, or how many women it took before me to make him this good at it, or if the French are just naturally gifted in this regard, but god-fucking-dammit, give this man a medal.

I can't function, but he's sheathing himself one-handed while I continue to convulse around him. I whine at the sudden loss of his fingers, but I'm quickly rewarded with his dick instead. I gasp at the intrusion, then sigh in relief.

I'm still a bundle of nerves. External thoughts and feelings are not invading my brain yet.

"*Fuck*, Maggie..."

Julien's voice is gravel above me. I open my heavy eyelids to find his head thrown back, neck taut with tension. He's ridiculously hot. And unfortunately, he's probably ruining me for future men.

His hands tighten on my thighs, and then he tilts his head back down to look at me.

I know in romance novels, authors write about how the hero's eyes "darken" or whatever, and I've always thought that's kind of silly. Eyes obviously don't change color when their owner is turned on.

But holy shit, in this moment...in this *specific* moment, I understand.

Julien and I have had sex many times at this point, but I'm not sure I've ever seen his eyes like this. They're not soft with emotion or hard with anger. No, they're molten with desire, and they're going to light me on fire. And it's fine. He can incinerate me.

He's doing a pretty good job already, murmuring and growling words in French that I have no hope of translating, and it doesn't seem like he can translate them right now either. So I just hang on for the ride, wrapping my legs around his back as he leans forward to kiss me. Twining my arms around his neck when he rolls us over. Grasping his wrist when he reaches between us.

And when we're both panting, trying to catch our breath, he kisses me softly, caressing my face, my back, my thighs. He's trying to prolong the inevitable moment when my brain clicks back into overdrive, and it works. For the most part.

Until I think about Ethan again. About how I thought these intimate moments would only be spent with him for the rest of my life.

I know the second he realizes my brain has re-entered the chat because he breaks the kiss and looks at me with concern in his eyes.

I have no idea what my face looks like or what he sees in my eyes, but he gives me a sad smile and kisses me softly one more time. Then, he rolls me onto my back and whispers that he'll only be a minute before disappearing into the bathroom.

When he returns, he holds me while I cry.

CHAPTER 13
WHAT THE FUCK AM I DOING?
ETHAN

Please Don't Be - Hazlett
January

"In five hundred feet, turn left." My GPS takes me one step closer to the restaurant.

"What the fuck am I doing?" I ask the lady from the Maps app.

"Turn left, then turn right."

"Helpful, thank you."

I'm meeting Holly for dinner.

Yes, Holly. From my Christmas shopping trip that resulted in me sprinting across the courtyard in an attempt to reach Maggie.

That Holly.

I texted her a few days later when I was tipsy and sad. We texted back and forth for a couple of weeks, and then she suggested we meet for dinner. Probably because I hadn't suggested it.

For whatever fucking reason, I agreed, and now I'm turning right into the parking lot of this restaurant.

"What the *fuck*..."

"You've arrived at your destination."

I scowl at the robot's voice, then whisper a thank you... just in case the robots rise to kill us all one day.

I snag an empty parking spot and then turn off the car and take a few deep, calming breaths. Holly is a nice person. And beautiful. I can have dinner with her and maybe even get laid. You never know. I mean, I won't push it, but maybe there's an opportunity if I don't totally fuck this up.

That's the spirit, Ethan. Keep your expectations low.

Rolling my eyes at myself, I get out of the car and start walking toward the front doors.

"Ethan!"

The voice to my right stops me before I start spiraling.

I force a smile as I meet her eyes. "Holly. Hi. It's good to see you."

Her smile is not forced. It's wide and toothy and flirtatious. Pre-Maggie Ethan would be eating this shit up, getting excited for the possibility of something hot later in the evening.

Post-Maggie Ethan is already cataloging all the things about Holly that *aren't* Maggie.

Blond hair, not brown.

Blue eyes, not green.

Curls aren't natural like Maggie's.

Height isn't horribly off.

She meets me on the sidewalk and kisses my cheek. It catches me off guard, and I have to force myself to not flinch away from her.

"It's good to see you, too. How was your week?"

She loops her arm through mine, even though I didn't offer it, and starts leading us toward the front doors.

"Uhh, it was all right. Same old, same old," I say, and then realize I should ask her the same question. "And you?"

"It was good. It's nice to have a break from the store. January is always slow."

She told me via text that she only worked at the store part-time. She has a full-time gig as an executive assistant in an office somewhere, and she works at the store for extra cash to pay off her student loans.

"I'll bet. I'm sure that's exhausting."

"Yeah..." she says as we approach the doors. I untangle my arm from hers and hold the door open for her. "But it has its perks." She smirks at me as she walks by, a heated look in her eye.

My dick certainly gets the message, but my brain is far from the conversation.

I let the hostess know we have a reservation under my name, and she leads us to a candlelit table. My manners are thankfully ingrained, so I manage to pull out her chair and help her get seated before sitting down myself. The person who seated us hands us menus and lets us know our server will be here shortly.

"Have you been here before?" Holly asks.

The place where Maggie and I have been countless times? Nah, I've never heard of it.

"A couple of times," I say, shrugging a shoulder like I don't have a thousand memories of this place. "You?"

"Just once. A long time ago."

I force myself to find a question to ask her. "Did you like it?"

"I remember the food being good. The company, less so."

"Oh?"

"Yeah, my date was kind of a douche."

I nod. "How so?"

"He flirted with the waitress while I was in the bathroom."

That makes me frown—for more than one reason. "Did...she tell you that?"

"Yeah. She came into the bathroom to tell me."

I'm sure my surprise is plain on my face.

"I was glad she did. I cut the date short. There wasn't a point in sitting there any longer."

"Makes sense. He sounds like a real douche."

She smiles. "Glad we're on the same page."

I bury my face in the menu to avoid her gaze. I know what I'm ordering, but she doesn't know that yet.

"Do you know what you're getting?" she asks, like she's reading my mind.

"Hmm. Maybe the pork shank."

Definitely the pork shank.

"Oh, that sounds good."

"Hi, how are we doing this evening?" Our waiter appears to my left.

"Good, thanks," Holly answers brightly. "And you?"

"I'm doing well, thank you for asking." He smiles down at her, and I can see the interest in his eyes. He glances at me and clears his throat. "I'm Jake, and I'll be taking care of you this evening. Can I get you started with something from the bar?"

"Can I have a glass of your house red?" Holly asks.

"Of course. And for you, sir?"

"I'll have the Stone IPA."

"Very good. I'll get those orders put in for you while you look over the menu. Do you have any questions about what you've seen thus far?"

He says *you* in a universal, plural way. But he's looking at Holly when he says it.

She asks him his opinion on two different entreés.

For what it's worth, she doesn't seem to notice that he's giving her more attention than he's giving me, and I'm more stricken by my complete lack of...me giving a shit.

If this were me and Maggie, I'd be doing something —*anything*—to make sure Jake the Waiter knew she was with me. Not just at a table together or on a date, but *with* me. In fact, I've done that before. Calling her a pet name or reaching across the table to take her hand. Wrapping an arm around her while we walked side by side. Interlacing our fingers together as we sat next to each other. Basically anything to get someone to stop looking at her like she's available because she fucking *wasn't*.

But it's not Maggie. It's Holly. And I find myself not caring that Jake the Waiter is obviously interested in her. I must say I'm grateful she's not entertaining him, though. That would suck a little.

The fragile male ego and all.

Jake the Waiter leaves, and Holly begins talking about what she might want to eat. I set my menu down because I think I can stop pretending to not know what I want. I listen to her thought process behind her dinner selection, smiling and nodding, adding little *hmms* and noises of agreement when it makes sense.

She decides on a cobb salad. I briefly wonder if she's the type of woman who eats salads on dates to make the guy think she's a dainty little bird and then goes home to eat something more substantial.

Maggie never did that, but she told me some of her friends did. Something about previous comments from guys about how much they ate and how it triggered them. So they got something light and then ate again at home if they were still hungry.

Maggie had a huge burger on our first date. Our first *real* date. After the club.

"So how were your holidays?" Holly asks me. "You said you saw your parents."

"Uhh, yeah. I did. They live about an hour from here, so I went down there for a few days. It was a good time." I don't really want to talk about myself. I'd much rather she talk, which means I need to come up with questions for her. "You mentioned seeing your nieces and nephews. Did you have a good time with them?"

"Oh my goodness, yes." Holly launches into a story about two of them and how they were passing out all the presents to people. Another one was assigned wrapping paper cleanup duty.

"That sounds very organized." My project manager brain is into that, I have to admit.

"Oh yes, we're full of Type A personalities. We need organization and planning."

Just then, Jake comes back to drop off our drinks and take our food orders. She gets her salad, and I order the pork. When he leaves, she picks up her glass of wine and offers it up in a toast.

"To new beginnings," she says with a broad smile.

I force my mouth to smile, but her word choice feels like an arrow through my gut. "To new beginnings," I parrot, then take a *very* generous gulp of beer while she takes a small sip of her wine.

We manage to have a decent conversation while we wait for our food. As I'd hoped, she does most of the talking. When she asks me a question, I answer it and then turn the tables back on her. She seems happy to oblige.

Holly tells me more about the company she works for and how she enjoys being an assistant. In turn, I wonder how things are going for Maggie in Paris.

Holly talks about her Christmas decorations—how she has a tiny pre-lit tree with colorful lights. I think about the giant tree Maggie used to set up every year—as big as the apartment would allow—and how we covered it with soft white lights and glass ornaments.

Somehow we get on the topic of bourbon and whiskey. When Holly says she can't stomach the stuff—how the only liquor she can drink is vodka, and only when it's mixed into a drink—I think about how Maggie can drink scotch neat.

We both order another drink when dinner arrives. Holly somehow manages to eat while still talking almost nonstop. I can't help but remember that I never had to *try* to have a decent conversation with Maggie. It flowed naturally.

I eat all of my pork, but Holly doesn't finish her salad. To be fair, it's a huge salad. And maybe it's that memory about Maggie's friends not eating much on dates combined with the two IPAs that has my tongue loosening.

"You can eat more."

Her head tilts to the side, and she frowns. "What?"

"My ex told me once that some of her friends didn't eat on dates because guys made comments about how much they were eating. I just want to make sure you know I'm not going to judge you for how much you're eating. Or not eating."

She's perfectly still for a moment and then nods her head once, like she's wondering what the hell happened to me. I can't really blame her.

"Okay...thanks."

"Sorry, I'm not trying to make you feel weird. That comment always stuck with me."

"I had a snack a couple of hours ago because I was super hungry. So I'm not famished." She pauses to study me. "But I appreciate your concern."

"Yeah, yeah...sorry." I wave her off. "Do you have any fun plans coming up?"

Holly takes the topic change in stride, blinking a couple of times before telling me about how her friend is getting married in two weeks, and she's the maid of honor. She shows me a picture of her wearing her dress. She looks beautiful, and I make sure to tell her so.

She blushes a soft shade of pink at my compliment, smiling wide.

The problem is, I feel like I'm telling a *friend* how beautiful she looks...not someone I want to date.

"Do you want to get married?"

Her gaze snaps back up to mine, alarm in her eyes, and that's when I realize how the question sounded.

"Not to me," I blurt. "Or, not now. Shit, sorry." I stammer, closing my eyes and dropping my head.

I mentally facepalm myself.

What the fuck are you doing, dude?

"Um..."

"I meant *someday*. Like *do you want to get married someday* to a person you're in love with and want to share your life with." I can't even look at her. I'm certain I'm the one blushing now, since my face is on *fire,* and I've never been this embarrassed in my whole life. Not even when I threw up on another kid in kindergarten.

There's a moment of awkward silence, and I start to wonder if she left, and I didn't notice.

I manage to look up and find her staring at me, lips parted.

"Sorry. You really don't have to answer any of those questions."

"Ethan...are you okay?"

Isn't that the million-dollar question?

"Yeah, I'm fine."

I'm so fucking miserable. You have no idea.

She keeps looking at me, studying me like I'm going to freak out. "Do *you* want to get married someday?" she asks tentatively.

"I mean, yeah. I do. I did, anyway."

After another moment of silence, her soft voice asks me another question. "But you don't anymore?"

I scrub my hands down my face. I'm really fucking this up, but in for a penny, in for a pound. "To be totally honest, I don't know anymore. I did...I really did."

"But it didn't work out?"

"She said no."

Her eyebrows shoot up her forehead. "She turned you down?"

"She sure did."

"Wow..."

"Everyone wants to get married eventually...that's what I thought anyway. Which I now realize is a very antiquated way of thinking. Of course, there are other options. She doesn't want to get married at all. Ever."

Her expression is full of sympathy, but she doesn't say anything.

"I have two sisters. I should have known better. They've both told me so. They've both reamed my ass for not being attentive enough."

She smirks at that comment, then tips her head down, trying to hide it.

"No, it's okay. You can laugh. They're right."

She clears her throat and then looks up at me again, shaking her head slowly. "You're nowhere near over her."

"Not even a little bit," I admit.

She huffs a laugh. "That tracks."

"I'm sorry, Holly. You're really great. If there was ever a time when 'it's not you, it's me' was a real thing, this is it."

Her smile is a little sad. "That's okay. Better to find out now than a year from now."

I return her sad smile. "Friends?"

She nods. "Yeah. Friends."

"Can I get you anything else this evening?" Jake pops up to my left again with timing so precise, I wonder if he's been listening. "Anyone in the mood for dessert?"

Holly and I share a smile. I nod.

"We might as well take a look at the options."

"Sounds good," Jake says, handing her a small menu. "Would you like a box?"

"Yes, please."

"Excellent. I'll give you a few minutes to check out dessert, and I'll go grab that box."

I wait for him to walk away before I speak again.

"As your *friend*, I feel like I should tell you that Jake the Waiter has been paying you a *lot* of attention this evening." I waggle my eyebrows at her for effect. I'm so much more comfortable now that we have that awkward conversation out of the way. Now that there are no stakes and no game to be played.

"Really?" she asks, looking up and finding him by a serving station, pulling a to-go box out of a cubby.

"Yes, really. Figure out what you want for dessert." I tip my chin toward the menu in her hands.

"I want the brownie with ice cream," she says immediately.

"Perfect."

Again with the impeccable timing, Jake is back with a box for Holly.

"Did you decide on a dessert?"

"Yes, can we have the brownie with ice cream please? Two spoons."

I try to stifle my smile, knowing she's seeing him through new eyes as she gazes up at him. Her eyes look the way they did at me when I was at the toy shop. Flirty Holly is back, and I'm unbothered. On the contrary, I'm excited for her.

"All right, tell me about the ex," Holly says after Jake walks away.

So I do. I tell her how we met and how I fell in love with her. By the time dessert comes, I'm telling her how I fucked it all up.

"So she's in Paris now?" Holly asks around the brownie in her mouth.

"Yeah. As far as I know." I shrug. "She won't respond to any of my messages. A mutual friend told me she got the Paris project."

She spoons ice cream into her mouth with a thoughtful look on her face. "When does she get back?"

"Well, I'm not totally sure. But Miles said she left in September and should be gone for a good six months. Could be longer."

"Okay, so what's the plan when she returns?"

I blow out a breath and shake my head. "I honestly don't know. I'm pretty sure she blocked my number. I've been... sending her messages." I can feel my face flush with embarrassment. "I'm not sure if she's getting them."

I chance a look up at her and find her watching me intently as she chews.

"And honestly, the more I talk to you about it, I'm feeling like a bigger and bigger asshole for being on a date with you when I'm still in love with her."

She waves her spoon in the air and rolls her eyes. "You're certainly not the first man to do something like that, and you definitely won't be the last. Besides, Jake the Waiter is hot."

Her little non-joke about Jake has me huffing a small laugh.

"I still want her," I say quietly, cutting off a piece of the brownie with my spoon. "But when she gets back...I have no idea where her head will be. Fuck, I have no idea where her head is at *now*."

I shove the brownie in my mouth and chew.

"Damn...that's really good."

"It is, yeah," she agrees.

"I have reservations about how interested she'll be in hearing me out, though. Maggie moves on from things. She might not want to try again."

Holly doesn't say anything right away, and in the silence, I'm more certain than ever that Maggie *won't* want to try again. There's really no *might* about it.

"Did she tell you she doesn't love you anymore?"

I look up, startled by the question. Holly has one arm crossed over her chest and the other pointed up, holding her spoon near her mouth.

"No." I shake my head again. "She said a whole lot of other things. None as horrible as I said, though."

"Okay, listen, I know you know her, and I've never met her, but you've got to try. I mean, this is kind of unprecedented. This is the only time you've ever broken up. You don't *really* know what she thinks about it all."

I think about that for a second, hope trying to wiggle its way into my chest.

"You have to try, Ethan." Holly leans forward while I pick at my side of the brownie with my spoon. "You're clearly still in love with her. The two of you deserve to at least talk about it."

She fully crosses her arms and raises her eyebrow at me, like she's accentuating her point.

"You think so?"

"Yes," she says, emphatically. "God, you'd have to fight me off with a *stick* if someone I was in love with came crawling back to me, begging for a second chance, telling me he was still in love with me and wanted to try again."

I raise my eyebrows. "I'm expected to crawl?" I tease.

"Oh you should absolutely crawl. And grovel while you're down there."

"Is there anything else I can get you this evening?" Jake asks, looking directly at Holly.

She beams up at him. "No, we're all set. Everything was wonderful, thank you, Jake."

I look down at the napkin in my lap, trying not to laugh.

"I'll just leave this, but there's no rush."

I snatch up the billfold right away, snapping it shut so she can't see it.

"Let's split it," she suggests.

"No." I get out my wallet and slide my credit card into the slot at the top.

She raises an eyebrow, but I shrug and grab another bite of the brownie.

"Well, thank you very much for dinner. And for your honesty."

"Thank you for not freaking out and running toward the door."

She laughs. "I did briefly consider it, but you just looked so sad."

"Ouch," I say, pressing a hand to my chest to feign being wounded. "Are you going to give him your number?"

She sits up straighter, her eyes bright and twinkly. "Yeah. Yeah, I think I will."

She digs into her purse and finds a little notebook, immediately getting to work at writing a note. When Jake comes back to get the billfold, she hides the note with her hand.

I can't help but laugh at her. "Are you nervous?"

"Shut up. I'm always nervous when I'm giving my number to someone new."

"You didn't seem nervous with me at the store."

"Well, I was."

Jake drops off the billfold. I sign the receipt and slip the note Holly wrote inside, but I don't read it. It's none of my business.

"You ready to go?" I ask.

"Yep."

I help her get her coat on, and I walk her to her car. There's no pressure for a good night kiss. Instead, there's an easy, budding friendship between us, and it feels normal when she gives me a hug.

I wait until her car starts and she's driving away to head back to my own car. I'm exhausted, but I also feel like a weight has been lifted. It might not have been a successful date from a romantic standpoint, but I have a new friend and ally.

CHAPTER 14
CHERRY BLOSSOM PINK
MAGGIE

you broke me first - Tate McRae
February

"The projections are still pretty accurate. We've obviously had some shipping delays, but the winter has been pretty warm, so we're still set to break ground the final week of March," Marv says.

We're doing our weekly status meeting via Zoom with the two offices.

"But the American team should be able to come home after that. Even if there's a delay, we can still get you home, and the French team can let us know if they need you back over there. Sound good?"

Everyone agrees that it does.

I keep my mouth shut.

I don't necessarily disagree. It's true that we won't be needed here. It's cheaper for everyone if we go home—no one has to pay for us to be in two (incredible) apartments anymore—and we can get back to our regular lives. The bulk of our work will be done by that point, and there's no reason the French team can't handle the rest of it on their own.

It's a win-win.

Except that I have to go back to the States, where I'll be in the same city as Ethan again.

At least I have an apartment to go back to so I don't have to live with my parents when I return. Kate picked up my keys last week. I'm paying rent already for an apartment I'm not currently living in, but I'm not paying for the apartment in Paris, so there's that.

I know the likelihood of us actually seeing each other is low. Yes, we'll live in the same city again, but we lived in the same city for years before we met, and we never knew each other. It's not a small town.

It will be fine.

It will.

"I think we should bring the American team back for the grand opening. And you, too, Marvin," the lead French architect, Maxime, says.

"Oh, we'd love to do that, Max," Marv responds. "Thank you for the invitation."

"Of course. This collaboration has been an absolute joy, and we'll be sad to see our American colleagues go."

Maxime is a truly kind person. I think he means every word he's saying, and honestly, we'll miss him and this entire team.

Going home is bittersweet.

I miss my family and friends. But I've made new friends here, and I love living in this city. I can see the same sentiments reflected in my colleagues' faces. Isaac, Wesley, and Kelsie have all made friends here...established relationships with people—romantic or otherwise—and it will be difficult to leave them.

Out of the corner of my eye, I can see Dominique tilt her head my way, but I don't look over at her. I haven't talked to her on a regular basis about what's going on with her brother. She gave me the all-clear to follow through, so I did, but we don't talk about it. I have no idea what Julien may have told her.

The truth about Julien is that I like him. Of course, I like him. But I'm not in love with him, and I honestly can't see that happening. At least not where my head is currently at.

I was upfront with Julien from day one, and he's been upfront with me. We agreed that we'd say something if our feelings started to morph into something different—that we'd be sensitive to each other's feelings no matter what.

So far, neither of us have said anything to that effect. I know people say that it's difficult to have sex with no strings, but we're doing just fine. And it's really no one's business what we do.

"All right then, it's settled..." Marv's voice, which I must admit, I hadn't been listening to very closely, manages to pull me back to the present. "The American team will leave on or around the 15th of April. We'll make the arrangements."

And just like that, our time in Paris has an end date.

March

"Vite, vite, chérie,"* Julien urges me forward with long strides, tugging me along through the streets of Paris. It's

---

* Quickly, quickly, dear.

mid-March and we're seeing just a few blooms popping up. He said he wants to show me his favorite cherry blossoms.

I appreciate his enthusiasm, but I'm wearing heeled boots and trying not to break my neck. My legs are shorter than his.

"Okay, okay," I try to appease him. "Don't let go of me though because these boots were made for *walking*, as they say."

He barks out a laugh. "All right, Nancy, I'll slow down."

The fact that he caught that random reference warms my chest. And he *does* slow down. He stops tugging me along and instead walks right next to me, adjusting his grip on my hand, intertwining his fingers with mine.

He smiles down at me and not for the first time, I curse every god in every religion that I cannot fall in love with this man.

On one hand, I wish I could. And on the other, I'm leaving within the next four weeks. Falling for this man would do nothing but hurt me. And possibly him, too.

It's better this way.

"The cherry blossoms don't usually come out this early in the year, but the winter was so warm, it appears they're starting ahead of schedule," Julien tells me. "Notre Dame still has limited access, but there are others I can show you."

Regardless of the temperature, I'm also determined to enjoy some of the patio culture before I head back. The patios are constantly open, thanks to the sheer number of smokers, but that doesn't mean I want to sit outside in the cold.

I'm not complaining about a single moment I've had in Paris, but sipping coffee outside on a patio is kind of quin-tessential Paris, and I want to do it at least once before I leave. Who knows when the building will be finished—if there are delays, it could be the dead of winter when all is said and done.

Julien leads me around the corner and a leg of the Eiffel Tower comes into view, rising above other people's heads and demanding attention.

At the end of the block, we're standing on the edge of the Parc du Champ-de-Mars, which is a dedicated green space in front of the Eiffel Tower. In the warmer months, people will bring blankets and have a picnic here. Right now, it's mostly people wearing scarves and wool coats, passing through while tourists take selfies. Some of the locals get tapped to take pictures so the tourists can get the entire tower in the frame.

"Over here," Julien says, giving a gentle tug on my hand. I hadn't realized I'd stopped moving.

"Oh, sorry..."

"No need to apologize, *ma choupette*,"* he says, kissing my temple. "Follow me."

When he stops walking, we're in front of trees that look dormant at first glance.

"Voilà."†

His voice is so gentle when he says the word, tipping one branch so I can see it better. It's a regular brown branch in his hand—nothing I haven't seen before—except that there are tiny buds where I'd expect regular green leaves to sprout.

Instead, what I see is a tiny shock of pink on the very end of the bud.

I've seen pictures of cherry blossom trees in Washington D.C. and Japan, but I've never seen them in real life.

----

* sweetie.

† There.

They aren't even open yet, and they're beautiful.

"Sometime in the next few weeks, all these buds will open, and this entire area will be full of pink trees," Julien tells me. "It's breathtaking. I'll have to send you pictures once it's fully in bloom."

It's a stark reminder that our time is coming to a close.

"Please do," I manage to squeak out.

He wraps one strong arm across the front of my shoulders, drawing my back to his chest. Then, he drops a kiss in my hair.

"I'm sure it will be beautiful."

He's quiet for a moment, but when he responds, it's like a suckerpunch to my chest.

"It's always beautiful. Now, when it's mostly dormant and in a few weeks when it's in full bloom. It's just a different kind of beauty...one that takes a more discerning eye. Someone willing to be patient."

LATER THAT NIGHT, we're lying in Julien's bed, naked and relaxed. He's been telling me about what else he wants to show me before our time is up—we'll go to Versailles to see the gardens, even though they won't be full in all their glory yet. He says it's still worth it.

When I ask him what his plans are for the rest of the week, he mentions needing to go to his parents' house for their anniversary.

"How long have they been married?"

"Forty years, this week."

"Wow..." I breathe. I'm no stranger to lengthy marriages. My own parents have been married for longer than that, even, but I personally have a hard time grasping that concept. "That's a long time."

"It is," he agrees.

"Are they happy?"

"Insufferably so."

My smile isn't forced, although it's bittersweet. It's adorable that he describes it that way, but Ethan described my parents in a similar manner. And he wasn't wrong.

"That's wonderful for them."

"It is," he repeats, and I get the sense that there's more to that story.

"Are you close?" I press gently.

He takes a breath before responding. "We talk regularly. They're good people."

I can't help but notice that he didn't answer my question, but I don't want to push him if he's not interested in talking about it. As it turns out, I don't have to.

"They...they'll ask me when I'm going to settle down."

"Oh..."

I can certainly understand that situation.

"They want to see me happy. Like they are."

I nod. "I get that. My parents have been married even longer than yours. They're disgustingly in love. Even now."

He offers a commiserating smile. "Dominique is the youngest and is just starting to see that scrutiny. Our older sister is married and has two children."

"So they have a couple of grandkids to hold them off... but not for long, huh?"

"Exactly. Not for long."

I think back to my conversation with Ethan when we broke up. I think about all my siblings and their children—except Nick, of course, but they would have had children if he hadn't died. I'm sure of that. It's so *normal*. It's what most people do.

When you're younger, people make it seem so simple... the expectations society has for you—*especially* if you're a woman.

You meet someone. You fall in love. You get married. You have kids.

I think that's how it used to be, though.

That's how it was for our grandmothers, who didn't have much of a choice. They were expected to marry—and marry young. They were expected to have kids, not careers. They were expected to look the other way when their husband fucked their secretaries under the guise of working late.

And even if they were miserable, they couldn't leave. They had no job skills. No work history. How would they survive? How would they pay for the children they were expected to have?

Not that they'd be able to get their own bank account without their husband's signature anyway.

We've evolved as a society. Women are educated and earn their own income. So why are we still clinging to this idea that we have to get married and have children?

If we're evolving, we need to expect our relationships to evolve as well. And my ideal relationship doesn't involve an expensive wedding and giving up my name.

I know what people think...that I could elope and that I don't have to change my name.

Both fair points.

Except that my views aren't much different than other people's in that regard. I can choose to not marry, and they can choose to elope. Both buck societal standards. Both are valid.

The problem remaining is that I still want a meaningful

romantic relationship with an equal partner. I want that comfort and companionship. I want to know that someone loves me for exactly who and what I am. I want to have someone to work through tough times with. To celebrate the happy moments with.

Of course, the older you get, the smaller the dating pool.

What if I've already missed my chance at a happy relationship?

What if I ruined my one chance at a good relationship?

If it were anyone else, I wouldn't ask the question burning a hole in my brain, but it's Julien, and Julien doesn't want a relationship with me.

We've been clear about this, I remind myself.

"Do you believe there's one perfect person for everyone?"

As soon as I ask it, the asshole voice in my head reminds me that I was also clear with Ethan and look where that landed us.

"You mean soulmates, yes?"

"I guess, yeah."

I take some comfort in seeing the calm in Julien's eyes. He doesn't seem to be freaking out or watching me with love-soaked eyes. No, that hazel gaze is strong, confident, steady, and thoughtful.

After a moment, he says decisively, "Non."

The certainty in his voice has my eyebrows arching up.

"Why not?"

"Because I find the concept depressing. There are billions of people in this world. What if my soulmate is in Fiji? How will I ever find her? And what if I don't? Am I destined to live a lonely life, believing I missed out on that chance? What if your soulmate is somewhere else in Paris, and you're missing him because you're here with me?"

I have to hand it to him... "Fair point."

"I believe we're compatible with many people, and the success of each possible relationship depends on many things—shared interests, temperament, commitment, and luck, to some degree."

"I suppose that's a bit more hopeful. Perhaps less romantic."

"I disagree. There is something romantic in choosing to be with the same person every day. Even when there are other options."

The way he says it so plainly shoots pain straight through my chest. When did Ethan stop choosing *me*?

Still, I have to admit, "You raise a good point."

"Do you believe this Ethan was your soulmate?"

I avert my eyes. It doesn't matter that there's no future with Julien, and we're just fooling around for a while, it's still awkward to talk about my ex while I'm lying naked next to another man. To his credit, though, Julien doesn't seem to feel any of that awkwardness. Not outwardly, anyway. So I push aside my awkwardness, clear my throat, and answer honestly.

"I used to think so. But now, I kind of hope there's no such thing."

"Why do you say that?" he asks.

"Because if soulmates exist, I think I broke up with mine."

A tiny line forms between his eyebrows. The smoothest frown I've ever seen.

What the fuck do the French use on their skin? And how much can I smuggle back into the United States?

"But you said the two of you do not want the same things. He wanted to get married, and you did not."

I shrug the shoulder I'm not laying on. "Maybe soulmates don't always work out."

"Or maybe he wasn't your soulmate," he posits, raising an eyebrow that barely wrinkles his forehead. "It seems to me that—*if* soulmates exist—yours would accept you for who you are and what you want out of life. That one didn't seem to love you the way you deserve to be loved."

I'm sure the shock of his words is plain on my face. For some fucked up reason, my first instinct is to defend Ethan, but I don't bother. Why should I? Julien isn't wrong.

Again, I'm reminded that Ethan couldn't possibly know anything about me if he proposed to me. And if he didn't know anything about me, how could he love me? And with that, my heart sinks.

"I've upset you."

"No, I...I guess you're not wrong. I just— I hadn't thought about it like that."

"Like what?"

"That he didn't even love...*me*. The real me. How could he?"

Julien closes the gap between us and gathers me to his chest. "*Viens ici chérie...*" he coos. He presses my cheek into his warm skin, and I close my eyes, trying to let his arms transport me to a different place. But he continues.

"You deserve a man who appreciates and loves you for exactly who you are. If it's not him, it will be someone better."

He plants a tender kiss on my head and begins stroking a soothing hand up and down my back.

The room descends into a content—albeit sad—silence. But then, I hear him take a deep breath and release it, like he's trying to build himself up to say something. And when he does, I get the distinct impression that his mind has taken a quick trip elsewhere to pull a memory in so he can relay something important.

"Someone once told me that they believed we have many soulmates..." He pauses, but his hand continues to move up and down my back. "...But that they weren't all romantic in nature. They could be parents or friends or romantic partners. They said souls traveled in packs...and in every lifetime we re-encountered them, though perhaps in different forms. Maybe your best friend in this life was your romantic partner in a previous life. I liked that idea—that perhaps we have soulmates who are always around us."

I let that sink in for a moment. It's an oddly comforting thought. Maybe Ethan *is* one of my soulmates, but not one I'll be with for the rest of my life. Maybe he'll reappear in my next life.

"Who told you that?" I ask quietly.

His soothing hand on my back faltered in its rhythm for just a second before continuing its regular pace.

"My ex."

I can hear something different in his voice, and it makes me sad, so I wrap an arm around his body and squeeze a bit.

"How long ago?"

"Hmm...I suppose about three years ago now."

"What happened?"

"She met someone else," he says simply.

"Oh, Julien...I'm sorry."

I squeeze him tighter. He returns my squeeze and drops a kiss on my temple.

"It's okay. Things happen."

"You loved her."

It's not a question, so I don't phrase it as one. I can tell in his tone that he loved her with his whole heart.

"Oui,"* he confirms.

"Did you want to marry her?"

"Oui."

Of course he did. Most people are normal like that.

"Do you still miss her?"

"At times."

I take a deep breath and let it out slowly. I don't want to miss Ethan now, let alone three years from now. If I could snap my fingers and make myself stop loving him, I would do it.

"Were you mad at her?" I ask.

His hand stops caressing my back and moves to my waist. "A bit, yes. But I wanted her to be happy. She was happier with the other man."

It's frankly shocking to me that anyone would leave Julien for another man—especially when Julien loved her and clearly still holds a special place for her in his heart.

But then again, I have no intention of staying. This is a temporary situation. I can't help but wonder if I would want something long-term with him if I were staying. It's a moot point, so I let it go, opting instead to turn my head and nuzzle into his neck, pressing a kiss on his soft skin.

"I'm so sorry," I whisper.

"It's okay. She is happy. They married, and they have a beautiful child. Last I heard, they were expecting a second."

Picturing Ethan happily married to some other woman with two kids in tow feels like someone is stabbing me directly in my sternum. I squeeze my eyes shut to stifle the burning behind my eyes. I decide to ask another question just to distract me.

"Was it painful...when she married him?"

---

* Yes.

His hand moves from my waist and returns to my back, resuming his slow, soothing motions up and down my spine.

"Not when she married him, no."

I roll my lips between my teeth to force myself to stay quiet. I've already pried enough. He's humored me thus far—maybe he doesn't want to talk about it any further. I decide to let the topic drop, but then his voice cuts through the silence between us.

"It was painful when she left," he says. "And for a long time after. But I've moved on. It's all for the best."

I pull away from him just enough to look into his eyes. His hand trails back to the dip of my waist, then down to my hip.

"Is it?" I ask. "Is it for the best? You still care about her... and she's with someone else. Don't you ever just...wish you could turn it off?"

"Turn what off? My feelings for her?"

"Yeah."

Seriously, this feeling sucks. I don't want it. How could anyone?

But Julien's mouth curves into a compassionate smile. "Non. I am a better man for having known her. For being loved by her. And I will always love her for that."

I lose my battle with the tears pricking the backs of my eyes. They well up, and one trails down my face onto the pillow.

"That's beautiful," I admit, placing a hand on his bare chest over his heart.

"It's the truth."

"I don't think Ethan feels that way," I whisper.

"How can you be sure of that?"

I shake my head. "He was so hurt. So shocked. I just can't

imagine him still loving me. Not even in a distant…grateful-for-the-time-we-spent-together kind of way."

His calloused hand moves over my waist, up my side, over my shoulder, and to my cheek before nudging my chin up, forcing me to look into solemn hazel eyes.

"If he doesn't love you anymore, he's a fool."

I try to avert my eyes and shake my head, but he pinches my chin between his thumb and forefinger, again forcing me to look in his eyes.

"A fool," he says again. "And if someone were to fall out of love with you so easily, they were never worth your affection to begin with."

The intensity of his gaze makes my heart skip a beat. I swallow hard against my tightening throat.

"I don't want to talk about it anymore."

"D'accord."* His thumb feathers across my cheekbone. "Are you tired?"

"No." I steal a glance at his mouth—soft, gentle, and inviting.

"Good," he says, leaning forward and kissing me.

The physical feeling of Julien's lips and the tender caress of his tongue are far better than any of the feelings in my chest when I think about Ethan.

I decide to leave them behind for now.

---

* All right / Okay.

CHAPTER 15
SMELLS LIKE HOME

MAGGIE

The official groundbreaking goes off without a hitch, though it was a few days later than initially planned, thanks to some unfortunately timed weather.

There's a small ceremony for the entire company with the American crew present via Zoom. Each member of the team working on the project gets to shovel a ceremonial pile of dirt moved during the demo into a pot that will be (hopefully) used in the lobby for plants. We take pictures of each other doing so, including some goofy shots of us in our hard hats with the gold shovel.

Obviously, stuff like this is just for posterity. It's a nice bit of levity after the massive amount of work that both teams have already put into this project. The gold shovel will be placed somewhere—maybe in Max's office or possibly, a storage closet—but it's really just a representation for the long hours, late nights, and hard work.

I feel...accomplished.

I've been here for about seven months, actively contributing to a building that will shape the Paris cityscape, and I'm so fucking grateful.

I smile while people take pictures of the American and French teams together.

I laugh at all the right times.

I make jokes at appropriate moments and join in on the revelry with my team.

And underneath it all, I wonder if I've chosen my career over my family. If I'm truly a heathen—the way my childhood religion would describe me.

The difficult part about that line of thought is that this work makes me *happy*. It provides me with a sense of fulfillment. And what does that say about me? That I enjoy having a career...one I wouldn't give up if I chose to have children. Even if Ethan and I had stayed together and started a family, I'd still be doing this. I'd still want to work.

I do my best to push it out of my mind so I don't miss out on these final weeks in the city of lights.

ON OUR FINAL day in the Paris office, Maxime takes the whole team out for a traditional, four-course lunch. I make sure to order my favorite dishes—ones I know I can't replicate at home: the soup of the day (onion...because you don't need to specify that it's French here), Coquilles Saint Jacques (sautéed scallops in a garlic and tomato sauce), the local cheeses, and the dessert special (choux puffs with hazelnut cream).

Max orders bottles of wine for the table, and I watch all of my American colleagues mentally remind themselves that we are not in America and need to keep ourselves in check. The French aren't ones to overindulge, and definitely not at *lunch*.

He gives a beautiful speech about collaboration and the value of learning from one another. He thanks each of us by name, citing something he appreciates about us one-by-one.

I love working for Marv and wouldn't trade it for anything, but I would seriously consider working for Max if Marv was to retire, and there was an opening in this office. It's a pipe dream—they'd hire a local, I know. But thinking about it gives me warm fuzzy feelings. Who wouldn't want to live in Paris?

The fact that it's thousands of miles away from my family and ex-boyfriend is basically just icing on the cake.

It's not that I don't love my family. It's just that I'm nothing like them. I'm the oddball. I want kids, but I don't want to get married. I want a successful career, and I don't plan to take an extensive amount of time off when they're born. I'll take maternity leave, but I don't plan on checking out for five years. I like working. I love my job. I don't want to stop, and I don't think I should have to just because I'm a woman. If my partner wants to, and we can financially survive that decision, then fine. But it shouldn't be me by default.

For all of those viewpoints and more, I have a hard time relating to my super Catholic family, and these months in Paris have offered me a brief reprieve from their meddling.

"What time is your flight?" Dominique asks us.

"One thirty," Kelsie says. "What can we bring tonight?"

Dominique is having a party at her place tonight in our honor. The current plan is that I'll spend one more night with Julien afterward. We have tomorrow to pack and get everything in order before our flight leaves on Saturday.

"*Ne sois pas stupide*," Dominique answers. "*S'il te plaît*, my goodness.* You don't need to bring a thing."

Kelsie and I roll our eyes in tandem. We already bought her a rare orchid to add to her collection. It's in our apartment, and we've been praying to all the gods we don't kill it before tonight.

Dominique doesn't miss the eye roll and starts speaking rapid French, far beyond our comprehension. Maxime and the rest of the French team are laughing at her congenially, giving clear indication that she's not actually angry, but is probably making a show of being upset and teasing us. It doesn't matter though—Kelsie and I love Dom and don't want her to be upset with us. We immediately start talking over one another, apologizing repeatedly.

"Je suis désolé, Dominique..."†

"Je regrette, mon amie..."‡

"...s'il te plaît, ne sois pas en colère..."§

"...nous vous aimons tant..."#

Our French apologies run out quicker than we'd like, forcing us to switch back to English.

"We were only teasing..."

"This is our last day, please don't be mad..."

"...we didn't mean it..."

"...please tell me you're teasing..."

Eventually, Dom can't keep a straight face anymore, and she dissolves into laughter along with the rest of her teammates.

---

* Do not be stupid. Please...

† I am sorry, Dominique...

‡ I'm sorry, my friend...

§ ...please don't be angry...

\# ...we love you so much...

"Vous allez me manquer toutes les deux,"* she tells us, wrapping an arm around each of our necks and hugging us close. Phones pop up in front of us and people take pictures of her kissing our cheeks and laughing.

It's the type of moment I hope I can sear into my brain. The type of moment I want to remember when I'm old and boring. It's unfiltered joy and love and adoration.

"Of course, I'm teasing you, chéries."†

I wrap my arms around her waist and hug her, closing my eyes, trying to memorize the scents and sounds around me. This experience in Paris has been one of the best of my whole life, and I wish I could remember every detail for the rest of time.

We eventually head back to the office, but it's late afternoon, and no one is expecting us to get any work done. Everything that needs to be complete before we leave has been finished and approved by all parties. We pack up our personal belongings and laptops and head back to the apartment to drop everything off before heading to Dominique's with her rare orchid.

At Dom's, the air is vibrant and happy. There's plenty of wine, aperitifs, charcuterie boards, and giant balloons that spell out *bon voyage*. I have my fair share of wine, but I don't want to be too drunk for Julien, so I switch to water after a while.

When our eyes meet for the first time, they're without the immediate heat I usually see on nights like this. Instead, I see an undertone of bittersweet sadness. One I imagine is mirrored in my own eyes.

Unlike our usual dynamic, he's more affectionate

---

* I will miss you both.
† Darlings.

around people tonight. We don't typically touch in front of others, but tonight, his hands find mine. His arm wraps around my shoulders. He doesn't kiss me in front of others, but when we're alone in the kitchen, he presses his lips to my temple and tells me I look beautiful.

Eventually, we both decide we've had enough and head back to Julien's place, holding hands the entire way.

Oftentimes when we're together, we're frantic, hot, and even playful. But right now, there's an undercurrent of something sad. This is our last night together, and it's accentuated in every kiss, every touch, every movement of our bodies.

Julien moves slowly, savoring every sensation, and for once, I'm not in a hurry. It's loving, caring, sweet, and I allow myself to stay in that mindset with him instead of pushing for something different. Instead, I just soak him in...this person who has taken every opportunity to make me feel valued at a time when I was questioning myself after my life plan changed so dramatically. This person who lifted me up and reminded me that I'm worth whatever I demand of others. Who has shown me his city with the same love and care in which he seems to do everything.

Even though I'm not in love with him, I do love him, and I'll always care for him.

Afterward, we lay in bed, a tangle of limbs and soft caresses.

"I'm going to miss you," I admit.

"I'll miss you, too," he says, brushing hair back from my forehead. "But I'll always be here for you, chérie.* You have my number. You can call or text me any time."

____

* Dear.

I force a small smile. "Same, you know. I'm always here for you."

"I do know that."

A barely-there frown appears between his eyebrows. (For the record, I did get all the beauty secrets from Dominique, and I'm bringing back as much as I can.)

"What is it?" I ask, smoothing out the world's smallest wrinkle with my thumb.

He looks into my eyes for a few breaths. It's probably not a long time, but in the silence, it makes me anxious. It makes me second-guess the depth of his feelings.

For a brief moment, I start to panic. I can feel it rise in my chest as I wonder if I'm about to experience another Ethan-esque argument where he tries to tell me he wants something I can't give him.

And then all of a sudden, his entire hand palms my face, snapping me out of my spiral.

"Stop," he says, sternly.

I can't help but laugh as I remove his hand from my field of vision.

"What was that for?"

"You're starting to panic. I don't want you to panic. I just want to tell you something."

"Julien..."

"Non," he stops me again. "There's no reason to be afraid."

He can't possibly know what I'm feeling at this moment —the panic, the terror, the desperation to know (and also not know) what he's thinking. But somehow, I think he might know exactly.

"Maggie, when you arrived in Paris, your wounds were fresh," he starts.

The start of his sentence doesn't do a single thing to calm my nerves.

My mind starts filling in possibilities.

...so I agreed to a "with benefits" situation to appease you.

...and I didn't want to scare you.

...but time has passed, and I want something more.

I force myself to focus, swallowing the lump in my throat.

"I've watched you these past few months. I've seen you be confident and sexy and adventurous. I've witnessed the care and attention to pay to the people you love." He pauses to lay a gentle kiss on my forehead. "I believe you are all of those things and more. But I also believe that this experience with your ex weighs heavily on your mind, and I worry that it's made you question yourself and what you want out of a romantic relationship."

I can feel my body deflate, sinking further into the mattress. He's not wrong, obviously. But hearing him tell me these things is leaving me with a very raw feeling. It's hard to let someone stare into your soul and tell you they see things you try to hide from the world.

"You are wonderful, Maggie. Talented, kind, generous. You deserve to be loved and not only accepted, but celebrated. You deserve someone who will want *you* exactly the way you are...someone who will *need* your presence in their life. Someone who can't imagine living their life without you."

I grind my teeth against the burning in my throat and the sting in my eyes. He notices—because of course he does—and pauses to kiss each of my eyelids.

"I know you're still grieving the loss of your relationship, and you have every right to choose whatever path you believe is best for you. I only hope that when you return home, you remember that someone worthy of being your soulmate will want you to be *you*. Not someone else."

I can't stop the tears at this point. They fall down my face toward the pillow. Julien swipes at the ones that can't get over the bridge of my nose before pulling my body into his, pressing every possible inch of him against every available inch of me.

"*Il n'y a qu'un bonheur dans la vie, c'est d'aimer et d'être aimé*," he whispers.

When I frown, he translates for me. "The only happiness in life is to love and be loved."

I close my eyes and press my face into his neck.

"You are a *force*, Maggie. Don't dim yourself to blend into someone else's light."

After taking one more moment to memorize the feel of his body and the scent of his skin, I tilt my head up and press my lips to his. He doesn't miss a beat, kissing me back, licking my bottom lip and teasing my mouth open.

We're nearing frantic territory again, his tongue expertly invading my mouth, spreading warmth through my body. But there's still the underlying feeling of respect and adoration I felt earlier.

"*Tu es un homme merveilleux*," I murmur in between kisses. "*Je suis si heureuse de t'avoir rencontré*."[*]

"*Ton français s'est amélioré*,"[†] he says with a dark chuckle.

"*Oui. J'ai eu un bon professeur*."[‡]

He practically purrs as he rolls me to my back, fitting his strong body between my legs.

"*C'était son plaisir, j'en suis sûr*."[§]

---

[*] You are a wonderful man. I'm so happy to have met you.
[†] Your French has improved.
[‡] Yes. I had a good teacher.
[§] It was his pleasure, I'm sure.

"*Non, non, tout le plaisir était pour moi.*"[*]

But then he grinds into me and watches with a smug expression when my mouth drops open.

"*Pas tout à toi,*" he says, punctuating his retort by sucking on the pulse point in my neck. "*Détends-toi, mon amour.*"[†]

The endearment is stronger than anything he's ever said to me, but I accept it because it makes me warm and fuzzy inside. He kisses his way down my stomach, and when he reaches my navel, I grab fistfuls of his hair to get his attention.

"*Je tiens à toi,* Julien,"[‡] I whisper.

"I know," he turns his head to kiss my wrist, and it's not lost on me that I spoke to him in his language, but he's responding in mine. Like he wants to make sure I understand him fully. "In the same way I care about you, Maggie."

WHEN WE FINALLY GET OUT OF customs, Kelsie and I drag our tired bodies to baggage claim to search for our luggage. As we come down the escalator, I see a familiar face light up with a massive smile. She holds up a sign that says *Bienvenue à la maison, Maggie!*[§]

"Evil shrew," I say, stepping right in front of her, taking the sign out of her hands.

"Spiteful hag," she returns, then throws her arms around me, squeezing me tight.

My mom offered to come pick me up from the airport,

---

[*]   No, no, the pleasure was all mine.
[†]   Not all yours. Relax, my love.
[‡]   I care for you, Julien.
[§]   Welcome home, Maggie!

but Kate thankfully offered first, so I had an excuse to turn her down.

I'm still feeling raw, and I'm just not ready to see my mother. I'll text her to let her know I'm on the ground and then call her when I get to Kate's so she can hear my voice. Then, she'll be appeased.

For now.

Tonight, I'm staying with Kate.

"Come on, dear." She lets go of me, looping her arm through my free one. "Let's get your bags. Liam is making you a special dinner."

"Oh yeah?"

"Yep. Since you weren't here for St. Paddy's Day, he's making slow-cooked corned beef with cabbage."

I freeze in my tracks.

"Cooked in Guinness?"

"Cooked in Guinness."

"Let's get to it, Katherine. Pick up the pace."

Her laughter is behind me as I tug her toward the baggage carousel, where I can see Kelsie is standing with Isaac and Wesley.

"He won't eat without you."

"Move your butt, I'm starving!"

After we get my bags and load them into the car, Kate drives us back to her house. And when she opens the door from the garage to the kitchen, I'm gently immersed in the comforting scents of *home*.

THE FOLLOWING DAY, my brothers pick up the truck I rented to move my stuff into my new apartment. They help me load the truck with Kate and Liam while talking shit to each other, and I find myself laughing until I cry on multiple occasions.

These bozos were infuriating when I was a kid, but now I just love them. Maybe it's losing Nick. Maybe it's being older and less hormonal. Maybe it's Maybelline. But whatever it is, I'm glad we're on good terms these days.

The boys have never put pressure on me to settle down. That pressure has typically come from my sisters and my mom. I'm sure that has something to do with it.

They load up all my crap from Kate's, and then they (and Kate) follow me over to my new apartment building, where they proceed to *unload* all my crap in my fifth-floor apartment.

Mark had the good sense to pick up beer, and Matthew tried to teach us—for the eight-hundredth time—how to open bottles using his wedding ring. We still can't do it—of course, I don't have a wedding ring, so I use the silver ring I wear on my middle finger. We're lost causes.

We toast to new beginnings as we start unpacking the critical boxes, and Kate makes it her mission to set up my bed so I have a comfortable place to sleep, regardless of how much I get done in the apartment today.

By the time we're finished, everyone is sweaty and exhausted, ready to return to their normal lives (and showers). We all hug goodbye, and the boys walk Kate down to her car. I can see them part ways from my living room window. Mark and Matthew will return the truck on their way home. I'll pick up my beloved Mustang from my parents' house tomorrow.

I take a moment to look around at my new home. It's one-bedroom, one-bath, a kitchen-dining room combo, and a living room.

And it's all mine.

CHAPTER 16
FIRST, SECOND, THIRD IMPRESSIONS

ETHAN

The Alcott (feat. Taylor Swift) - The National, Taylor Swift

May

"They'll be here soon?" I ask my new boss, Dan.

We're in his office. It's a big space, though not the biggest office on the floor. He has big windows and a nice view of the city. There are bookshelves along one wall that house books, binders, plaques, and various awards. He's behind his desk, and I'm sitting in one of the chairs in front of it.

He's been telling me about the architecture team that's been hired to create our new building just outside the city. It will be our new headquarters, since we've outgrown our downtown space.

I just started this job. I needed a change. I'd been at my old place for a long time, and at the end of each day, I kept coming home to my new apartment and thinking about how I used to tell Maggie I wanted something different. I was sick of the people there...of the culture. Of the lack of accountability from management. Being a project manager, I just couldn't take the agency life any longer.

This conversation with Maggie went on for far longer than it should have. She was patient for a long time, but after an entire year had passed, she started encouraging me to find a different job. She said life was more important than a shitty job that made me miserable. She even told me she'd support me if I just wanted to quit without something new lined up.

The memory of that moment and the earnest look on her face is a stark reminder that Maggie was telling the truth —she really did think of me as family. Why else would someone offer to support their partner who just wanted to leave a crappy job?

She wanted what was best for me, and I tried to guilt-trip her into marrying me.

Fuck, I'm such an asshole.

"Yeah, they're scheduled to be here at ten." Dan's response pulls me out of a self-loathing spiral that's become quite familiar to me over the past nine months.

In the very back of my mind, it occurs to me that I don't know who is designing the space. I've only been here for a month, so I'm still being assigned projects and getting caught up.

Could it be Maggie's firm?

"Dan, who did you say the contractor is?"

I think something in my gut already knows the answer because my stomach flips over suddenly.

Dan looks up and meets my eye, but before he can answer, we hear voices down the hall. I twist in my chair, already knowing what I'm going to see.

"Oh, they're already here. It's Obsidian. Do you know them?"

I'm silent as I watch the only woman I've ever wanted to spend my entire life with pass by Dan's office. She doesn't see me, but I soak up every single second of her.

She's wearing black slacks and heels with a red button-down top that pulls out the red undertones to her hair. If you just met her, you might think her hair is brown, but in the sunlight—especially when she wears red—you can see hints of auburn, and the way it contrasts with her green eyes is stunning.

I can't see her eyes from where I am, but her curly hair is tamed and still fucking vibrant. It was always shiny. Soft. I immediately remember how it felt between my fingers.

She smiles at something her coworker says, and I swear if I weren't already sitting, I'd fall to the floor.

If there was a single doubt in my mind that I was still head over heels in love with that woman, it's obliterated now. I missed her. I still miss her, even though she's *right there*. I want her back.

She disappears into the conference room, which is when I realize Dan has been trying to get my attention.

"Ethan? Are you okay?"

"Yeah," I say, twisting back to face him. "Of course."

He looks skeptical, his eyes narrowing the slightest bit.

"Are you sure?"

"Absolutely."

He studies me for another moment before moving on. "They're expecting us. You ready?"

"Always," I promise, standing from my chair.

I'm fibbing, just a little. I'm not actually ready to face Maggie, but I can't sit here while she's a few doors down the hall.

Dan leads the way to the conference room, where Maggie and her coworkers are already shaking hands with my new coworkers. My heart is pounding, and even though I'm nervous as fuck, I feel a pull toward her. Like my feet would move that way on their own even if I wasn't supposed to go into that room.

"Marv!" I hear Dan greet Maggie's mentor and realize I hadn't even noticed Marv come in with her. Or anyone else she was with, really. My eyes are glued to Maggie's as she smiles at the person she just met before averting her eyes to Marv and Dan. I can hear them talking to each other somewhere on the left.

"I hear you hired someone new recently," Marv says.

"We sure did. We're really excited to have him. Ethan, I want you to meet Marvin James. Marv, this is Ethan, he started last month. He'll be stepping in as the project manager. He'll be your primary contact."

I hear what Dan said, and before I create an absolutely wretched first impression for our lead architect, I force my gaze away from Maggie.

I don the best smile I can muster given the circumstances and reach out to shake Marv's hand.

Marv takes my hand, but blinks in surprise a few times before recovering. "Ethan. It's good to see you again."

"You two know each other?" Dan asks.

I hold Marv's eye, but he breaks it to glance over at Maggie. I nod so he knows I know she's here.

Letting go of Marv's hand, I look back over to Dan. "I met Marv about...five years ago now. But it's been awhile since we've seen each other."

Dan is looking back and forth between the two of us, trying to read the room and decipher the odd energy.

"Yes, it has been a while." Marv nods, pausing for a moment. "I'm glad we'll get to work together."

The comment strikes me as odd. I assumed he'd hate

me. That Maggie would have told him how I fucked everything up. That I didn't listen to her. That I thought she'd change her mind. That I broke her heart. I can't find an immediate reason he'd be *glad we get to work together*, but I'll take the win for now.

"Thanks, Marv. I am, too."

And I fucking mean it.

He nods again and takes a breath before averting his eyes to where I know Maggie is standing.

"Let me introduce you to the rest of my team," he says to Dan.

I steel myself to turn and look at her, knowing she'll be looking at me. I can feel her eyes on me already, and I know this is only the beginning of this potentially (probably, definitely) awkward encounter.

When I turn and see her—eyes on me, as I knew they would be—it strikes me in the chest. My heart skips at least three beats, and I have to swallow a lump in my throat.

Her eyes hold confusion with a healthy dose of anger for a split second before she schools her expression into something more professional. A tall woman with blonde hair steps forward first, hand already extended to shake.

"Dan, Ethan, this is Kelsie Matthews and Maggie Rafferty. They're two of my best."

I can see Maggie out of the corner of my eye shaking Dan's hand while I shake Kelsie's, offering her a smile. I remember her from the night we met—she was at the bar. I haven't seen her as much as I have Marv over the past few years, but she must suspect who I am. Her eyes are narrowed like she's trying to place me.

We switch, and the butterflies in my stomach erupt into complete chaos. Maggie is suddenly standing right in front of me, hand extended like she's never touched me before.

Like she didn't sleep next to me every night for four years. Like that exact hand hasn't yanked on my hair or caressed my face or wrapped itself around mine while we walked side-by-side.

"Ethan," she says. Matter of fact. No discernible emotion. Just my name.

I slide my palm against hers and squeeze gently.

"Maggie."

Neither of us makes a move to pump our hands or squeeze harder. We're just standing there, basically holding hands and—I know this sounds ridiculous coming from a man, but I get tingles all the way up my arm to my shoulder, and I have to stifle a shudder.

For me, it's warm and welcome, and I want nothing more than to drag her to a private room and talk all this out.

But for her? Her eyes are hard and cold. This is a business transaction. Maggie is working. If she's been pining for me the way I've been pining for her all this time, I wouldn't know it by looking at her at this moment. If she's feeling anything other than cool, calm, and collected, she's hiding it very well.

"It's good to see you," I add.

Her eyes narrow in what looks like disbelief before she huffs out a quiet laugh, her trademark sass taking over. "I'm sure." Her voice is low, like she doesn't want anyone to hear our exchange.

"I mean it."

Her eyes narrow further, but we don't get a chance to say anything else.

A clap from behind me breaks our staring contest. She lets go of my hand like it's burning her as I turn to face Dan.

"Let's get started, shall we?"

Everyone shuffles into seats, Maggie intentionally

seating herself between Marv and Kelsie. I join my team on the other side of the table, back far enough that I can sneak glances at Maggie without being overly conspicuous about it. I'm certain Dan will have questions when this meeting is over.

Marv and Maggie fiddle with the projector, hooking up Marv's phone to it for visuals. Marv gives the presentation, but Maggie also has her phone out, getting answers for Marv when people have questions. She has numbers ready to spout off and cost differential options on her phone.

Dan asks questions, along with my other coworkers, but since I'm still new to this project, I don't feel I have much to add, so I stay quiet to soak things in.

The longer I sit here, the less shocked I feel. Being in the same room with her makes all those memories and feelings rush right back. They've always been there, simmering in the back of my mind, but now they're front and center, assaulting my frontal lobe.

The pain and guilt I felt all those months ago is still there, for sure. Now though, nipping on their heels is a healthy dose of anger.

Maggie broke up with me (her choice) after turning down my proposal (my bad) and then just...cut me off.

That twelve word exchange we just had is the most she's spoken to me since the night we broke up. I'm not totally innocent in that—I played a part as well. I couldn't be there when she came to get the rest of her stuff. It was too painful. It was still so raw.

When Miles told me she'd landed the Paris gig, I reached out to congratulate her. Of course, I never got a response.

Every message I've sent her has gone unanswered, whether it was a text, a voicemail, or an email.

Her phone is still resting face up on the table, and I realize I might not get another chance to test my theory that she blocked my number. So, I discreetly pull my phone from my pocket, hiding it out of sight, and tap out a quick message to Maggie.

I wait for the screen to light up with a notification, but it never does.

I feel both vindicated that I was right and stricken that she hasn't read or heard a single word I've sent to her since we broke up. That she cut me off completely.

Five years together and then nothing.

Still, I can't say I'm surprised.

Maggie moves on.

Maggie finds something else and focuses on it. That's how she gets through grief. And as much as it hurts to know *I'm* the thing she's moved on from, I'm very sure it's been painful for her. I remember her face that night. The look of betrayal in her eyes. It's wretched to think about. I don't want to, but I do it anyway because I need to remind myself that I wasn't just something she tossed out the door. That I wasn't easily forgotten.

No, I know Maggie Rafferty well enough to know she's doing her absolute best to ignore me. To become indifferent to my existence.

I also know her well enough to know that it's not working. That there's still something there. And if there's even the slightest fucking chance that she still feels *something* for me—even if it's anger—I'll be right there waiting. Because the opposite of love isn't hate. It's indifference.

If she still feels *something* for me, there's still hope.

∼

WHEN THE MEETING WRAPS UP, Maggie's phone is lighting up, so she says goodbye and slips out of the conference room to take the incoming call. I shake Kelsie's hand before making my way to Marv and shaking his as well.

His face is inscrutable, but I don't really expect him to say anything in my favor. Maggie is his mentee, and I know he'll always be on her side. The fact that he said it was good to see me, would be glad to be working with me, was good enough for me. It was downright shocking, frankly.

Unless, of course, he's planning to kick back with popcorn and watch Maggie rip me to shreds over the next year.

I suppose that's possible, too.

Once they all clear out, Dan jerks his head toward his office, signaling me to follow him. He waits for me to enter and then shuts the door behind me.

"What did you think?"

He sits down behind his desk and motions for me to sit, as well.

"I think it looks beautiful," I say, sinking into the club chair across from his desk.

"I thought so, too. It's different enough to make it stand out, but it still aligns with that area's architecture."

I'm nodding before he even finishes his sentence. "I totally agree. I'm excited about it."

"Good," he says with a smile. But then he doesn't continue. He just looks at me with that amused smile on his face.

I feel like I know what's on his mind, and I decide I'd rather be the one to say it first.

"So uh...like I said, I know Marv."

Dan nods slowly.

I wipe my clammy palms on my pants and avert my eyes while I search for the right words.

"I know him because...well, I...I met Maggie first." I glance up at him to find his expression the same. Smiling and patient. It's just encouraging enough to keep going. "Maggie and I used to be a thing. For a long time, actually. Five years. We broke up last year."

Finally, Dan's expression changes. His smile becomes somber, and he leans back in his chair.

"I see."

"Listen, I would have told you ahead of time, but I didn't know. Regardless, I'm confident I can stay on this project. Marv is a great guy and—as I'm sure you could tell—Maggie is a consummate professional. I realize it may not be ideal... having all this baggage from a new employee. But my history with Maggie will not negatively impact this project or this company."

Dan nods again, but doesn't say anything.

I'm not really sure if he expects me to say anything else, but I'm not really comfortable airing all my dirty laundry to a person I barely know, let alone when the person in question is my new boss. I don't plan to offer any additional information without some justified inquiries.

After a semi-tense moment where we stare at each other, he finally takes a breath and leans forward, resting his elbows on his desk.

"All right. I won't make any changes unless I find evidence that suggests otherwise. In the meantime, I have to trust you to let me know if anything is amiss."

"Yes, sir." I nod.

A knock on the door interrupts us.

"Come in."

I turn to see the CEO poking his head in the door. "Dan, can I have a moment?"

"Of course." He looks back at me. "Ethan, if you'll excuse me. We can continue this later."

"Anytime, yeah." I get up and nod to the CEO, who I haven't actually met yet, but I just want out of this room so I can go back to my office and try to pull myself together.

I know I told Dan that everything would be fine and I can stay on this project—and I am and I can—but holy shit, seeing her again has thrown me. I shut my office door behind me and head straight for the window, which I'm exceedingly grateful for at this moment. I crack it open as far as it allows, which isn't much (for safety reasons, of course).

I suck in the fresh air like it's the first breath I've had in hours and close my eyes. For all the anger that rushed through my veins, the misery of missing her is currently winning out. I have to brace my hands on the window frame to keep myself steady.

Maggie.

It's *Maggie* and Obsidian.

Of course, it is.

I get the concept of karma, but this seems very on the nose.

Oh, you messed up the greatest thing in your life because you were a fucking idiot and now you're forced to work with her for at least one year?

I'm both elated to know I'll get to see her and miserable I won't get to touch her.

I'm glad she seems to be doing well, while wishing she were just as miserable as me.

Which is horrible to say. I shouldn't feel that way. You shouldn't feel that way about a person you care about.

My feelings about Maggie aren't questionable to me. I'm not confused. I'm not conflicted. I've been in love with Margaret Rafferty for nearly six years, and that's not going to change. I love her, and I want her to be happy and safe and healthy. Always.

But would it kill her to...miss me a little?

Fuck.

One thing is for damn sure, I'm *still* not giving up on Maggie. I might be mad at her. She might be mad at me. She might even hate me.

But I'm still not done.

I still want her.

I'll always want her.

CHAPTER 17
WHERE'S THAT RAGE ROOM?

MAGGIE

Wouldn't Come Back - Trousdale

"**W**hat the *fuck*?!"

My scream echoes in the Obsidian parking lot the moment I get out of the car. I was silent the whole drive across town. We all were, really. Marv only mentioned that they seemed happy with the presentation, and Kelsie agreed with him. I just chewed my lip and stared out the window.

But when I got out of the car, Kelsie asked if I was okay.

I'm clearly not.

My fists are balled at my sides, and both of my colleagues are just staring at me.

"Maggie, was that—"

Marv cuts her off with a quick confirmation that that was indeed my ex-boyfriend who broke my fucking heart last summer. The person I thought I'd spend the rest of my life with. The person I'm still hopelessly in love with. The person I tried to get over by getting under (and on top of) someone else.

Which didn't fucking work, apparently.

For the record, Marv just said yes to Kelsie's question. I added the rest of it in my head.

My chest is tight, and my head is starting to throb. My eyes start to sting, and I can feel my nose already starting to run. I'd blame the nip in the air if it weren't for the tears threatening to escape my eyes.

"What the fuck?" I say again, but this time, it comes out as a pathetic whimper. "How did this happen?"

"You didn't know he worked there?" Kelsie asks, cautiously.

"No." I shake my head. "He was working somewhere else the last time I…" I trail off because I realize that the last time I talked to him was also the last time I saw him, and the memory is coming back so intensely that I feel nauseous. "… last summer," I finally finish the sentence.

I hear Marv sigh to my right, then hand something to Kelsie.

"If you wouldn't mind, Kelsie, I could use a little walk to stretch my legs. I'll take Maggie with me, and we'll be in soon."

She takes something from Marv and heads toward our office building.

I keep staring at anything and everything, trying to keep my tears at bay. I wind up watching the ripple of the lake move around in the distance.

I feel Marv come up to stand next to me.

He's not overly tall—about five-foot-nine inches. He has a little gut forming these days. But his face is clean-shaven, and his hair is well-tamed. He's wearing dress shoes and I'm still in heels. We're not exactly in good walking shoes—or clothes, for that matter—but I know he's trying to calm me down.

"Come on," he urges, jerking his head toward the sidewalk in front of the building. "Let's take a walk."

I follow him because I don't know what else to do. I want to scream and maybe break things, but I also want to crawl into my bed and sob for the next few hours.

All those emotions that I've carefully kept pushed down for months have burst to the surface like lava. There was no slow simmer or bubble to them. They just erupted, leaving a path of destruction along the way, frying every nerve ending and incinerating the walls I'd built up to contain them.

I'm a live wire, ready to explode at any moment.

The anxiety attacks I started having after Nick died—the ones I thought were completely in check since starting therapy—are choosing now to resurface.

My heart is racing, I'm getting hot, and I feel like I'm going to crawl out of my skin.

I wonder if Kate remembers where that rage room is.

I should definitely ask her about that. I could use a baseball bat right about now.

Marv takes a right on the sidewalk, leading us away from the building and toward the park. He doesn't say anything for a while. So long, in fact, that I'm not sure if he's waiting for me to start. He's just looking around at the barely-there buds on the trees and the grass as it tries to revive itself after a cold winter.

He's not clearing his throat or nudging me. He's just silent.

I don't want to give in, but eventually, I can't stand it. I have too many questions and thoughts and feelings.

"Did you know?" I ask, trying to keep the accusatory tone out of my voice, but probably failing.

"No. I didn't."

I feel a modicum of relief that Marv didn't put me in this

position on purpose. Marv and I have known each other for years—long enough that I worked for him when I *met* Ethan, so he witnessed every stage of our relationship. Ethan and I attended parties at his house. He and Ethan got along really well.

And perhaps most importantly, Marv really liked Ethan.

Like I said, I love my family. They're important to me. But I'm different from all of them. My brother, Nick, was the one who got me best...who made the most effort to understand me. And once he died, Marv and Ethan were the only family left who knew me as well as he did.

Or so I thought.

I suppose now, it's just Marv.

"What's the verdict?"

I frown. Is it just me, or was that question out of left field?

"Did I miss something? Did you ask me a question?"

Marv smirks and shakes his head.

"No, I didn't ask you a question before that last one. I'm asking you what conclusion you're coming to in your brain right now."

I take a deep breath, allowing the crisp air to fill my lungs before blowing it back out slowly.

"I was thinking that you're probably the only person on this planet who knows me as well as my brother did," I admit, averting my eyes so he doesn't notice me trying to hold back tears.

"I'm sure that's not true."

"I'm pretty sure it is."

Marv heaves a sigh and stops walking to look at me, so I stop, too, turning to face him.

"If that's true...why do you think that is?"

"Why do I think people don't know me?"

"Yes. Why do you think that's the case?" He holds up a finger. "*If* it's true. I'm not sure I agree."

"Because Nick knew me better than anyone. And then you did. And I thought Ethan did. But Ethan clearly *didn't,* and Nick...well he's dead. So that leaves you." I wave my arm up and down in the direction of his body.

He gives me a pointed look. "Maggie, if that's true, then I'm...sad for you."

"What?" I basically shriek. "You're *sad* for me?"

Anger is exponentially easier than the absolute chaos I've been feeling since we left Ethan's office, so I latch onto that pretty hard.

"How can you say that to me?"

He tilts his head, studying the outrage on my face. "Maggie, you're asserting that I'm the only person who knows you anymore. For the record, I don't believe that's true, but if we take your statement and examine it, what we'll find is that the only person on this planet who knows you is your boss..." He pauses, as if he's trying to get me to come to a conclusion on my own. When I don't respond, he continues "...which means you spend far more time at work than with your loved ones, and *that* is sad."

"Okay, fine," I say, rolling my eyes. "Other people *know* me. My friends do, but not...not my family."

"Well, the rest of them are still living. You can rectify that situation, if you'd like."

"Look, it's just how we are—I'm very different from all of...wait, why are we talking about this?"

"Because you're trying to say that no one knows you, and I'm trying to prove you wrong."

I groan and start walking again. Now is not a good time for an existential crisis. And since when did I become a person who has existential crises, anyway?

Since around the time you broke up with Ethan.

Holy fuck, Nicholas, now is not a good time. And breaking up with a man is certainly no reason to have an existential crisis.

It's less to do with the breakup itself and more to do with who he was to you.

If you have a point, just make it.

Meh. I think Marv can handle it. I just wanted to throw in my two cents.

Of course you did.

"You're the one that brought it up," Marv continues.

"*Marvin…*" I plead.

He chuckles—fucking *chuckles*—and I resist the urge to scream again.

"Maggie, you're spiraling. And I'm trying to snap you out of it. To make you realize that what you're saying is absurd."

Don't say a fucking word, Nicholas.

I didn't.

I heave a huge sigh and trudge over to a bench to sit.

Marv slowly follows and sinks down next to me.

"People know you, Maggie. Your friends might understand you more than your family does, but you can work on that—if you want to—and if they're willing. As for Nick…I know it's still difficult for you."

He pauses while I try to wrangle in the extra burst of emotion trying to breach the surface at the mention of my brother. I close my eyes and swallow compulsively. When I'm convinced I won't start crying, I open them back up to find him looking at me.

I don't trust myself to speak yet, so I just frown in the form of a question.

"Ethan knew Nick. Sometimes I wonder if that has played a part in this breakup being so…challenging for you."

Bingo.

Fuck.

The anxiety attack is quickly turning into a panic attack and something needs to give. The battle with my tears requires surrender. I can't stop them, so I bend over, clasping my hands together and hoping the tears fall straight down to the sidewalk instead of tracking down my cheeks and ruining my makeup. I can't remember if I have any tissues in my purse. Probably not. All my sisters would, the fucking supermoms.

Marv is hitting the nail on the head. I know that's one of the reasons this has been so gut-wrenching for me. No one else I date will ever know my brother—this person who played such a massive role in the person I became. Who influenced so many aspects of my personality, values, and life decisions.

Ethan is the last one who will ever be able to understand that part of me. And that is *killing* me.

Marv sits silently next to me while I stare at the sidewalk, tears blurring my vision, mourning yet another facet of the relationship I was sure would last forever.

Like every other time I miss my brother so much it hurts, I want to see my mom. I want to sit with her and soak up her strength. Drink bourbon with her while she tells stories about Nick as a child, or the two of us together, so I can force my face into a smile and cry on the inside.

"Maggie."

I blink a million times, trying to shake off the last tears, then dab under my eyes gently and sit back up.

I take a few deep breaths, swallow hard, and clear my throat.

I'm fine.

Everything is fine.

"I know this project is going to be hard for you. But I need to know if you can handle it."

I look over at him, trying to read his face and failing. There are no hints. No tells. His face is open and waiting for my genuine answer.

It's a moment when I can choose to turn tail and run. I can say right now that I don't want to work on this project and beg him to take me off it. I can tell him I can't handle working with Ethan. That being forced to interact with him will torture me.

I flash back to the first week after Ethan and I broke up where I sat on the floor in Marv's office, pouring over old drawings, trying to distract myself from the maelstrom in my mind. I'd gotten there at least an hour before him, my hair up in a messy bun. I was sleep-deprived and trying to fight off a migraine.

He'd taken one look at me and knew damn well I wasn't doing nearly as well as I'd promised everyone. He didn't say anything at all. Just sat in the chair near my array of documents and gave me his signature Marv stare.

I was sobbing within seconds.

He sent me home (to Kate's) and had ice cream delivered later that day.

I chew on my bottom lip while he holds my stare. I wonder if he's thinking we'll have a repeat of that day in his office. It's certainly not something I want to relive. I work in a male-dominated field...the last thing I need is someone thinking I'm too emotional to be in this firm. Or asking me if I'm on the rag or need a Midol or whatever other sexist bull-shit those bros will spout.

The truth of the matter is that I'm very stubborn.

If you tell me I can't do something, I'm more likely to put my nose to the grindstone and work harder.

And if you point out that you know I'm not doing as well as I'm trying to claim I am, I'm going to want to prove you— and the rest of the office—that you're wrong.

And if I'm being totally, completely honest, I don't want Ethan to know he's affecting me that much.

"I can handle it," I tell him.

He watches me for another moment, then nods. "Good." He stands with a low groan. "I wasn't planning on taking you off the project, so I'm glad you agree you can handle it."

I throw my head back with a dramatic eye roll.

"You're a crotchety old man, you know that?"

He laughs. I would never say that to him in the office, but we're outside and nowhere near our coworkers. I can talk to him like this here.

"Get your able-bodied butt up and let's get back to the office. We have shit to do."

I'm able to crack a smile as I join him on the sidewalk, and we begin the short walk back to our building.

"How's your new apartment?"

"There's not enough booze in it yet."

"Sounds like a shithole."

"Hello?" I call out as I open the front door of my parents' house. I texted my mom after my sidewalk meltdown earlier to ask if she'd be around tonight so I can pick up some of the stuff I have stored here.

"Back here, Mags!"

Dad's voice sounds like it's coming from the living room in the back of the house, so I follow it. I find him sitting on the couch with a crossword puzzle from the newspaper, his reading glasses perched toward the end of his nose. He looks so much like Nick it takes my breath away. This is exactly what Nick would look like if he were my dad's age. Except that Nick had more snark than our dad.

"Hey there, pumpkin," he says with a big smile, looking at me over the top of his glasses. The childhood nickname brings a matching smile to my face. I was a tubby baby.

"Hey, Dad. What's going on over here tonight?"

"Oh, it's very exhilarating. I'm working on this crossword, and your mother is in the backyard checking on her plants to see what's popping up. She'll be back in soon." He folds up his newspaper and sets it on the coffee table, then turns to face me. "What brings you here this evening?"

What a loaded question that is.

I choose to go with the easier answer.

"I wanted to pick up some of my stuff and take it to my apartment."

"Oh sure," he nods. "Of course, you're welcome to leave anything here for as long as you need to. We're not going anywhere."

I smile, knowing he means they have no plans to move, even as the obnoxious voice in the back of my head tells me that nothing is guaranteed. That people die unexpectedly all the time. I avert my eyes to look at literally anything to make my mind stop working against me.

"What you got over there?" I ask, jerking my head toward the dining room table, where papers and paint samples are laid out.

"Oh, your mother and I were thinking about painting the front room. We're sick of that color, and we thought it would be fun to make it a bit brighter and make it a kids playroom."

Yes. Paint samples and planning. It's a perfect distraction.

"That sounds like a good idea. What color are you thinking?"

He gets up and heads toward the table. "Why don't you help us decide? That's really your area of expertise."

"I'm not a designer, Dad."

"I know you're not, pumpkin. I'm well aware you're an architect—a talented one, at that—but you still have an eye for these types of things."

I stand next to him at the table, looking over the samples laid out.

"I like this yellow. It's soft and warm. Not too bright, but still cheery."

He nods. "Yeah...I think that makes sense."

I turn to look at the living room in question and an idea starts to form in my head. I pick up the yellow paint swatch and head in there, Dad's quiet footsteps behind me.

He flips on the light when we walk in, and I'm reminded of how ugly that light fixture is, which gives me another idea.

"Okay, what if we use this yellow paint, but then we use chalkboard paint on the bottom part of this wall? The kids will love that. We can keep a basket of chalk in here for them. Those toy bins can stay, but we should probably do some rearranging." Looking up to the ceiling, I start to envision a new fixture. "And then I'm thinking we should get a different light...maybe a fun chandelier we can decorate for the seasons. Something lightweight—I don't mean a heavy duty chandelier, but something in that shape with small bulbs. Something we can paint."

Dad doesn't say anything, which makes me wonder if he hates everything I just said, but when I look at him, his eyes are soft and a warm smile is spreading across his face.

"Thoughts?"

"Pumpkin, that sounds wonderful. I love those ideas. And I think your mom will, too."

"What do you think I'll do?"

I straighten up as my mom comes into view. Dad turns and puts an arm around her, pulling her into his side. Her hair is pulled back in a ponytail, she has a smudge of dirt on her forehead, and she's carrying her gardening gloves in one hand.

My mom is gorgeous. And smart. And the strongest woman I know.

"I was telling Maggie about our plans to paint this room and turn it into more of a playroom for the youngsters, and she had some great ideas."

He turns his vibrant smile on me, and I have no choice but to rehash all my ideas to Mom.

When I'm done, she has the same warm smile he does. "You're right, I think that sounds lovely." She looks up to the light fixture. "I'll be honest, I'm not sure I know how to make that chandelier happen, though."

"I'll do it, Mom."

"Really?"

"Yeah, of course," I shrug. "I'll look around and find something cheap we can redo. My designer friends can keep an eye out, too. Kelsie loves refurbishing stuff, so she's always on the lookout."

"Oh, honey, that would be so wonderful. Thank you." My mom looks mildly surprised, which makes me feel like shit. She shouldn't be surprised that I'm offering to help her with something.

Maybe Marv's not entirely wrong.

I smile away my awkwardness, trying hard to hide it. I'm sure they see it anyway.

"Are you hungry?" Mom asks.

I scoff. "Like I'd turn down the opportunity to eat your food."

She laughs as she turns toward the kitchen, getting food out of the fridge to heat up for me. I pour us each a drink, and as I eat, I get my wish.

Mom and Dad talk about Nick, the two of us as kids, and all the trouble he used to help me get in, enabling all my wild ideas. About what a great big brother he was to me. About how much they miss him. About Kate's plans to set up a fund at the animal shelter where he got Beaker.

I don't cry, but something tells me I will when I'm alone later.

CHAPTER 18
THREE HUNDRED SIXTY-FIVE DAYS LATER

ETHAN

I Loved You Then (And I Love You Still) - Woodlock
June

"You ready?"

My head snaps up from the email I was writing to find Mitchell in my doorway. He's on the team with me and Dan, although Dan is starting to step back now that I'm better onboarded.

"Yep." I hit send on the email and slam my laptop shut, ripping the power cable out of the side.

Today, we're having a working meeting with Obsidian. Marv, Maggie, and Kelsie will be coming over to discuss progress, permits, and timelines. If we can keep everything on track, we'll be breaking ground in mid-to-late July.

The construction crew can start on the underground work while we're finalizing designs and applying for permits applicable to interior work. Truth be told, this is the first time I've ever been a project manager for a building being built. It's exciting. And what's even more exciting is getting to see Maggie at work.

I heard her talk about work all the time, obviously. But I never actually saw her in action. It's fun, in some ways. It sucks in others.

Picking up my laptop, I walk around my desk toward Mitchell. He makes room for me, and we walk side-by-side to the conference room. My stride is a little quicker than normal, but I'm in a hurry.

I want to get to the conference room as soon as possible because I want to see Maggie. I want to soak up every single moment of her. We've had to email a few times, and she's been on email threads I've been included on, but we haven't actually *seen* each other since last month when she walked into our office.

And in an odd twist of fate, today marks one year since my disastrous proposal-turned-breakup. Technically, the anniversary is tomorrow, but today is Friday. And fifty-two Fridays ago, I ruined my fucking life.

It's like the universe is drawing us back together.

I'm going to let it.

It's strange to go from seeing someone every single day to never seeing them and then randomly seeing them again...and then not again for a month.

I can't properly express how much I miss her. It's bone-deep. I relive happy moments together when I'm awake, remembering the way she felt next to me. The way her hand fit inside mine. The joyous sound of her laughter.

I dream about her at night and wake up disoriented, reaching across the bed for her. She's not there, of course. Just cold sheets. Just like that first morning after. Just like every other morning for the past three hundred and sixty-five days.

It's probably weird to say this, but I miss her hair in my face. It's perplexing.

When we were together, I'd wake up with her curls stuck to my morning stubble. It would tickle my nose at night, and I'd wake up annoyed, brushing it out of my face and trying to position it above her head so it was out of the way. Undoubtedly, that would rouse her enough to make her move around. Sometimes, she'd snuggle into my chest and bury her face into my neck, and the entire predicament would be immediately forgotten. I'd just be happy to have her there.

Does all this make me a complete sap? Yes, it probably does. And I don't care.

The thing about losing the person you love is that all the things that annoyed you are easily dismissed. I wouldn't give a shit if I woke up breathing Maggie's hair in tomorrow morning because it would mean she was there in my bed. Or I was in hers. I don't care where we are as long as I'm with her.

The things that irritate you are usually trivial. And if the things that irk you *aren't* trivial, they're probably not 'annoying' so much as they're deal-breakers. And those warrant a breakup.

Kind of like when Maggie broke up with me because the thing that was standing between us was more than just a misunderstanding. It wasn't an annoyance. It was a deal-breaker for her.

I didn't appreciate what I had when I had it, and no one is more aware of that than me.

As we near the conference room, my heart beats faster. I know she'll be here soon. Mitchell and I get set up, laptops open, projector on, connections at the ready while we wait for Obsidian.

A ping from my phone interrupts my studious attempts at staring a hole through the wall, waiting for Maggie.

Holly: Today is the day, is it not?

Me: You truly have no idea how on the nose you are with that.

Holly: Confusing, but we'll talk about that later. Is she coming to your office today?

Me: Yes. Should be here any minute.

Holly: Oh! Okay, good luck. Message me later and tell me all about it.

I respond with a thumbs up just as the elevator dings.

The moment she comes into view, I'm on my feet.

She's wearing navy pants with a white and navy striped shirt, complete with nude heels. I remember those heels. She wore them with a green dress to a wedding once. I try to push those memories aside because they're not even a little bit safe for work, and if I can't repress them, I'm going to get a hard-on, and that's inappropriate as fuck.

As she crosses the threshold, her eyes meet mine and hold. Her lips—painted with a conservative pink shade—part just the tiniest bit, and I have to grind my teeth to keep myself from walking around the table and dragging her into my office. Everything fades away as we take each other in. I know Marv and Kelsie all entered the room, that Mitchell was in here with me, but I can't see them, and their voices are muffled to my ears.

For a long moment, it's just the two of us, standing a few feet apart, taking each other in.

For the most part, she wears a mask of professionalism, but I can see the cracks. Her lips are still parted. Her chest is moving faster, like her breathing is quicker than normal. Her eyes are that same vibrant green they always were when she was on the verge of tears.

But that knowledge makes me frown. Is seeing me that painful for her?

I take a small amount of sick joy in that idea.

I want her to miss me the way I miss her. But I don't want her to cry. I don't want her to be sad.

The same instincts I've had for the past six years kick in, and I find myself diverting attention from her so she can pull herself together.

"Thanks for coming, Marv," I say, extending my hand to shake his. "Please have a seat. Kelsie, good to see you again."

I gesture toward the center of the table, where various connections to the projector are draped. "Feel free to plug in, as needed. Can I get anyone anything? Water? Coffee?"

As Marv and Kelsie think on their drink selections, I glance over to see Maggie getting seated next to Marv. She's not looking at me, but she looks like she's more put together than she was a moment ago.

"Maggie?" Marv asks.

"Hmm?" She looks up and then clears her throat. "No, nothing for me, thanks." Then her eyes are glued back to her laptop as she sets everything up.

So I leave to go grab some bottles of water. I think Maggie needs a break from me. Just a moment without my presence to get her head in the game.

This demure version of Maggie isn't someone I'm used to. I'm not trying to make her feel uncomfortable or disoriented. I will always want her to succeed. So if leaving the room helps her, I'll do it, and I'll take a few extra moments and bring extra drinks back with me in case she changes her mind.

When I get back to the conference room, the Obsidian team is ready to go, and Dan has joined us.

I promise I didn't plan this, but the last remaining seat in the conference room that isn't directly in front of the projection screen is right next to Maggie. So I set all the bottles of water on the table, nudging them toward each person before sitting down next to her—a respectable distance away, so she feels like she has breathing room.

We talk through our questions and concerns. I take notes and start drafting a recap email as we go, including action items on each team's end.

Everything is looking really good, and Dan is excited to break ground as soon as possible. After all, people are pretty cramped in this office building, and the sooner we get moving, the sooner we can...move.

"All right, I'll leave next steps to Ethan. I apologize, but I need to get to another meeting." Dan stands, buttoning his suit jacket and shaking people's hands on his way to the door, dropping compliments with each point of contact. "It was wonderful to see all of you. We're loving this direction. You've done excellent work."

When the door closes behind him, I take things over, communicating next steps and promising a follow-up email. Kelsie asks for directions to the restroom, and Marv offers to show her. Mitchell gets a time-sensitive phone call, so he bids his farewell, and then it's just Maggie and I, sitting next to each other.

To say the silence is charged is an understatement. It's tense. My hands are practically shaking from holding back the urge to touch her. But we're both just sitting in our chairs. I can't speak for her, but I'm sneaking glances at her out of the corner of my eye.

I'm not sure how much time I have, so I don't want to let too much of this awkward silence pass before I speak to her.

The *first* time I'll speak to her alone in an entire year.

"Hi."

Great opener, Ethan. Nailed it.

I can feel her eyes on me, so I turn to look at her.

"Hi." Her voice is more of a whisper than anything, but it's there.

"How are you?"

She swallows, and my eyes go unbidden to the ivory column of her throat. It takes a monumental effort to meet her eyes again.

"Um..." She clears her throat. "I'm good. You?"

I'm completely fucking miserable, thanks for asking.

I don't say that, though I want to.

I lick my lips while I try to decide on an answer and watch her eyes drop with the action.

Fascinating.

I eventually decide to go with the cold, hard truth.

"I miss you."

Her eyes snap back up to mine, just long enough for me to see the flare of surprise. Then, I watch her stuff those feelings back down into a dark place and divert her attention back to her hands in her lap.

"Right," She mutters.

"It's the truth," I state. "How was Paris?"

She tenses...doesn't meet my eyes again.

"It was really great."

I nod. "I'm glad to hear that."

She reaches up and closes her laptop, stuffs it into her bag.

"Did you change your phone number?" I ask.

She sighs and throws me a knowing glance.

"Okay, well, we work together right now...so if you could unblock my number for the sake of this project, I think that would be helpful."

Her elbows land on the table, and she rubs her forehead.

"Are you getting a migraine?"

"No," she says firmly. "I'm fine." Suddenly, she stands,

then paces a few feet away and looks out the window, head down, still rubbing her forehead.

"I'm sure someone has some ibuprofen. Do you have your meds with you?"

"I'll be fine," she insists.

"Maggie, I'm just trying to help," I say, standing from my chair.

"I don't need your help." She shifts another step away from me, eyes cold and annoyed.

Her stubbornness is something I've always loved and hated. I loved it because she was always so confident in herself and who she was, and hated it because I was sometimes on the receiving end of it.

Like right now.

I wouldn't trade it, though.

"Okay," I concede. "I'm not trying to start an argument. Can I do anything for you before it gets worse?"

"No," she says again. "Just drop it, Ethan."

With a sigh, I grab an unopened bottle of water from the table and hold it out for her. She makes no move to take it.

"Come on," I urge. "You know the water will help. Please just take it."

After glaring at me, she takes the bottle and cracks it open, taking a few sips. As she screws the cap back on, her tongue peeks out to swipe at a drop of water left on her bottom lip. I stuff my hands in my pockets to keep them to myself.

"Look, I'm...I'm sure you're still mad at me..."

I can hear her scoff, but I ignore it.

"...and I don't blame you. But now we're working on this project together, and I think we're both professional enough to handle this."

I'm stretching the truth, of course. I am not sure I can

handle this at all. I also plan to use every opportunity to show her that I'm still in love with her and that I want her back. But I can't really lead with that.

"Says the one who told me he misses me," she says, calling me out immediately. I'd expect nothing less.

"I do miss you. I'm not going to pretend that's not true."

"Well, you're sure handling it well, aren't you?" she says under her breath.

"I can handle this on a professional level. I'm good at what I do." I step closer to her, so there's only a foot between us, and I lower my voice. "But if you think for one second that I'll just sit here and pass up the opportunity to tell you how I feel—how I still feel—then you're kidding yourself."

She looks up into my eyes, her gaze skeptical.

"I fully plan on working with your team to make sure this new building is constructed according to plan. We'll break ground and get things moving. But make no mistake... I'm still in love with you, Maggie. I still want you. I want you back. I want *us* back."

I take the final step toward her so I can speak directly into her ear. The proximity lets me take in the scent of her conditioner, bringing me back to hundreds of memories of her scent lingering in my nose.

"And I'll do whatever it takes to make that happen."

CHAPTER 19
INSULT, MEET INJURY
MAGGIE

Locksmith - Sadie Jean

"He said what?" Kate shrieks over the bluetooth in my car. I'm driving home from work. After the meeting, we all went back to the office to finish out the day, but mostly I sat in my office and stared at my computer while replaying that conversation with Ethan over and over and *over* in my head.

"You heard me the first time." I'm not repeating it. I still can't believe he said it in the first place.

Make no mistake…I'm still in love with you, Maggie.

I still want you.

I want you back.

I want us back

And I'll do whatever it takes to make that happen.

"Some lady in the store gave me the stink eye for yelling." Kate's voice has lowered to a harsh whisper. "Holy shit, Maggie."

"I know." I stop at the red light and fidget in my seat, resting my elbow on the windowsill and my head in my hand. "The actual audacity. And in the fucking conference room, right after the meeting ended."

The memory of his warm breath against my ear sends shivers down my spine, and I latch onto the anger that surges like a lifeline.

"It's hard enough to see him in these fucking meetings... to see his name pop up in my inbox...but to have him saying shit like this to me...god, I don't know, Kate."

The light turns green, and I obediently follow traffic forward. I can't get home fast enough. There's bourbon there, and God knows I need some after this fucking day.

She makes a sympathetic sound. "I'm sure it's a lot to deal with."

"It *is*. Every day I think about having Marv pull me from this project, but I told him I could handle it."

I hear her heave a sigh. "Can I ask you though...what exactly is it that makes working with him so hard for you?"

I don't know how to answer that, so I sit there in silence, biting my lip and gripping the steering wheel harder.

If I'm being brutally honest with myself, I can admit that it's difficult to work with him because I'm still in love with him. Because I want what he said he wants...for us to be back together. I miss him. Of course, I miss him. I've missed him this entire year. But it's so fucking painful.

The facts remain the same. He thought I'd change my mind about marriage, and I am never going to. And he didn't even bring that thought up at any point. It's not like he asked me if I thought I would change my mind. He never told me he wanted to get married. I would have ended the relationship if he told me he needed to get married.

I mean...I literally did that. But it would have been a lot less painful if we hadn't waited five years to get to that conversation. And following a marriage proposal, at that.

Insult, meet injury.

Realistically, getting back together with Ethan will result in the same ending. We'll be in the same place we were a year ago. But it will be too late for me to find someone else and have kids by that point. Whether I like it or not, I have to be thinking about that kind of shit.

"Maggie?"

Oh, Jesus, I still haven't said a word.

"Sorry...I was just...thinking."

Thinking for so long, apparently, that I'm pulling up to my apartment building. I turn into the lot and park in my designated spot. I make sure to lock the doors when they automatically unlock so I can sit and talk to Kate more safely.

"Why is working with him so difficult for you?" she asks again, her voice gentle and kind.

I let my head fall against the headrest behind me and close my eyes. "Because he *hurt* me, Kate."

"Yeah...that's understandable."

I'm hoping she'll leave it at that, so I don't say anything in response, but I'm not that lucky.

"Do you think that maybe you're having such a hard time because you still have feelings for him?"

My eyes sting when she says the words. They're true. Obviously.

"Otherwise, you wouldn't care that he hurt you...you'd just let it go."

I let out a huge sigh and rub my temples. This migraine is coming no matter what I do.

"You don't have to tell me, Mags. I'm just thinking that... maybe you should think about it. And maybe try to figure out what that means. Maybe try to talk to him."

We're both quiet for a few moments. I can hear the

sounds of the grocery store in the background behind her—shopping carts and beeps at cash registers. Random people talking to each other.

"I'll think about it," I say eventually.

"Okay," she replies immediately. Like she was listening intently the whole time. Not distracted by her shopping list or anything else around her. "You know where to find me. I'm always here. Anytime."

"I know you are. Thanks, Kate."

"My pleasure."

"All right...I'm home. I'm gonna go inside and put an ice pack on my head."

We say our goodbyes, and I take one final look at my surroundings before getting out of the car and trudging into the building.

I need to be in my apartment. My very own space where I can be alone to do whatever I please. It's an Ethan-free space.

I stop at the mailboxes before heading to the elevator. I'm still getting mail for the previous tenants, so I've been keeping the things that look important in a pile to take to the management office once a week. Have people not heard of mail forwarding?

"Excuse me, miss..."

I freeze at the familiar voice coming from my left, my key still in the lock of my mailbox.

This cannot be happening.

"Miss?" That smooth voice with just a hint of teasing speaks again, and I can feel the happy memories from the first two times we had this interaction, in addition to the despair and the anger warring in my blood. My conversation with Kate just now isn't exactly helping matters. It brought my feelings so close to the surface.

"You've got to be fucking kidding me," I whisper to my mailbox.

"Are you all right?" His voice is softer. There's no hint of teasing in it this time. He's asking for real...he's not just following the script from the night we met.

Something in me snaps. I've held it together—mostly—for so long, but this is too much. He's too close. I can smell his cologne, and it's bringing up memories of my hands in his hair, my face in his neck, his hands all over me, and I just *crack*.

I tear the key out of the mailbox and turn to face him.

"What, are you stalking me now? Is that what you mean by 'whatever it takes'"?

His face is calm and open. He's not angry or annoyed that I'm snapping at him.

Instead of responding verbally, he turns to the wall of mailboxes and slides a key into one of them, opening it up and grabbing a few items before locking it back up.

"You've got to be fucking *kidding* me," I repeat, pinching the bridge of my nose. "How in the *actual fuck* do we live in the same building?" Miles pops into my head, sending fresh rage spiraling. "Did you plan this?"

I'm going to kill Miles. First thing tomorrow morning. Right there in the office.

A small measure of annoyance flickers in his eyes.

"When did you get back from Paris?"

"What? What does that have to do with anything?"

"Because I moved in here months ago. After our lease was up at the old place. So, if I'm doing my math properly, that tells me you didn't get back from Paris until at least March. Which would mean I moved in before you did. So if anyone planned this..." He ends on a smirk, letting his voice trail off.

"Fucking Christ," I mutter, whirling around toward the elevator, punching the up button far too hard.

I can sense him behind me, waiting for the elevator in silence.

"Can't you just take the stairs?" I mutter.

"I suppose I could. I'm pretty tired, though. My day was stressful."

I scoff, rolling my eyes and then regretting it as a bolt of pain stabs through my eye socket. I press my fingers to my eyebrow to try and relieve some of the pain.

When the elevator arrives, I storm in and press the number five as quickly as possible. I can't help but notice he doesn't press anything at all—except every single one of *my* buttons, of course—and I curse myself for not looking at the number on his mailbox. I have no idea where he lives in this building, but if it's on my floor, I'm going to have to move. Lease, be damned.

"Do you have ice packs ready in the freezer?"

"Stop it," I snap.

"If you haven't taken your meds yet, you're going to be in for a bad night."

"I mean it, Ethan. Stop."

He's not wrong, and I'm furious about it. My head is really starting to pound. And my dumb ass didn't have any meds in my purse today.

Fucking hell.

I'm out the doors the moment they open enough to let me through, and of *course* he gets off and follows me down the hall.

"Go home, Ethan."

"I think we've already covered this, but I live in this building."

"Not in my apartment, you don't."

"Unfortunately, that's true," he says. "For now."

I turn my head to glare at him over my shoulder and feel the pain shoot across my skull.

"Fuck," I whisper, but I'm sure he hears it.

I fumble with my keys at the door, and when I cross the threshold, I try to slam it in his face, but he catches it. When I turn around, he's calmly closing the door and locking it behind him. He stuffs his mail in his messenger bag before taking it off and setting it on the floor by the door.

I throw my purse down on my dining room table and my coat over a chair.

"Ethan, please leave." I grip the chair for balance as I say the words. I can feel a panic attack starting...my heart hammering against my ribs, my lungs squeezing.

His head tilts as he studies me. "I understand you want me to leave, and I will. But first I want to get you settled. Your migraine is getting worse, and I'm concerned."

"You don't *get* to be concerned about me, Ethan!" I yell at him. It hurts my head, but I do it anyway because I *need* him to leave before this panic attack really takes over.

"I can see why you feel that way, but I'm worried about you, Mags. I just want to make sure you're all right."

"Of course, I'm not all right!" Another dam breaks inside me, my tears coming out in a torrent. "I break up with my boyfriend of five years because he doesn't know me at all, and then I hide in Paris for seven months, and when I come back, my very first assignment is for his new employer." A hysterical laugh bubbles out of me, unbidden. "Because why *wouldn't* that be how things go for me? And *then*, as if it wasn't already stressful enough, he lives in my fucking building!"

My safe space. My sanctuary. Sullied.

"Nothing about me is all right! How is this fucking *happening?*"

"Mags—"

"And stop calling me Mags! You don't get to call me Mags anymore, not ever again!" I wish I could say my voice is steady and sure, but it's not. It breaks on the final words as my throat constricts.

"Okay...okay," he says, his voice quieter, his hands up like he's trying to tame a wild animal. "I hear you."

I want to yell at him again. To tell him to get away from me. But my head hurts, and my heart is beating *so fast,* and I can't *breathe.* I just want everything to *stop.*

"Maggie, please...go lay down. I'll get your meds and an ice pack. Just go lay down."

He wraps an arm around my shoulders and turns me toward my bedroom. Together, we move down the hall. When we reach the bedroom, neither of us reaches for the light switch. He knows better. He brings me to my bed and encourages me to lay down. Then, he takes my heels off and sets them gently on the floor next to my nightstand.

I don't have the energy to fight him, so I just lay there and listen to him moving around in my apartment as my anxiety and panic give way to tears. They're mercifully quiet, although my breaths are audible as I try to get my lungs under control.

I hear water running in the kitchen. I hear the freezer open and close, followed by my medicine cabinet. When he returns, he helps me sit up to take the meds, and then lays me back down in bed, placing the ice pack over my head. Then, I hear the blinds twisting closed and curtains being pulled shut. Through it all, I keep my eyes shut...partly because it hurts to see him walk around my space. To have him here, taking care of me. And partly because my head is pounding.

He wasn't wrong...it's going to be a long night.

Finally, I feel the other side of the bed sink under his weight and hear his shoes hit the floor. He doesn't say a word as he lies down next to me, gently reaching his hand around my head to rub the base of my skull and neck, just like he used to.

Knowing the room is darker than it was when we came in and that I'm lying down, I risk opening my eyes. He's laying in front of me, eyes focused on my face. His brows are pulled together slightly, his mouth in a tight line.

The silent tears are still coming, but I don't have the energy to try to stop them, anyway. At least my breathing is getting better.

"Why are you doing this?" I whisper.

"You know why I'm here," he says, his voice not a whisper, but very low, so he doesn't make my migraine worse. "I already told you. I'm still in love with you, and I want to make sure you're okay."

"I'm so mad at you, Ethan."

"I know..." He adjusts his hand to rub my trapezius. "And I...I know what you said a year ago. I know why you ended things between us. But can you tell me why you're still mad at me?"

I squeeze my eyes shut. I don't want to tell him. I don't want to admit that I'm still in love with him, too, or that I still want him just as much as I did last year.

Because yes...I remember what today is. It's why I'm mad at myself for forgetting my migraine meds. I knew it would be a stressful day—the one-year mark of our breakup and also knowing I'd see him—and it just slipped my mind.

"Maggie."

"Ethan, please, I can't..." I feel a stab of pain in my head and wince.

"Okay, okay. It's all right. Let's stop talking now." His arm slides under my neck while the other wraps around my waist. He pulls me closer and uses his chin to keep my ice pack in place. This means my head is tucked into his chest and the rain scent of his cologne is surrounding me, just like it used to.

My brain shuffles through memories like a slideshow, that familiar, calming scent pulling them to the front of my brain and forcing me to relive them.

Ethan at the club that first night with a giant smile on his face.

Ethan running through New York City with me over a long weekend, laughing as we dodged construction barrels.

Ethan at the Rafferty Christmas, playing with my nieces and nephews like he'd never outgrown childhood himself.

Ethan by my side in the aftermath of my brother's death, waiting on me hand and foot.

Ethan next to me on the couch while we watch countless movies, sharing a bottle of wine on the weekends.

Ethan popping open a bottle of champagne in our shared apartment the first night we lived there.

Ethan just being *Ethan.*

He was always there for me, just like he is now...taking care of me exactly the way I need to be because he knows exactly how to do it. He's done it countless times before. He knows what I need, and he's doing it, regardless of the fact that I was rude and downright *mean* to him in the office today.

And then again at our mailboxes.

Guilt and shame settle over me as tears start pouring from my eyes again.

He must hear me sniff because he leans his head back to look down at me.

"Maggie, we need to get you to stop crying. It will only make the migraine worse. What can I do?"

I wish I could say that didn't make me cry more, but it does. He's just so kind.

"Fuck, Maggie..." He rests his forehead against mine so tenderly. "Please stop crying. Please."

"Ethan, I..." I try to tell him I miss him, but I choke on the words. I want to. So badly. But the words just won't come out.

"One time, when I was a kid, I was at my friend's farm outside the city," he says. "I borrowed his brother's bike, and we were riding all over the place...around the buildings and between the fields."

I frown, confused at what's happening right now.

Why is he talking to me about this random farm?

And then I realize he's doing it to distract me. To make me stop crying.

And it's fucking working.

"But his brother was younger and didn't have a ten-speed yet, so it was the kind that you brake by reversing the pedals. Anyway, the chain came off, and I couldn't stop."

As he talks, his hand starts moving up and down my spine, further soothing me.

"I was headed straight for the broad side of the barn, but there was nothing I could do. It was either hit the barn or try to fall off the bike and hope I didn't mess myself up too badly. I ended up hitting a bump and basically ramming my balls into the bike seat."

The abrupt turn to the story makes me want to laugh, but I can't. It would hurt too badly.

"Oh my god..." I whisper.

"Yeah." He huffs a quiet laugh. "I didn't have to worry about the barn anymore because I was in so much pain, it didn't really matter what happened to me on the bike...no matter where we ended up."

"What happened?"

"I absolutely ran into that barn, which actually made it worse." He shakes his head as much as he can in the confined space. "The bike stopped, and I fell over immediately, the bike coming with me. I just laid on the ground, trying to catch my breath while Max laughed like a hyena. Kind of like you're trying not to do right now because it would hurt."

"I'm sorry," I whisper-laugh.

"It's fine. I survived."

Neither of us speaks for a moment while we both try to make ourselves stop laughing.

When it's finally quiet and sleep is starting to tug at me, I whisper one more thing.

"Thank you."

He doesn't say anything out loud, but pulls me back into his chest, his chin slotting back into place above my head.

CHAPTER 20
STIFF UPPER LIP

MAGGIE

marjorie - Taylor Swift
July

"Hello, hello." I kick the door open with my foot and shuffle my way into the house I grew up in.

"Hello, darling! I'll be right there," my mom calls from the back of the house. I can hear water running. She's probably cleaning up the kitchen.

When I clear the door, I kick it shut and head into the soon-to-be playroom for the kids. It's starting to come together. We painted the walls yellow last weekend. We're doing the chalkboard wall today.

"Hey there, pumpkin."

I turn around to find my dad walking toward me, arms wide open for a hug. I'm happy to oblige.

"You ready to paint?" I ask him. I already know the answer, and he knows I know. He was a general contractor before he retired. He's always ready to paint. He's still very handy around the house and has even gone over to Kate's house to help her with things from time to time.

"Like you even have to ask," he says, a big smile on his face.

"I'm ready, too," my mom volunteers.

She appears at my side wearing an old T-shirt from the school district she retired from, a pair of yoga pants that are already stained from crafts and construction over the years, and a great big smile of her own.

I've been coming over more often to work on this room. Truth be told, it's been really fun. I'm enjoying myself. Since Nick died, I haven't been spending as much time here...I think because he was always a great buffer between me and our more conservative counterparts. It's harder to be here by myself. And frankly, it's hard to be here, immersed in the memories of growing up with him, seeing family photos on the wall, baby photos of each of us, and tiny bronzed shoes.

I grew up in a large family—Catholics, you know. My dad's family is one thousand percent Irish. Matthew Rafferty, Sr. is second generation, and when he drinks, he slips a little bit into his accent. If you're really lucky, he'll break out his Gaelic. He's tall and broad with dark hair the same color as mine. Nick and I both got his green eyes, though most of our siblings ended up with Mom's brown ones.

Dad is warm and kind at all times. He might have had the more rugged job, but he was the softer of my two parents. He was the one who would listen to me cry about boys or friends or whatever drama was unfolding in my life. He was the one I'd tell first when I got bad grades or got in trouble at school. He'd tell me to fess up to my mom, but I still enjoyed having the opportunity to tell him first. I knew he'd be tough, but fair and kind in his punishments. He trusted in his kids to do the right thing and to know when they got it wrong.

My mother's family came from England a couple of generations ago, with her ancestors being born throughout a mixture of European nations. Grandma Abbott used to say that her family was full of mutts—the kind you couldn't help but take in and love, but they brought their English demeanors over to the States. From there, my mom either learned these traits, or inherited them, or both.

My mom has always been relatively regal. She's always got her shit together. She's calm in a crisis. Stoic. Not big on talking about her feelings—at least not with me. Helen Rafferty, nee Abbott, is more "stiff upper lip" and less "let's talk it out."

And for my part, we've made a lot of life decisions that were very opposite in nature.

She married my dad not long after college and started having babies pretty quickly. Marie, Matthew, Molly, Nick, Martha and Mark (twins), and then me. She and my dad both claim I wasn't an *oopsie baby,* but I don't know that I believe them. It doesn't really matter, either way. She had a choice. I'm here now.

She worked as a teacher her whole career, only retiring a few years ago. She taught history to high school kids right up until the end, turning down multiple suggestions that she move into school administration instead. Helen enjoyed teaching, I know that. But being an administrator would have made her summer shorter, and we needed her home because that's when Dad was really busy with work. It was convenient to have them on opposite schedules—he got us off the bus in the winter, and she was around all summer to take us to the pool or to museums or force us to read so our brains didn't turn to mush.

I, on the other hand, am already approaching my midthirties.

I have no prospects for a long-term relationship and no desire—or intention—to ever marry. If this were regency times, I'd be a spinster, and I'd be happy about it.

I *do* want children, though. It might be the only thing we have in common.

And maybe that's why I've had a hard time relating to her throughout the course of my life.

I feel this intrinsic pressure from her to settle down. I get it, and I also don't. She already has plenty of grandkids. She doesn't need any from me.

"I brought the chalkboard paint, so we can get that done tonight, and I also hauled the chandelier in. I don't know that we can get it set today, but at least it's here."

"The wiring is done," Dad answers. "It shouldn't need anything different than what's already there. I looked into it."

"Oh, how exciting..." Mom smiles even bigger, clapping her hands and looking over toward the chandelier I've been working on for the past two weeks. Kate let me spray paint at her place, since I'm in an apartment building.

I take a moment to look at her...still gorgeous even with her graying hair and sloppy clothes. Somehow, she's still impeccable. Kate sometimes jokes that she thinks my mom was actually meant to be a British royal, but was switched at birth. I don't *not* believe Kate's theory. She might have a point.

"Yeah, so let's get the first coat of chalkboard paint done before we mess with the light," I suggest.

"You're the boss," Dad says, causing a loud huff of laughter to fly out of my face.

"At no point have I ever been the boss in this house," I respond. "That honor belongs to Mom."

"Ouch," Dad says.

"It's true, honey," Mom answers, not even looking at him. She's picking up the chalkboard paint and reading the label.

"Wow," he whispers. "Good to know."

I give him a sympathetic look to soften the blow, but Mom kisses him on the cheek, and his face transforms into one of complete and total adoration. Something tells me he doesn't give a flying fuck if Helen has been in charge their entire marriage, just as long as he gets to be a part of it.

That hollow spot in my chest aches at the sight of them —my parents, still happily married after all this time. They're going on fifty years.

There was a time when I thought I had what they have. In my own way, at least.

The three of us work for the next few hours, painting and installing the new chandelier. It looks fucking amazing, if I do say so myself. This room is shaping up to be something really beautiful.

When we're done, Mom and Dad dish up a stew from the crockpot, and we eat outside near the fire pit. It's cozy and fun. I'm legitimately enjoying myself. I'm grateful to have the opportunity to hang out with my parents like this.

At some point, Dad goes inside to clean up the kitchen, and Mom and I are left alone at the fire pit. As much as I'm nervous to be alone with my mom and her inscrutable gaze, a voice in the back of my mind—probably Nick's—is telling me to stick it out.

Mom asks me about Paris. I tell her everything except the spicy bits.

She asks about my current projects. I tell her everything except the *Ethan* bits.

But she's a mom. She's *my* mom. And she can tell I'm hiding something. So she prods. And pokes. And eventually,

I can't keep it inside any longer. I tell her I'm working with Ethan.

She watches me in silence for a long moment before saying, "It seems like this experience has potential to be difficult for you."

I keep my eyes on the fire when I respond with as much nonchalance as I can muster. "It is what it is. This town isn't that big in the grand scheme of things."

She pauses, undoubtedly scrutinizing my behavior for missed clues or cracks in my cool façade. Her gaze practically burns a hole in my temple. My mother could have been a behavioral analyst for the freaking CIA, I swear. In many ways, her teaching career was a waste of talent. Or perhaps a much different use of it.

Finally, she sighs.

"Maggie, I haven't..." She pauses, looking down at her hands while she thinks. "I don't want to pry, or ask you to tell me what's happening...but I want you to know that if you want to talk to me about Ethan or relationships or the absence of them, I'm happy to do that with you."

I stop fidgeting with the loose strand of my sweater in exchange for the actual perpetrator.

She's looking at me with kind, gentle eyes and a concerned look on her face. I want to make some sort of excuse and bolt. Say I need to get home, except I'm not going home *to* anything...so she'll know that's an excuse to get out of here. That little voice in the back of my mind reminds me that this is my mother—my concerned mother—facing the upcoming anniversary of her son's sudden death.

I remember what Kate said about Helen being kind when she told her something that likely upset her and decide to throw a little caution to the wind. What's the worst that could happen? She'll judge me? Criticize my decision? I can always leave.

"Mom, it's not..." I start, but quickly have to stop and clear my throat. "I'm not like the rest of you."

"I know, sweetheart," she says gently. "I raised you, remember? You've always been your own person. There's nothing wrong with that."

I watch her while she says it, and I can feel my throat closing immediately. My eyes start to sting, and I can feel the tears flowing before I even realize it's too late to stop them.

"Sometimes I feel like maybe there is..." I whimper. It's pathetic, truly.

Helen is out of her chair and by my side in one second flat, wrapping her arm around my shoulders and running a soothing hand up and down my arm. "Why do you say that?"

"Because the rest of you wanted to get married and have big families, but I don't," I sob. Vaguely, I can sense her pulling a chair closer to me and sitting, never letting go of me. "I've never been like you. I don't want to get married. I would like to have kids one day. I really would. I love kids. But I don't think I should have to get married to make that happen. And I know that flies in the face of the religious beliefs I was raised on, but, Mom, I think you know those have never really resonated with me."

There's not a tissue in sight, but my face is leaking far too many fluids to ignore it. I start using my sleeve. This shirt is already paint-stained anyway.

"I don't talk to you about this stuff because I feel like I'll just be disappointing you all over again. Nick and I were close in part because I felt like he didn't care that I was different, but everyone else looks at me funny. Like I'm not really one of you because I haven't achieved the things the rest of you have."

I sniff loudly and choke on my own snot.

I'm horribly embarrassed by myself at the moment.

"I broke up with Ethan because he wanted to get married, and I don't. And I was *fine*. I was heartbroken, but fine. I went to Paris and lived a *dream*. I got to help create a building that will stand in Paris for decades—hopefully centuries. I met wonderful people who I still keep in touch with. And I was able to avoid too many thoughts about Ethan." I pause because that's not totally true. "Well...I was able to keep *busy* and therefore, distract myself from Ethan. But when it was over, I came home to find that I'll be working with Ethan for at least the next *year*. And if that's not difficult enough, I found out not too long ago that we live in the same building."

"Whoa..."

"I know!" I shriek.

"What are the chances?"

"I don't know, but if you figure it out, please let me know."

Mom takes a deep breath and lets it out. "This is a lot."

"I know it is," I whine. I'm fucking *whining*. "I see him for meetings all the time, and he pops up in my inbox. And one day, all those feelings just came crashing back in. He was being so nice to me, and I was...rude. Borderline mean. And right after that is when I ran into him at the mailboxes. He followed me to my apartment, and we argued..."

My head drops in shame. That's not really true either.

"Well...I kind of yelled, and he was calm and courteous. I was getting a migraine, and he took care of me, Mom. He got my meds and water and an ice pack. Helped me lay down in bed and then stayed with me. I was being so mean to him, and he took care of me anyway." I look up at her, desperate for answers. Her head tilts to the side, and she gives me a sad smile.

"Seems like he still cares about you," she says quietly.

I still want you.

I want you back.

I want us back.

And I'll do whatever it takes to make that happen.

I lean back in my chair and pull my knees into my chest. I can't do much but let my sobs finish out at this point.

"Sweetheart..." my mother coos, running her fingers through my hair and gently massaging my scalp. She knows what crying does to me. She knows I've got another migraine headed my way.

"I told Marv I can handle this, but I can't, Mom. I can't handle it at all. The only way I feel better is if I'm far, far away from him."

"Well, you can look for a different apartment."

I nod. I can. I've looked online at some buildings, but there weren't any openings in the ones I liked. And I really do like this place I moved into. It's cute and cozy.

"Have the two of you tried to talk this out?"

I roll my head to the side to look at her. "What's the point?" I ask with a shrug. "He wants to get married, and I don't. And god, the look on his face, Mom. It haunts me. The way he looked like I was just ripping his heart out...when he was doing the same thing to me."

"Maggie, I know it would be difficult to talk about this with him, but I think it could do you both a lot of good. To help you move on."

I huff a bitter laugh. "He doesn't want to move on. He said he wants to get back together."

"And how do you feel about that?"

"I don't see the point. It'll just end the same way. He hasn't changed, and neither have I."

"How do you know he hasn't changed if you aren't willing to talk to him about it?"

"Mom, you're being far too rational," I grouse. It's unfair and stupid, but I'm not ready for someone to tell me how to fix it. I just need her to listen.

"Oh, um...sorry." She clears her throat. "He should move out of that building. Why should you have to leave?"

Her face has taken on a false anger on my behalf, and she's clearly trying very hard to find other things to say to support me.

"How dare he tell you he wants to get back together when he broke your heart? You deserve better than that."

I can't help the smile that tugs on my mouth.

"I hope his pillow is hot, no matter how many times he flips it over. And that he hits every single traffic light on his way to *and from* work tomorrow. And that his coffee is always cold. And not in a good way, like he intentionally wanted iced coffee. I mean like he didn't drink it fast enough, and then it's cold, and it never tastes as good that way."

Her over-explanation of the coffee being cold is what finally does me in. I laugh, and it seems to startle my mom. Her brown eyes go wide as her head snaps in my direction.

I can't stop the giggles that keep coming. I'm sure I look like a loon, but her willingness to change her approach— especially the direction she chose—took me totally off guard. She sits quietly while I wipe my eyes and calm down. Eventually hugging my knees to my chest and laying my head down on them, facing her.

"I'm so sorry this is happening, Maggie. It's got to be so hard."

It is. It really fucking is.

"And sweetie, I'm...I'm sorry we've made you feel like you can't talk to us about this stuff. I swear, we didn't mean for that to happen, but it *did* happen, and we owe you an apology for it." She reaches out and moves a lock of hair away from my forehead. "We're the parents. We should have tried harder. *I*," she says, laying her hand over her heart, "*I* should have tried harder."

I don't really know what to say to that, so I just stare at her.

"You and Nick always got along so well. He sort of became our litmus test when it came to you...if he said you were fine, we'd take his word for it. If he said he was concerned, we tried to step in. But so often that path involved an argument, and it became easier to...not engage. I'm so sorry, Maggie. That's on us, not you." Tears fill her eyes and I freeze.

I haven't seen my mother cry very often. Only a few times, really. And most of them have been since Nick died.

"Mom..."

"No, baby. It's our fault." Tears break free from her eyes and fall down her cheeks. "We never meant to make you feel like you couldn't come talk to us, and we certainly never meant to make you feel like an outsider in this family...that's just inexcusable. We'll do better, Maggie, I promise."

We sit in silence while she tries to compose herself, and I just sit there staring at her. I don't even know what to say to her. I just word vomited the past year's trauma on my mother—who I'd assumed wouldn't understand—and instead of arguing, she's apologizing and crying.

"Do you think you can forgive me?" she asks, her voice unsteady.

"Are you kidding me?" I unwind my right arm from my

legs and take her hand. "Mom, of course. I never thought you didn't love me, I just...thought you maybe didn't like me."

"Oh, Lord," she whimpers, her head falling in her free hand. "I don't think that's much better. It might even be worse."

I squeeze her hand. "Mom, please. You didn't do it on purpose. We're talking it through. Kind of like you're telling me to do with Ethan, which I'm just now realizing as I'm talking that it's working with me and you so maybe I should do it with him, too."

I let go of her hand and cover my face, letting my head fall back against the chair.

"Damnit, was that your plan? Did you mean for that to happen?" I peek out from under my fingers to look at her. She's wiping her eyes and dabbing at her cheeks with her sleeve.

"No, it wasn't," she assures me. "But that's sort of a perfect result."

I groan. I don't want to talk to Ethan. I really don't.

"Maggie, can I ask..." Mom trails off.

I make eye contact with her and nod.

"Do you still love him?"

"Unfortunately."

"Oh, don't say it like that," she chides.

"Why not?"

"Why *would* you?"

"I already told you. It will just end up the same way."

"And I told *you* that you don't know that."

Damnit.

Why does she have to be right?

"I'm annoyed you have a point."

She shrugs. "I felt the same way about my mom."

I frown. "I thought you and Grandma Abbott always got along."

She rolls her eyes. "Absolutely not. I did all kinds of things she didn't approve of. Got in trouble all the time when I was a kid. As an adult, it wasn't relevant. We didn't really talk it out like this. We just...looked past it."

"Hmm."

Fascinating.

Maybe Helen and I have more in common than I thought.

"Anyway...you can do what you think is best. It's your life, baby, and I'll respect your decision. But I hope you consider talking to him."

I hate to admit she's right, but I think she might be. Kate was right about Helen, too.

What else have I been wrong about?

"I'll think about it," I whisper.

CHAPTER 21
INCONVENIENT
TIMING, BRO

MAGGIE

*The Last Time (feat. Gary Lightbody of Snow Patrol) (Taylor's
Version) by Taylor Swift, Gary Lightbody*

"Do you have the adjustments on that conference room?" Kelsie asks from across our shared office space. "I can't find the email."

"Sure do." I bring up the email in question and reply to it so it shows up again. "Should be at the top of your inbox."

"Thank you. I need to do a serious inbox cleanup."

Today is Friday. It's been almost a week since my heart-to-heart with Mom and two days since we broke ground on the building for Ethan's company.

I saw him there, but we stayed a professional distance apart. There wasn't a reason for us to be front and center. Marv and Dan were there as the primary representatives for our companies. We were there for support.

It was sunny out, so I took advantage of the dark sunglasses covering my eyes to study Ethan. He looked at me frequently, especially when he thought I wasn't looking.

The ceremony was the first time I'd seen him in person

since the morning after I yelled at him in my apartment and then he took care of me when my migraine took over. I'd woken up that morning engulfed by him, our limbs draped around and across each other, my face in his neck, his hand on my bare back under my shirt, his leg in between mine.

My migraine was gone.

I'd laid there for a while, not wanting to move. I wanted to just lay there with him, pretending everything was okay. That we hadn't broken up. That I still had him. That we weren't doomed.

I don't know how long it had been, but eventually, I realized he was awake. His lips brushed against my forehead, landing in my hair and leaving an impossibly gentle kiss. Like he couldn't resist doing it, but he didn't want to wake me.

Apparently, we'd both been lying there, trying not to destroy the moment...and that made me smile.

Which accidentally broke the spell because he felt my cheeks move.

He'd pulled his head back to look at me, meeting my eyes with a healthy dose of concern and a touch of apprehension. Not that I could blame him. I'd yelled at him the night before.

"Hey...how's your head?"

"Better."

He stayed still for a long moment, just looking at me. I don't think either of us really knew what to say. It was sort of awkward, but also not. It also felt very comfortable. I didn't want him to move, and frankly, that scared me.

Finally, he moved the hand on my back—still inside my shirt—running it up and down my spine, sending shivers throughout all my limbs.

I placed my hand over his heart and felt it tap against my palm.

He pushed his fingers into my hair and massaged my scalp.

I snuggled in closer to him, silently hoping for more of his kisses to my head.

He didn't leave me disappointed.

All that touching eventually led to an erection pressing against my leg, but instead of moving things forward, he shifted his lower half away from me and squeezed my hip to keep it still.

It took an act of God and Congress to keep me stationary. My fists curled into his shirt to keep him from slipping completely away. I wanted to maul him.

Respectfully, of course.

"Maggie..." he growled. "Don't fucking tempt me here."

My only response had been a whimper, which made him growl again before cursing and taking several deep breaths.

Sex between us had always been hot. There was plenty of passion between the two of us and that moment was a terrible time to remember it.

"It should go without saying that I want you very, *very* much," he ground out. "But we have things to talk about, and I'm not fucking you until that happens."

I didn't respond. I couldn't. My mouth wouldn't do anything but open and close like a fish. But the question in my eyes—*why*—must have been plain enough.

"Because this is not temporary for me. I don't want to fuck you and walk away. I want to fuck you and keep you. Forever, Maggie. So it's not happening until you're ready for us again."

I had no response to that. I was dumbfounded and

annoyed and *horny*. But I was also scared. And there was no hiding it.

"See?" he said gently. "You're not ready. And that's okay, Maggie. I am. And I'll be here when you're ready to talk."

He released my hip and held my head in his hands while he softly kissed my forehead. My eyes had drifted shut while his lips were pressed to my skin, but they flew open when he abruptly pulled back and climbed out of my bed.

"You know how to find me."

So yeah...that's what I was thinking about at the ceremony, which wasn't great timing. And apparently what I'm thinking about now. Which is also not great timing.

I shake my head, trying to clear Ethan from my thoughts. Fortunately, my phone pings with a text and I look down to find Julien's name on my screen.

Julien: How are you, chérie?

I smile, a warm feeling spreading through my chest. I miss Julien. I miss his...dirty talents, but I miss talking to him more than anything. He was a great listener and always had wise comments about my dumpster fire of a love life.

Me: I'm hangin' in there. You?

Julien: That doesn't sound like you're doing well.

Me: I'm doing as well as I can. And you didn't answer my question.

Julien: You're right, I didn't answer. I'm doing very well, actually, but we'll talk about that at a different time. Tell me how you're faring with the ex-boyfriend. How is work going with him?

I'd texted Julien the night I realized I was working with Ethan. He didn't respond until the next day, given the time difference, but we FaceTimed that morning. I filled him in on everything, and he told me to keep him posted. Since then, we've been checking in with each other at least once a week.

Me: It's terrible. And not terrible. Good and bad. Face-Time would be easier for a catch up.

Julien: Tomorrow?

Me: Yes. I can do that.

We decided on a time and then he announced he had a date to get ready for.

Me: Kinda buried the lead there.

Julien: I don't know what that means.

Me: It means you skipped the important parts.

Julien: I did no such thing. I asked you about the ex-boyfriend.

I roll my eyes and groan in my office, forgetting that Kelsie is sitting across from me.

"Everything okay?"

"Julien."

"Oh...is that still..."

"No, no," I wave her off. "We're friends. We text. Occasionally FaceTime."

I feel Kelsie's eyes on me for another minute, but she doesn't say anything else about him. Instead, she goes for my throat.

"And Ethan...how are things going for you?"

I intentionally sink further into my chair, letting my butt go all the way to the edge of the seat.

"That good, huh?" Kelsie laughs.

Dragging my body back into an upright position, I rest my chin in my hands, looking directly at Kelsie.

"It's really hard," I finally say.

She narrows her eyes. "*What's* really hard?"

I throw a pad of Post-it notes at her. "The *situation* is really hard."

"All right, all right! No need to get violent," she says through her laughter.

I look back down in an attempt to avoid her scrutiny, but I'm unsuccessful.

"You still have feelings for him, don't you?"

"Of course I do," I whisper.

"And it's obvious he still has feelings for you…"

I sigh. "That's what he claims."

"So what's the problem?"

"The problem is that we want different things from a long-term relationship. That hasn't changed."

Even as I say it, I hear my mom's voice in the back of my mind. I don't *actually* know that's true. I know my feelings are the same, but I don't know about Ethan's.

Kelsie throws her hands in the air. "Straight people make everything so freaking difficult."

I don't get to ask her what she means by that because we get interrupted by a knock on the door.

From Ethan.

"Sorry, I don't mean to interrupt," he says, looking directly at me.

I realize I have no idea how long he's been standing there.

How much did he hear?

"That's all right," Kelsie says, standing up. "I was just about to head out, actually. Come on in."

Ethan steps into our office as Kelsie gathers her laptop, sketchpad, and pencil and heads toward our office door, tossing the thrown Post-it pad back on my desk on her way. "I need to talk to Marv. It was good to see you, Ethan."

"Good to see you, too."

Kelsie throws me a mischievous smile and pulls the door closed behind her.

As Ethan takes slow steps toward my desk, I can feel the tension rising in my neck, so I stand.

"Ethan."

"Maggie."

"What can I do for you today?" I ask, clasping my hands in front of me in what I hope is a *totally-chill-and-not-at-all-tense* kind of way.

He doesn't answer right away. He just looks at me for a long moment before he lifts his hand, which is when I finally see he's carrying a bag.

"I came to drop off these tile samples for you." He steps closer to my desk and sets them on a clear space to my right. "The team all weighed in and our consolidated feedback is inside the bag. I also emailed a copy to you."

"Oh..." I stare at the bag, then glance at my computer. I haven't seen the email yet. "Thanks."

"Thank *you*. The team liked all the options. It was a great selection."

I nod to buy myself some time while I study the expression on his face. "I'm glad to hear that."

That familiar pull in my chest is still as strong as ever. Deep inside, I want to jump over this desk and into his arms. I want to feel him surrounding me like he used to all the time. But I don't move at all.

Our confrontational conversation by the mailboxes (and then in my apartment), followed by our interactions the next morning have broken down some of the wall between us. In many ways, it feels good to know how he feels. He hasn't hidden his feelings. He's stated his intentions clearly.

And yet, I still don't know what any of that means. I don't know how to act around him. Or what to say. Or what to do. At least not when we're alone. When we're in meetings or in work settings, I'm one hundred percent professional, like I always am.

Since we're alone, my mind takes the opportunity to take him in. He's wearing a purple button-down with a purple plaid tie...a set I distinctly remember buying him after we had a conversation about his black and gray closet. He's wearing charcoal gray pants and black dress shoes, as per the rest of his wardrobe. He looks...handsome.

I swallow thickly as I drag my eyes back up to his, only to find that he's watching me check him out. I look down, scratching my temple and trying to hide the heat I know is rising in my pale, Irish cheeks.

"How are you?" he asks.

"Um...I'm okay." I nod, trying to convince myself that I am, in fact, all right.

It's not like my ex-boyfriend who I'm still in love with is standing in my office or anything.

Everything is totally fine.

Again, he doesn't say anything right away, but I see his hand twitch before he clenches it into a fist.

"Maggie, I delivered the tile samples. I did what I came here to do. Professional Ethan is done. He's already left the building." He takes a step closer to my desk and puts his hand on his chest. "I'm asking my ex-girlfriend—who I'm still in love with—how she's doing. Because I can see in her eyes that something's not quite right."

My breath catches in my throat, and my eyes immediately sting. I close my eyes to stop myself from crying. I don't want to ruin my makeup. The workday isn't over.

And also when the fuck did I become a crier? I was never like this before.

Before what?

You have a tendency to pop up at inconvenient times.

Like when you need me most?

I blow out a breath and pinch the bridge of my nose. He's been honest with me. It's past time I'm honest with him.

But I'm not sure this is the time or place.

"I...um...I was..." I stammer around, hoping words form in my mouth on their own, but they don't, and I have to force myself to form coherent sentences. Again, I never used to be like this.

Before what? Nick's voice presses, and I mentally kick it in the ass.

"Ethan, I think maybe we should talk," I finally say, looking up to meet his gaze, trying to keep my expression open.

He nods slowly. "Like I said, I'll be here. I'm not going anywhere, Maggie."

The commitment in that statement is like a kick to my chest.

"Um...maybe tomorrow night?"

"Sounds good."

He agreed so quickly.

Of course, he did. He wants to talk to you.

"Okay...is there a time that works for you?"

"Anytime you're ready. We can order takeout."

I take a deep breath to calm down. This feels like it's moving fast. All I said was that we should talk.

Yes, because he wants to talk to you, so he's setting a time before you panic and back out.

Seriously, Nick's voice can shut the fuck up any time.

"Would you feel more comfortable at my place or yours?" he asks.

Truthfully, I don't know. Maybe at my apartment? It's home turf. Home field advantage, right? Or would it be better if I went to his place so I could leave whenever I wanted?

"Let's talk at your place."

"I can text you my apartment number," he says with a nod, digging his phone out of his pocket. "That is...if you'll unblock my number."

I fidget, straightening things on my desk needlessly. "I already did." I'm very aware that I just confirmed the fact that I'd blocked his number previously. He'd clearly been suspicious.

Seconds later, my phone, still on my desk face up, pings with a text from Ethan.

Ethan: 712

"So...maybe seven?" I ask.

"Perfect."

His expression is cautiously optimistic. Like he's not sure I'll show up, but hopes I do. Of course, if I don't, he knows where I live. He could just show up at my door.

"I'll see you then."

"I'm looking forward to it," he says with a hard look that absolutely says *I'll come find you if you don't show up* before turning and walking out of my office. He gives me one last look over his shoulder as he walks out of sight.

I slowly lower myself in my chair, then take a few deep breaths.

Tomorrow night, I'm going to talk to Ethan.

And now I just have to figure out what I'm going to say.

CHAPTER 22
WHAT IS WRONG WITH YOU?

MAGGIE

Just Yet - BIZZY

"You're avoiding the question. Tell me how your date was."

"*You're* avoiding the question," Julien's accent echoes through my living room, where I'm lying on the couch with the softest blanket in the world pulled up to my shoulders. I got it at Target, and I wish I'd bought five of them because I can't find them anymore.

I roll my eyes. "*Fine*, I'm avoiding the question. I'm not ready to talk about it. Can you please just tell me about your date, first?"

He squints at me, considering my request.

"Fine," he finally concedes. "It was wonderful. We had dinner and took a walk along the river."

He stops so abruptly, it makes me frown.

"That's it?"

"Oui."*

---

* Yes.

"Julien, come on," I press. "I need you to convince me love is real and long-lasting. Didn't you share an earth-shattering kiss or feel your soul shift or something?"

"Chérie,* you know very well that love exists and is real. You don't need me to convince you," he scolds. "But I did kiss her. We had a lovely time."

"Good. When will you see her next?"

"What do you mean?"

My eyebrows shoot up my forehead. "I mean when is your second date, Julien?"

"I'm not sure how to answer that when the first one hasn't ended yet."

My mouth falls open. "Julien, are you still with her?"

His eyes dart off camera and hold, turning hot in one second flat.

"Julien!" I shriek. "Why are you talking to me when you're still with her? What is the matter with you?"

"I told her I had a FaceTime date with a friend."

"Yes, but we could have rescheduled," I argue.

"Sure, but you would have done everything possible to avoid this conversation. I have asked multiple times how things are going with Ethan, and you continue to change the subject."

He nails me with a pointed glare.

I roll my eyes again, giving in. I give him a brief synopsis of my recent interactions with Ethan, including my absolute panic attack upon finding out we live in the same building, ending with our plans for later this evening.

"Good. The two of you have much to discuss."

"Do we, though? Don't we—"

"Stop this instant," he commands, his voice hard and

---

* Dear.

unyielding. "He's told you how he feels, but you haven't done the same. It's time to hash it out, Maggie. You still love him. And he still loves you."

Every argument dies on my lips. He's right. We need to talk it out. We need to rehash the past so we can see what might be salvageable. To see if we can move forward. *If* there's anything to move forward to.

"Fine. *Fine*," I concede.

"Excellent," Julien says, getting up from his position on the couch. The phone dips for just a moment, and I realize he's naked.

"Jesus, Julien."

"What?" He frowns at me.

"I can't believe you're talking to me when your date is technically not over. Please, go. Tell her I said I'm sorry."

He collapses onto another surface—a bed, I realize—the phone bouncing and blurring with the movement.

"It's okay," a feminine voice says before a beautiful woman appears on camera. She has brown hair, blue eyes, and a heart-shaped face. "He told me earlier."

Julien's arm goes around her shoulders and pulls her to him.

A genuine smile splits my face. "Hi...I'm Maggie."

She returns my smile. "Bonjour.* I'm Chloé."

"It's wonderful to meet you," I say, and I mean it to the depths of my soul. Something in Julien's expression when he looks at her is different than I've seen in my months of knowing him. There's something here, and I'm so happy for him.

"Pareil ici,"† she says.

---

* Hello.
† Same here.

"We'll talk later, Maggie," Julien says gruffly.

"We sure will," I tease before the call cuts off.

The idea of Julien falling in love with someone again makes me all warm and fuzzy inside. I hope this works out for him.

And as for me, I have a pseudo-date with my ex in a few hours.

I RAISE my fist to apartment number seven-twelve and knock on the door three times.

Before I've even had time to take a full breath, the door flies open, and I'm face-to-face with Ethan.

"Hi," he says.

"Hi," I return softly.

"I'm glad you're here."

I nod, averting my eyes.

"Come on in," he says, opening the door further and stepping aside to make room for me.

I step into his apartment, looking around as I move, and immediately realize how emotionally unprepared I was to be here.

The couch from our shared apartment is in front of the television we bought together three years ago. The bookshelves from our old guest bedroom are in the living room behind the couch, containing some of his favorite books, in addition to our favorite movies and some random plants.

I note that the plants are healthy. Well-watered and tended to.

The coffee table was ours. The dining room table is familiar, too.

In fact, the more I look around, I realize a lot of the furniture is the same, which makes sense, considering I didn't take any of it. I didn't have anywhere to move *to* at the time, and I didn't feel the need to pay for a storage unit when Ethan could just keep using it.

Despite the furniture being mostly the same, it's not an exact replica of our shared space. It's smaller, for one thing, so he either got rid of some things or still has them in a storage unit somewhere.

All hints of the two of us ever having existed together are notably absent—no pictures of us on the wall. In fact, there's nothing on the walls at all. There are a few framed photos on shelves, but he hasn't done anything to really *decorate*.

That makes sense, too, I remember. Because I was the one who wanted to turn our apartment into our *home*.

"Can I get you something to drink?"

When I look over at him, he's standing with his hands in his pockets, watching me with his head tilted slightly to the left. He looks...content. Maybe satisfied.

Maybe because I'm standing in his apartment.

"Sure. Whatever is fine."

He raises his eyebrows. "Any particular requests?"

There's extra meaning in the look he's giving me, and after a second, I realize he's trying to right a wrong. I ended things between us because he didn't listen to me, so right now, instead of assuming he knows what I want, he's asking.

I recognize an olive branch when I see one, and I choose to accept this particular one.

"I'm sure you remember what I like to drink, Ethan."

He nods slowly as if he understands the meaning behind what I'm saying.

I'm meeting you in the middle. I'm here to listen, too.

"Do you know what you want for dinner?"

This time, I don't bother deferring to him. I know him. He'll ask me if I have any requests, just like he did with the drink.

"Have you tried that pizza place down the street?"

"Yeah, I liked it."

I shrug. "I'm good with that if you are."

He nods. "Pepperoni and mushrooms?"

"You can just get mushrooms on half of it," I say with a smile. He hates them. It's a texture thing.

He returns my smile, getting out his phone and tapping around.

"Salad?" he asks.

"Sure," I reply.

"I have ranch and Italian dressing in the fridge. Do you want anything else?"

"No, that'll work."

He taps a few more times and then locks his screen and drops the phone back in his pocket.

"What do I owe you? I can Venmo you."

He gives me a dry look that tells me he won't be taking any money from me for dinner.

"It'll be here in thirty. Make yourself comfortable." He juts his chin toward the couch before turning toward the kitchen.

I look down at the old familiar couch and wonder if it's as comfortable as I remember it being. Sounds of clinking glasses and liquids being poured drift to me from the kitchen, so I take the opportunity to sit down and see for myself.

My body sinks into the cushion in the same old perfect way—not so much that you can't get leverage to get up, but just enough that you feel like your whole body is being hugged. I release a sigh and close my eyes.

God, I miss this couch.

Are you sure it wasn't just the person you sat on it with?

Nick's voice is getting on my nerves.

The couch is amazing. You know this. You sat on it.

Yeah, but you're really missing the point here.

"Comfy?" Ethan asks from above me.

My eyes fly open and meet his. He's holding two glasses of wine.

I clear my throat and sit up straight. "Yes...you know how comfortable this couch is."

"I certainly do."

He hands me one of the glasses. I have to admit I'm mildly surprised he went with red wine instead of whiskey, but then again, he probably remembers how amped up I get with whiskey, and he might know it's best if we don't start there.

This conversation will be hard enough.

I thank him and then watch as he sits on the couch, turning so he's facing me completely. He leans against the arm of the couch and sets his feet flat on the cushion so his knees are up between us.

My heart skips when I realize what he's doing.

We used to argue like this. When we were really upset, we'd sit on opposite ends of the couch with our legs outstretched so we'd have to touch each other. Oftentimes, he'd rub my feet while we talked through the disagreement. He isn't a huge fan of foot rubs, so I'd keep my hands on his shins—wanting the contact.

I forget where I read it, but at some point I saw an article that suggested this method was helpful in conflict resolution. I'd mentioned it to Ethan, and the next time we were arguing, he sat us down just like this.

Well...not exactly the way he is now. His legs are bent instead of outstretched, like he's making sure I have some space.

I slide my flip flops off and turn to face him, mimicking his position—feet between his, my soles flat on the couch with my knees together.

I can feel his eyes on me the whole time, and when I finally look up, his eyes soften, and he releases a breath.

It feels momentous to be sitting on this couch with him again. We're not actually touching, but we're sitting in a position we've been in many times before. It's familiar and foreign. Unbelievably comfortable and uncomfortably believable.

And we're not actually talking. We're just looking at each other, letting all these feelings simmer between us. I can feel the air crackle and charge.

The spark is still there. The heat never left.

Any question I had of whether or not something exists between us is answered before the discussion even starts. I curl my hands around my wineglass to keep from reaching for him.

"Where do we start?" I ask.

"You're here," he says. "It feels like a good start."

I give him a small smile. It's true...there was a long time where I never thought we'd be in the same room again, let alone getting together for the express purpose of talking about our relationship.

"What are you hoping happens tonight?" I ask. The question is loaded, but I leave it.

His jaw clenches, but he maintains eye contact. It makes me think about that night at the gas station.

"To be honest, I'm just happy you're here," he says. "I want to talk things through. I want to catch up and hear about how you've been, but the fact that you're here is all I really wanted."

I take a cleansing breath and swallow the lump in my throat. I don't know what I can really give him, other than an honest conversation.

"What about you?" he asks.

Fucking mindreader.

"You've been honest with me...I think, anyway. I have questions. But mostly, I think I owe you an honest discussion."

He thinks about that for a long second. "I think we owe each other an honest discussion. We were together for five years."

We thought we'd be together forever.

That's the next sentence that neither of us says.

"You said you have questions," he says. "What are they?"

I shake my head. "We'll get to them later." I don't want to come in hot with questions about what's different now. I want to hear other things first. "What do you want to know?"

His expression hardens, and I mentally prepare myself for difficult questions. I know this man inside and out. I lived with him for four years. I know every expression on his face. Every look in his eye. And this one tells me I hurt him.

My chest heats. I know I hurt him, but seeing it again is just as painful as it was the first time.

"I want to know why you chose to end things instead of talking them through with me. I want to know why you ran from us."

The pain in his eyes is clear, and it forces me to look down at my wineglass. I can't look directly at him. But I promised him an honest conversation, and that's what he'll get.

"Ethan, I..." I clear my throat and then take a sip of wine for courage before starting again. "I didn't see a path forward for us. Not if what we wanted in the future was so different."

I still can't look at him, and he's silent. He doesn't even move. He's just completely frozen in front of me. All those raw emotions from last year come rushing back, and I have to press a hand to my chest to try to alleviate the ache.

"You wouldn't even talk to me," he says.

"You wouldn't talk to me either...you weren't there when I came to get my things."

"How could I possibly stand there and watch you pack your life away and leave me?"

That thought brings tears to my eyes because I flash back to the moment I arrived at the apartment to find him missing. There was a note on the dining room table saying that he couldn't be there, and I should leave my key.

"That was horrible. Easily the third worst day of my life."

"That's what I mean, though." In my peripheral vision, I can see him lean forward. "Neither of us were happy to be ending our relationship. So why couldn't you just talk to me? You blocked my number, Maggie. Do you have any idea how many times I sent you messages? How many voicemails I left for you?"

I lose the battle with the tears. They start flowing down my cheeks.

"No, of course you don't," he answers his own question. "Because you moved out and moved on. And when I really thought about it—rationally thought about it—I wasn't surprised."

I look up at him, confused.

"I wasn't surprised because that's what you do. You don't dwell on things once they're over. The only thing I've *ever* seen you dwell on is Nick, and that makes sense."

I watch his jaw clench again...his Adam's apple bob when he swallows.

"I never expected you to move on from your brother's death. But I...I expected you to think twice about *me*, Maggie."

Ouch.

Fuck, that comment hurts...and maybe I deserve it.

"I expected the benefit of the doubt. I expected that you'd try to understand where I was coming from."

But *that* comment...it just makes me angry.

"Ethan...I told you how I felt about marriage, and you *disregarded* me. You blatantly thought I would just change my mind. That I would eventually *come around* to your viewpoint. How would I give you the benefit of the doubt there? You'd already ignored my opinion."

He finally looks away from me, chewing on his bottom lip and shaking his head.

That's really the crux of it for me. The fact that I'd told him my stance on marriage, and he proposed anyway. The fact that he just...didn't believe me when I told him how I felt.

"That's why I ended things, Ethan," I say, as gently as I can. "I felt so...betrayed. Like you'd just assumed I was a different person than I'd told you I was."

He takes a large sip of wine and runs an agitated hand through his hair.

"I fucked that up. I know that."

"Ethan, I just—" But my next sentence is cut off by a ping from his phone.

"Pizza's here," he says, setting his wineglass on the coffee table and getting up from the couch. "I'll be right back. Don't move." He throws me a pointed glare as he goes through his apartment door.

Fuck.

It's going to be a long night.

CHAPTER 23
IT'S NEVER SIMPLE, IS IT?
MAGGIE

White Flag - Dido

The second the door closes behind Ethan, I suck in a breath and slouch further into the cushions. Being here with him is a lot. My emotions are *everywhere*. They're pinging off walls and also trying to burrow into corners to hide.

I didn't think this evening would be easy, but, *fuck,* it's hard. Just the act of sitting on this couch with him is emotionally draining.

I take a few sips of wine and practice deep breathing to calm my racing heart while he's gone, but I remain seated, as instructed.

When he returns, his eyes dart to the couch, as if checking to make sure I hadn't moved.

He puts the pizza box and a small bag down on the coffee table and then disappears into the kitchen. He's back seconds later with plates, napkins, utensils, and a bottle of water.

"Eat. Drink." he says.

I want to take offense to his one-word commands, but I know deep down that he's trying to take care of me. I'm drinking wine, and I've already started crying. He knows I'm on my way to a migraine if I don't hydrate and eat something. I heave a sigh and reorient my body so I'm facing the food.

He seems to hesitate for just a second—like he considered sitting on the floor before choosing instead to sit on the couch.

"Thank you for dinner," I say quietly.

I see him turn his head toward me out of the corner of my eye. "Of course," he says, matching my gentleness in tone.

He's meeting me halfway. Again.

So I turn my head to meet his eyes.

"Let's just take a breather. Let's eat." He tips his chin toward the bottle of water. "Drink that."

So we do. We sit on our old couch and catch up on the things we don't know about each other anymore.

I ask him about his new job.

He asks me about the project in Paris.

I ask him about how he found this apartment, and I silently wonder how the actual fuck we ended up living in the same building.

He asks me how my time at home was over the holidays.

We ask about each other's families.

We both eat salad. He sticks to his side of the pizza, and I stick to mine.

I dutifully drink the water and therefore need a bathroom break, which allows me the opportunity to discreetly check out more of his apartment. There's a lamp on in his bedroom, so I can see the furniture in there is different. It's not our bed. Or at least not our headboard or nightstands.

But before I duck into the bathroom, I note there are *two* nightstands. I have no right to wonder if someone is using that other nightstand—especially considering my extracurricular activities while I was in Paris. But it still makes me wonder, which makes me just a tiny bit jealous.

I sooth my envy by telling myself it's entirely possible he bought two nightstands because they came in the set. Like a regular adult.

While I'm washing my hands, I stare at myself in the mirror. I didn't mess up my makeup too badly when I cried a little earlier. Still, I groan inwardly as I dab at the smudge of mascara on my cheekbone. I'm not on a date. I'm not here to impress Ethan. Lord knows he's seen me in every possible state of dress or undress at this point. First thing in the morning with my hair in complete disarray. Hungover after a night out. In a deep, can't-get-out-of-bed depression after Nick died. A smudge of mascara won't bother him.

I'm able to get some of it off, but not all of it. I'm left with a red mark for my efforts.

When I get back to the living room, I see he's topped off our wineglasses and grabbed another bottle of water for me.

His eyes immediately go to the red spot on my cheekbone, and I'm certain he saw the mascara smudge before I went into the bathroom. I go back to my seat on the couch and watch him resume his previous position—facing me with his knees bent and his feet flat on the couch.

I take a cleansing breath and mirror his position. Before I ask my next question, I meet his eyes. "What else do you want to know?"

"Are you seeing someone?"

"No. Why?"

"Because I'm wondering what your major hesitation is.

I've told you how I feel about you, and you're not exactly eager to get back together."

I'm sure my mouth is agape as I stare at him.

"So I'm wondering why," he says again. "Maybe you don't have feelings for me anymore. But if that's the case... then why are you here?"

I shake my head. "My turn to ask questions."

"You haven't answered mine," he responds calmly.

"Your answers might inform mine," I argue.

He picks up his wine from the coffee table and takes a sip. "Fine."

"Why do you want to get back together?"

"Because I'm in love with you," he says without hesitation.

"That doesn't—"

"Because you're the only person I've ever wanted to spend the rest of my life with. Because even though we've been apart for a full year, I still wake up every morning reaching for you and go to bed every night wishing you were there...missing your body molded against mine like a phantom limb. Because I'm still just as in love with you today as I was the day you ended things. Because if I didn't *still* want you this badly, I wouldn't be asking."

Jesus.

My throat is suddenly very dry. I pick up my wine and take a healthy gulp.

"Not what you were expecting?" he asks.

"Not really, no," I say weakly.

"What did you think I would say?"

I gesture toward him with my free hand. "That you... missed me, I guess. I don't know. Not *that.*"

"I do miss you," he says. "But that's the least of the reasons I want to be with you. If I believed we were better off without each other, I'd be able to handle simply *missing* you."

I squint at him. "So what are the reasons you want to be with me, then?"

He doesn't even pause.

"All the reasons will take a while, but I'm happy to list them out one-by-one if that's what you need," he says with a final nod. "First and foremost, because you're my best friend. You've been my best friend for years, and you'll never be the kind of friend I'm all right with losing. Second, this isn't a situation where we've outgrown each other. I fucked up, and I've learned from it. I hurt you, but you hurt me, too. I can't fix this alone. You need to partici-pate, too."

I can hear the determination in his voice, along with the pain.

"Third, because we're *great* together, Maggie. We can do *anything*. We're the best team I've ever been a part of...will *ever* be a part of. Fourth—"

"Okay, okay, you can stop." I put a hand up for emphasis.

He clamps his mouth shut, his lips going into a thin line, which draws my attention, and I have an inexplicable urge to kiss the tension off his face. But I don't move.

"Let's just...let's skip to the logistics," I say, desperately trying to get us back on course. "You say you still love me and want to be with me, but regardless of how I feel about you, I...I'm just not sure that's enough."

"*Love* isn't enough?" he asks, incredulous.

"It's clearly not, Ethan," I say as gently as possible. "Let's pretend for a moment that we get back together. What's even changed?"

I pause, waiting for him to put the pieces together himself, and maybe he does because his face hardens.

"I still don't want to get married. I'll *never* want to get married. And you clearly do—"

He opens his mouth to speak, but I hold up my hand.

"If we get back together...if we spend another five years together, and we break up for the same reason...I can't do that, Ethan. I can't. It's been hard enough the first time. I'm not sure I'd survive it a second time."

I have to stop because my throat is tightening. I swallow and compose myself.

"If you still want to get married, and I still don't, then nothing has changed. There's no point in getting back together."

"Maggie, I don't need to get married."

Ethan sits forward and places his free hand on my foot.

It's a lot.

The physical contact in our designated arguing position from the past. On *our* couch. Him saying things I want to hear, but can't let myself believe.

"I want to be with you. Period. I'll take you any way I can get you, Mags. I love *you*. I want *you*. I don't give a shit about rings or ceremonies. I'm already going to be in love with you for the rest of my life, and I don't need a ring to be committed to you."

He pauses, catching my eye with a meaningful look.

My own voice echoes from the night we broke up.

His hand stays on my foot, but I keep mine glued to my wineglass.

"Then...if we were to get back together, are either of us doing anything differently? Are you accepting me for who I am? Am I accepting you for who you are? Or am I hoping *you've* changed *your* mind?" I offer a pathetic shrug. "Isn't that the same thing? Me, not wanting to be with you because of a fundamental part of who you are?"

"Getting married is not a fundamental part of who I am," he says, his voice stern. "But you...? *You* are."

The shit of it is that Ethan is also a fundamental part of who I am at this point. Or at least what loving him has made me.

But that doesn't mean we couldn't find out who we are without each other.

I shake my head. "I don't want to hurt you again, Ethan. And I don't want you to resent me years down the line because I never married you. I want you to be happy...even if it's not with me."

"No." He sets his wineglass down on the coffee table and holds both of my feet. "I know you don't believe me, and I also know that's my fault. But Maggie, you know *me*. Trust me when I tell you that I could never resent you for anything."

He exhales a short, frustrated breath and then takes my wineglass from me, setting it on the coffee table next to his. Before I even know what's happening, he's hauling me out of my position on the couch and settling me on his lap, my knees on either side of his hips.

"Ethan, what the hell?"

He doesn't answer verbally. Instead, he takes my hand and places it over his heart. Holding my gaze like a lodestone, he starts over.

"I want you to feel me when I say this. Because I've never been more serious about anything in my whole life, and I won't abide by you purposefully twisting my words or refusing to believe me when I tell you something. I did that once, Maggie."

The look in his eyes is so intense. I don't think I could look away if someone started up a jackhammer across the room.

"*I* fucked everything up because I didn't believe you when you told me how you felt about marriage. I can't let you make the same mistake. You'll never forgive yourself. Ask me how I know."

He takes a shaky breath and presses my hand harder into his chest.

"Maggie, I will never resent you for not marrying me. And I'll never ask you again. I'll never assume you'll change your mind. I'll happily live the rest of my life with you—by your side, as your partner. I would rather never marry you than marry anyone else for even one day. You're it for me, Mags. You always have been. And I'm so sorry I lost sight of that. But I never will again. I can't snap my fingers and make you believe me, but I can promise you that I'll try every day to make sure you know I'm here for you."

A few tears escape my eyes. He keeps one hand on top of mine on his chest, but wipes away the tears with the other.

"*This* is what I want. You and me. *This* is the most important thing in the world to me. Being married doesn't mean we're more committed to each other. You and me...we say we're committed to each other, and that's it. I want *you* at the end of every day for the rest of my fucking life."

He finally takes my hand off his chest, only to bring it to his lips, kissing my knuckles.

"You're just going to have to trust that I'm telling you the truth."

I'm just going to have to trust him.

So simply complicated.

Once upon a time, I trusted Ethan implicitly. I'd have trusted him with my life, even. How else can you stay in a relationship with someone for so many years? How else can you consider spending the rest of your life with a person?

To be totally honest, I still trust him in many ways. The question at hand is whether or not I can trust him with *me.*

Or maybe more specifically, if I can trust *myself* with *him.*

My throat is burning, and I can't see very well on account of the tears. I'm an obnoxious mess, and as much as I want to bury these feelings, I'm here to *talk* to him. I promised him a conversation. Even if I can't actually cognate thoughts.

"Ethan, I don't know what to say..."

"You don't have to say anything right now, Maggie." He takes my head in his hands and wipes my tears away with his thumbs. "I'm not asking you to answer me right now. But I needed to tell you where I stand and why. All I'm asking is that you think about it."

"What is it exactly that you want out of this conversation?" I ask with a sigh. "If you get to choose, where do we go from here?"

The tiniest flicker of hope flashes through his eyes, but he tamps it down quickly.

"I want you. I've already told you this."

"Yeah, but everything is different now—"

"Not everything," he interrupts.

"Enough things," I rephrase. "We've been apart for a year. We don't live together anymore. We've both...had life experiences without each other now. How do you expect us to move forward?"

He considers my question for a few seconds longer than I expected. Thus far, he's been so quick to answer my questions and address my concerns. But here...

"Why are you hesitating?" I whisper.

He shakes his head, leaning forward to press his lips to my jaw. The move surprises me enough to make me gasp. I melt when his nose brushes against the column of my throat. Warmth shoots through my chest.

"I'm not hesitating," he insists. "I'm wondering what I can tell you without you bolting toward the door."

"Just say it."

Some might say I'm begging. Maybe pleading.

I'm frustrated though.

I'm exasperated, and I want him to spit it out.

"Maggie, if I had my way, you'd never leave," he says, trailing featherlight kisses down my neck, ending at my collarbone. "Or I'd go back to your place, and *I'd* never leave. I'm ready for forever with you, and I want it to start now," he finishes, looking back up into my eyes. "And there are so many ways to get started..."

I don't know exactly how this happened, but our mouths are very close together. We're only a breath apart. He inches slowly closer to me while I blink repeatedly, wondering if this is a good idea and wanting to do it anyway.

I'll never know what could have happened, though, because in that moment, my phone blares to life.

It's behind me on the coffee table, and the shrill sound puts a stop to the electricity in between us. I turn my head to gauge the importance of the call, and I realize immediately that I can't ignore it.

"Shit..." I start scrambling to get off Ethan's lap. I have a feeling in my gut, and it's freaking me out. I vaguely register strong hands steadying me as I find my way to standing and lunge for my phone.

"Cora?"

"Maggie?" Marv's wife responds, her voice shaky.

"Cora, what's wrong?"

I hear her sniff before she responds.

"Sweetheart, it's Marvin."

CHAPTER 24
HEAVY QUESTIONS WITH
EASY ANSWERS
ETHAN

I'd Run to You - CJ Starnes

The coffee is terrible. But the actual coffee shops aren't open. So this is what I'm stuck with as we wait to see what's going on.

I'm sitting in a waiting area at the hospital. Maggie fell asleep a little while ago, curled up on the shitty couch I'm sitting on, the top of her head pressed against my leg. I balled up my jacket and made a pillow for her.

I offered my lap, but she didn't take it.

Our conversation at my apartment was intense. We talked about a lot of stuff that was extremely difficult to resurface. We were both already on edge, emotions running high. And then she got a call from Marv's wife, Cora, who told her that Marv had been transported to the hospital.

It's been a rough night for her.

For me, too, but not in the same way.

A tall man walks through the doors holding a bottle of Dr Pepper. I've learned in the last two hours that this is Peter, Cora's youngest son from her first marriage.

He sits down on the chair adjacent to Maggie and me and then freezes. I look up from the Dr Pepper bottle that's captured my attention to find him looking at me with a confused expression on his face.

"Sorry," I say quietly. "The coffee is terrible, and I'm wondering where you got that." I gesture to the Dr Pepper.

"Oh, it's a couple hallways down. I needed to make a call, so I went outside and then walked around a little. You want one?"

I look down at Maggie. She's still sleeping, and I don't want to move and risk waking her up. "Nah, I'll be fine."

"I can grab you one."

"Oh, no you don't have to—"

"No, don't worry about it, I got you."

He's up before I can say another word. I can't even dig into my pocket to get my wallet without bothering Maggie, so I just stay put.

It was immediately obvious to me that Maggie's phone call was going to be a bad one. Her whole body went completely still, and she stared—unseeing—straight ahead. It's only the second time I've seen her so paralyzed with fear.

I got to my feet and stood in front of her, our intimate moment completely forgotten as I searched her eyes for clues. There were already tears forming, but none fell. She wasn't reacting at all to my presence there, so I took her free hand in mine. She blinked and squeezed my hand—hard.

Cora said that Marv started having chest pains after dinner. They wondered if it was heartburn, but it showed no signs of getting better, so Cora called an ambulance. Marv was conscious for a while, but wasn't by the time he got to the hospital.

When we arrived, she was pacing back and forth in the waiting room, talking to Peter on the phone. She'd called

Maggie and Marv's sister, but there weren't many other people in his life. He'd married later in life when he met Cora, who was divorced with three children. Maggie was the closest thing to a blood-related child he had.

Some people might panic upon receiving news that a loved one was being rushed to the hospital, and truth be told, I wondered for a second if Maggie would flip out. But Maggie is calm in a crisis. She's the type of person you'd want with you during the apocalypse. I mean, I'd want her with me, regardless, but she's also very action-oriented and would be able to prioritize quickly.

Maggie called Kelsie to let her know what was going on, and they consulted with another member of their team to determine if anyone else needed to be notified immediately. They decided it could wait until they knew more.

Then, she said she needed to leave so she could go to the hospital. I told her I'd drive her, which is how we've ended up where we are, on this shitty couch in a waiting room.

Next to me, Maggie shifts, adjusting her body and makeshift pillow, her hand landing on my knee. I adjust my hand so it's resting more comfortably on her shoulder.

Peter comes back into view holding another Dr Pepper.

"Thanks, man."

I crack open the bottle and take a very necessary sip of delicious chemicals that will hopefully keep me awake a little while longer. "Much better. I owe you."

"No, you don't," he says with a smile, then juts his chin to the sleeping beauty by my side. "This is the Maggie that works for Marv?"

"Yeah."

Peter nods. "Marv has always spoken very highly of her. My siblings have met her, but I haven't had the pleasure."

I study him for a moment, the instinct to protect Maggie

roaring to life. I just met this dude, and I'm not sure if he's angling for anything nefarious. In the end, I decide that he's important to Marv, and I don't need to contribute to anyone's stressful evening.

"I'm sure she'll be happy to meet you when she wakes up."

"You guys been together long?"

Is that his angle? That he wants to date Maggie?

"Feels like forever," I say vaguely before smirking and adding, "...in a good way."

He nods and looks down at his hands. "I've been with my girl for about three years now."

Relief I don't deserve to feel floods my body.

"Yeah?"

"Yeah...she's starting to talk about getting married."

"Ahh."

He gives me a look that very blatantly says *I know, right?*

"And you don't want to get married?" I ask.

"It's not that I don't want to..." he hedges, rubbing his palms against his jeans. "It's just that...I think she's ready, but I'm not."

"That's valid. It's a big step. Not something to take lightly."

"I guess..."

He's so fidgety all of a sudden. He scrapes his hands down his face and stares ahead.

"It's probably weird that I'm thinking about this right now. Like, Marv is having emergency surgery. My mom is outside on the phone with my siblings. But she and I just had an argument, and it's all I can think about."

"Your phone call?" I ask.

"Yeah. I mean, no." He shakes his head. "Yes, that was

her, but no, the argument was earlier today. I just wanted to call and check in with her."

"That's a good idea," I say, hoping I'm being encouraging.

He glances at me out of the corner of his eye, like he's trying to determine my sincerity.

"It is. If you let arguments fester, they just get worse. It's best to talk it out. Or at least keep talking to each other... show you're still there."

Peter nods. "Yeah, I mean, I...I don't want to go anywhere. I want to be with her. I just don't know how you're supposed to know if you're ready to get married."

I can't help the smirk on my face.

"Are you two going to get married?" he asks.

"Nope," I say, shaking my head.

"Why not?" he asks with a frown.

I feel like we're treading back into muddy waters. Maggie and I aren't technically *together* right now, but I'm serious about not giving up on her. I'm going to keep doing everything possible to convince her that we're still good together. That we should try again. That we can be even greater the second time around.

"Personal preference," I finally answer with a shrug.

He watches me for a moment, but I don't say anything else. I don't know what Maggie would want me to say.

"And that's enough?"

I laugh quietly. "*She's* enough." I look down at her sleeping form and feel that familiar warmth spread throughout my chest. "She's everything, man."

"How do you know?"

"How do I know what?"

"That...that she's who you want? That it's going to be okay if you don't marry her?"

Heavy questions. Easy answers.

I take a deep breath before I meet his eyes and start. "I've wanted her for the past six years. That's not going to change. I just...know."

I offer an apologetic shrug because I'm well aware of how obnoxious that sentence is.

"When I was younger, I remember someone telling me that they just *knew* when they met their person, and I was so aggravated by that. What does that even *mean*, right?"

He huffs a laugh. "Seriously."

"The thing is, when I met Maggie, I just...*knew*." My eyes lose focus as I think back on that first night at the club. "I'd met her once before—the night before, actually. So when I saw her again, I couldn't *not* talk to her. We talked all night. And there was this moment...she was laughing. Her eyes were squeezed closed, and she was clutching her chest..."

I can feel the smile stretch my skin as I picture it. That's how Maggie laughs—*really* laughs...not that polite kind of laughter like she's trying to be amicable. Her eyes squeeze shut like she's trying to freeze the moment in time. Like she's trying to burn the memory into her brain for the rest of her life.

"She was fucking radiant. I don't know that I can say I fell in love with her that night, but I knew beyond the shadow of a doubt that she was going to change my whole life. And I willingly let her. My life has never been the same in the best kind of way. I wouldn't go back and alter that night for anything."

Peter has a soft smile on his face when I glance up.

"And as for part two of your question...I guess I don't know that it will be okay if I don't marry her. There are no guarantees, man—married or not. But I know that I'll regret it every single day if I don't give her my all. If I don't try every single day to make it work with her."

I have to repress the urge to run my fingers through her curls. I don't want to wake her up. So I just keep my hand as still as possible on her shoulder and gaze at her profile.

"If you feel a fraction of that, you just talk it through with her. Work it out. Meet her in the middle."

I hear Peter hum, maybe in agreement, or maybe just in acknowledgment that he heard me speak. But before he can say anything else, Cora comes back through the doors and heads toward us.

"Mom...any news?" Peter asks, standing up.

"Hi, sweetie." She hugs him and lovingly taps his cheek. "No, I haven't heard anything yet."

Cora looks from me to Maggie.

"Is she getting some sleep?"

"A bit, I think."

"Good." She nods. "Let her sleep as long as she can. Who knows how long this will—"

"Mrs. James?" the nurse at the desk calls.

"That's me," she says, squeezing Peter's hand before she goes toward the desk. Peter follows behind her, staying back a couple of feet. I can't catch what the nurse is saying, but Cora is nodding.

Maggie sits up with a start, her eyes bleary and unfocused from sleep.

"Hey, it's okay."

She turns to look at me with something in her eyes that looks like relief.

I reach down for her hand and interlace my fingers with hers. "The nurse just called Cora over."

"Okay," she says, nodding. Then she squeezes my hand and sits up straight next to me. "No one's said anything?"

"No. This is the first time anyone's come out with news." I look over at the nurse and see her hand a phone to Cora.

"Okay," she says again before taking a deep breath in and letting it out slowly.

I want to tell her that it will all be okay. That no matter what, I'm here for her. That we'll get through it together. But the truth of the matter is that I *don't* know if it will be okay. I *hope* she'll let me be here for her and that we'll get through it together, but I don't know if she'll let me.

We've been down this road once already, and it was really difficult. Don't get me wrong, I never once thought about leaving, and we were never in danger of breaking up, but it was hard. Maggie was really depressed, and I was *very* worried abouther.

If Marv doesn't make it, I'm not sure what will happen to Maggie.

"All right, I talked to the nurse, who put me through to the doctor. He's out of surgery. They think it went well. They'll let me in to see him in a little bit."

Maggie sags next to me. I bring our joined hands to my mouth to kiss the back of her hand and then offer what I hope is a reassuring squeeze.

"What happened?" she asks.

Cora meets Maggie's eyes and visibly hesitates for a second. "He had a heart attack," she says softly.

Next to me, Maggie goes stock still. When I turn my head to look at her, she's at least three shades paler.

I wrap my arm around her shoulders and pick her hand back up with my free one.

"They said he needed stents put in—three of them— which is a lot better than having open heart surgery," Cora says. "He'll need to make some lifestyle changes, but he should recover."

Pulling Maggie closer to me, I kiss her temple and whisper in her ear. "He made it through surgery, Mags. You'll get to see him before too long."

She nods...her head barely moving at all.

"Take a deep breath for me."

I breathe with her and then tell her to do it again a few more times. She relaxes a little bit with each breath and eventually leans into me.

"They'll let me see him once he's out of post-op, and then I'll have to see what visitors they'll allow," Cora says.

Maggie nods again.

"What do you need?" I whisper in her ear.

She shakes her head but doesn't say anything.

"Okay. I'll just sit here with you."

And then her hand squeezes mine so hard it actually kind of hurts. It takes me by surprise, but I don't flinch and instead hug her closer to my side.

"We'll hang around for a bit," I tell Cora. "At least until you see him, and if they let other people back, I'm sure Maggie will want to go."

She nods against my shoulder.

"Okay," Cora says. "I appreciate you all being here."

Peter wraps his arm around his mom's shoulders and squeezes her. "Can I get you anything, Mom?"

She gives Peter a grateful smile and pats his cheek with her hand. "No, baby, but thank you. I'm just going to wait until they call me back, and then I'll let you all know what's going on."

Everyone back settles into chairs, and we manage to find *Friends* reruns on the TV.

Two episodes later, the nurse calls Cora back.

The whole time, Maggie stays nestled against my side,

her head resting on my shoulder, her fingers intertwined with mine. She doesn't fall back asleep.

After another two episodes, Peter's phone dings and Maggie's phone vibrates with a text, and she practically jumps out of her skin. When she sees the message, she angles the phone toward me so I can see it.

Cora: He's in and out of consciousness right now, which is normal. They're moving him to an ICU bed. One visitor can go back at a time, so let me get him up there and settled, and then you're welcome to come back and see him.

Maggie: Sounds good. Thank you.

Two episodes later, Cora comes back out. She looks tired, but no longer terrified.

Maggie is on her feet before Cora even reaches us.

I stand with her, not because I'm planning to go back with her, but because I want to be close to her.

"Okay, he's all set. The nurse will tell you where to go. I'm going to stay here tonight, so go on ahead, and when you get back out, I'll head back in for the night."

Maggie nods. I squeeze her shoulder and whisper in her ear again.

"I'll be right here when you get back."

She turns her head into me, reaching a hand up to touch my cheek. I take the opportunity to kiss her hair.

Her eyes meet mine for a few charged seconds. In them, I can see her fear, her anxiety, and what I'm cautiously hoping is appreciation...for me being here, maybe?

In the past, I'd have kissed her in a moment like this. But now, I just pull her in for a hug. She melts into my body, wrapping her arms around my torso and burying her face in my chest. I might be imagining it, but I feel like she's trying to thank me.

When she pulls back, she turns toward Cora and takes a deep breath.

"I'll see you here when you get back," Cora says. "Ask the nurse how to get to his room."

With one nod, Maggie goes toward the nurse, who writes down instructions and ushers her through the door.

I sit back down, shaking out my jacket from its ball and draping it on the couch next to me. I try to ignore Cora and Peter so they can have a semi-private conversation. Instead, I focus on Chandler, Rachel, and Ross trying to get a couch up a flight of stairs. In other circumstances, I'd be crying with laughter. That level of enthusiasm feels inappropriate right now, so I keep it bottled up.

Peter agrees to come back in the morning with a few things for Cora. They have their game plan figured out by the time Maggie comes back, two episodes later.

As she walks back toward the group, I note her red, puffy eyes.

She pauses in front of Cora.

"He was in and out. A nurse came to check vitals." Her voice is gravelly and tired. "I'll be back tomorrow, if that's okay."

"Of course, honey."

Cora wraps her up in a hug and says a few things in a low voice that I intentionally try not to hear. I put my jacket back on and look around the couch to make sure we're not forgetting anything.

When I look back up, Maggie is turning away from Cora. She walks straight toward me, stopping just a foot in front of me.

"Can you take me home, please?" she whispers.

I take her hand and jerk my head toward the doors we came in. "Let's go."

CHAPTER 25
DÉJÀ VU
ETHAN

Dancing In The Dark - biz colletti

The drive home is silent. I hold her hand the whole time.

I've been in this situation before, and I think I know what's coming. The day Nick died is playing on a loop in my head.

How Maggie reacted. How the waves of grief hit her and refused to let up.

How she held it together for a little while and then completely lost it.

How she yelled and cried and raged against the world.

And then stopped.

So I drive her back to our building and follow her to her apartment. This time, she doesn't try to slam the door in my face. She holds it open for me, and I lock it behind us.

She walks straight to her kitchen and pours whiskey into a glass. She downs the whole thing in a few gulps and grips the counter, her head hanging.

I pull a glass from the cabinet and fill it with water from the tap. I set it on the counter for her. She needs to drink it, though I'm not sure she will.

"What do you need?" I ask again.

She lifts her head and looks at me, fresh tears welling in her eyes. Her lips part, but then tremble and instead of words, a sob escapes her.

I don't waste time grabbing the nape of her neck and pulling her into me. I feel her fists bunch up my shirt, clinging to me as she tries to get words out.

"H-he was so pale, Ethan. He o-only opened his eyes a c-couple of times, and they were...unfocused. Confused. I-I tried talking to him, but I couldn't s-stop thinking about Nick. Wondering if h-he was that pale before he went into surgery. Did Kate get to see him afterward? Was he cognizzant? Why didn't he call me? I wish he would have c-called me. I would have given a-anything to get to talk to him one last time..."

"I know, sweetheart." I gently hold her head against my chest with one hand and rub my other hand up and down her spine, hoping to soothe her.

"H-he has to make it," she wails. "I wouldn't be able to take it, Ethan. I won't survive it."

Flashes of Maggie in bed after she was finished raging at the world pop up in my mind. She laid in bed for days. I worked from home, not wanting to leave her. I didn't think she was suicidal, but I had never seen her like that. I'd never been more worried about her.

"Shhhhh...Maggie, he made it through surgery, and he's being monitored. The doctors are optimistic, so we have to be, too."

"I n-need him to be okay..."

"I know you do."

We stand in the kitchen for a while, me holding her while she cries and eventually calms down.

She lets go of my shirt and pulls back to reveal a red, splotchy face. Her eyes are puffy and bloodshot. She's still beautiful, even now. I take her head in my hands and kiss her forehead before sliding my hand into hers and guiding her toward her bedroom.

"Throw on some pajamas. Wash your face. Brush your teeth. I'll grab your migraine kit."

I plant one more kiss on her head before turning toward her bedroom door to grab her migraine supplies.

"Ethan?"

"Yeah?" I turn halfway to see her. Her shoulders are slumped. She looks exhausted. I can see her eyes getting tight in the corners the way they do when her headaches start.

"Thank you," she whispers.

I make sure she's meeting my eyes when I respond because it's more important than ever that she understands.

"I'd do anything for you, Mags." And then I turn to leave before she changes so she can first of all, have privacy, but I'd be lying if I said I wasn't trying to avoid seeing her naked. I don't want to see another inch of her skin because it's already hard enough to keep my hands off her. I meant what I said—I won't fuck her until she's mine again, and I certainly won't be taking advantage of her while she's vulnerable like this. So it's best if I high-tail it out of this room as quickly as possible.

I stop in the bathroom first so I'll be finished before she's ready to wash her face and brush her teeth. I grab her migraine meds from the medicine cabinet and then put a few ice cubes in the glass of water I already got for her. Grabbing her favorite ice pack from the freezer, I head back to her bedroom to find her already padding down the hall in a cute pajama set I remember very well. Blue shorts with white flowers and a matching button-down top.

It's soft, as I recall.

I leave her meds and water on her nightstand and turn off all the lights except the ones on the nightstands. Then, I make myself comfortable on my normal side of the bed. After years of sleeping next to her, I doubt she'd changed sides. I leave my coat on the chair in the corner and check my notifications—nothing important—before putting my phone on the nightstand.

When Maggie returns, she stops short in the doorway. I meet her gaze and refuse to look away or appear to be questioning my choice to lie in her bed.

I'm staying here.

After a deep breath, she acquiesces. She's slow to move to her side of the bed, but I'm pretty sure it's an issue of her head hurting and less about reluctance to having me here. I meant what I said before.

I won't touch her in a sexual way. I'm here to make sure she's all right and support her any way I can. And I think she knows it.

She sits on the bed and takes the pills. I remind her to drink all the water.

"Why are you so obsessed with my water intake? Did you become a full-fledged Dom while I was gone?"

I try to suppress my smirk. "There's no appropriate way for me to answer that question."

"What does that mean?" she asks, turning to look at me.

"It means I'm not talking about sex with you right now."

She squints. "Not all Dom-sub relationships are about sex."

I squint back, but I'm not at all hiding my smirk anymore. "What'd you get up to in Paris?"

Her face hardens, and she turns away, switching off the lamp, grabbing her ice pack, and sliding under the covers. Her movements are short and fussy as she gets settled and puts the ice pack over her forehead. It's hanging over her eyes just enough to obscure them.

Regardless, it seems I've touched a nerve. I try to swallow down the bile I can feel rising at the idea of her being with someone else. We weren't in a relationship. She was free to do whatever she wanted.

Never mind that you were pining away for her back home, and she was in Paris doing...what? Hanging out in kink clubs?

I mentally slap myself to stop the thought spiral. It's none of my business. I have no right to feel that way, and it needs to be cut off now.

"Maggie, I wasn't trying to imply anything. It was a joke."

She sighs.

"I promise, Mags."

She raises her ice pack just a tiny amount and stares at me. She must find whatever she's looking for because she lowers the ice pack and resumes her prone, stationary position.

"Do you want me to message Kelsie to update her?" I offer.

"Shit," she says, starting to sit up.

"No no..." I put a hand on her shoulder and stop her, gently laying her back down. "Where's your phone?"

"In my purse," she says, a suspicious look on her face.

I get out of bed and go to the living room to grab it. I don't open it—I just bring the whole thing to her.

As she takes her purse and fishes her phone out, I crawl under the covers and lie down. I'm totally wiped, and I'm really hoping I can get some sleep.

After a few moments, she makes a frustrated sound and lets her phone drop onto her stomach.

"Everything okay?"

"I can't...I can't really see the screen. I have floaters right now."

"Maggie, I can help you. I'm not going to go through your phone."

With a sigh, she hands it to me. It's open to the messages app, but I have to search for Kelsie's name—which I do by using the search function, not by scrolling through her messages.

"Okay, what do you want me to tell her?"

Maggie gives me a script, which I type out and read back to her before hitting send. I don't even exit out of the message thread before I lock it and reach over her to set it on her nightstand.

"Thank you," she says softly.

"You're welcome." I reach over to my nightstand and switch off the lamp. "Close your eyes. Get some sleep. The more you get, the better you'll feel. We can visit Marv tomorrow."

She doesn't respond, but I don't wait for her to do so. I just roll over so I'm facing her and try to make myself relax enough to sleep.

Her ice pack is still on her forehead, pulled back low to obscure her vision again, but we've done all we can—she took her meds, and she drank some water. The next thing she needs to do is sleep. So I close my eyes.

"Ethan?"

"Yeah?" I ask, keeping my eyes closed. I was nearly asleep.

"Why are you here?"

That makes me open my eyes. I'm quiet until they adjust so I can see her profile in the darkness.

Heavy question. Easy answer.

"Because I'm in love with you."

She inhales a slow, deep breath before letting it out just as slowly. Like she was counting her breaths evenly.

"We broke up."

"I remember. It's why I'm not touching you right now. I used to spoon you when you had migraines. Or you'd tuck your head into my chest. I liked that best."

She seems to hesitate before she speaks again, taking in a short breath and then holding it for a second, releasing it and trying again.

"You touched me last time."

She's right about that.

"You're right, I did," I concede.

She's silent for a moment, and I assume the conversation is over, but then she rolls to face me, adjusting her ice pack to stay on the side of her head.

"Why did you before?"

"Couldn't stop myself, I guess. I was finally lying in bed with you again. I never thought I'd have the chance." It had been an emotionally challenging day, and then there she was...in pain in more ways than one. I just wanted to help her feel better.

"To touch me?"

"Yes...but also to make you feel better. To help you."

"And what's stopping you tonight?"

"You've had an emotionally draining day," I say with a sigh. "We had a tough conversation, and then Marv...

you're vulnerable, and I'm not about to take advantage of that."

"You're not touching me because of chivalry?"

"I suppose that's part of it, yeah. Trying to be respectful over here."

"What's the other part of it?"

Not a single part of me is surprised she caught that. Even with a migraine, she's sharper than most.

"You know where I stand, but I don't know where you stand," I admit.

"And that makes you not want to touch me?"

"I never said I didn't *want* to touch you. I've touched you plenty of times today. But it's the end of the night, and we're in bed."

"Again, that didn't stop you before."

I rub the back of my neck, trying to contain my exasperated sigh.

"Maggie, are you trying to tell me you *want* me to touch you?"

"Yes, Jesus. Take a fucking hint, Ethan."

The words aren't even fully out of her mouth before I'm moving.

"Fuck, twist my arm."

I slide one arm under her neck and the other around her waist, then haul her into me. She lets out a tiny squeak of surprise at the movement.

"Did that hurt your head?"

"No, no..."

"Are you sure?"

"Yes, I'm fine. I promise."

Her arm tucks between our bellies and the other snakes around my back. I feel one foot slide forward to tangle with mine. She buries her face in my chest, and just like I've done a thousand other times, I use my chin to hold her ice pack in place.

"Ethan?"

"Yeah?"

"I'm really glad you're here."

I slide her ice pack out of place for just long enough to leave a lingering kiss on her forehead.

"I don't want to be anywhere else."

CHAPTER 26
ENOUGH IS ENOUGH.
RIGHT?

MAGGIE

mine - Kelly Clarkson

"Have a seat. She'll be with you in a few minutes."

"Thanks." I nod to the receptionist in Gwen's office and then sink into a semi-uncomfortable chair in the waiting room.

I called first thing Monday morning to book a therapy session because my weekend had been so intense. I haven't seen Gwen since before I left for Paris. I've been neglecting my sessions, and it's fucking showing. The panic attacks have been coming on more frequently than they used to.

The receptionist booked an appointment for me, but it's not for another six weeks. But she called me back Monday afternoon saying she had a cancellation for Wednesday.

So here I am.

I woke up late Sunday morning still wrapped up in Ethan's arms. Actually, I was practically on top of him. My head was on his chest, one arm slung over his stomach, and one leg wedged between his.

My ice pack was abandoned on the far side of the bed. My migraine was gone.

Again, I found myself not wanting to move and break the moment. I just laid there, running the previous night on a loop in my head.

The thing is, I heard Ethan and Peter talking. I'd been sound asleep, but their low voices woke me—I know they were trying not to, and they were doing the best they could. It's just that I was feeling hyper alert to any kinds of sounds, needing sleep, but not wanting to miss any updates.

She's enough.

She's everything.

I'd be a stone cold liar if I said that shit didn't stop my heart and bring tears to my eyes.

The only thing that kept me from sitting up and talking to him was the look on his face the night we broke up. I just don't want either of us to go through that again.

I've never been a person who puts enough stock in people to let them break my heart. I have a tough exterior and more than enough resilience. I've dated plenty of guys —some even for months or over a year—and not been horribly broken hearted when we broke up. Something Nick taught me from a young age was to have enough respect for myself to know when a relationship wasn't serving me. He told me that when it wasn't enriching my life or the partner in question wasn't sufficiently—even exuberantly—supporting my goals, it was time to cut ties. He said this philosophy should apply to *all* relationships...not just romantic ones.

At this point in my life, I can say with certainty that my heart has only been broken twice. The first was the day my brother died. The second was the day Ethan and I broke up.

I know people have their hearts broken far more often

than mine has been. I know people go through far worse things than I have. I grew up with a roof over my head, food in the fridge, and a stable home life. I have plenty of friends who have experienced horrible tragedies.

Knowing how much pain I was in after both of my heartbreaks, I can't help but wonder how many times a heart can be broken before it's just irreparable.

Kate managed to survive her parents' divorce, her mother's move across the country and subsequent abandonment, and the death of her spouse. And that's just the stuff I *know* about. But she's doing okay now. She's been to therapy and worked through her issues, and she's *happy* with Liam.

So I know it's possible.

It's why I'm sitting in this room right now.

When I heard Ethan tell Peter that we would never get married, followed by everything else he said...I swear I felt a piece of my cracked heart stitch back together.

Maybe we *can* fix it.

I just don't know how. And after what Ethan said about me not even talking to him or trying to work it out...it seems like I need to work on my communication skills.

"Maggie!" Gwen's voice brings me back to the present. "It's good to see you!" She's smiling at me and motioning me to follow her into your office.

"Hey...it's good to see you, too."

"It's been a while," she comments after she closes the door.

"Yeah...I was in Paris for a few months."

"Right, I remember."

I settle onto the couch and watch her gather my chart, her notebook, and a pen, then head over to her chair.

"The last time we talked, you were about to leave for Paris. That was..." She trails off as she flips to the last page in my file. "...August. You and Ethan had broken up, and we talked about finding things you could control." She looks up at me and smiles gently. "So how are you feeling today? What's going on these days?"

I take a deep breath and blow it out, letting my cheeks puff out with the action.

And then I dive into the last year of my life. I try to give her the too-long-didn't-read version so we don't spend the entire fifty minutes rehashing events and miss the time to create an action plan.

I rush through Paris and spend more time talking about how Ethan and I are working together *and* living in the same building. I tell her about yelling at him and him taking care of me. And then how he took care of me *again* after we had a real talk about our breakup. And of course, I tell her about Marv's heart attack.

"Is that triggering you at all after Nick's death?" Gwen asks gently.

"Yes. Fuck, yes."

She nods. "That makes sense. Marv is very important to you...he's like family. And he experienced a similar health event."

"He's going to be fine, though," I say emphatically.

"I'm very glad to hear that."

"I...I *need* him to be fine."

She tilts her head. "I'm sure his medical team is doing everything in their power to help him make a strong recovery."

"They better be," I grumble.

That makes her smile a little bit as she asks if I've been able to see him.

"I saw him after surgery, but he was still coming out of

anesthesia. Ethan took me back over there on Sunday to see how he was doing."

She blinks before writing something down and asking her next question. "And how was he on Sunday?"

"He was awake. Coherent. Doing well, given the circumstances. He made arrangements for Kelsie to lead the team for now, which makes sense, although I was...disgruntled at first."

"Why is that?"

"Because Marv is *my* mentor. I want to be in charge."

"And why do you think he chose Kelsie over you in this instance?"

I roll my eyes. "I don't have to *think* about why. He told me flat out."

Gwen raises a perfectly shaped eyebrow instead of asking the obvious question.

"He said that Kelsie has seniority—she's been there longer than I have."

Gwen blinks at me meaningfully.

I let out a groan. "*Fine*, he also said that this project is already hard enough for me, having to work with Ethan. He didn't want me to take on additional stress."

"Yes, that makes sense," she says with an authoritative nod. "It sounds like Marv is trying to look out for you."

I look down at my nails. I've never been one to get manicures or paint my nails, so they're bare and filed into an almond shape. "I suppose you're right."

"Are you feeling a bit better about Marv and his medical state since seeing him again?"

"Yeah...for the most part. I've talked to him every day. He should be released tomorrow, actually."

"Excellent," she says. "Then I'd like to go back to Ethan, if that's okay with you."

I take a deep breath. "Sure."

She pauses, probably waiting to see if I'll change my mind. "You said he drove you to the hospital when Marv's wife called with the news."

"Yeah."

"You were together when Marv's wife called?"

"Yeah…it was while we were talking about our breakup."

She nods. "And you let him drive you."

I shrug. "Yeah, I did."

"Why is that?"

I shake my head and look back at my nails. I note that they could use a little grooming. They're getting longer than I prefer.

"I guess…it was just easier."

"Easier than?"

"Than leaving his apartment and going back to mine to get my car keys. Than driving myself when I was so frazzled."

One of my nails has a tiny chip in it, and I wonder how that happened. I run another finger over it to test the sharpness.

"Maggie?"

My eyes snap to hers.

"You're dissociating."

"What?" I frown.

"You usually pick at your nails when you're hoping to distance yourself from whatever you're talking about."

My wide eyes fly back to my nails, and then I shove my hands under my thighs.

Gwen's eyebrows are drawn together as she watches me. "Did you know you do that?"

"No."

She nods. "What is it that you don't want to talk about?"

I look up to meet her eyes.

The truth is, I think she's right. I think I'm trying to remove myself from this story because talking about Marv's heart attack is painful, and Ethan's part in the evening makes it complicated.

The real truth is that I wanted Ethan to come to the hospital with me. He was with me all through Nick's death and afterward. While he annoyed me sometimes back then, I know his hovering was out of love and concern. Looking back on it, I was just angry at everything and everyone. Ethan was an easy scapegoat for my rage. I don't even think he took it personally. He just kept doing what he was doing.

Of course I wanted him there. He *knows* me.

I didn't just *want* him there...I *needed* him.

I just don't want to admit it out loud. I know I have to, though, so I tell Gwen.

She writes something down and then looks up to the ceiling, like she's thinking about something.

"When you say you 'needed' Ethan...what did you need from him?"

I have to think about that for a moment, trying to figure out how to put it into words.

"I needed someone who knew about Nick. I needed someone who knows my history with Marv. Someone who would be supportive and kind."

"But that person didn't *have* to be Ethan, did it? Or is he the only person?"

I search my brain for someone else who could have filled that role. Kate would come the closest, but I'm not sure she really knows how big of a role Marv has played in my life.

"I think Ethan's the only one."

"Okay. And if you weren't with him when that call came in...would you have called him?"

The silence is...something. I chew on my lip while I think about it.

"I—I don't know."

Gwen nods. "All right, that question may not be totally fair anyway. It's hard to tell what we might do in a hypothetical situation." She adjusts her seated position, crossing her legs the other way. "Let's phrase it this way instead: were you *glad* Ethan was with you?"

"Yes."

"And did you want him to leave at any point during the evening?"

"No," I say, shaking my head. "He stayed all night, actually. He drove me home and took care of me when I started getting another migraine."

I paused to think about the conversation we had in bed.

"I asked why he was there."

"And what did he say?"

"That he was still in love with me."

"He's told you that before."

"Yes. And I asked why he wasn't touching me—not in a sexual way or anything. Just...he wasn't cuddling me. Or rubbing my neck like he did the time before."

"And what did he say to that?"

"He said I know where he stands...but he doesn't know where I stand."

"Ahh," Gwen says, nodding and writing something else down. When she meets my gaze, it's pointed. "You know what my next question is."

I do know.

Where do you stand with him?

I chew my lip and start rubbing my finger over that chip in my nail again, my eyes wandering.

"Maggie."

I look back at her.

"Look at me. And just tell me how you feel. You know I'm not going to judge you. I'm asking because I think you know the answer, and you're afraid to say it out loud."

Tears obscure my vision, stinging my eyes.

I manage to nod.

Gwen closes my chart and rests her forearms on top of it, leaning toward me.

"Without thinking about all the complicated reasons you broke up, do you want to get back together with Ethan?"

A tear escapes my eye as I nod.

Of course I do.

I love him.

I always have.

"Then what's stopping you?"

"I-I'm afraid it w-will end the same w-way," I manage to squeak out.

"But he claims it won't?"

I nod again.

She's quiet for a moment, letting me get tissues out of the box and try to pull myself together.

"How can I possibly know it won't end that way? Or with him resenting me for not marrying him?"

Her response is remarkably close to the response Ethan gave Peter. So close, it's alarming.

"You don't, Maggie. You can't know that with any certainty. There are no guarantees, and you know it."

I dab my face with a tissue and blow my nose, then grab more from the box.

I wonder if the price of tissues is built into the session price.

I'll bet they have a line item in their budget for tissues.

Goddamnit, I'm dissociating.

"You'll never know what will happen with Ethan unless

you try again. I would never tell you what to do. But I will pose this question: if Ethan is still in love with you—and you're still in love with him..." She trails off, causing me to look up at her. I realize she's asking me the question.

I nod.

"If the two of you love each other, and you were happy together for so many years...how can you be so sure that it would end the same way? If the two of you set new, clear boundaries and *then* get back together, why do you think you'll get the same outcome?"

"Why wouldn't it?"

She shakes her head. "Maggie, I think you're scared, and I think that's totally valid. It's a risk getting back together with Ethan. But the potential for reward is also there."

I dab at new tears with my tissues.

"Again, I'm not trying to tell you what to do here, but I want you to consider both sides of the argument."

Gwen puts her notes and pen on the coffee table between us. It seems to break down a barrier between the two of us. Like she wants me to know she's not speaking to me strictly as a therapist anymore.

"Falling in love...being in a relationship...it's always a leap of faith. You're hoping your partner catches you. And it seems like Ethan dropped you at one point. But it also seems like he's trying to make sure he never lets that happen again. The thing is...it sounds like you dropped him, too. So the thing you can control here," she says, gesturing to me. "Is whether or not you'll try to catch him again."

CHAPTER 27
GOING TO BE COMMITTED

MAGGIE

Northern Attitude (with Hozier) - Noah Kahan, Hozier
August

I've never liked cemeteries.

I can't claim it's because they're creepy, or that it freaks me out that we leave our rotting corpses in the ground as a matter of standard practice, though I'd be lying if I said neither of those things also bother me.

No, the thing I don't like about them is they're just another piece of the capitalism puzzle. Even in death, you cannot escape the cost of living.

But I'm here anyway, for reasons I'm not even sure I can explain.

After I talked to Gwen about my weekend, I started thinking hard about myself and what I'm holding back from. I've spent so much of my life focused on my career—not taking much time to stop and appreciate what's around me.

Nick used to tell me I was going to die without any fun memories, but he was wrong. (And also frankly, a hypocrite.

He was on the fast track to become CFO of the financial advising firm he worked for.)

I'd had my friends and family to lean on, but for all intents and purposes, I was riding the high of success for years.

I was—and still am—able to tolerate the twatwaffling suck-ups at work because I know damn well I'm better than them, and I work harder, too. I love my job.

Meeting Ethan was the icing on my cake. He supported my ambitious goals and never once made me feel bad for working late or bringing work home with me. His job requires extra hours sometimes, too. And it's not like we had kids to look after.

I find myself wondering frequently what Nick would say if he were here.

Which is why I'm standing in front of his grave, staring a hole in the headstone on a random Saturday.

There are fresh flowers in the little cup holder—someone must have been here in the last day or two. Probably my mom or Kate. I'm honestly not sure if my siblings ever come visit.

'Visit' seems like a strange word for standing in front of a gravestone.

"Are you really here?" I whisper.

I'm met with silence and a profound feeling of embarrassment.

I drop my head into my hand and rub my forehead. "Oh my god, what am I doing?"

The question holds more weight than I intend.

What am I doing standing here talking to my dead brother?

What am I doing with Ethan?

What am I doing with Mom?

What am I doing with my freaking life?

I plop down next to the headstone, to the left of his body, careful not to sit on his neighbor.

"Hey, Jack. Rita," I say to them. "Someone brought you pretty flowers, I see."

Never ever ever tell anyone you're talking to headstones. Nick's voice rings clear as a bell in my mind.

"Honestly, I think talking to dead people in cemeteries is the least of my problems these days."

Remember on Grey's Anatomy when Izzy had a brain tumor, and she saw her dead fiancé?

"You're a dick, and that's unfair. You can't put shit like that in my head. I already get migraines."

I'm just saying your problems aren't nearly as bad as a potentially inoperable brain tumor.

"You know a lot about this show you claim to have not liked."

Kate liked it. I like Kate.

"I know you did, Nick," I say, my voice softer than it had been when I was giving him shit about *Grey's Anatomy*.

I reach out and adjust the flowers so the smaller ones are in the front.

"Gwen would have me committed if she knew I was talking to a headstone."

I tip my head back toward the sun and take a few deep, cleansing breaths.

The fact that my brother only lives inside my head now is a mindfuck I still can't wrap my brain around. I know it's not *only* my head—he lives in Kate's head and my whole families' heads. I know he's not forgotten.

It's just that sometimes I feel so lost—so adrift—that I wish I could throw myself at his feet and sob. It's something I never would have done before he died, but when I'm feeling particularly lonely, it's what I want now. I need his steady presence. His quiet support.

I need to know he's *somewhere.*

I've always wondered why people visit cemeteries because they've never felt particularly comforting to me. But as I sit here now on the grass beside his final resting place, I feel comfort. I feel like there's still a place I can go to be with him. I think I get it now. I get why people bring flowers and polish the stones.

Yet another way I'm finding common ground with my mother.

"I had a heart-to-heart with Mom."

Yeah?

"Yeah..." I sigh. "I told her how I feel about the way they treat me. She seemed receptive. She cried, if you can believe it."

Mom cries sometimes.

"Not often. A lot more since you died, though."

My brain can't conjure a response for that.

"I need you to tell me what to do about Ethan," I tell Nick's headstone.

You already know what to do. You're just too chicken-shit to do it.

"You know, you could pull a punch every once in a while."

Why would I do that? You can take it.

I glare at his headstone before getting up and brushing my butt off.

"Thanks for the chat, jerk."

Anytime, Mags.

"I'm on my way to Mom's. I'm going to tell her about that time you smoked pot in high school."

You wouldn't dare.

I cackle as I turn to walk away. "Like you could stop me."

"Hello, hello," I call as I walk through the door to my parents' house.

"Hey, pumpkin!"

Dad's voice is coming directly to my left. He's already in the kids' playroom.

I head toward him with a big smile on my face. He wraps me into a hug and kisses the top of my head.

"How's your day going?"

"Good. You?"

"Better now."

"Hi, sweetheart," Mom says as she sweeps into the room, wrapping her lithe arms around my shoulders and kissing my cheek.

Things have been a lot better with my parents since we had our chat recently. Especially Mom. As difficult as that conversation was, I'm very glad we had it.

And yes...even though the conversation with Ethan was very difficult, I'm glad we had that one as well.

"What's in the bag?" Mom asks.

"I stopped by the store and picked up the fabric for the new curtains." I hold up the bag for her to take.

"Oh, thank you so much," she says, taking the bag and peeking inside.

"I got some extra, just in case."

"Good idea. How much do I owe you?"

"I'd love a glass of wine."

She looks up at me with pursed lips. "Margaret, we're retired, but that doesn't mean we can't buy fabric for curtains."

"I know." I shrug. "Think of it as partial repayment for all those college courses you paid for."

Dad laughs loudly. "We're going to need a few more yards of fabric, pumpkin."

"Matthew!" Mom scolds, softly hitting him in the shoulder. "Don't even joke about that. We would never ask any of our kids to repay us for college."

Dad winks at me.

I stick out my tongue at him.

"Well, I think the only thing left to do in here, really, is install the new light switches, hang the chandelier, and make the curtains. I think I've chosen the fabric for the little reading nook," Mom says.

We decided to make a tent-like thing in one corner—an area where the older kids can lounge and read (or perhaps more realistically, play games on their screens) away from the adults. Mom is making it instead of buying something to save cash, and then she's going to make big pillows to go inside of it.

The kids are going to love it.

Also, I might hide in that tent when I need a break from the family on holidays.

(Don't tell my mom.)

"What are you up to tonight, Maggie?" Mom asks.

"Nothing, really. I was at the cemetery, and then I thought I'd drop the fabric by. I can stay to install those light switches, if you want. Maybe get that chandelier hung if we have time."

"That would be great," Dad says. "I'd love some help."

"Could you stay for dinner?"

"Sure."

"Wonderful," my mom says with a broad smile. It lights

up her whole face and shows the crows feet around her eyes. Still gorgeous. Mom's always been gorgeous.

"We're having caprese chicken salad, if that's all right with you."

My eyebrows shoot to my hairline. "Are you kidding? That sounds amazing."

"Oh, good! I'm trying to make the most of the garden before we need to harvest."

"Lucky me."

"All right, I'm going to get that going while you two work in here." Mom squeezes my arm and heads toward the kitchen.

"Okay, pumpkin, let's tackle this so we have time for a drink before dinner," Dad says.

"Speaking my language."

He laughs and then pulls me in for a side hug before gathering all the materials we'll need. We get the light switches installed and have enough time to take down the existing ceiling light before dinner, but not to hang the new chandelier. We have a game plan though. I'll be back tomorrow afternoon.

Dinner is delicious, as always. Mom's a great cook. Dad makes a joke about her being able to cook, despite being a Brit, and she throws her napkin at him. She throws a barb back about the Irish not being much better.

Dad tells stories from my childhood—mostly ones about my siblings...things I might only remember because of the sheer number of times I've heard them told over the years. The line between my actual memories and the memories of the retellings having been too blurred.

Mom tells me about Nick and me as kids. How he used to take care of me and never stopped paying attention to me, even when he became a hormonal teenager with dates lined up. How he was probably the best of all of us.

Dad lightens the mood by suggesting they get a dog—something Mom has never wanted because she had enough living beings to take care of.

Mom tells him *he* can get a dog, provided she never has to take care of it.

He says she'll fall in love with a dog and end up taking care of it anyway.

She groans because she knows he's right. So she vetoes the dog idea.

Through it all, I sit at the table, holding my glass of wine, smiling with and laughing at them.

This is what I've always wanted. Minus the legal paperwork of a wedding, of course.

This easy banter and inside jokes. The way they know each other so well—inside and out...the good, the bad, and the ugly. And they *still* want to be together after all these years.

It's what Ethan and I had before he proposed.

Could we have that again? Could we pick up where we left off? Or do we have to start over?

As if he knows I'm thinking of him, my watch pings with a text from him.

I frown at the tiny screen.

Ethan: Hey. I was just thinking about you. Wanted to see how you were doing.

He was thinking of me.

My stupid heart lurches, and I fight the smile trying to split my face.

"Everything okay?" Mom asks.

I dismiss the text on my watch and meet my mom's eyes.

"Yep. Everything's fine."

Her eyes narrow. "Anyone interesting?"

I pick up my wineglass and cross my arms over my chest. I want to say something, but I can't find the words. Saying "no" isn't really true. But if I say "yes," she'll want further details, and I just don't know what to say. So I shrug instead.

My mom gets a knowing look in her eye.

She's watched seven children lie to her face over the past forty-some-odd years. She knows when we're being stupid or dishonest or even downright evil.

"You don't have to tell me, Maggie," she says with a sigh. "Truthfully, I'm being nosy because I want to hear if you've talked to Ethan at all."

Mom always knows. You should know better than to think you can hide anything from her.

Shut up, Nick.

Just tell her. It's a show of good faith after your last conversation.

Stop it, or I'll tell Dad about the time you scratched his truck and lied about it.

Maggie, stop being stubborn.

I rub my forehead and avoid their gazes when I admit he texted me. And then I admit that we talked. But that we were interrupted by Marv's heart attack, which quickly changes the conversation from interest in the Ethan saga to concern for Marv.

They ask how he's doing and if I've talked to him. I tell them everything I know and how he was when I visited him at home on Wednesday.

When my mom is satisfied that Marv is on the mend and will make a full recovery, she pivots hard back to Ethan.

"So?"

I blink at her. "So what?"

The amused expression melts off her face. "Margaret Helen, don't sass me right now."

I roll my lips between my teeth to keep from sassing her further.

"You know very well what I'm asking."

"Mom, I just don't know," I admit with a sigh.

Apparently I'm admitting a lot of things tonight.

"What's tripping you up, pumpkin?" Dad asks.

With a groan, I set my elbows on the table and give them the Cliffs Notes on our conversation.

"It's okay to be scared," Dad says.

"Yeah, that's what my therapist says," I grumble.

"You're seeing a therapist?" my mom asks.

Shit, I forgot I didn't tell them about that.

It's okay, Maggie. You don't give them enough credit.

"Um..." I clear my throat and tuck my hair behind my ears. "Yeah. Kate recommended I see the person she saw after Nick died."

They're both quiet for a moment, and I start dying a little bit inside.

I shouldn't have said anything.

Give it a second.

You give it a second.

You're the most stubborn person I know.

You don't know anyone anymore, you're dead.

Harsh.

But not wrong.

"That's wonderful, sweetheart," Mom finally says.

I blink at her a few times. "It is?"

"Of course. I've been seeing a therapist since Nick died."

I can feel my jaw drop. "Seriously?"

"Yes. It's traumatic to lose a child."

"Well, I…" I scoff. "Yes, I understand that, but you never said you were talking to a therapist."

She shrugs. "I didn't want to worry any of you."

Do I even know her at all?

Don't look at me, I feel like I don't know her either right now.

Do you think we ever really know our parents?

Do we ever really know anyone?

Okay, that's not helpful.

You asked.

That's not what I—

"It's your life, pumpkin," my dad interrupts my internal argument with Nick. "You can do whatever you feel is best for you, and we'll support that decision."

"Thanks, Dad."

I offer him an appreciative smile and then realize it's nearly nine o'clock at night. They'll want to wind down and get ready for bed soon.

"I should get out of your hair. It's getting late."

I start picking up our dishes and carry them over to the kitchen. I help them get things cleaned up, and then I grab my purse and head for the front door, where both of them hug me goodbye and make a point of letting me know they're excited to see me again tomorrow.

When I get to the car, I take my phone out and look at Ethan's text.

As I read it again, I'm mildly surprised by the fact that I *want* to text him back. I *want* to talk to him.

And that realization is both terrifying and comforting.

CHAPTER 28
THE FINER POINTS OF
HALLMARK MOVIES

ETHAN

The View Between Villages - Extended - Noah Kahan

"Did you text her?" Holly asks me.

I scrape a hand down my face.

"Yes, I texted her."

At least an hour ago.

"She hasn't responded?"

"No."

"Not *yet*," she corrects.

I let my head fall against the back of the couch with a sigh.

"I don't know. She could be out with someone for all I know. That would be my luck."

Holly's quiet for a moment before asking, "You really think so?"

"I just...I don't know. Things are different between us. She's more closed off now. And I get it. I get why. But it makes it harder for me to read her."

"You're not giving up, are you?" Holly's voice doesn't sound sad—it sounds angry.

"Fuck no," I reply.

"Okay, good." She blows out a breath. "I thought I was going to have to kick your ass."

I roll my eyes and laugh. "How would you ever reach me up here?"

"A short joke? Are you kidding me with this shit?"

I'm so glad my one date with Holly went completely wrong. That I fucked it up so badly. She's a great friend, and I really enjoy talking to her.

"Hey, babe," she says, her voice a little further away from the phone.

"Hey, gorgeous." I can hear the smile in Waiter Jake's voice as he greets her.

Yep, they started dating right after our one and only date. They seem obnoxiously happy. I've hung out with them a couple of times—dinner out with friends and whatnot. Jake shook my hand and thanked me for getting weird at dinner with Holly.

He's welcome.

I'm glad it's working out for them. They're very sweet together.

"Okay, so what's your game plan, then?"

"For what?" I ask, having completely lost the thread.

She heaves an exasperated sigh. "With *Maggie*. Are you going to text her again? Wait for her to respond? What are you doing?"

"Oh..." I rub the back of my neck with my free hand. "Is it psychotic to sit outside her door and wait for her to come home?"

"Yes," she says emphatically. "What's the matter with you, Ethan?"

"I wasn't really going to do it," I grumble.

Probably not, anyway.

"All right, so if she doesn't text you back tonight, what's the plan?"

"I'll stop by her place tomorrow. If she's not home, I'll leave a note on the door."

"I still can't get over the fact that you two live in the same building."

"I know. It's nuts."

"*And* she's an architect on your new building."

"She sure is."

"It's like the universe is trying to get you back together," Holly says, a dreamy sound in her voice.

"My life is a Hallmark movie?"

She gasps. "Oh, this would make a *great* Hallmark movie."

"Meh. Hallmark movies are too clean."

"What does that mean?"

"Not enough sex, Holly."

She lets out a bark of laughter. "Yeah, well make sure your condom stash is replenished for when you two finally figure this shit out."

I laugh. What I don't tell her is that Maggie has an IUD, and we hadn't used condoms for years when we broke up.

Of course, I don't know what she's been up to since then. Or if she still has the IUD.

Maybe I should pick up some condoms.

"Oh, tomorrow can I come pick up those tickets?" she asks.

I won two tickets to a musical in a work contest, and that's not really my thing. Also, I have no one to take to a musical.

"Yeah, absolutely. I'll be around."

Holly agrees to text before she leaves her place, and we say our goodbyes.

I grab a beer and put on a movie.

Maggie never returns my text.

THERE'S a persistent knocking on my door. It's rhythmic and mildly obnoxious.

It's obviously Holly.

She's endearing in a sometimes annoying way. She's fun. Maggie will like her when they finally meet.

I yank the door open without even looking through the peephole.

Her fist is still raised, and she isn't even looking at the door. She's dancing. Her fist hitting the door was clearly setting her beat.

When she realizes her fist isn't hitting the door anymore, she looks up and drops her arm.

"Hey!"

"What song was that you were tapping out on my door?"

"'Shake It Off' from *the* Taylor Alison Swift," she says, incredulous. "Duh."

"My apologies for not recognizing it." I open the door fully and gesture for her to come in.

"Did she text you back?"

I walk over to the table, where I left the tickets.

"No. She didn't," I say, handing her the envelope.

Her face falls, and it takes her a second to take the envelope from me.

"What the hell?" she says with a frown.

"She's had a hard week."

"Well...then she should be..." She looks around the living room and gestures obscurely toward it. "...here and seeking comfort."

"My life is not a Hallmark movie, Holls," I say, walking over to the couch and plopping onto one end. She follows me and sits on the other end.

"Well, I hope not because you said there isn't enough sex in Hallmark movies," she quips.

"There's not."

She narrows her eyes. "How often do you watch Hallmark movies?"

"I have sisters. I watch at least three every Christmas."

"Which one's your favorite?" she asks, her mouth quirking up into a smile.

"There was one with Kelly Kapowski from *Saved By the Bell*. I don't know what it was called, but she was hot in it."

Holly rolls her eyes.

"There was also one with Dolly Parton, and she's a fucking icon, so that one was cool."

"Okay, that's fair."

"The other standout for me is the one with Winnie Cooper from *The Wonder Years*. She's still hot, and she's almost fifty."

Holly gets out her phone and starts tapping away.

"Are you searching for these movies?"

"Duh."

I huff out a laugh as she starts scrolling.

"Oh my god," she gasps. "There's a list of the fifty best Hallmark Christmas movies."

"I'm not at all surprised by that."

"Have you seen *Christmas Comes Twice*?"

"I'm pretty sure that's the name of a porno."

Her startled gaze meets mine. "What did you say?"

"*Christmas Cums Twice*. Sounds like the title of a porn."

"Jesus, Ethan. It's a Hallmark movie starring Tamera Mowry. You know...from *Sister Sister*?"

"Not sure that show was marketed to little boys."

"Maybe not, but you have sisters."

I shrug. "Name sounds familiar, but I don't think I've ever seen it. The porn, though? Probably."

"Wait a minute, how do you even know about *The Wonder Years*? Isn't that a little old for you?"

"Yeah, but all that shit eventually started streaming, and I was a horny teenager."

"Gross."

"I don't know what to tell you, Holls." I set my feet up on the coffee table and stretch my arms out over the back of the couch. "Also the actress who played Winnie Cooper is actually a fucking genius in real life and that makes her even hotter. She writes children's books about math. I've bought them for my nieces."

Holly's head tilts to the side. "Huh."

"What?"

"You know, for all of the discussions we've had about marriage, we've never talked about kids."

I raise my eyebrows at her. "Is there a question in there somewhere?"

"Do you want kids?"

"Yeah...I do."

She pauses, seemingly considering her next question. "Does Maggie?"

"Yeah. She does. At least two."

"She just doesn't want to get married?"

"Nope."

"Oh. Well, families all look different. Families are made, not born."

That last part makes me look up at her.

Families are made, not born.

"Hmm. I like that."

"It's true," she says, shrugging. "You know that quote 'blood is thicker than water?'"

I nod.

"Well it's not actually that. The context is completely different. The actual quote is 'the blood of the covenant is thicker than the water of the womb'. It implies that chosen bonds—the ones with your friends and chosen family—are stronger than the bonds you have with your blood relatives because you *chose* them."

I stare off into space behind her.

Holy shit.

That's what Maggie was trying to tell me the night she broke up with me.

*You **are** my family.*

"What?" Holly asks.

My eyes focus on her again. "What?"

"You said something."

"Did I say that out loud?"

"You said something about family."

I plant my feet on the floor and my elbows on my knees. "The night Maggie broke up with me, she tried to tell me she already considered me family—without a ring or a promise of a wedding. She already felt that way about me."

Holly is silent while I continue to process Maggie's year-old words.

"Fuck." I scrub my hands down my face. "Fuck, fuck, fuck."

"If she felt that way last year, she still feels that way, Ethan. Chosen family is still family to her."

"Yeah, but she didn't text me back last night."

She draws in a breath, but doesn't say anything, so I look over at her.

"You already have a plan to talk to her today. You should

do that." She glances down at her phone. "In fact, I have to get going."

She stands up.

"Talk to her. *Today.*"

"Yeah, okay."

I get up and follow her to the door.

"Text me later and let me know what's going on."

"Yeah, yeah," I say, my brain already on Maggie and what I want to say to her today.

I open the door and before she heads out, she turns toward me and gives me a hug, squeezing hard. "I'll talk to you later."

"Okay."

She lets go and heads toward the door, but stops short suddenly.

When I look up to see why, I see Maggie's face, drained of color, staring at Holly.

"Hi..." Holly says.

Maggie blinks a few times and then shakes her head. She plasters on a polite smile and sticks out her hand. "Hi...I didn't mean to interrupt. I'm Maggie."

A huge smile stretches across Holly's face, and she clasps Maggie's hand. "Oh, it's so nice to meet you. I'm Holly."

Maggie throws me a quick glance before taking a step back. Her whole body is tense, and I can tell she's about to bolt.

"Mags—"

"No, sorry I should have called first. I have somewhere to be, so I'll just text you later. It was nice to meet you, Holly."

She's turning and heading toward the elevator before my brain even has time to catch up.

Something hits my shoulder, but I'm still looking at Maggie. I assume it was Holly's hand.

"*Ethan.*"

Her urgent whisper-shout gets my feet moving.

"Maggie, wait." I run down the hall after her, but she doesn't so much as slow her steps. If anything, she speeds up. I catch up with her just before she reaches the door to the stairwell, which she undoubtedly wanted to take instead of waiting for the elevator.

"Stop, Maggie."

She doesn't show any signs of hearing me, so I jump in front of her.

She runs straight into me, her arms coming up to cushion the impact, and I hold her shoulders to steady her.

"Ethan, I have plans, I need to go."

"No."

She finally meets my eye, and I watch the anger flare to life.

"*No?*" she says. "What the fuck do you mean *no*?"

With a heavy sigh, I bend down, pick her up, throw her over my shoulder, and begin the walk back to my apartment.

"I mean *no*, you're not leaving. *No*, you can't run away. You clearly came to talk to me about something, and I want to hear what it is."

She pounds on my lower back with her fists. "Goddammit, Ethan. Put me down."

"*No*." I throw her word back in her face. Er...her feet. Or technically her ass, since it's right next to my head. If we were still together, I'd smack it for emphasis, but I feel like picking her up like a caveman is probably crossing the line enough for today.

Holly is standing outside my apartment door, staring at us with wide eyes.

"Ethan, I never said *barbarian* was a good idea."

I step into my apartment and kick the door closed behind me.

"Bye, Holly," I call over my shoulder.

When I hear the door slam behind me, I put Maggie down.

As I stand to my full height, I see her in all her glory. She's no longer pale, but red-faced from being upside down. Her hair is wild. Her expression is angry. No...furious.

"What the *fuck*, Ethan!?" she yells.

And I can't stop the smile that stretches across my face.

CHAPTER 29
BACKED UP AGAINST A WALL (IN A GOOD WAY)

MAGGIE

this is me trying - Taylor Swift

"Why are you smiling?" I demand. My harsh tone does nothing to the obnoxious smile on his stupid, handsome face.

"Because you're here to talk to me."

I'm honestly not sure if I've ever been this angry with Ethan. I'm downright furious.

First, he tells me he's still in love with me and wants to get back together. He texted me last night to ask how I was doing, and no, I didn't respond, but that was only because I was so confused about my feelings.

I wanted to text him back. I really did. I thought about it the whole way home and then I *got* home and even started typing out the message. But then I freaked myself out and deleted it. And then I had another glass of wine and called Kate.

We talked for about an hour in a very circular way. I told her I wanted to text Ethan, and she told me all the reasons she thought it was a good idea.

Then I told her I *didn't* want to text Ethan, and she told me all the reasons she thought *that* was a good idea.

And then I got stuck and didn't know what to do. Feelings have never really been my strong suit, so debating them for a full hour wiped me out, and at that point—when I was feeling emotional and confused and warm with wine—it seemed like a really bad idea to text him.

Stupid fucking feelings!

So I decided I'd stop by this morning to talk some things out before I went over to my mom's.

And then this gorgeous blonde comes waltzing out of his apartment after giving him a hug.

A *tight* hug. Full chest-on-chest.

The torrent of emotions that punched me straight in the sternum were far too much to handle. My immediate reaction was humiliation. That I came up here to talk to him, and he'd been letting out his date from the night before. I'd been feeling conflicted in my apartment, and he'd been fucking a hot blonde in his.

That's when the sadness hit me.

He's sleeping with someone else. I'm too late.

And that's when the anger hit me.

*He's sleeping with someone else **while** he's trying to convince me to get back together with him.*

Which is when the urge to get the fuck out of there hit me, and I turned on my heel to leave.

And that brings me to the *second* reason I'm mad at Ethan. I'd *almost* made it to the stairwell when he picked me up and fucking threw me over his shoulder like a caveman.

"What the hell is the matter with you?"

"Do you want some coffee?" He ignores my question and sidesteps me to head to the kitchen. He knows damn well my answer to that question is always yes.

"*Ethan.*" I watch him pour coffee and then walk back over to me. He holds the mug out, which I take, of course, albeit begrudgingly.

"I'm glad you're here, Mags."

I can feel my mouth drop open.

"What? You were *just* letting some woman out of your apartment!"

"Holly, yes." He nods once.

I glare at him over the top of my coffee mug as I gulp as quickly as my body will allow.

"You are *infuriating*, Ethan."

"Why do you say that?"

"Why are you *asking* that?"

He's so even-keeled, and it's pissing me off even more.

"Okay, let's back up," he says, holding his hands out in surrender. "I texted you last night."

I grind my molars together to keep from snapping at him. He's not talking about the parts I want to talk about.

"Yes," I admit, teeth still clenched.

"So you did see it?"

I close my eyes and take a deep breath to try and relax. I unclench my teeth and force my jaw to loosen up.

"Yes. I did. I didn't respond because I...I had...things."

"Things?" he asks, eyebrows raised.

"Yes, *things.*" I start pacing around because I can't stand still while he looks at me the way he's looking at me right now. Like he knows something I don't. Like that *thing* is what I'm going to do about the remaining feelings between us. "Things I needed to think about. And since I didn't respond, I figured I'd come up here and talk to you this morning before I head over to my parents' house."

"How are they doing?"

I stop pacing to look at him. I forgot for a moment that

they were his family for a while, too. He's asking a genuine question.

"They're good." My voice is quieter than it's been since I entered this apartment. Higher, too.

"Good," he says. "I've been thinking about them."

I blink a few times to force my stupid eyes to stop stinging.

"Is tonight the family dinner?"

I have to clear my throat before I can talk again.

Stupid fucking feelings.

"Um yeah. I'm going over early to help them hang a chandelier."

"That's nice."

A lot of my anger has drained away in the last couple of minutes and now I feel...sad.

Sad that I've missed my chance with Ethan.

And the idea that I'm too late makes me even sadder because of the simple fact that I'm sad. I was conflicted until I realized that he was moving on and now I'm *devastated*.

I take a deep breath and let it out slowly.

This is a truly shitty time to have this realization. To *finally* figure out that I want to try again with Ethan.

"Yeah...I'm helping them redecorate that room to the left of the front door. It's going to be the kids' playroom. It's mostly finished. We just need the chandelier and the curtains."

I swallow against my dry throat and catch him looking at me with curiosity in his eyes.

"Look, I'm—I'm sorry I yelled at you. That was uncalled for. And I should have called first," I say, setting the coffee mug on the dining room table. "Holly seems great. She's really pretty." Offering him a small smile, I head toward his door. "I'm sure we'll talk soon."

"Nuh-uh," I hear Ethan say from behind me. "No, you don't." Suddenly, he's in front of me again, holding my upper arms and leaning down to make eye contact with me.

"We got sidetracked again. So let's back up again. Holly? She's my friend. And *only* my friend. I met her while I was Christmas shopping—she was working in the store. She does it part time for extra cash. She helped me pick out Christmas presents for my nieces and nephews, and at the end, she gave me her number."

I open my mouth to tell him it's none of my business, but he doesn't stop long enough for me to get a word out.

"When I walked out of the store, I was heading back to my car, and I saw you. I saw your hair, and I heard your laugh. I chased you through the courtyard, Maggie, but it was dark, and I lost you. I heard you one more time...over in the parking lot, but I couldn't see you. I was fucking devastated."

His grip on my arms loosens, and he stands a little straighter.

"A couple of weeks later, I was tipsy and sad. I texted her, and we eventually went out on a date, which I ruined in a *spectacular* fashion because I couldn't stop thinking about *you*. We ended up talking about you and agreeing that she and I were better off as friends. And then I hooked her up with the waiter, who'd been checking her out the entire evening. His name is Jake, and she's been with him ever since."

"Oh..."

That's the only thing I can manage. One simple, barely-there word.

"I talked to her on the phone last night, and she asked if she could come over and pick up tickets to a musical that I won at work, but won't be using. That's why she was here this morning. She stopped by. We talked for a few minutes. I gave her the tickets. She was leaving."

My annoying, hopeful heart kicks into high gear.

He's not dating her. He didn't sleep with her last night.

I take a moment to check in with my stupid fucking feelings to see where I stand.

I'm glad he's not with her.

The jealousy is gone.

I feel relieved that I haven't missed my chance.

I press a hand into my chest and let out a long breath.

One of Ethan's hands releases one of my arms, his fingertips grasping my chin instead. He tilts my head up and looks deep into my eyes.

"Maggie, why are you here?"

It's a question I've asked him many times, and now that the tables have turned, my mouth has suddenly gone very dry.

"I-I wanted to talk to you."

"About what?"

I swallow hard and blink compulsively against the tears threatening to pour down my cheeks.

"About me and you," I whisper.

The relief in his eyes is palpable. It's a tangible thing I can feel in my own soul. His body practically vibrates as he takes a step closer, his hand sliding down my arm until his fingers interlace with mine.

"What about me and you?"

My mouth opens, but nothing comes out. I'm overwhelmed by being close to him like this. It's different than lying in bed with him when I'm in pain and vulnerable. We're both alert and cognizant. The things I say now can't be blamed on pain or medicine or a traumatic life event.

He takes another step closer, leaving only a couple of

inches between my chest and his. The fingers holding my chin slide up my jaw and into my hair, brushing my curls back and off my shoulder. And suddenly his mouth is next to my ear, murmuring sweet words that leave devastating cracks in the walls I've erected between us.

"Tell me what you want, Maggie. I'll give you anything."

"I'm not...promising anything, okay?" I try to set the boundary, even knowing I'll probably cave in the long run. "But I want to talk to you more about us. About the possibility of there being an us again."

Ethan releases a ragged breath and touches his lips against the soft skin below my ear. He doesn't kiss it, but his lips are there just the same.

"That's the best news I've heard in years," he whispers.

"I didn't completely agree—" I try to interject.

"That's okay. I asked you to think about it. And you are. And I'll wait."

My chest fills with a familiar warm, fuzzy feeling. I release his hand and slide my palm up his torso until it's resting against his heart, beating steadily, maybe even a bit more quickly than usual.

His arm snakes around my waist, his fist bunching into my shirt.

"Maggie, I meant what I said...I won't fuck you until you're mine again. But please...may I *please* kiss you?"

I couldn't have faked my sharp intake of breath. This is all very overwhelming, even though I'm the one who came here to talk to him. He's so close...in perfect position, really. He could just take what he wants, but instead he's asking permission.

It's hot.

It's really fucking hot.

Ethan has a bit of a dominant streak. I'm not saying he's

an *actual* Dom—though yes, I did joke about it with him recently—but he tends to...take charge in sexual encounters. I've never been sad about it.

Although I *was* annoyed when he picked me up and carried me back to his apartment.

It was also...a little hot.

Anyway, now is not the time to examine why I found barbaric behavior hot. Now is the time for appreciating the gesture at hand.

He's *asking*.

I swallow hard—a gulp, really—and then try to speak.

"Yes."

I don't even get the full word out before his mouth is on mine.

It's not tentative, but he's not invading me either. It's sweet in a hot way. Panty-melting in an *I-haven't-kissed-you-in-a-year* kind of way. In some respects, it feels like a first kiss. A *first-time-in-a-long-time* kiss.

He doesn't bother keeping his lips closed. Ethan and Maggie are so far past that. No, his lips part immediately, capturing my bottom lip between them before switching to capture the top one. And then he methodically tastes every square inch of my lips.

At first, one hand stays in my hair, while the other remains fisted in my shirt at my back. But then his fist releases, and he slowly, slowly, slowly, trails his fingertips across my back, up the back of my arm, over my shoulder, leaving goose bumps in his wake until he's finally mirroring his other hand. He holds me in place, moving me this way and that so he can get whatever angle he wants.

It's all very lovely. And sweet. And hot enough that I'm turned on, but still conservative enough that it could be in a teen movie, which feels...appropriate. We *should* be taking this slow.

Right?

Right. We should.

This feels *good*. Like finding something I've been searching for. Like returning to a familiar place that I'd missed dearly and desperately needed to see again. To *feel* again.

But then his tongue teases at my top lip, and I don't want to hold back anymore.

This is not another teen movie, and I am not Janey Briggs. And I'm certainly not Laney Boggs.

So I open my mouth and let myself sink into him.

He responds greedily, stepping even closer, dropping a hand to my lower back and pulling me up against him.

His tongue brushes mine, and I swear every single nerve in my body lights up. The goose bumps from his hand have nothing on these. I'm a live wire and ready to jump in his arms.

I've missed him. *Fuck*, I've missed him.

I'm pretty sure it's the whimper that escapes my lips that triggers his growl, which escalates everything.

Before I know what's happening, I'm off the ground, in his arms, and up against the door. He's devouring my mouth in the most polite way possible.

I might be up against a door, his strong hands supporting my thighs, my legs wrapped around his waist, but somehow, nothing feels out of control. Things between us are heated, but not frenzied. We're rediscovering each other in a new way.

Ethan has me.

And maybe this time, he won't drop me.

We make out like teenagers for a few minutes before he

pulls back, leaving me pinned to the door, planting gentle kisses at the corners of my mouth, my cheeks, my brows, and finally, my forehead.

It's unbearably reverent.

I keep my eyes closed, trying to savor the moment.

Finally, he rubs his nose against mine and leaves one last kiss on my lips.

"Maggie…" he breathes. My hands are on his jaw, so I can feel him swallow, then clench his teeth.

We're both breathing heavily, swept up in this unexpected moment. So we stay there for a bit…him holding me up, thumbs brushing against my legs. Me, with my hands sinking into his hair and scratching against his scalp.

Finally, he speaks, and I'm almost startled by it. I can feel my shoulders tense up at the sound of his voice, even though his voice is low and quiet.

"My memories were not exaggerating."

I know what he means without further explanation. Things between us were always explosive—and they still are.

"Mine either," I sigh.

He squeezes my thighs and lifts me just a little bit, encouraging me to unwrap my legs, and then he slowly lets me down, my body sliding down his so I feel every single inch of him.

I watch the muscles in his cheek jump as his molars grind together, and he closes his eyes, all while his thumbs feather along my waist under the hem of my top.

"I know you have somewhere to be," he says eventually.

I nod, not wanting to actually say anything just yet. I'm not sure I have a lot of coherent words right now, anyway.

"I'm going to let you go…for now," he says. "But I'll text you later."

I nod again, managing only to whisper a simple, "Okay."

With a sharp exhale of resignation, he captures my mouth again before touching his lips to the sensitive spot below my ear and whispering one more thing that sends tingles down my spine. "And if you don't answer, I'm coming down there."

CHAPTER 30

HOLDING OUT HOPE
ETHAN

Somewhere Only We Know - Keane

Me: How was dinner with your parents?

It's nine o'clock, and I haven't heard anything from Maggie yet.

If nothing has changed, the Rafferty Sunday dinner starts around six o'clock. People trickle in starting around five, but dinner is served at six.

People usually hang out for a couple of hours. The people with younger kids are out by 7:30 so they can get the youngsters to bed before it gets too far past bedtime. Nick and Kate used to stay for cleanup duty, and because Nick was there, we usually stayed.

It was a good excuse to spend time with her family, but at the time, Maggie often used Nick as a buffer between her and her parents. Particularly her mom.

I didn't really get their strained relationship at the time —I just accepted it as a thing and didn't think it was my place to push her on it either way. I've had a lot of time to think in the past year though, and the more I look back on it, I can see how Maggie's views on marriage could have been a sticking point between them.

I hope they're working it out. I hope Maggie will trust me enough to talk to me about it.

I've got a beer in my hand and a documentary on the TV, and I'm trying not to stare at my phone. I texted her. She still has time to get back to me.

She knows I wasn't kidding about going down there to find her. I felt the shiver go down her spine.

I'll give her another thirty minutes, and then I'm going down to her floor. It's possible she's finishing cleanup duty or still driving home.

So I push my phone farther away from me on the couch and force myself to focus on the documentary. It's about a windshield factory a few hours south of here. Miles recommended it to me. It's really good. Fascinating. But I'm distracted anyway, tapping my phone screen to check the time every once in a while.

When my phone finally does make noise, it's not Maggie.

Rachel: We haven't had an update in a bit.

Another ding comes through before I even unlock the screen.

Abby: Rachel's right. What's going on?

Abby: You guys had that talk but we haven't heard anything since.

With a sigh, I start typing a response.

Me: We talked again this morning. She said she wants to talk more about us.

Me: Or, the possibility of us.

My phone starts dinging repeatedly as both of my sisters

start sending me gifs of people being excited. Rachel and Phoebe jumping up and down. Barney and Robin jumping on a bed with champagne spraying everywhere. Taylor Swift cheering at what appears to be an awards show. Dogs jumping around. Michael and Dwight raising the roof in the whitest way possible.

It's impossible to get a word in. Finally, Abby uses actual words again.

Abby: Okay, so what's the next phase of the plan?

Me: Haven't even thought about it. She's coming over after she has dinner with her parents.

Rachel: Gross and also exciting!

Abby: Super gross!

Me: Both of you shut up. You have kids—you think I don't know how they got here?

Me: Now leave me alone. We'll catch up later.

Rachel: Rude.

Abby: Very rude.

Abby: But we love you and good luck!

Rachel: GROSS.

I drop my phone onto the coffee table and rewind the documentary to catch up on what I missed while my sisters were blowing my phone up. I'm watching a particularly tense interview when a knock on the door nearly makes me jump out of my skin.

There's only one person who would randomly stop by and not need to alert me beforehand. No one buzzed my door.

I don't think it's too hopeful to say it has to be Maggie.

I pause the documentary and bound over to the door, tearing it open as quickly as possible. And I'm not disappointed.

Her eyes are wide, and her mouth is open just slightly. She's wearing the same thing she was earlier, but those curls I've wrapped around my fingers more times than I can count are up and off her neck, held up by a hair tie.

There's a smudge of something on her jaw—maybe paint or primer or joint compound. Something they surely used for the chandelier hanging.

She's fucking gorgeous.

"Hey..." she finally says.

"Hey, Mags."

"I hope you don't mind me stopping by...it just felt weird to text you from two floors down. Or worse...call."

"I don't mind at all," I tell her, shaking my head quickly. "I'm glad you're here." I step to the side and motion her into my apartment.

She acquiesces, stepping past me, but stopping only a few feet away from me. I close the door and lock it before asking if I can get her anything.

"No, I'm good. Thanks, though."

I nod. "Okay. Why don't you have a seat?"

"I thought maybe we should finish our conversation from earlier," she says as she gets settled on the couch.

I sit far enough away to give her space, but close enough so I'm still within reach.

"I was thinking at dinner...how do we do this?"

Her body language is more timid than usual for her, so I reach out and take her hand, interlacing my fingers with hers and squeezing.

"I'm not sure there's a rule book," I say. "I think we can just make it up as we go...do what we feel comfortable with."

She nods. "Yeah um...I think I need to tell you something."

The tone of her voice tells me I won't like what she has to say, but I try to keep my facial expression from pinching up.

"All right," I say, sweeping my thumb over the back of her hand.

Maggie takes a deep breath, like she's preparing herself. I make extra effort to keep the tension out of my body and my face from giving away how nervous I am for what she might say.

"I made a lot of friends in Paris," she starts. She's not looking at me, but I won't tear my eyes off her. "And my friends made friends. We hung out with their families because we didn't have anywhere to go for special occasions."

She's still not looking at me, so I give her hand a squeeze, hoping she finds it encouraging.

It must have some sort of positive effect on her, because she looks up, straight into my eyes and lets it all hang out.

"I met someone while I was in Paris."

She's not saying the exact words, but I don't need her to spell it out. She was sleeping with someone in Paris.

Jealousy. Despair. Sadness. Anger.

I'm feeling all of them all at once and at a full volume eleven on a Spinal Tap scale.

The jealousy is probably obvious. Maggie is *mine,* and someone else touched her. I'm not violent, but that makes me want to break something.

Didn't Kate visit a rage room at one point? I wonder if Maggie knows where it is.

The despair is frustrating because this news makes me momentarily question my determination.

Is this a fruitless venture?

But then I remember that she came to my place earlier

today to specifically talk about the possibility of *us* and then she came *back* tonight to continue the conversation. So no... it's not pointless. I can shut the despair down quickly then.

The sadness though? That's going to stick with me for a while. I'm sad for me and for her. For the pain I caused both of us. I suppose there's also some guilt intertwined with the sadness.

And the anger? Well, that's all on me. I'm not mad at Maggie. She didn't do anything wrong. We weren't together anymore. We were not on a break with questions surrounding our status. We were very much broken.

No, I'm mad at myself. *I* did this to us. If I would have listened to her in the first place, I never would have proposed, and we could have skipped this entire mess, and she'd never have been in a position to meet someone new in Paris.

I'm sure the look on my face is betraying some of my emotions, though I try really hard to maintain a neutral expression.

Eventually, I nod. I know I need to say something, so I clear my throat before I bother trying. It feels like I swallowed sandpaper.

"Why are you telling me this?"

I watch her throat move as she swallows, the only remaining indication that she's nervous to talk to me about this.

"I thought you should know..." She nods once. "In case this changes anything for you."

That makes me frown.

"Why would that change anything for me?"

Maggie blinks a few times before looking down at our joined hands.

"I mean, I...I was thinking about how you went on a date

with Holly, and it didn't work out. And that's still none of my business, but I thought...I don't know."

She trails off, so I squeeze her hand again. She takes a quick breath in and places her other hand on top of ours.

"I was with someone else, and you weren't."

"So?"

Her eyes fly up to mine. "So...doesn't that bother you?"

"Would it make you feel better if I slept with someone else before we get back together?"

"No," she says immediately.

"And it doesn't bother me that you slept with someone else."

She squints at me, like she doesn't believe me.

"Look, I don't *love* it..." I admit with a sigh. "But it's because I'm...jealous someone else touched you."

Maggie's eyebrow pops up. "Oh, really?"

"Yes, really."

"You're not mad?"

I run my free hand through my hair. "I'm not going to lie to you, Maggie, I'm a little mad." As soon as the words are out of my mouth, I feel her freeze, so I rush the next words out. "But I'm not mad at you..."

Her eyes narrow.

"I promise, Maggie. I'm not mad at you. You didn't do anything wrong."

She still looks skeptical. Which is fair.

"I'm mad at myself, Mags. But that's on me," I say, laying my hand on my chest. "I'm the reason we're in this position. But no, my anger isn't directed at you."

With a big sigh, she angles her body to face me fully. "Ethan, you can't take all of that on yourself though. I've been thinking about what you said...and you're right. I should have talked to you. I shouldn't have run away the way I did…blocked your number and refused to just have a conversation."

It suddenly hits me what a waste the past year has been. How much precious time we gave up that we could have spent together.

I pick up our joined hands and kiss her fingers. When I look up, there are unshed tears in her eyes, so I scoot closer to her and pull her into my arms, then lean back on the couch. Her head rests on my shoulder, her arms wrapping around my waist and squeezing. The longer we sit there, the more I can feel the tension leaving her body.

We used to sit like this all the time while we watched TV at the end of the day, or when we watched a movie on the weekends. Sitting with her again, our arms around each other, feels like returning home.

Finally.

"Do you have any questions?" she asks quietly.

I run my fingers up and down her back, actively trying to keep myself from tensing back up at this subject coming up again.

"Just one," I respond gently.

I feel her chest expand against me. Like a fortifying breath. "Go ahead."

"Do you want to be with him now?"

Her head shakes as much as she can in her position. "No. He was convenient and kind. And I was sad."

And then she tilts her head up to look at me. "He's a good person, though. We've stayed in touch. We're good friends."

To be honest, that part stings more than anything.

The caveman part of me wonders if he's hanging around her to see if she'll take him back at some point.

She stares into my eyes like she's trying to read my mind,

and she can see through my bullshit. She knows my face too well.

"No."

"No, what?" I ask.

"No, he's not holding out hope."

My teeth grind together involuntarily while she continues to study my face. Her eyes track to my jaw, and I'm certain she can see the muscle in my cheek jumping.

"Who in their right mind wouldn't hold out hope for you?" I ask quietly.

Her eyes soften as she brings a hand up to my jaw. She rubs her thumb across my cheek, silently encouraging me to relax my jaw. I can't resist—I grab her hand and hold it in place, turning my head to kiss her palm.

I can feel her body melt against mine.

This is the stuff I've missed the most. The stuff that seems mundane.

When I meet her gaze again, she sits up straighter. "I talked to him the day you and I had dinner. He was with someone else—she's very pretty and seems sweet—and we were talking about *you*."

I don't say anything in response. Mostly because I don't know *what* to say.

"I was nervous about seeing you...talking to you. I still am, to be honest."

"Why?" I ask with a frown. "We've known each other for years."

"Yeah, we have," she says, grabbing onto one of the strings from my hoodie and twirling it around her finger. "We know so many ways to hurt each other."

"Hey." I cover her hand with mine and use my index finger to tilt her chin up so she has to look at me. "Maggie,

I've never intentionally hurt you, and I never will. I fucked up last year, but that's not a mistake I'll make twice."

My Maggie is a confident person. She's spunky and strong and genuine to her core. But right now, I can see the uncertainty in her gorgeous green eyes, and it kills me to know I put it there.

"I didn't hurt you on purpose," she whispers, her eyes getting glassy.

"I know you didn't. I never thought you did."

"What have we done to each other, Ethan?"

I take a moment to think about that. Because realistically, we've done some damage to each other. We got lost for a bit. We got wrapped up in our own shit and stopped focusing on *us*. A project manager—someone responsible for keeping track of details—and an architect—someone responsible for designing buildings that stand the test of time—managed to lose sight of the most important project in their lives.

The irony isn't lost on me.

"Nothing we can't fix, Maggie," I promise her, gently brushing a loose curl away from her eyes. "We can do anything together...remember?"

She stares into my eyes for a few seconds, hopefully remembering all the times we talked about being a team. About being able to conquer the world together. About being stronger together than we were apart.

I know Maggie is as independent as they come. I love that about her. I would never want to dull her shine or have her be dependent upon me.

We're not getting married—I know that. But much like a marriage, a long-term committed relationship is a team sport. It's like beach volleyball. There's a lot of ground to cover, and you need to be able to rely on each other. You need to be in sync with each other, knowing where the other person is without looking. Maggie and I were like that once before, and I have no doubt we can be like that again. Maybe it won't be the same as it was before.

But maybe it will be better.

A tear falls from her left eye, and I immediately wipe it away.

"Please don't cry, gorgeous."

"Ethan, I don't know how to do this," she says. Her voice is so quiet.

"Don't know how to do what?"

She licks her lips and starts playing with my hoodie string again. "I told you I want to talk about the possibility of us...but I don't really know what that looks like. Or how to move forward. Or what to do."

Fuck, I really hadn't spent time thinking about any of the logistics.

"I mean, we were in a five-year committed relationship where we were living together. We can't exactly pick up where we left off. So what does that mean? What do we do here?"

"I'm gonna be honest, Mags, I hadn't thought about it at all. The only thing I care about is being with you again. I don't have a plan," I admit, running a hand through my hair. "I think we can just take things one day at a time. Let's hang out. Go out to dinner. Talk. Get to know each other again. And see how it goes."

She doesn't respond with words. She just makes a humming sound and continues wrapping and unwrapping my hoodie string around her index finger.

We sit there for a while, her playing with my hoodie. Me, playing with her hair. Her head on my shoulder. Mine resting on hers. There's nothing sexual about it, though it certainly could be if we wanted it to be.

For now, I'm content to just be with her.

When she says she's going to go down to her own apartment, I walk her down and kiss her at the door. It's slow and sweet.

It feels like a first date, but so much better.

CHAPTER 31
THERE'S NO NEED FOR GIVEN NAMES

MAGGIE

Intrusive Thoughts - Natalie Jane

"I brought that soup you asked for. Although, I'm still baffled that you want soup when it's this warm outside."

"Thank you, Margaret."

I look up at Marv with wide eyes.

"You're welcome...Marvin?"

Why are we going with full names right now?

"Did you know that Saint Margaret of Scotland was actually English? She married Malcolm III of Scotland, which is why we know her as Margaret of Scotland."

I blink at him, wondering if I should call Cora. I'm here to stay with him while she runs some errands and goes to the grocery store.

"I've always been fascinated by the Catholics and their saints. It's the last part of Catholicism I still pay attention to."

"Okay..." I say, checking his pulse and coloring.

I wonder if I should get out the blood pressure cuff.

Not that I can actually take his blood pressure. It's an automatic one. All I have to do is press a button.

"As the story goes, she died of a broken heart. Her husband and her eldest son died in a battle. She passed a couple of days later."

"That's dark as fuck, Marv," I say, eyes still wide, still assessing the need to call Cora.

"Don't look at me like that," he grumbles. "I've had a lot of time to read in the past couple of weeks."

"You're supposed to be resting," I scold.

"Reading is like resting," he argues. "You know me, I can't sit around all day and not do anything. I'm already not working. You and Kelsie are handling my projects. I've been checking out library books online, and Cora is picking them up for me."

I give him a side-eye in response.

"I'm resting, I promise."

"Mmmhmm."

He rolls his eyes.

"Fine. Then let's talk about you."

Shit.

"Nothing new with me, Marv."

"Bullshit. Cora said Ethan was at the hospital with you."

And just like that, I'm back in the hospital, laying on a shitty couch with my head practically in Ethan's lap, pretending to be asleep, but listening to him and Peter talk.

Then, sitting next to Marv's hospital bed.

He was so fucking pale. He had an IV in his arm, a cannula in his nose, and an oxygen monitor on his finger. I'd never seen him look so fragile. It completely freaked me out. And of course, I couldn't stop thinking about Nick.

Is this what he looked like?

Did Kate see him like this?

I sat by Marv's bed, holding his hand and sobbing. Occasionally, he'd murmur something or look around the room, but nothing was coherent. He was still coming out of the anesthesia and was drowsy as fuck.

I remember sitting there, terrified he was going to die and then wanting nothing more than to be with Ethan. I stayed for a few minutes after I stopped crying and tried to get myself together. Then, I kissed Marv's cheek and told him I'd be back the following day.

And then I booked it back to Ethan.

"Earth to Maggie."

Marv's insistent voice pulls me out of the hospital and back into his bedroom.

I clear my throat. "Yes, Ethan was at the hospital with me."

I'm not looking at him, but I can feel Marv's eyes on me, nevertheless.

"That's an interesting development."

"Is it?"

"Cut the shit, Margaret."

"Jesus, what is it with my full name today?"

"Tell me what happened."

With a sigh, I finally look him in the eye, but I still don't say anything.

"Maggie, I was there after you ended things," he says, his voice much softer than it was when he told me to cut my shit out. "I saw you. I'm asking because I love you like my own family, and I want to know how you're doing."

Acquiescing, I sink down into a chair next to his bed.

"We've talked some things through. The night you nearly checked out of the universe, we had dinner and talked for a while."

Marv stays silent, letting me go at my own pace.

"He drove me to the hospital. Stayed with me the whole time. Drove me home."

And then I'm back in my bed with Ethan, him too far away and me needing to feel him, but being too chicken shit to do it myself. Instead, I asked him probing questions until he finally caught my drift.

"I had a migraine...he stayed overnight and took care of me, which..." I tip my head back to stare at the ceiling. "Is actually the second time that's happened since we started this project."

"Oh?"

"Yeah...as it turns out," I swallow the lump in my throat and look back at his face to wait for his facial expression when I drop this news. "We live in the same building."

His eyes go wide, and his bushy eyebrows shoot up on his forehead.

"Holy shit."

"I know."

"What are the odds...?"

"*I know.*"

Seriously, what are the odds? I still haven't reconciled that in my mind.

"So what's the plan, then?"

"We don't really have one," I admit. "We're just going to hang out and talk...see what happens."

Marv doesn't say anything, which makes me look at him again—mostly to make sure he's okay. And he is. He's just watching me with a pensive expression on his face.

"What?" I ask.

"You're still in love with him."

He's not asking a question. He says it like it's fact.

I don't bother lying. I just nod my head.

"And he feels the same way?"

"That's what he says," I admit quietly.

"But you doubt it?"

"I don't—" I cut myself off and take a deep breath. "I don't doubt the way he feels. I'm just..."

"Scared," he finishes when I trail off.

Again, I nod.

"Well then maybe it's good you're going to talk. And spend some time together."

"Yeah...I suppose."

I hear him sigh as I look down at my fingernails, uselessly pushing at a cuticle.

"Maggie, I've known you for years. Since long before you knew Ethan. And I'm old...I'm an old person who recently had a brush with death. So forgive me if I'm being a bit preachy here, but Maggie...take the chance."

His voice is so tender, it actually hurts. I look up to meet his gaze, which is pinned on me.

"Life is hard, Maggie. And it's short. I'm telling you right now that there's nothing—absolutely *nothing*—in this world that is more important than the people you love. You love him, and he loves you. You both made mistakes, and that's okay. People who love each other make mistakes—we're all human. But if you find someone who loves you the way the two of you love each other...you can't let that go. You just *can't*. You have to try to make it work—you have to learn from your mistakes and try again. And if you try a second time, and it doesn't work out, then you know you gave it your all."

My eyes are stinging, but I hold his gaze anyway. He gets more blurry by the second. So I blink away the tears and keep listening.

"It's your life, sweetheart. You can do what you want. I

just want you to think about what I said. And then make the best decision for you."

It's as I'm sitting there, tears streaming silently down my face that Nick's voice pops back into my head.

He's right, Mags.

"Tell me you got spring rolls."

Kate is digging through the bag of sushi takeout, looking like she's about to riot.

"You spiteful hag, I swear to—oh good."

I roll my eyes as she finds them.

"Chill out, evil shrew."

"Cut me some slack, I've barely eaten today, and I want spring rolls."

"Whatever. Where's the wine?"

"I pulled out a couple of bottles. One red, one white. The red is on the counter over there," she points to a corner by the coffee pot. "The white is in the fridge."

I head straight for the fridge. It's hot outside, and I want something cold.

"How's Marv doing?"

I came straight here from Marv's. Well...after I picked up the carryout.

"He's doing better, I think." I grab the wine from the fridge and start peeling off the foil wrapper. "He seems cognizant and coherent, but he's also spouting out philosophical shit."

"Like what?"

I start screwing the corkscrew into the cork, trying to figure out how I want to phrase it.

"Well...he started off by full-naming me and then telling

me about Saint Margaret of Scotland. About how she was English, really, but married a Scot. And then how she died of a broken heart after her husband and eldest son were killed in battle."

I get the cork out with a low pop and glance over at Kate, who is staring at me with wide eyes.

"What the fuck?"

"I know," I say, grabbing a wineglass. "Do you want red or white?"

"White is fine."

Getting a second glass for Kate, I walk back over to the open bottle and start pouring. Generously.

"He said he's had a lot of time to read over the last couple of weeks and that he has always been fascinated by Catholic saints."

She blinks. "Um. Okay."

"Girl, I know."

She finishes setting out all of our sushi on the table by the back windows, then gets us glasses of water while I put the wineglasses on the table and return the bottle to the fridge to stay chilled.

Once we're seated, she asks about the rest of my visit.

I fill her in on the night of Marv's heart attack because it's relevant to his line of questioning and subsequent advice. And also...because I have things to ask Kate, and I want her to understand why I'm asking *now* after all this time.

As I talk, I can see Kate's body slump in her seat. When I'm finished, she sets her chopsticks down, not that she's used them in the last few minutes.

"Kate?"

She doesn't respond, but she looks up to meet my eyes.

"Can I ask you questions about the day Nick died?"

The change in her is immediate—tears in her eyes, shallow breathing, subtle trembling of her hands. I actually feel bad for asking.

But then she takes a fortifying sip of wine and nods.

And then I realize I don't even know what to ask. So I just sit there and stare at her.

"What do you want to know?" she finally asks.

I try to speak, but it comes out as a croak. I have to clear my throat before I can get any actual words out.

"I was at the hospital, waiting to see how Marv was... after he got out of surgery, Cora was called back, and then I got to go see him."

Her lashes flutter shut heavily, and she sniffs.

"When I was sitting there, next to his hospital bed, I...I couldn't stop thinking about Nick." My voice cracks at the end, and the tears start falling from my eyes as well.

She nods, likely knowing where I'm going with this.

"He was so pale, Kate. And he looked so fragile." My voice is so high, I barely recognize it, but I press on. "Which made me wonder if that's what Nick looked like. I didn't get to see him. Or talk to him one last time."

A sob escapes her throat, her head drooping down, and I feel even more terrible for bringing this up, but I *have* to know.

"Why didn't he call me?"

She looks back up, eyes pleading. "He didn't want to worry anyone. Neither of us thought it was going to be that serious...that's why I texted instead. Maggie, I'm so sorry." Her hands fly to her chest, pressing into her sternum. "I promise, I would have called...or had someone else call. We just didn't think it was going to be a big deal. Doug was confident, and Nick was alert—"

"He was..." I ask with a gasp. "He was alert?"

She nods emphatically. "Yes. That's why we thought everything would be okay. He was fully alert until..." Kate stops abruptly.

"Until what?"

"I only know what Doug told me...I wasn't there in the operating room. But he was alert until...he wasn't. The last time I saw him, he was talking to me...telling me everything would be okay. That he loved me, and he'd see me soon."

She looks so fucking miserable, sitting across from me, crying. I move from my seat over to the one next to hers and wrap my arms around her shoulders.

"I'm so sorry, Maggie," she sobs. "I swear, we didn't leave you out of it on purpose. And honestly, I don't really remember much after Doug came to talk to me—"

She stops quickly and looks at me. There's something in her eyes...like panic, maybe.

"If you want Doug's number, I can give it to you. You can call him and ask every question. I just...I don't have all the answers. The only thing I can tell you with absolute certainty is that we really thought everything was under control. Even Doug thought so."

I nod because I believe her. I've always believed her. I never thought they intentionally left me out. I just...wish he would have called.

"I know, Kate. I know..."

She lays her head down on my shoulder and sobs some more. We both do. Just sitting there at the table, the sushi mostly eaten, but forgotten.

When we've both pulled ourselves together, she sits back up and looks me in the eye.

"Your brother loved you so much, Maggie. I hope you don't doubt that. I hope our misguided decision to not call you immediately doesn't make you question how much he adored you."

I take a deep breath and slowly let it out. "Thank you for saying that." Even though I know it's true, it's still nice to hear it...since the one person who would have told me can't say it anywhere other than in my head anymore.

She grabs her phone from the table and taps a few times before I hear a ding from my own phone.

"Doug's number. I'm sure he'd talk to you. I don't think he really wants to talk to me, so just call him and ask whatever you want to."

"Thank you," I whisper. "I know this is really difficult for you to talk about."

"Of course, honey. Anything for you."

We sit in silence for a moment, dabbing at our faces with our napkins, trying to erase the evidence of our conversation.

"Wait..." I look at her with a frown. "Why wouldn't he want to talk to you?"

Kate freezes, her eyes staring unfocused at the remaining sushi on the table before shaking her head and picking up her chopsticks.

"We're gonna need more wine for that conversation."

I WALK OUT of the elevator of my apartment building and meander to the apartment door. It's only when I reach it that I realize I haven't gone to my own apartment.

I knock on the door anyway.

When Ethan opens the door, he's wearing basketball shorts, a T-shirt, and a confused expression on his face.

"Maggie...are you okay?"

I'm not really sure how to answer that question. But I do know I'm emotionally drained from this day.

"Hey...I just, um...I kind of just ended up here."

Confusion gives way to concern on his face, and he moves aside to let me in the door. I walk in without a word and set my purse down on his dining room table.

"What's going on?"

He's standing only a couple of feet away from me when I turn around, so I close the gap and wrap my arms around his waist, pressing the side of my head into his chest, listening to his heartbeat. His strong arms engulf me, his head dipping down to kiss my hair. He doesn't ask any other questions. He just stands there with me.

"Can I stay here tonight?" I finally ask.

"Of course."

He doesn't hesitate for a second. There's no question or pause.

"Do you need anything from your apartment? I can go down for you while you get ready for bed."

This man.

I squeeze him tighter. It's late, and I'm so exhausted from this day. All I want to do is go to sleep.

"If you have a spare toothbrush, I'm good."

"I do."

He drops another kiss on my hair and then leads me over to his bedroom. I take my earrings out while he roots around in his dresser.

"Here's some clothes you can sleep in. I'm going to get a fresh toothbrush for you."

By the time I turn around, Ethan is already gone. I pick up the top garment and find the old, worn-out college T-shirt of his I used to wear all the time. It's soft from countless washes, and close to threadbare. But I loved sleeping in it.

Under the shirt is an old pair of my sleep shorts that I must have left in our apartment.

I'm still frowning at them when he returns.

"I left a toothbrush on the sink for you. What's wrong?"

I look up to meet his eyes. "The um...these shorts."

"What about them?"

"You still have them."

"Yeah."

This man kept a pair of shorts that I loved to sleep in because they were super soft. I've had them for years because I can't find a suitable replacement. I figured I'd lost them in the move—out of the apartment, into Kate's house, over to Paris and back, then into my new apartment. I haven't seen them in months, and I couldn't remember when I'd seen them last. They must have been in the dirty laundry when I moved out of our place.

They look fresh and clean. Like he washed them and put them in a drawer for safe keeping.

It's such a small gesture. It could be nothing, really. But it feels monumental right now. Like he always held out hope.

Who in their right mind wouldn't hold out hope for you?

I drop the shirt and close the distance between us, grabbing the back of his neck and pulling his mouth to mine.

CHAPTER 32
THAT SMART MOUTH
MAGGIE

Handle - Emily Hackett

Ethan's surprise is evident, but only for a split second. He catches up quickly, hands sliding around my hips to my low back and pulling me flush against his body. But he lets me keep the upper hand, leading the kiss wherever I want to take it.

And I want to take it and run with it.

My hands find their way into his hair, soft and full. Our kisses are more open-mouthed than closed while still keeping a PG rating, but it's not long before I need more. He might have plastered our bodies together, but I'm the one who really goes for it. With a tilt of my head, I have a better angle for a deeper kiss, and I take advantage of it.

I'm rewarded with a hungry growl from deep in Ethan's throat. It makes me smile just a little bit, which Ethan must feel against his lips because he peels his eyes open to look at me. Even then, they're hooded and *hot*.

I'm content to lose myself in him tonight, but he's clearly not on the same page.

"You remember what I said?" he asks, voice low and gravelly.

I won't fuck you again until you're mine.

As his words are making their way through the recesses of my brain, he presses his hips into me, giving me a not-so-subtle reminder. As if I could possibly forget.

I nod slowly.

"I'm not going to pressure you, Maggie. Just trying to set expectations here."

"Ever the project manager." The comment is meant to tease him, but his eyes grow more serious, his hands squeezing my hips.

"You have no idea how badly I want you."

"Maybe we could just...fool around a bit?" I ask, trailing my fingertips down his chest. When I've nearly reached the waistband of his shorts, he grabs my hand, interlaces our fingers, and gently—so gently—pins our joined hands behind my back.

"What did you have in mind?"

I do my best to control the smirk on my face. I don't want him to know *I know* that I'm winning. But I *do* know. I can see his resolve crumbling.

"When we first got together, we did other stuff first." I glide my free hand up his neck, running my index finger over his lower lip, and his reaction doesn't disappoint. He dips his head and takes my finger into his mouth, sucking on it and swirling his tongue.

Fuck, I forgot how good he is with his tongue.

I falter for just a second, my mouth parting as I watch him.

"If we're starting over—"

He freezes, eyes flashing to mine, filled with anger. Or

frustration. Or mutiny. I'm not sure in my current lust-filled haze. What I know for sure is that he doesn't like that word choice.

"—kind of—" I correct.

His eyes narrow, but he resumes his ministrations, sliding his tongue in between my index and middle fingers to flick the skin between them. I have to swallow before I can speak again.

"—we can go back to the beginning, in a way. Start fresh...but better. Because we know what we like."

He growls again, letting go of my hand and tunneling his fingers into my hair, but he doesn't kiss me. He stares into my eyes like he's trying to read something written in invisible ink and then seems to arrive at some sort of decision.

"Why did you come over here tonight?"

I blink and instinctively try to put space between us, but his hand is still in my hair, the other holding mine behind my back, and I'm stuck here.

"I had a hard day. I wanted..." I trail off because I realize I don't really know what I meant to finish that sentence with. Fortunately, Ethan shows me mercy.

"Why did you have a hard day? What happened?" he asks, unwinding our arms from behind my back and guiding me to sit down on the bed. When we're both settled, he takes my hand and holds it in both of his, laying a gentle kiss on my knuckles.

And then I melt.

He's not letting me use sex to mask my emotions—he wants me to want *him*...not what I know he can do for me.

While I'm frustrated he's not currently doing dirty things to my body, I appreciate what he's doing for my soul. For the prospect of rebuilding our relationship.

Of course I still love this man. How could I not?

With a sigh, I tell him about seeing Marv, but I leave out the parts about his life advice. I just tell him Marv was grilling me about him being at the hospital with me. When I tell him about my conversation with Kate, he scoots closer to me and wraps his arm around me. I let my head rest on his shoulder, my tears falling to his T-shirt as he runs a soothing hand up and down my arm.

"I'm glad you're here, Mags. You're always welcome here."

I sniff and pick up my head, wiping at my face before I look at him. I'm met with understanding and kindness.

And love. Always love.

"I had a hard day.... And I wanted *you*," I admit. "I wanted my best friend. The person who knows me—or who I thought knew me—better than anyone on this planet."

His face falls when I say it, but I take his hand and interlace our fingers.

"We both messed up, Ethan...and I take full responsibility for my part in all of this. But I've missed you so much," I say, my voice cracking with the emotion of it, fresh tears thickening my throat. "I came here without even thinking about it. I just ended up at your door. If we're going to see if we can do this again...you need to be the person I go to. I don't want to hide from you. I ran from you once, and it was awful. I was..."

I stop myself, because *no...that's not right.*

"I *have been* so heartbroken," I correct. "I just wanted you."

"Maggie..." he breathes. "I always want you. All the time. And I told you I'd be here when you're ready."

The unspoken question hangs thick in the air between us.

Am I ready?

"I'm getting there," I whisper.

He nods slowly, then gently dislodges his hand from mine, wrapping it around the nape of my neck and pulling me toward him.

"That's good enough for now."

His voice is low and sends a shockwave through my core just before his lips crash into mine.

Before I know what's happening, I'm on my back on his bed with his tall frame looming over me, his mouth devouring mine.

He's still holding on to my neck with one hand while the other plants on the mattress next to my head. It's not soft and gentle or anywhere close to calculated. It's raw and needy, and somewhere in the back of my mind, I wonder if he'll lose control and change his mind about sex.

I hope so.

His hips press into mine, and I can feel that he definitely *wants* me, even though he claims he'll be keeping his dick to himself.

We'll see about that.

Since his hands are both occupied, I take the opportunity to run mine down his strong back and squeeze his ass, pulling him tighter against me. I'm rewarded with a growl low in his throat, his hand sliding into my hair and grabbing a fistful of it. It stings in a delicious way, and the force of it tilts my head back, giving him better access to my neck.

He doesn't waste a second, burying his face in the thin, sensitive flesh, licking and nipping at the skin as he moves down to my collarbone.

We've kissed, and we've been close in proximity—me sitting on his lap or next to him—but this is the first time his mouth has been on any part of my body other than my head or face in over a year, and I'm on *fire*. This man knows every single erogenous zone on my body, and he's going to find each and every one of them while he has me under him on this bed.

I feel him tug at my shirt with his teeth—his *teeth*—before his low, gravelly voice directs me to take it off.

I fumble with it, my hands trembling slightly from all the emotions that have soared through my body today. When I get it over my head, he takes it from my hands and throws it somewhere. And then his mouth is on my breasts, his tongue exploring the soft swells above my bra cups as he slips a hand under me and pinches the clasp to release it. His mouth on my nipples is so overwhelming I can't even keep my eyes open.

We haven't even gotten to the "good" stuff yet, and I'm ready to combust.

I'm gasping and arching my back, holding his head against my chest, and wondering why I'm so fucking dizzy. Is it because my breaths are so shallow or because Ethan's mouth is on me?

This feels so much more intense than it did the last time I remember us being together. Then again, I wouldn't have known that the last time we were together was going to be the last time. Would I have been paying attention enough to really commit those sensations to memory? Probably not, to be honest.

But this time? This time, I'm fully in tune with every single movement of his body. Every place his mouth touches. Every part of my body his hands squeeze.

"Fuck, Maggie..." he grinds out, trailing wet kisses down my stomach. He's unbuttoning my shorts before his mouth reaches my low belly and then urging me to lift my hips so he can yank them down my legs. He doesn't bother to take my panties off separately. They're both off in one go, and then he's pulling me to the end of the bed and planting himself between my spread thighs.

I can't help but lift up on to my elbows so I can watch him slowly kiss my inner thighs as he treks toward my center.

"I know you're still working on it..." he says. "But I've never doubted us, Maggie." He punctuates his words with languid, open-mouth kisses on my thighs. "Not for a single moment. Not even when you left. We're so good together... and I know you'll see it again. And no matter how long that takes, I'll keep fighting for you. I will *always* fight for you."

His mouth finally reaches my center, his tongue taking a long swipe up. The heat of him coupled with the throaty groan he lets out and his eyes fluttering closed is too much. I suddenly can't keep my head upright. It falls back, and I fist the duvet in my hands to keep myself from collapsing.

He nips at my inner thigh, making me gasp and whip my head back up, only to find him looking at me with so much possessiveness...so much hunger that my breath stalls in my chest. I swallow hard against a dry throat before trying to speak.

"Ethan..."

He licks me again, and my eyes flutter closed.

Which earns me another nip, which makes my eyes fly open.

And that look is back in his eyes.

Fuck, why is that so hot?

"Eyes on me, Mags."

I feel my jaw drop as I stare at him.

"Understand?"

I nod hastily. Anything to get him back to work.

"Good girl."

And then I'm done for. I'm just a ball of nerve endings while Ethan puts his talented mouth to good use, which is made even hotter by the sight that he seems to be truly enjoying himself.

Ethan has always been enthusiastic about going down on me. He's never hesitated or been weird about it like some guys can be. But right now? It's like he's been waiting and waiting and *waiting,* and he can finally have me.

And based on what he's said…I think he *has* been waiting.

Through it all, I do my best to keep my eyes on him. And when I accidentally let my eyes drift shut—and he manages to catch me—he gives me another nip to draw my attention.

And even that is hot.

To finish me off, he plunges two fingers into me, and I just about pass out. My arms finally give out, my back collapsing onto the bed. I can't even pick my head up to look at him, but he grants me mercy, not stopping when I'm *so* close. Somehow, I'm able to thread my fingers into his hair, earning me a growl.

And then I'm flying. And falling. And sobbing, just a little.

As I catch my breath, I can feel his fingers still inside me, his mouth leaving kisses on my thighs, and the light pressure from his teeth at his discretion.

When I've finally calmed down enough to lift my head, I whisper his name.

He meets my eyes with that same possessive, hungry look before pulling his fingers from my body and licking them clean.

"So. Fucking. Perfect."

I lick my lips, so very dry from all the panting and gasping I just did, intent on getting my mouth on him.

Sitting up, I pull myself the rest of the way toward him using his neck for leverage. He meets me halfway, up on his knees on the bed between my legs. His hands tunnel into my hair as I start pulling on his shorts, yanking them down his thighs. Before I can pull down his boxer briefs, he grabs my hands.

"What are you doing?"

I let out a self-satisfied smirk at his breathless question.

"You agreed we could do other stuff...*beginning* stuff." I cup him with one hand and feel his body tense up like a bowstring.

"Maggie—" His voice has a warning tone to it, but I don't let it deter me. Instead, I push his hips backward, and he lets me, slowly lowering each of his feet to the floor so he's standing. I follow him, sitting on the edge of the bed and divesting him of the rest of his clothing, watching his face the whole time.

When I push his shirt up his torso, kissing the bare skin I unveil, his eyes soften.

When I start to drag his boxer briefs down, his jaw clenches.

When I push them down to the floor with his basketball shorts, he takes a deep breath in.

And when I take him in my hand, he mutters a few curse words.

But just before my mouth finally makes contact with his swollen head, he slips his hand into my hair and holds me away. I look up at him, confused.

"Why?" he asks.

I squint at him. Part of me can't believe he's pressing pause, but the rest of me knows he doesn't want to take advantage. But he's not taking advantage, and I'm not sure how to prove it to him.

"Why did you?"

"Because I'm in love with you," he responds. And then that muscle in his jaw ticks just before his eyes turn to molten hot chocolate. "And I missed the taste of you."

Every thought in my head basically just turns to screaming. The inside of my skull is that GIF of the woman in the white shirt whisper-screaming and shaking her hands.

I somehow manage to hold his gaze while I gather myself enough to give a response. Now is probably not the right time, but then again...maybe there's no *right* time. No perfect time.

I lick my lips and press a chaste kiss to his frenulum, secretly delighting in the way his fist tightens in my hair.

But then I return my gaze to his, still watching me with trepidation.

"I never stopped loving you, Ethan." I pause just long enough to see his eyes flare a bit wider. "And have you ever considered that maybe *I* missed the taste of *you*?"

After that, he seems to momentarily lose the ability to speak. His fist is still tight in my hair, but not so tight that it restricts my movements as I suck the swollen head of his dick into my mouth and get to work at proving my point.

I know some people look at sucking a dick as demeaning. To some extent, I can see where they're coming from. (Ha. Coming.)

I think some of it has to do with men behaving badly—thrusting when their partner isn't ready, grabbing their head and shoving themselves farther in, coming without warning.

And all of that is valid. No one wants to go down on a partner like that. But I think with the *right* partner, it's fun.

I (perhaps purposefully) forgot how much I love going down on Ethan. He's responsive. And vocal. And because he's typically dominant during sex, this is one time when the tables are turned. He cedes control to me, and it's so fucking hot. He might give direction or tell me what to do, but I'm the one running the show, and I *love* being the one Ethan gives up control to.

So while I'm sitting on the edge of this bed, I'm watching him as closely as possible. I'm listening to every single sigh, groan, and filthy word that falls from his lips. I'm tracking every movement in his body and using it as a guide for when to slow down, speed up, or change up my tactics. I still remember what he likes, and I'm making sure to put that information to good use.

"God, Maggie, your *mouth*," he says between gritted teeth.

I hum in response and am rewarded with a gentle—but decisive—tug on my hair. The movement drags me backward just slightly, and he clearly didn't think about the consequences because his abs contract right before my eyes. The sensation makes him pant, but it just makes me smile. He must feel the difference because his eyes fly open to meet mine.

"Wipe that smirk off your face, gorgeous."

I slowly pull off him, knowing I'm about to taunt the proverbial cobra.

"Or what?"

"Jesus fuck, Maggie, you are so insolent."

"Yeah..." I drag my tongue from root to tip as he watches with hooded eyes. "But you love my smart mouth."

I said the words without really thinking about them, and I can see that they didn't go over his head. His hand moves from my hair to my jaw, his thumb trailing tenderly along my cheekbone.

The air between us starts to shift, but I'm not ready to

cede my power yet, so I turn my head to the side just long enough to kiss his palm before diving back in.

"Ahh, *fuck...*"

And then it's nothing but his ragged breaths and *yesses* and *just like thats* and bits of praise that make me blush as he gets closer.

"Maggie." His voice holds an unmistakable warning that I both appreciate and do not heed in the slightest. Instead, I double my efforts.

His fingers slide into my hair just before he comes with a long moan. I don't pull away. I stay right where I am until he finishes spasming, and then he's pulling himself out of my mouth and dragging me up toward the pillows. Ethan crushes his mouth to mine as he lays down on top of me, giving me just the right amount of his delicious weight. His kiss might be possessive and scorching, but his hand holds my jaw with a reverence that takes my breath away.

He kisses me for so long that I can feel him soften, then harden again, but he doesn't do anything about it, even though I'm starting to writhe beneath him. Instead, he pulls back and rests his forehead against mine, running that thumb along my cheekbone again.

"I do love your smart mouth," he says quietly.

The comment takes me right back to that energy shift between us a few moments ago. I swallow a sudden lump in my throat and close my eyes against the sudden burning in them.

"I love the sass that powers it. And the way you choose to harness your sass. The way you use your powers for good." He punctuates his sentences with sweet kisses on my eyelids, cheeks, nose, and forehead. "I love everything about you, Maggie. I always have. Always will."

When I open my eyes, a tear tracks down my temple and

into my hair. It doesn't slip by him. He leans in to kiss the wet path on my skin, which just makes another tear form in the corner of my eye. But he catches that one, too.

"Ethan..." I whisper.

"Yes?" he asks, kissing a gentle path down my face toward my neck.

"I love you."

He freezes, his lips resting against my jaw. Slowly, slowly, slowly, he turns his head so he can meet my eyes, shifting his body so he's directly on top of me again. The whole time, his eyes search mine, looking for who knows what—a sign that I'm ready to jump back in, an indication that I'm done fucking around, or maybe complete surrender. I honestly have no idea. But I can feel more tears forming in my eyes.

"I...I don't really know...what I'm doing in this situation," I admit. "I don't know where to go or how to navigate this."

His eyes soften, and he nods. "I don't either, Mags. The point is that we can figure it out together."

I return his nod, so he drops two more sweet, lingering kisses on my lips and then gets up to his knees. He's at least half-hard, but he still doesn't do anything about it. He just reaches over for the clothes he got out for me and sets them on my belly.

"Get dressed," he instructs, sliding off the bed to find his shorts. "I'm not sure we'll survive the temptation of sleeping naked next to each other."

I quirk an eyebrow at him. I don't really care for his little rule, but apparently he's going to stick to it.

He pulls up his shorts and goes to the bathroom to brush his teeth while I'm dressing. I join him to brush my own and then crawl into bed.

It feels completely natural to curl up next to him, my head on his shoulder and his arm around me. My arm slung across his torso. My leg over one of his so we're intertwined. We've fallen asleep like this hundreds of times.

It feels familiar and comfortable, but with a renewed sense of novelty.

I didn't think we'd ever be here again. And thanks to Ethan's tenacity, we have a second chance.

I just really hope we don't screw it up.

CHAPTER 33
THE FACE...OFF
ETHAN

When I first met Maggie, I thought she was hot. I won't lie about that.

She was standing over the hood of her Mustang wearing jeans and a simple T-shirt that rode up just enough to show a sliver of skin on her lower back.

It was like one of the regency era romance novels my sisters read. Substitute *lower back* for *ankle,* and I might as well have been a rakish duke trying to make a move on a virginal heroine.

Of course, she wasn't a virgin, and I wasn't much of a rake. It was more of a middle-of-the-road scenario. But the statement that Maggie took my breath away the moment I saw her isn't an exaggeration in the slightest.

Choosing to be a gentleman that night was an agonizing decision. I wanted to flirt with her. I wanted to get her number. But I also knew that if I did either of those things, I'd be labeled as a creep in her eyes.

For the rest of her life, I'd be *that guy* from the gas station who hit on her and now she looks over her shoulder every time she gets out of the car.

Although, maybe she should be looking over her shoulder every time she gets out of the car. The world is a dangerous place.

What I wanted from Maggie that night was a genuine interaction. I wanted to talk to her, but I also wanted to make sure she was okay. Anyone—man or woman—bent over the hood of a car with jumper cables on the ground could be in need of help, and I wanted to make sure she had whatever assistance she needed.

Would I have provided her with anything at all, even if I didn't know how to actually do it myself? Absolutely. That's what the internet is for. And if we couldn't have figured it out, I'd have made some calls, and we'd have found someone who could.

In the end, my first impression couldn't have been the worst one she'd ever had of another person because she spent plenty of time talking to me the following night at the club.

I wouldn't change a single thing about that night or the first night we met. I think I did it right. I think she would have run the other way if I'd gone the creepy route (as she should have).

The moment she opens the door, I'm thrown back into that first night...when I observed her from afar (again...not in a creepy way) before I gathered the courage to actually talk to her.

She's wearing a sundress with some kind of sandal with a heel and she looks fucking incredible.

"Hey! Come on in." She steps aside to make room for me to enter her apartment. Her smile is massive and genuine.

The look in her eyes screams excitement with a touch of nerves. "I'm almost ready."

"Take your time," I say. I'm not going anywhere without her. "These are for you."

I hold the bouquet of flowers out for her. They're nothing particularly special, but I did pick them up from a florist as opposed to a grocery store, so it must count for something. She takes them with a soft look in her eye.

"Thank you..."

I don't even bother resisting the urge to lean in and kiss her cheek. And while I'm there, I linger, pressing my lips to her cheekbone one more time, breathing in the soft scent of her shampoo or conditioner or whatever the fuck she puts in her hair that makes it smell so goddamn good.

One hand goes to the side of my neck, holding me in place as I take a selfish moment in close proximity to her.

"I should put these in water," she eventually whispers.

I nod and take a step back. My whole body tries to revolt against the action, but I shove my hands in my pockets to keep from reaching for her again.

The column of her throat bobs as she swallows, and it takes a significant amount of effort to tear my eyes from the soft, pale skin.

I ask about her day, and she fills me in as she busies herself with finding a vase and cutting the stems.

I lean against the wall while she fusses over the flowers in a vase that I remember well. Maggie doesn't have many vases, but Kate bought her this one when we moved in together. It was her go-to when anyone bought her flowers, which honestly wasn't often because she said flowers make her sad when they die. But she still loves getting them, so I did on occasion. And she always loved them. She'd leave them in the vase until they were basically a fire hazard because she didn't want to throw them away. So when I was home alone, I'd throw them out for her, wash the vase, and put it away. A clean slate.

When she's satisfied, she sets them on the coffee table in her living room.

"Okay, I just need my purse," she mumbles as she goes into her bedroom. I keep my feet planted to the floor exactly where I am, not wanting to make her think I'm only here to jump her bones.

(If we're being totally clear, I'd have a hard time saying no to her if that was her intention. I know I told her I wouldn't fuck her again until she was mine, but that line seems more blurry than it did when I first said it.)

"Where are we going?" she asks.

"I figured we'd visit some old favorites," I answer. I know it's cryptic, but I can't be bothered to care.

If her arched eyebrow is any indication, she knows I'm being purposefully cagey.

"I just want to spend some time with you, Maggie," I say, hoping to calm her down. I'm not sure what she's expecting me to say or what reaction I'm expecting her to have, but no matter what I would have said, I was wrong.

She stops what she's doing and slowly turns her head to look at me. She doesn't say anything, but I can tell she's watching my face for any reaction—any facial expression or clue that will tell her what I'm really thinking.

I'm hoping she realizes that I'm telling her the truth here —I just want her time. Time doing anything at all—going out to dinner, seeing a movie, making out in the back seat of my car, under the bleachers at a football game...whatever, wherever. It doesn't matter to me. I just want to be with her.

Time is our most finite resource, and I know she understands that. I know she's acutely aware of the loss of her brother on a daily basis. I know she wants to eliminate regrets in her life.

And I don't want to be one of her regrets.

I want to be her forever.

"So I don't get any hints?"

I drag my eyes from her perfect ass under that dress up to her curious eyes.

"No...you don't get any hints," I tell her.

"Then how do I know if what I'm wearing is appropriate for the evening?" she asks.

It's a valid question...she doesn't know what we're doing.

"You look perfect," I assure her, planting one more kiss on the top of her head before wrapping my arm across her belly and pressing her against my torso. I'm holding myself far enough away that she won't feel my semi, but all I want to do is rut into her like an animal. I'm the one that imposed this stupid no-sex rule until she's mine again, and I regret it right now almost as much as I regretted it the other night when her mouth was wrapped around my cock.

She hums and wraps her arm around mine, twice encircling my arm across her abdomen and dropping her head to lean back against my shoulder.

"Fine," she acquiesces. "I'll just have to be surprised. Do I need to bring anything with me?"

"Just yourself." I drop a kiss on the place where her neck and her shoulder meet and feel goose bumps pop up beneath my lips. She inhales deeply and interlaces her fingers with mine, still holding on to her side.

This no-sex rule is getting more stupid by the minute.

"I suppose I'm ready, then."

It's too good to be true that she's actually ready in the sense I want her to be, but I know what she means.

"All right, then." I use our interlaced fingers to spin her

around and bring her with me to the door. She grabs her keys from a little table by the door with her free hand, closing and locking the door behind us.

"Strip club first?" she asks when we get into my car.

"Stop fishing."

"I hate fishing."

"I know you do." She hates the quiet and the worms and the bugs on the water. And taking the hook out of the fish's mouth. And the general idea of harming an animal and then releasing it back into the wild and hoping it's okay.

"What are you smiling about?" she asks me.

I glance in the rearview mirror. I didn't even realize I was smiling, but apparently I was.

"I was just thinking about all the reasons you hate fishing," I say, reaching over to take her hand.

She huffs a laugh and squeezes my hand.

"Does this feel weird to you?" she asks after a moment.

"No," I say immediately. And then I can feel her eyes on me. "I've never felt weird around you, Maggie."

"That's not what I meant..."

I glance over at her. "What did you mean then?"

She hesitates for a moment, but doesn't let go of my hand. Instead, she traces my knuckles with her free hand.

"We haven't talked much over the last year," she says quietly. "We've both...lived separate lives for a while now."

She's not wrong, obviously. But I don't care what's happened over the past year as long as we end up back together.

"That's all true..." I agree. "But you're still you. I'm still me. That hasn't changed."

"Yeah...that's what worries me, Ethan."

I pull the car into the driveway and off to the side. Then, I turn to face her and kiss her hand.

"I know. And I get it...I really do, Mags."

Her eyes look sad, like they always do when we broach this topic.

"I'm just asking for a chance to show you that we're still good together—great, even. We hit a big bump in the road. We both made bad decisions. But we know better now. We'll be better the second time around."

I can see the hope flicker in her eyes, trying to catch fire. And you can bet any amount of money on me—I'll turn it into an inferno.

A car drives by us and catches her eye.

"Where are we?"

"A new place," I tell her, truthfully. "But it will bring back memories."

She narrows her eyes at me as I turn away and pull back onto the driveway to follow the car that passed us. We drive along the crude driveway until we reach a booth, where I buy the tickets.

Out of the corner of my eye, I can see her turning around to look at the cars that have lined up behind us.

"Enjoy the show," the ticket attendant says.

I thank him and pull forward.

"Ethan, seriously, where are we?"

"You'll find out in a minute."

I turn the corner and when I hear her quiet gasp, I know she's figured it out.

There are already plenty of cars lined up, people getting situated and set up. At the front sits a massive screen with a rear projector showing advertisements.

"Are you kidding?" she asks, eyes wide, lips parted as she looks around.

I take a moment to look at her excited face as it takes the whole thing in.

Something about Maggie that most people wouldn't know is that she's always wanted to go to a drive-in theater, but they're few and far between these days. This one opened up in the spring, and she was the first person I thought of.

"Not kidding," I say just before I kiss the back of her hand. Her gaze snaps over to me. "Very serious, in fact."

Her eyes drop to my mouth, still very close to her hand, and I can't stop myself from leaning forward to kiss her. If this were actually a first date, I wouldn't have done this. Probably not, anyway. I've always been more comfortable with Maggie—more forward. More myself.

She doesn't miss a beat, returning the kiss immediately, her hand releasing mine and grabbing onto my shirt to pull me closer. She's the one who reaches out with her tongue, but I don't let my (happy) surprise show. I give back as good as I'm getting, taking her head in my hands and cursing myself for the fiftieth time for my dumb no-sex rule.

When she pulls back, we both need a moment to catch our breath, but she doesn't lean away. No, she rests her forehead against mine, and I still have a perfect view of her lips...and they're curved into a gentle smile.

"I brought food," I manage to say through a lustful haze.

"You did?"

I nod. "It's in the trunk."

"Any chance you brought alcohol?"

I lean back with a laugh. "Are *you* kidding?" I get out of the car, not bothering to close the door while I grab the cooler out of the trunk and set it in the back seat of the car. I slide the seat back, and twist around to open the cooler.

"I brought sandwiches...turkey and swiss. I also brought clementines and pepper slices. Oh, and Pringles."

When I look up, I find her gaze on me, a look of amusement shining in her eyes.

"Pringles, huh?"

"Yeah…" I nod. "Pringles. Original flavor. None of that low-fat or artificial flavoring crap," I parrot her own words back to her—I've heard her say those exact words countless times over the years. Nick had Pringles in his hand the night we met. I'm sure she remembers.

She hums—a thoughtful sound in her throat. "And what did you bring to drink?"

"Well, water, of course. But I also brought wine." I pull a bottle of red out of a bag on the floor and uncover a bottle of white from the cooler. "Whatever you want."

I'm rewarded with a smile, her eyes darting around to take in our surroundings.

"Well, isn't this just perfect?" she muses. "How come we never did this before?"

I shrug. "I don't really know…but this place is pretty new. I'm not sure how many other options there would have been before."

Maggie nods slowly, like she's carefully weighing that response.

"And what are we seeing tonight?"

"I'm so glad you asked." I pull out my phone and find the schedule. "It's Nicholas Cage night. First up is *Gone in Sixty Seconds* and after that, it's *Face/Off*."

Her eyes get comically wide. "Shut up, seriously?"

"Yep." I turn my phone so she can see it for herself.

"Holy shit, Ethan. This is *amazing*."

"I thought you'd like it."

"Like it? I *love* it. You know I love-slash-hate *Face/Off*, and *Gone in Sixty Seconds* is almost like porn."

That comment manages to shock a laugh out of me.

"This is a great idea, Ethan," she says, her tone much more serious than it was a moment ago. And then she leans forward, places one hand on my chest, and kisses me softly. "Thank you."

I pull her mouth back to mine using the nape of her neck, needing just one, two, three hundred more kisses. "Thank you for coming."

It sounds vulnerable when I say it, and I suppose that's accurate. I fight the urge to avert my eyes though because I want her to see me—my thoughts, my intentions, and my feelings. And more importantly, I want to see *her* while she's seeing me.

I watch her gorgeous green eyes as they flash with surprise, then her own vulnerability, and then a bit of sadness.

Instead of responding verbally, she takes my hand and kisses the back of it.

A car horn pulls us out of the moment, and when I look up, I see that the parking lot has filled up.

"It's going to start soon." I turn around to dig into the cooler again, getting the food out and putting bottles of water in the cupholders between us. Maggie chooses white wine to start, so I open it and pour some into the cheap plastic cups I brought. She laughs, and we toast to new beginnings just as the credits are starting for *Gone in Sixty Seconds*.

And then I get to watch two movies in the dark, under the stars with the woman I want to spend the rest of my life with. I get to hear her laugh and groan and insert her own commentary as she wishes.

When Nicholas Cage is saying "face...off..." repeatedly, she laughs so hard she wheezes, and I swear I feel a piece of my life shift back into place.

It's perfect.

She's perfect.

CHAPTER 34
CHICKENSHIT
MAGGIE

Lego House - Ed Sheeran

When I was in college, I pulled multiple all-nighters. It's very common among architecture students—in fact, come to think of it, I don't know a single architect who hasn't pulled all-nighters. It's not *really* a procrastination issue (although...sometimes it is), it's more that you have a ton of work to do, and the deadline is mid-morning.

What ends up happening is that you'll be at the studio the day before—drawing, modeling, prepping—and then before you know it, it's nighttime. You order food with everyone else there and then work through the night.

Sometimes, people would bring boozy drinks, but we learned quickly that you need to be careful with drinking and drafting—your lines end up crooked, no matter what tool you're using and let's just say that no one is trying to design another Leaning Tower of Pisa.

Ideally, you'd finish your project with enough time to go

home and shower before your class. (That's not always the case. Thank the beauty gods for dry shampoo.)

Those nights were exhausting, but exhilarating. With the youthful energy we had, we didn't suffer too badly, assuming we got a solid nap in later that day, or went to bed super early. In my thirties, there's no way I could do that and be at all functional.

Which is why I'm currently dragging my feet, trying to convince myself to get ready to head to my parents' house to finish up the kids' playroom.

I wasn't up all night drafting or drawing. Instead, I was up all night with Ethan, and that's far more exhilarating and just as exhausting. Sure, there were sexy times—though he's still holding out because we're not officially back together—but most of the time, we were talking, laughing, catching up.

He stayed at my place. I got out an extra toothbrush for him.

It feels new and fun.

It feels like the beginning.

Like we're getting a second chance at the amazing new feelings at the beginning of a relationship—the exciting, tentative, and yes, exhilarating new parts.

The parts romance novels and romantic comedies are predicated on. You know, the kinds of movies and books men shit on.

The parts women want the most and miss when they're gone.

I'm getting those all over again.

I'm getting the chance to fall in love with Ethan all over again.

I never stopped loving Ethan, of course, but this time around, it feels more...solid.

I'm grateful.

And currently very tired.

Ethan's arm wraps around my waist and pulls me tighter against him. We've been laying on the couch watching a movie—*National Treasure* because we wanted to continue Nicholas Cage night, but wanted to see a movie worth watching. Truthfully, we've been dozing throughout the day. I had to set a timer so I get up and over to my parents' house at least sort-of-on-time.

"What are you doing after?" Ethan's voice is grumbly with sleep.

"Probably face-planting my bed."

His hand slides down my belly and under the hem of my shirt, flattening back out against my skin. "Maybe you should face-plant my bed."

His warm breath against the nape of my neck sends a shiver down my spine.

"Or I can face-plant yours," he suggests.

I take a moment to think about that before I turn in his arms. There's a confident vulnerability in his eyes—he knows I might say no, but he won't let it get him down if I do. Somehow, I know he'll keep trying.

Respectfully, of course.

"Do you think that's moving kinda fast?"

A smirk pulls up one side of his mouth. "I wouldn't have suggested it if I thought it was too fast." He drops a kiss on the tip of my nose. "But if you think it's too fast, I'll respect that."

"Oh, yeah?" I tease.

"Yes," he says, but his jaw tics, and his hand flexes on my back.

"I'm sure."

His eyes narrow, and I swear I hear him growl a little bit.

I'm being a brat, and I know it. So I lean forward and kiss him to soothe his annoyance.

"I'll face-plant in your bed," I acquiesce.

"Good," he says, pulling me under him and kissing me. "Come on up when you're back."

"Okay," I whisper just before my alarm goes off, notifying me that I need to get moving.

"Do you want me to take anything upstairs for you?" he asks.

I blink heavily, once again assessing the seriousness of this do-over and how quickly it's moving. But then I decide that it doesn't really matter...that we're making up the rules as we go along, and we're just trying things out to see how it feels a second time around.

"Sure," I say, pushing on his chest. I go to my bathroom and get everything I need for my bedtime prep—my nighttime moisturizer, retinol, and eye cream. He already has a spare toothbrush for me at his place. I put everything in a little bag, get the shorts he'd kept, and grab a tank top to sleep in. I hand him a little duffel bag and then wrap my arms around his waist. I hear him take a deep breath in and feel him squeeze me tight.

"Be careful driving, please."

"I will."

He releases me but pauses to kiss me before turning for the door. Before he closes it, he looks back at me. "I'll see you later?"

I smile and nod. "You will."

"I can't believe how quickly you two pulled this together," Mom says. We're standing in the kids' playroom with Dad, checking out the finishing touches. The lights are finished. All the switch plates are installed. The toys have been arranged—neat and clean for the first (and probably only) time. The bins we got to store everything are labeled and nestled in their respective cubbies. The room is bright and cheery.

It's perfect.

"We did all right, didn't we?" Dad wraps his arm around my shoulders and pulls me into his solid frame.

"Yeah, I think we did okay," I say with a laugh.

"Dinner's almost ready. Let me go take that roast out of the oven and let it rest for a few minutes. You two wash up and head to the table," Mom orders.

Dad gives her a little salute. "Yes, ma'am."

"You watch it," she says, pointing a finger at him. Her serious tone is undercut by the smile that turns up the corners of her mouth and playful look in her eyes.

Dad and I follow directions, though, washing our hands and getting things set up at the table. Mom finishes getting the sides plated up while Dad cuts the roast, and before I know it, we've all stuffed ourselves and shared a bottle of wine on the back patio.

When Dad gets up to clean up the kitchen, Mom pointedly turns toward me with narrowed eyes.

"What?" I ask, mildly alarmed.

"You look happier today."

I blink. Multiple times. "Why are you looking at me like that if you think I look happier?"

"Because I want to know *why* you look happier."

The smile that splits my face is completely involuntary.

She gasps. "You're talking to Ethan again, aren't you?"

And then it's my turn to gasp. "How did you know that?"

My mother's head falls back as she laughs. She looks young and happy. Relaxed and triumphant. "Maggie, I haven't always been very adept at understanding you, but I've always been able to read your face. And right now?" She smiles as she studies my face, shaking her head slowly. "Right now, you look *happy*. Happier than I've seen you in over a year."

I don't have to think about it to know she's right. I can feel the heat rising in my face, turning my skin pink. I am happier than I've been in over a year. And I don't need to think about the reason—it's a no-brainer.

"Yes, I've been talking to Ethan again."

She fist pumps the air.

Fist pumps the air.

"Wow, I don't think I've ever seen you so excited about any of our relationships."

Helen Rafferty groans, picking up the bottle of wine and pouring the very last drops into her glass before picking up the second one.

"Margaret, I just want my kids to be happy. *All* of my kids. No matter what that means for them—and I do understand that might mean something different for each of them."

She frees the cork and pours us each a small glass.

"I've known you before Ethan, with Ethan, and without Ethan. And I'm telling you right now, there's no mistaking the way you look tonight versus the way you looked when you got home from Paris."

That comment makes me frown.

"I was happy when I got home from Paris."

She tilts her head to one side, then the other, considering. "You weren't *unhappy*, but you didn't look *happy* either.

Not to me, anyway. You looked..." She trails off as she squints into the dusky evening light.

I notice in this light the little similarities she and Nick shared. He looked so much like Dad, but Mom was in there, too. Helen Rafferty has hard edges—likely a product of being raised by the English—but her beauty softened all of us.

As I watch her brain whirl, I wonder if I'll ever think my mother isn't gorgeous. These days, knowing acutely how short life can be, I can't help but think that each year she ages is one to be grateful for. She and my dad are fortunate that they get to age. I realize not everyone will appreciate the wrinkles and the aching joints and all the other fun, potentially debilitating, aspects of growing old.

But if I got to spend my life with people I loved, I'd choose to take the good with the bad and enjoy life for as long as I could.

So...why aren't you doing that then?

Nick's voice pops into my head unbidden.

What the fuck are you talking about?

Hello...you aren't spending your life with a very specific person you love. You're being a chicken shit.

Do you show up just to antagonize me?

A little, yeah.

How are you still a dick in the afterlife?

Because now I live in your head. By the way, I was wondering if you should bring our little convos up with your therapist.

Oh, fuck off.

Never. I'll always be your brother. It's my job to tell you when you're being stupid. And Maggie...you're being stupid.

How am I being stupid?

You're still in love with Ethan.

So what? I'm allowed to be hesitant about this.

I guess. But I have the benefit of hindsight and the afterlife. I can see you're being stupid.

I thought you only lived in my head now.

...

You don't have anything to say to that do you?

If I live in your head now, I think you need to ask yourself if you think you're being stupid.

"...lost."

Mom's voice pulls me out of the dumpster fire that is my subconscious and snaps me back to the present.

"You looked lost."

I'm staring at her—surely with my jaw slack—when she turns her body toward mine, settling in for a lecture. I know that look, and yet I can't resist the bait.

"What do you mean by that?"

"I'm not sure I can describe it well...on the outside, you appeared normal. You looked mostly happy. Like you'd had a great time in Paris and were maybe a little sad to be home, and also glad to be back." Her eyes drift off to the side as she pauses. "But there was just...something off. Something didn't feel right. And the more I saw you, the more I realized that something was actually wrong."

See?

God, shut up, Nicholas.

Make me.

"You hide your emotions well, Maggie. You always have. But I'm still your mother...I know your face. I know every facial expression. Every look in your eye." Her voice gets softer as she speaks, the tone dripping with nostalgia and motherly love. "Like I said, I haven't been very good at understanding, or following through...but I saw it. And now, I *don't* see it."

I can't help asking the question burning on the tip of my tongue. "What do you see now?"

She smiles as her eyes roam over my face. "I told you... you look happier. You look more content."

With a sigh, I let my head fall back onto the chair.

"He took me to a drive-in movie theater last night," I admit.

I can't see her face, but I couldn't possibly miss her gasp.

"Where in the world did he find a drive-in theater?"

I tell her generally where we were and promise I'll get the details from Ethan. I don't need to be psychic to see a date night in the near future for Mom and Dad.

She asks questions about the evening—what movies we saw, what we had for dinner, what my plan is from here, although I leave out the more salacious details.

We're chatting and laughing, still sitting around the table when the patio door slides open, and Marie steps out of it.

"Maggie."

"Hey, big sister."

"Hello, dear. This is a nice surprise," Mom says. In the past, I might have thought Helen was making a comment about unannounced visits and how rude they are, but now I realize that might have been my own perception coloring the words. She looks genuinely happy to see Marie. She doesn't appear annoyed or put upon.

"I had to stop by and see this playroom everyone keeps talking about," Marie says, bending down to kiss Mom's cheek. "You know, since you were all secretive about it last week at family dinner."

"Oh, yes!" Mom sits up, twisting further to give Marie

her attention. "Maggie and your father have been working very hard on it. Did you look when you came in?"

"I did. It's gorgeous," Marie says, turning her head toward me. "You guys did a great job."

"Thanks," I say, with a smile.

A loud exclamation from inside draws our attention.

"Incoming," Marie says with a sigh.

"What?" I ask, turning to look at the sliding door.

Marie doesn't respond. Instead, she picks up my water glass, chucks the water out of it and into the grass. Then, she pours some wine into it.

Badass.

Right? I don't think I've ever seen her do anything like that.

And then I see Molly round a corner and head toward the back patio, Dad closely behind her with slumped shoulders.

I don't have a chance to say a single word when Molly opens the sliding door.

"What a lovely playroom, Mom. Dad was just showing me."

Oh, hell.

Fuck.

"Yes, your father and Maggie have been working very hard on it," Mom agrees. "Would you like to have a seat?"

Dad squeezes Mom's shoulder as he moves past her and reclaims his seat, pouring more wine into his glass.

Molly plops herself into a seat between me and Marie.

"What brought this about? At the last family dinner, you said you were redecorating, but you didn't say anything about making a playroom."

Ten bucks says no one told her because they didn't want to deal with the meltdown.

God-fucking-dammit.

"It was an idea your father and I had, but originally the idea was to just paint the room," Mom cuts in. "Your dad told Maggie about it and that got her mind going, which then turned into a more elaborate idea. I think it turned out beautifully. I'm very happy with it."

Molly watches our mother with an expression I'm sure she thinks is impassive, but from the three-and-a-half decades of knowing her, I know damn well she's a ticking time bomb.

"Yes, it's lovely," Molly agrees.

Marie drinks a sizable gulp of her wine.

Dad's shoulders tense up.

Mom is watching Molly patiently.

Here it comes.

We need popcorn.

"I'm just wondering what the impetus was for a playroom when so many of the grandchildren are too old to use it."

Marie rubs her forehead.

Dad is staring at his wine.

Mom is still watching Molly with infinite patience.

She's a fucking saint.

I know, dude.

I wouldn't have always agreed with Nick on that front, but the more I get to know my mom as an adult, the more I realize she was always letting us do our own thing...make our own decisions and mistakes.

"There are still plenty of young kids, Molly. And who's to say the older ones can't play with the younger ones in the playroom?"

Pay attention, Mags. She's delivering a master class.

You could use this one day. You know…if you ever get your head out of your ass about Ethan.

You're a dick.

It's not nice to speak ill of the dead.

Holy fuck.

"It just would have been nice to have something like that when my kids were younger, that's all," Molly says, her spine straight, her words clipped.

"I understand, Molls," our mom says. "Technically every room in the house is a playroom. We're just trying to get everything centrally located into one room so the toys have a place to live."

Molly doesn't have a response to that, but I didn't expect her to.

"I think it's great," Marie chimes in. "I'm sure my older ones will have fun with the younger ones in there. Besides…"

At her pause, I look up to find her giving me a sly look.

"…Maggie over here still hadn't had any kids."

My eyes bug out of my head, and Nick's voice in my head devolves into uncontrollable laughter.

"Oh, that is true."

Sure, *this* is the moment our dad chooses to speak up.

"Thanks, everyone, I'll get right on that."

Marie's shoulders are shaking with laughter.

Dad is smirking at me.

Mom is smiling, but she has a knowing look in her eye.

Molly is watching me from the corner of her eye.

"Okay, it was wonderful to see all of you," I say, just before downing the rest of my wine and standing up. "I'm going to head out." I kiss Dad's cheek. "Work day tomorrow and all." I hug Mom, and she squeezes just a little tighter than usual.

"I'm happy for you, Maggie," she whispers in my ear.

I force a breath into my lungs when I stand back up and meet her eyes. She smiles, and for some stupid reason, I can feel the backs of my eyes starting to burn, so I make hasty goodbyes and bolt for the front door.

I have a bed to face-plant.

CHAPTER 35
LACK OF SELF-AWARENESS
MAGGIE

Everlong (Acoustic) - Foo Fighters
October

"Did you bring the goods?" Marv asks from his recliner in the living room.

I came over to hang out with him while Cora went out to dinner with some friends. He's on a strict heart-healthy diet since his heart attack, and he's salty about it.

Pun intended.

"Absolutely not."

"Oh, come on."

"*No*, Marv. This is serious. You need to live a healthier lifestyle, or you're going to have an even bigger heart attack next time."

"*One* cheeseburger isn't going to kill me," he argues.

"No, it's the thousands of them you ate before that tried to kill you once already."

"Oh, for fuck's sake. What kind of life is worth living if you can't eat a cheeseburger now and then?"

I pour him some more water and sit down in the recliner next to his.

"Right now, it's important to change your habits. Once you're more established and comfortable with them, you can talk to your doctor about cheat meals."

He grumbles something under his breath.

"What was that, Grumbles? I couldn't understand you."

"I said you're a pain in my ass," he says more loudly, enunciating his words and even turning his head toward me so I can see his mouth moving. It only makes me laugh harder.

"Just trying to keep you alive, old man."

He rolls his eyes and turns his attention back to the television. He's watching last night's *Jeopardy*.

It feels good to be here with him. He's got his spunk back and is thankfully not talking in weird riddles anymore.

"Well if you didn't bring me a cheeseburger, what did you bring for dinner?"

"I brought you a delicious salmon filet that will be cooked in a maple balsamic glaze. The oven is preheating right now. You can have brown rice and broccoli with it."

I watch him out of the corner of my eye, waiting to see how he reacts. He's quiet, but some of the tension in his shoulders seems to relax.

"Okay, fine," he says eventually. "That actually sounds pretty good."

"It *is* good. It's my mother's recipe, and she's a brilliant chef."

I feel the moment his eyes shift to me, but I try to act normal. I realize there have been lengthy periods of time when I didn't bring my parents up. He knows I've struggled in my relationships with them over the years.

While one contestant clears an entire category, Marv

continues to watch me. Finally, I drag my eyes over to him with a sigh.

"What?" I ask.

"You got a recipe from your mom."

"I did."

"And you said she's a brilliant chef."

"I did."

"Do I really have to ask you to elaborate, or are you going to just tell me?"

I adjust my seated position and take a sip of my water, just to buy myself some time. He lets me do so in silence, likely knowing exactly what I'm doing.

"I've been...spending more time with them lately."

"Oh yeah?"

"Yeah," I say with a nod. And then I tell him about decorating the playroom, the conversation I had with my mom, and about how my view of her has shifted in the past few months.

When I'm finished, I look up to find Marv with a small smile on his face.

"What?" I ask again.

"I'm really proud of you, Maggie."

"Why do you say that?"

"Because you're trying."

I squint at him. "I'm always trying. I'm a hard worker."

Is he confused? Should I be worried?

He rolls his eyes dramatically, his head falling back to the recliner. "That's not what I meant, and you know it. Of course you're a hard worker, but I'm proud that you're trying to work on your relationship with your parents."

"Oh..."

"Yeah, *oh*."

"You know it's hard for me with them," I mumble. It's a pathetic defense.

"Yes, I do know. That's why I'm proud of you."

That brings a smile to my face, which I try to hide by picking up my water glass and taking a few sips.

"Not everyone gets along with their parents, and that's all right. But sometimes, we just need to try a little harder to find some common ground," he says. And I know he speaks from experience. "I'm glad you were able to find some, Maggie."

"Me, too," I whisper. It takes more effort than it should to speak. My throat is starting to sting with tears.

"And Ethan?"

I blink, trying to keep my face as impassive as possible. We've been spending a lot of time together, but we haven't exactly advertised that fact. "What about Ethan?"

He gives me an unamused look. "Maggie, I know you. You've been much happier lately. And I could be wrong that you've been hanging out with him again, but I don't think I am."

"You're the second person to say that to me recently."

"Who was the other?"

"My mom."

"Hmm. Interesting."

It's my turn to roll my eyes. "What does that mean?"

"Oh, nothing."

"Marvin, I swear..."

"I just mean that she and I must be seeing similar things."

"And what are those things?"

"That you seem like your old self again. But also...better than that. You seem to have found yourself again, but you've grown."

I frown, because I don't know what he means about me growing.

"Maggie, you haven't always been very forgiving," he says with a big sigh.

"What?"

"You have a tendency to see in black and white. You're unlikely to forgive someone after they've hurt you." Marv blinks at me with wide eyes. "Did you really not know that?"

"Okay, so I'm not quick to forgive. Why should I be? *Fool me once, shame on you. Fool me twice, shame on me,* and all that. I don't see it as a character flaw."

"I think for people you barely know, that's fine, but it's important to make exceptions for people who love you and want to support you."

"Sometimes people who claim to love and support you still hurt you," I say. My voice is louder, and I'm sure he can hear the defensiveness in my voice.

"Yes, they do. And those people deserve the chance to earn your forgiveness."

I can feel myself getting worked up—ready to start an argument with him—so I take a deep breath to calm down. In the quiet, I force myself to really think about what he's saying.

I think about how my relationship with my mom has changed and the conversations we've had. About the things I've learned about her and the way she apologized for not trying harder with me. How those conversations and the time we spent together have helped soothe an ache in my soul that's been there for as long as I can remember.

And then I think about Ethan.

Ethan.

Kind, thoughtful, loving Ethan.

Ethan who sat patiently with me while I fell apart after the sudden death of my brother.

Ethan who took me to the hospital when Marv had his heart attack and stayed with me all night.

Ethan who has taken care of me more than once since I returned from Paris when I got migraines that knocked me on my ass.

Ethan who has stayed with me in my bed but hasn't tried to take anything physical farther than he said he would.

Ethan who told me he wouldn't give up on me—wouldn't stop trying to get me back—and he's absolutely stuck to his word.

Ethan who has been patient while I work through this mess in my head.

It has never been a question of me loving Ethan. It's always been a question of where this relationship is going.

"I still don't want to get married, Marv."

"Is he pushing for that?"

Bleh.

I don't want to say it out loud because it makes me sound like a chickenshit looking for excuses, but I still shake my head.

Marv stares at me until I meet his eyes again.

"You know what my next question is."

Then what's the problem?

I huff an exasperated sigh. "Because I'm scared, okay? I was with him for five fucking years, and then he drops this bomb on me, and I'm fucking *terrified* that we'll get through another five years, and it will happen again."

"Oh, Maggie..." He sits forward and rests his elbows on his knees. "Whether you're in a legal marriage or a long-term relationship, you're asking for the same thing..."

I look at him, a frown on my face.

"...a leap of faith, kiddo."

Something about that knocks the air out of my chest, and I have to blink a lot to try to keep the tears at bay.

"Relationships—all of them, but particularly romantic ones—require a serious leap of faith," he says, absent-mindedly twisting his wedding band around on his finger. "You're asking this person you love to love you back. To respect you. To support you. To tell you the truth. And to not hurt you. It's a tall order, Maggie, and it's not easy for anyone to fill or ask for. Especially as time goes on...when you've been with someone for years—decades—and both of you are growing and changing...evolving into new people. Long-term relationships are hard sometimes, kid. But whether you're married or not, the commitment is the same."

The battle with my tears was lost sometime around *it's a tall order*. I sniff and dab at my face with a tissue from the small table between us.

"How do I know it's not going to end the same way?"

"Sweetheart, you don't."

Of course that just makes me cry harder.

"Maggie, it's that leap of faith. Have the two of you talked through the breakup? What went wrong the first time?"

I nod.

"Okay, well...if the two of you have been clear about your expectations and boundaries, that's all you can do. You can put your love for each other first, commit to each other on a long-term basis, and then take the leap together."

Eyeing him warily, I grab more tissues from the box.

"I know, I know," he chuckles. "Like I said, it's not easy. But if you love him...if you want to see if it's possible to be with him the way you want to be, you'll never know unless you try again."

"Well, we're...hanging out."

Marv's head tilts to one side. "But you won't take the leap. And until then, you've got one foot out the door."

That's the moment the oven dings to let me know it's sufficiently preheated. I clear my throat and scramble out of my chair.

"I'm going to put that salmon in," I say as I bolt past Marv, blowing my nose along the way. I throw away my tissues and wash my hands in the kitchen sink before pulling the lid off the glass dish and placing it in the oven.

In the meantime, I heat up the brown rice I made last night in the microwave and grab the steam-in-a-bag broccoli out of the freezer.

I check in on Marv in between basting the salmon—he's back to watching *Jeopardy*. I also peek around at their family photos hanging on the wall. Marv and Cora on their wedding day. One in a big living room with two dozen people posing in front of a fireplace at Christmas. One of the frames has a bunch of ovals in it where baby pictures have been placed—each one with a name carefully scrawled in elegant cursive underneath.

Andrew James
Jennifer Elaine
Elizabeth Marie
Jackson James
Alexander Thomas
Edward Joseph

Memories assail me from years past—Ethan and I talking about baby names and debating how many children is the perfect number. The two of us at each of my niece and nephews' baptisms. Baby showers and birthday parties. I suddenly remember my nephews screaming *Uncle Ethan is here!* with striking clarity.

I was on this trajectory once, and with a man I was hopelessly in love with. I always thought we'd end up here...in a cozy house with family photos on the wall and babies nipping at our heels.

...Aaaaaand you still want that. And you can still have it. *With* Ethan, if you'd like.

Nick. What a surprise you'd show up right now.

I just want you to make the right decision.

So do I, Nick. I'm fucking trying here.

I know you are. I also know that you're doing everything you can to talk yourself out of this.

I don't even have a response to that. I just rub the space between my eyebrows.

Marv is right.

Marv is right about a lot of things.

Yes, but the thing he said about the leap of faith...that was true.

I stare at Edward Joseph's squishy face and feel a pang of sadness in my chest that I'll never get to meet Nicholas Junior.

There are no guarantees, Maggie. Whether you're married or not. I didn't have nearly enough time with Kate... But I'm grateful for every one of those years. I wish I could have had more. I didn't get a choice.

Nick, I just stopped crying. I really don't want to start again.

I'm not trying to make you cry. I'm trying to pull your head out of your ass.

Still eloquent, even in the afterlife.

Shut up. I know you're scared. I know it's hard for you to believe it will be different, but that's another thing Marv is right about...you won't know unless you try. And Maggie...you need to ask yourself if you'll regret not trying.

I'm staring blankly at the photos when the oven timer goes off for the final time. I snap out of it and plate up all the food, but my conversations with Marv and Nick's voice keep replaying in my head.

By the time I carry the plates into the living room, I know the answer to the question Nick posed.

CHAPTER 36
NO REGRETS

ETHAN

Men On The Moon - Chelsea Cutler

"You want another one?" Miles asks me.

He texted to ask if I wanted to meet up for a burger and a beer. I said yes, but that I have plans later and wouldn't be staying out too late.

"Nah, I'm good. I'm gonna head out soon."

Miles takes another pull of his beer and glances at the TV before asking the question I know has been burning in his mind.

"Your plans later...they involve Maggie?"

I don't even bother to control my face. It just splits into a huge smile.

"Yeah. Yeah, they do."

He doesn't look as happy as I expect him to, which gives me pause.

"What's that look for?"

Miles picks at the label on his beer bottle. "You guys hooking up or what?"

I rear back. "What? No. We're not hooking up. Why would you ask me that?"

"Because you're getting together later tonight. Sounds like a booty call, man."

What I really want to do is smack him in the back of the head. But I keep my hands to myself because I'm not that much of a dick.

"It's not like that, man."

"Look it's just that both of you seem like you've been doing better lately, and I don't want to watch either of you go down that spiral again."

Another beer sounds good right about now, but I'd rather get home to Maggie on time and with my wits about me.

"You said it seems like we've both been doing better lately."

"Yeah."

"What do you mean by that? About her, specifically."

I can hear him grumbling just under the bar noise. He scrubs an agitated hand over his hair.

"I don't know what I should tell you, Ethan. But lately... she seems happy again. She's smiling more. She doesn't have that cloud of sadness around her anymore. And I haven't seen her like that since before you broke up."

I take a deep breath and let those words sink in.

Maggie is happier.

She doesn't look sad anymore.

It has to be because of me, right? At least in part?

"And you, too. You're different tonight."

I study my empty beer bottle and do a mental comparison of how I've shifted and changed since Maggie got back into town.

I'm definitely happier, though I'd say that's a more

recent development. At first, I was miserable. I'd see her for work-related things, during which she was completely professional, which made things a little (tiny) bit easier. But then we'd be alone and every bit of self-loathing and anger rose back to the surface, which would be amplified by the pain I saw reflected in her eyes.

There were moments I'd see hope in our interactions—even when she was mad at me. Because at least that meant she still cared. But I was very glad when things evened out between us.

I wasn't glad Marv had a heart attack, of course. But I'm extremely glad I was with her when it happened so I could support her.

These last few weeks with Maggie have been nothing short of incredible. We're spending time together, getting to know each other again, while also giving each other space. Sometimes she sleeps at my place. Sometimes I sleep at hers. And sometimes we sleep apart—not that I like that arrangement much, but Maggie has insisted upon it, so I don't argue.

We've been on dates. We've had nights in where we watch movies in comfy clothes.

And yeah, there's been sexy stuff. But I maintain the no-sex rule because she hasn't admitted she's mine yet. I can say with confidence that we're building back toward that, though.

"I'm doing better. I'm happier, yeah," I admit.

Miles stares at me for a beat, and when he realizes I'm going to stay silent, he shakes his head. "That's all you're going to tell me?"

"Listen," I start with a laugh. "I don't know what she wants me to say. We haven't really talked about it."

"What the fuck does that mean?"

I tap on my phone to check my notifications. No text from Maggie yet.

"Maggie and I are hanging out. We have been for a while now."

"For real?"

I nod, my chest swelling with pride, if I'm being honest.

"So are you...back together or something?"

"Not yet," I say reluctantly. "But I'm not giving up. She wants to take it slow."

Miles huffs a laugh. "Take it slow? You guys were together for years."

"Preaching to the choir, dude. On some level though...I get why she wants to start over. That breakup was fucking traumatic. I understand why she's hesitant to throw herself back into the deep end."

Flashbacks from the morning after the breakup flood my mind, but I push them away. It's not worth thinking about. It was a long time ago now, and we're past it. We're moving forward.

"I don't have a problem waiting until she's more comfortable."

I'll wait as long as she needs me to.

It's not a hardship to wait for the love of my life.

And it's not like I'm cut off from her the way I was when she was in Paris. She lives a few floors below me, and she answers my calls. I get to kiss her and feel her body against mine at night and show her I love her in a number of different ways (both dirty and not).

It's enough for now.

"Wow, man...I had no idea this had been going on."

"Well, neither of us have talked about it with many people."

My phone lights up just then on the tabletop.

Mags: Leaving Marv's now. Be home in 20.

Me: Can't wait to see you.

Me: Be careful driving.

"That her?"

"Yeah." I dig my wallet out of my pocket and make eye contact with our server. "She's on her way home."

Across from me, Miles leans back against the booth, getting his own wallet out. "Fuck, man...I'm really glad that's what's actually going on."

The server arrives at the table, and I let her know we're ready to cash out.

"What did you think was going on?"

"I don't know...maybe you were just messing around, and I was worried you'd both crash and burn."

I laugh.

"Nah, we've already done that once. Neither of us is interested in doing it again."

"Fair enough."

Tabs paid, tips left, we're parting ways by our cars in the parking lot.

"Hey."

I turn to look at him.

"I'm really happy for you," he says. "And for her. You're good together."

"Thanks, man. She's not mine yet, though. Don't congratulate me just yet."

He smirks at me, then rolls his eyes. "Go home."

"Happy to."

I'm meeting the love of my life back at home, and I can't wait.

∼

THE KNOCKING on the door has me sprinting from my bedroom. I put clean sheets on the bed while I was waiting for Maggie.

When I open the door, she's standing there, a brilliant smile blooming on her face.

"Hey," she breathes.

"Hey," is all I can say in return. I reach for her, pulling her into my apartment and closing the door behind us. It's the most natural thing in the world to hold her head in my hands and kiss her—probably because it is. We've done this a million times. It's just that we eventually took it for granted. Never again, though.

She melts into me immediately, and I hope it's a sign that she feels the same way.

"How's Marv?" I ask when she pulls away.

Her eyes light up as she takes her purse off her shoulder and hangs it on a dining room chair. "He's doing really well! His rehab is going great. Cora said his physical therapists are happy with his progress."

"Good," I tell her. I'm sincerely grateful and glad to hear this news. Marv is so important to her. I want him to make a full recovery.

"Yeah, it was great to hang out with him," she says, wrapping her arms around my waist and pressing her head into my chest. "He's a lot like his old self again."

I thread my fingers into her curls, holding her head securely against me. "That's great news. I'm glad to hear it."

"Me, too," she whispers, and then she squeezes me so tight that it kind of hurts, but I wouldn't dare complain about it. She can squeeze me until I can't breathe if she wants.

We stand there for a few moments, holding each other

in silence. I take in the scent of her and try to re-memorize the exact curves of her body against mine.

It's interesting how things change after your life has imploded. There was a time when I took this kind of moment for granted—where I would have hugged her and moved on within a couple of seconds.

But once you think you'll never get the chance again, each one of these slow embraces feels like a fucking gift. And I don't care who thinks I'm giving up my man card by saying that. I'll trade that thing in a fucking heartbeat. It never meant much to me anyway.

And that reminds me that I didn't call Rachel back like I was supposed to today. I need to do that or she's going to kill me in my sleep.

"Ethan?"

"Yeah?"

"Can I talk to you about something?"

"Of course." I release her, and she pulls back, a nervous look in her eye.

A quick bolt of panic shoots through my body, but I force it back down. She wouldn't be here, wrapping her arms around me and kissing me if she was hoping to pump the breaks.

I interlace my fingers with hers and lead her over to the couch. She sits, but angles her body toward me, her knee against mine, both of her hands holding one of mine. She licks her lips and swallows.

She's nervous, and I don't understand why.

"Mags...what's going on? Are you okay?"

Her eyes snap to mine, and I see them soften.

"Yeah, yeah, I'm fine. I promise."

I give her hands a squeeze.

"Ethan, I..." she starts and stops, swallowing hard. "I've

been thinking a lot. About you and me and everything that's happened between us. First and foremost, I want to thank you for being so patient while I'm working through this. These past few weeks have been...amazing."

I open my mouth to tell her she doesn't need to thank me—that I'd do anything for her. That I'd wait for her forever if she asked me to. But she puts her fingers up against my lips to stop me.

"I just need to get this out...please. And then you can talk."

I take hold of her wrist and kiss the fingertips that rest against my mouth. Nodding, I place our intertwined hands back on our knees.

"I've been talking to my mom a lot. Working things out with her. I've talked to Kate about Nick. And Marv has been telling me some really cryptic shit, but telling me important things, too. And—" she cuts herself off quickly, like she's changed her mind about telling me something. "Marv told me some things about myself that I didn't really realize were true. And I'm going to work on that."

She stops and meets my eyes again, takes a small breath.

"And I want to start with you."

I frown, because I have no idea what she's talking about, but she asked me not to talk until she was done. She goes into an explanation about how she's not a forgiving person, and that's what she wants to start with me. While she tells me that she wants to forgive me, I can feel my chest crack a little bit. I squeeze her hands a little harder.

"So, yes, I'm trying to forgive you, but I also need you to try to forgive me. Because if we're going to try this again, we need a clean slate."

She keeps talking, but I'm stuck on one part.

If we're going to try this again.

"But I'm scared," she admits softly, yanking me back to the present. "I'm *really* scared. If being with you is a leap of faith, I'm willing to jump off the cliff, but I need to know you're jumping with me. I need to know you're holding my hand and that you won't let go. Because Ethan...I'm so in love with you. I know you know that. I don't want to keep pushing you away because I'm scared. I want to be fearless with you. I want to figure out what we both want again and what we want to accomplish together, although I really hope it's still kids because I think our kids would be fucking cute. But whatever we figure out—whatever we decide—I want to figure it out *with* you. I want to argue with you about it and then make up in sexy ways and then laugh about it later."

Staying silent is becoming more impossible by the second, but I do it because she asked me to.

"I don't want to hurt you again. And I know you don't want to hurt me again. More than anything, I want us both to be happy..." The rest of the air in her lungs rushes out in a *whoosh,* and she blinks repeatedly. And then that signature *Maggie* look of determination passes across her eyes.

"I want to celebrate the successes with you and curl up next to you when things go to shit—because we both know they will at some point. The point is though...I want to be with you for all of that. Even though I'm scared, I think...I think I'd regret not trying again. In fact...I know I would. At the end of the day, you're the only one I want to talk to. I don't want to fight it anymore, Ethan. I love you, and I want to be with you. Forever, if at all possible. Can we please, *please* try not to fuck this up again? Because I really can't go through another breakup with you. It was absolutely horrible the first time, and I think it would kill me a second time."

She stops talking and looks into my eyes with a hopeful look on her face.

"That's all, huh? Just forever?" I tease.

Her eyes dance as she tries to hold back a smile. "Yeah, I mean whatever. If you feel like you can't hack it, I can just head out." She makes a pathetic attempt at getting up, but she and I both know she isn't going anywhere.

I make sure she stays with a hand wrapped around the nape of her neck and my lips pressed to hers. She opens for me almost immediately, which I take full advantage of, tasting her mouth and pushing her backward on the couch as I crawl over her.

It already feels different. My blood is rushing in my ears, and if it's possible for a soul to sing, that's what mine is doing.

Maggie's hands are everywhere, and I'm pressing her into the couch like a starving man who's finally gotten his hands on his favorite meal.

Actually, yes...she is my favorite meal. And I'm absolutely going to feast on her tonight.

We're teenagers right now, making out on a couch because we have the house to ourselves. It's hot. Honestly, if someone walked in right now, I'm not even sure I'd notice. I'm completely absorbed in her.

Her arms.

Her mouth.

Her scent.

Her legs, which are wrapping around my hips and pulling me in closer.

I slide my hand under her shirt so I can get to her skin, not stopping until I reach her breast. I love Maggie's breasts. They're perfect—size, shape, weight, softness. Everything about them is incredible. And right now, they're trapped under a fucking bra.

So I start yanking her shirt up, but when I reach her head, the couch arm is in the way of actually getting it off. On a different day, under other circumstances, it would be funny. We probably would have laughed at the hiccup and picked up where we left off. But today? No...I'm too wound up. Too desperate. Too happy.

I need her. I can't have anything in my way.

With a growl, I sit up, bringing her with me. I pull the shirt off and chuck it behind me before standing up. She's scrambling to her feet when I pick her up, trying to expedite the process. I want her in my bed, and I want her there right fucking now.

She wraps her legs around my waist and her arms around my neck, and she doesn't stop kissing me for a single second of our journey from the living room to my bedroom. I pop the clasp on her bra while I still have easy access to it. She's still clinging to me as I lower us to the bed—with clean sheets, for the win.

Her dark curls fan against my duvet and something about that simple color contrast ratchets my need even higher. I drag her bra down her arms and throw it before diving down to capture a nipple in my mouth, and she arches her back, pushing into me. Her fingers thread into my hair, nails scraping my scalp and throwing what little patience I had out the fucking window.

But I need to make sure *she's* sure.

With a massive amount of effort, I pull off her nipple and jerk her arms above her head. I intertwine my fingers with hers, holding our joined hands against the pillow.

She swallows, a question in her lust-filled eyes as she stares up at me.

"You're mine."

She nods, but it's not enough.

I lean down so my mouth is directly next to her ear.

"I want to hear you say it, Maggie."

The gasp that comes out of her mouth is a beautiful reward, but the goose bumps that spread across her entire torso is electricity in my blood.

"I'm yours," she breathes.

At her words—ones I've been longing to hear for months now—a warm feeling starts right in the center of my chest and spreads outward, up my neck, down my arms, through my belly and into my legs. All the way to my toes.

Some people would call it love—and that's definitely part of it. I feel an incredible depth of love for this woman on a daily basis, and right now, it's even more intense.

But the rest of it...I think that's relief. Relief that she's mine again. That we're committing to each other.

That we're building our *family* again.

The absolute torture of being on the edge of a relationship is finally over, and she's *mine*. Finally mine.

I take a shuddering breath and lean back so I can look in her eyes. Those green pools of lust are waiting for me, but I also see my relief mirrored in her gaze. And I wonder if she felt the same warmth I did.

"Fucking *finally*," I breathe before I crush my mouth back to hers. Her intensity and hunger match mine perfectly, so even though she whimpers a protest when I pull away to slink down her body, I'm confident she won't be upset for long.

In fact, when I unzip her shorts and kiss the revealed skin, she seems to have forgotten she was protesting mere seconds ago.

I make short work of peeling the rest of her clothing off.

I have some feasting to do. And finally, *finally*...it doesn't have to end there.

CHAPTER 37
CLOSING THE LOOPHOLE
MAGGIE

Skin and Bones - David Kushner

"F*uck...*"

"Not yet, Mags." I look down to see his smug face looking up at me. "I want to do other things first."

I fist the duvet and swallow hard.

"And then...*then*, I plan to fuck you. Because you're finally mine again."

Something inside my brain is basically jumping up and down with glee. It's every championship sports team in the locker room, spraying champagne everywhere. It's elated but it's also horny as fuck and needs to let me focus because I've *missed* this. I've missed Ethan and everything he is.

Sure, we've been messing around and doing all kinds of sexy things, but there's nothing really like being *with* someone you love to your very core. I'm not one to use the term "make love" so I'm not going to. What I will do is admit that sex is better with someone you love.

Don't get me wrong—sex is great. Sex is absolutely

awesome when you're with someone you feel safe with and who treats you with respect (unless you're asking for some disrespect, and that's *also* great). Sex is wonderful with someone who knows what they're doing—particularly if you're a woman who is sleeping with a man. It's best if they know their way around a woman's body.

I enjoy sex, and that's not something I've ever been shy about. I don't think there's any reason to shame anyone, regardless of their gender identity or preferences. I think that what matters is that everyone involved is having fun and freely giving consent.

Active, participatory consent.

And Ethan knows this. He knows I go feral for consent-checks.

Which is why, when he looks up at me telegraphing his next move with a pointed look at my core, I know he's pausing long enough for me to give a red or green light.

"Yes. Ethan, please."

And that's all the permission he needs before diving in. His tongue laps at my core as his arms wrap around my thighs, anchoring me where he wants me. Everything is hot and hypersensitive, and I feel *desperate*.

I want to look away, but I can't. I need to watch him.

I want to move my hips, but he's holding them in place.

I want to dig my hands into his hair, and I do try that at first, but it's not enough. I can't touch him enough, so I take one hand and grip the pillow behind my head. I suddenly wish his headboard had openings so I could grip it. It's all fabric and tufting though.

The emotions rushing through my chest right now are heightening everything—his soft tongue, his rough hands, the sting of the occasional bite from sharp teeth—it's all more intense than it was the last time he had me like this. And if I'm not mistaken, he feels the difference, too.

His eyes are molten lava when he looks up at me before doing that *thing* with his tongue that has always made my legs shake.

"Ethan...*fuck.*"

His moan is the only response, and the vibration of it sends me higher.

I can feel both of my hands tighten in their fists, and I'm certain I'm hurting him now. But he doesn't complain. Instead, he uses that dirty mouth for different purposes.

"Give it to me, Maggie," he growls. "I want it. I need it."

With a few more flicks of his tongue, I'm lost. Arching off the bed, panting, flying, my whole body contracting. The feeling seems to last forever, and Ethan doesn't take his mouth off me the whole time. When I regain a sense of where I am, he's slowly lapping at me and leaving kisses everywhere.

"*Ethan.*"

His eyes flick up to meet mine—that milk chocolate melting into black pupils. With one last kiss on the most sensitive part of my body, he crawls slowly up my body, like a tiger stalking its prey. On his way up, he leaves languid kisses along my torso, my breasts, my collarbone.

"Maggie..." he breathes, settling his hips against me, notched perfectly between my legs, demonstrating just how hard he is. "I have waited so long to have you again." He cages me in with his arms, drops sweet kisses to the corners of my mouth. "But if you need more time, I'll wait as long as you ne—"

"No!" I cut him off with a startled outburst. "You act like I haven't been waiting for this, too. Don't you dare stop now." And then I fuse my mouth to his and feel the last of the tension leave his body. His shoulders relax, and his hands loosen their grip on my hair.

"Ethan, please," I beg again. I'm not above begging. I know he thinks it's hot. And like I said...I'm desperate at this point. I need him.

So I turn my attention to his shorts, unbuttoning them and opening the zipper. I don't waste time feeling him over his boxers. I slip my hand under the waistband and wrap my hand around him. He hisses, and I don't even try to hide my smirk.

"Give it to me, Ethan," I parrot his words back to him. "I want it. I need it."

"*Goddammit*, your mouth." He groans into my neck as he tastes my skin.

I let him go long enough to push his shorts and boxers down. When I get them far enough down, I use my feet to get them the rest of the way off. He spends the entire time with his head buried in my chest, licking, nipping, sucking.

"Ethan...now. Please." I thread my fingers into his hair and tug on the back of his head. He looks up at me with hooded eyes.

And then things suddenly slow down.

The desperation burning a fever in my blood cools off as he looks into my eyes. I can see the love I feel for him reflected back at me. I can feel the weight of this moment pushing down on both of us. I can clearly see the odds that were stacked against us. I can see how hard he worked to get me back. How hard I worked to get through my bullshit. How patient he was the entire time.

I can see our future.

He doesn't break eye contact as he reaches between us and lines himself up with my body.

He doesn't try to hide the emotion I see in his eyes when the tip goes in.

And he doesn't bother tamping down his physical reaction to being fully seated inside me.

His whole body trembles. His mouth opens to a perfect O. His breathing stutters and starts again.

And for my part, I'm feeling much of the same. Shivers go up my spine. My breath completely abandons me. I make some kind of noise, although I'm not entirely sure what it was supposed to be. A groan, maybe?

Ethan gently drops his forehead to mine as breathes my name in the barest of whispers.

When he starts moving, I kiss him for the simple reason that I *have* to. I feel like I'm going to melt into a puddle underneath him, and I want to stay present. Cognizant. I want to commit every single moment of this experience to memory. This is something I never thought I'd have again—a life I never thought I'd lead again.

With one forearm planted by my head, the other is free to explore my body, which he takes full advantage of. He's always had a thing for my boobs.

Reluctantly, I pull back for air, but he doesn't miss a beat, choosing instead to murmur loving words against my skin.

"I love you, Maggie."

"I've missed this so much."

"You feel so fucking good."

"I'll want you forever."

"I don't ever want this to end."

"I'll do whatever it takes."

"We're not giving up...not ever again, Mags."

With each word he says, the warmth in my chest seems to tighten, tighten, tighten until it's a ball fighting to get out.

Even as I roll my hips into him harder, I can feel my eyes and throat start to burn.

I've never been one to cry during sex, but I also know that if I do cry, Ethan won't judge me for it.

I push on his chest just enough for him to get the hint. With his arms wrapped around me, he rolls us. As I sit up, he's pushed even deeper, bordering on pain, stealing the breath from my lungs.

"Ethan...fuck."

"You can handle it, Mags," he says. "You've done it before." But he doesn't just leave me there to take it and hope I can adjust quickly enough. He sits up and wraps his arms around my back, which adjusts the angle just enough to take away some of the pressure. "Better?"

"Yes..." I sigh.

He somehow scoots us so he's closer to the headboard and then draws my mouth back to his, kissing me while I take over.

Ethan seems to remember every single thing about what I like and need in bed. He sucks on my nipples, kneads my breasts, and squeezes my ass. And when I'm getting really close, he goes in for the kill. He makes eye contact with me while he slowly sucks his thumb into his mouth, then drops it between our bodies and presses gently against my clit, letting the rhythm I'm setting control the pressure he exerts.

And holy fuck, it doesn't take long.

"Yes, Maggie. Yes..."

My eyes drift shut as my second orgasm washes over me. My hands involuntarily squeeze his shoulders as I try to keep from falling off the cliff I am obviously standing on. I vaguely register his voice as I tumble down.

"Fuck, yes. God, Maggie, you're perfect."

He thrusts up into me, chasing his own high as I spasm around him. And that doesn't take long either.

With a shout, he freezes, his hands on my waist, holding me down.

I place a hand over his heart and feel it beating relentlessly against his rib cage as his head falls back against the headboard. That simple rhythm infuses me with a calm feeling, chasing that desperation out the door.

We stay like that while our breathing returns to normal—or at least *closer* to normal—and then he's kissing me again. His hands are in my hair and moving my head in whatever way he wants me, his tongue slipping into my mouth.

It's...gentle. Loving. Perfect.

Eventually, he rolls me back over and sits up.

"Don't move. I'll be right back." He kisses me one more time and then smirks at me.

Smirks at me. He's so proud of himself.

I watch him walk toward his bathroom and then hear the water run for a moment before he returns, holding a washcloth. He uses it to clean me up, kissing sensitive skin as he goes. I giggle and squirm, but it only encourages him. When he's done, he tosses the washcloth in his laundry bin and heads to the kitchen. I use the opportunity to pee.

While I'm washing my hands, I look at my reflection in the mirror, and I'm surprised by what I see.

I'm flushed, my lips swollen, red marks are in plenty of places on my body. I expected all that. None of those things are causing me a single moment of pause.

What surprises me is the look in my eyes.

They're brighter than they were. There's an honest-to-goodness twinkle in them. I look...happy.

Some might say it's a post-orgasm glow, but even I can admit there's more to it than that. I smile at Mirror Maggie and dry my hands.

He's sitting on the bed when I return. There are two champagne flutes on his nightstand, and he's twisting the metal cage off the top of a bottle.

"What in the world are you doing?" I ask, pulling on his shirt from the floor.

He looks up from his task and smiles. A massive, genuine, happy smile.

"I've been saving this for when you finally agreed to get back together."

I huff a laugh. "Oh yeah? When did you buy it?"

He puts the metal cage on the nightstand and wraps his capable hand around the cork.

"The first day I saw you at work. When I realized we'd be working together."

What?!

I blink at him. I try to speak words, but I don't actually get any out. He gets the cork out with a gentle *pop.*

"I told you, Mags...I never gave up. I was never content to be without you."

He pours champagne into flutes while I sputter next to him.

"Fate or God or whatever had placed you directly in front of me, and there was no fucking way I was going to waste that opportunity," he says, handing me a flute. "You were mad. And so was I. But I believed in us. I wasn't going to stop until I had you back. So on the way home, I stopped at the store and picked this up. It's been in the back of my fridge ever since...just waiting."

Five months.

I can't say anything. I just sit there and blink at him.

So he leans forward and kisses me.

"I've loved you for years, Maggie. You're the only one I've ever wanted to spend my life with. You're my family, my best friend. My partner in everything. *Of course* I was going to fight tooth and nail for you."

Those tears I managed to fight a few moments ago are back in full force, falling down my cheeks with very minimal warning.

Ethan wipes them away with his thumb.

"You're it for me, Mags."

The tears come faster than he can wipe them away, so he takes my flute back and sets them on the nightstand, then scoops me up and into his lap.

"Why are you crying, sweetheart?"

It takes a minute for me to get comprehensible words out, but I manage it.

"You...you n-never gave up on me...but I...I gave up on you."

He frowns, still wiping my tears away.

"Maggie—"

"I dated someone else—"

"Technically, I did, too—"

"But it was one date," I wail.

It tells him that I had more than one "date" without using those words.

He sighs and takes my head in his hands.

"Maggie...I told you, I'm not mad. It was a really difficult time for both of us. We were both heartbroken, and we dealt with it in different ways."

"But—"

"No buts, Mags..." But then his eyes twinkle, and he adds, "Unless it's your butt, in which case, yes *please.*"

"Ethan," I whine, gently punching him in the shoulder.

But the joke has the effect he wanted. It makes me smile and breaks up my sobs.

"What matters is that I love you, Maggie. And you love me. And we're together again." His hands slide down the sides of my neck, my arms, and end with my hands. He pulls them both up in his and kisses my knuckles. "I'd have sent you a million more texts. Voicemails. Emails."

I study his eyes, looking for any indication that he's stretching the truth, but I don't find anything other than clear, beautiful honesty.

Wait.

"Emails?"

He stills for a moment, then meets my gaze again.

"Yes, emails."

"I didn't get any emails from you," I tell him, shaking my head.

"When's the last time you checked your junk email?"

I blink.

Who checks their junk email?

"When you block a phone number, the texts and voicemails are gone—lost to whatever cloud somewhere. But when you block an email address, the emails go to your junk folder."

I feel my eyes get wider, and then I'm spinning around, running toward my purse. I immediately start searching for my spam filter, slowly walking back to Ethan, who's sitting on the bed with a glass of champagne in his hand.

As soon as the folder pops up, emails start downloading. There's plenty of advertisements and actual spam, but amid them all, I see Ethan's name pop up over and over and over again.

A huge smile spreads across my face, I rush to him, leaping into his lap and wrapping my arms around his neck.

"I do love you, Ethan. More than anyone, ever."

He nods slowly. "I know you do."

"This is forever," I promise.

"This is forever," he promises.

We seal it with a kiss.

EPILOGUE

ETHAN

"Thank you to the English speakers for waiting patiently."

A man who even I can admit is extremely good-looking speaks into a microphone to the side of a red ribbon. He's flanked by a few members of his French team and Maggie's team from the US—Kelsie and Maggie, and thankfully, Marv, who is back on his feet and has returned to work.

He continues his speech, but in English this time, so I'm actually able to understand it. He's talking about how wonderful it was to work with the Americans, and I choose to believe that Maggie was responsible for ninety percent of that good sentiment because I love her, and my opinion that she is the greatest woman on the planet is completely unbiased.

We arrived in Paris a couple of days ago. She's taken me

a million places with her French friends and impressed me with her ability to speak to them and understand what they're saying. She ordered for us in French, even. (It's also really hot, I'm not going to lie.)

She claims her accent is awful, but it doesn't matter to me.

Note to self: have her speak French to me in bed.

It doesn't matter if it's complete nonsense. It will still be hot as fuck.

Today is the ribbon-cutting ceremony, and then we're staying for a couple of extra days just to make the most of the trip.

A gentle laugh to my right draws my attention. It's coming from a woman named Chloé, who is sporting a barely-there baby bump. Her fiancé, Julien, has an arm wrapped protectively around her body, resting on her tiny bump.

Yes, I know who Julien is. I met him via FaceTime a long time ago. I won't say we're *friends,* but I don't dislike him. It helps that he's engaged to a pregnant woman, and Maggie isn't paying him any extra attention. She's actually been fawning over Chloé, asking about French baby customs and if they've considered any names.

I never thought I'd be hanging out with someone Maggie slept with, but here we are.

And honestly...it's not awful. He really does seem like a good dude. And if I'm in a *really* good mood—like, a perfect steak with great bourbon after a blow job from Maggie kind of mood—I can admit that I enjoy their FaceTime calls.

"Without further ado..."

I look back to the stage to see Marv and the French dude —I think Maggie called him Maxime—holding a giant pair of gold scissors. The American team has lined up behind Marv and the French team has lined up behind their boss. Camera flashes go off repeatedly and phones are being held up to record the moment. When they cut the ribbon, everyone—including and especially me—cheer and clap.

It's obvious who the Americans are.

God, we must be obnoxious.

I know the ribbon was cut because I heard the sound of metal scraping against itself and then joined in the clapping when everyone else started, but I'm not watching it.

My eyes are on Maggie.

She's wearing a gorgeous green silk blouse with cropped pants and (really hot) heels. As per usual, she looks flawless, but the most important part is that she's smiling. And it's a genuine smile—the kind she only has when she's really, truly elated.

I'm so fucking proud of her. She worked her ass off to get to where she is, and now she can say she's contributed to a building in *Paris*. I'm so proud my eyes are stinging as she hugs her American colleagues and kisses the cheeks of her French counterparts.

The French dude speaks into the microphone. I don't understand a word of it, but I know what happens next, so I assume he's inviting us inside. Maggie finds me in the crowd and motions me forward. I make my way through the throng of people to the love of my life.

When I finally get to her, she leaps up and wraps her arms around my neck.

"I'm so proud of you, Mags," I murmur.

She squeezes me tighter and then slides back down my body to land on those precarious stilettos she can somehow walk in.

"Come on...I want to show you the inside."

She takes hold of my hand and guides me forward.

There was a time in my life where I felt like we were stagnant if we didn't get married—that we weren't moving forward...toward anything at all.

That was years ago, and I know better now.

Maggie is the person who keeps me moving forward—she always has been. We're just not moving toward the things other people might be moving toward.

Julien and Chloé will get married, and that's great for them.

But me and Maggie? We're good just the way we are.

I know she's mine. She knows I'm hers.

We wake up together each day and fall asleep with limbs entwined each night.

We make all our big decisions together.

Our goals are shared.

My family is hers. Hers is mine.

We're fully committed to each other.

We're a team. The best one I've ever been a part of.

Margaret Helen Rafferty is the best thing that's ever happened to me—hands down. It's not even a contest.

(Though, if it were a contest, Maggie would throw her hat in the ring and come out victorious. She hates losing. She's extremely stubborn.)

I follow her into the building and over to a plaque on the wall that lists the architects. Right there at the bottom, Maggie's name is clear as day. I run a finger along the letters and smile so big my face hurts. She stares at it like she can't believe what she's seeing until someone calls her name. And then she's interlacing her fingers with mine and leading me farther into the lobby.

I'm not sure where we're going or who we're going to talk to. It doesn't really matter. I'd follow Maggie anywhere—

into this building she helped create, into a future we build together, even into the burning pits of hell.

Because I know that no matter what happens, no matter what we encounter along the way, she'll keep me moving forward.

BONUS CONTENT

Thank you so much for reading! In the immortal words of Ted Lasso: I appreciate you.

If you enjoyed *Meet Me Again One Day*, please consider leaving a review. As a newer author, reviews can go a long way in helping people find my book.

Looking for more of Maggie and Ethan? Using your smartphone's camera, scan the QR code below to download the epilogue and see what they're up to a couple of years down the line.

ACKNOWLEDGMENTS

This book is very personal to me on several levels. Maggie isn't your typical romance novel heroine. She doesn't want to get married but still wants children. She's fiercely independent and wants to live life on her own terms. She doesn't want to give up her autonomy. She just wants a teammate.

I know women like Maggie. Shit, I've *been* Maggie. I know more women like her exist. I've been so nervous to tell her story, but I also know how important representation is. Her choices may not be your choices, but that's the whole point, isn't it? That we have a choice.

I wrote the majority of this book in the last three months of 2023 when I was struggling for multiple different reasons and the imposter syndrome was very, very real. I stalled out about one-quarter of the way through the book and had no idea how to continue. I joined a writing challenge through The Book Incubator that set ambitious daily word count goals just to hold myself accountable.

In the middle of that challenge, I was scrolling through TikTok and found a group of writers who were doing writing sprints. They were essentially body doubling—working together, though not in the same place. I started joining them because it held me accountable and I found that I wrote more words when I did so. I often joke that we get on a TikTok LIVE and then ignore each other for thirty minutes at a time.

I'm not exaggerating when I say that those Distracted

Inklings—that rag-tag band of misfits—they changed my life. This book would not exist in its current form without them and it would certainly not be out in the world right now. I love you all—Roxie, Rebekah, Amber T, Amber P, Nicole, Katherine, and the non-writing members Kim, Rochelle, and Mollie.

Special thanks to Rae for alpha reading this book and offering suggestions on how to improve the story. And generally for just being the most supportive human.

To S.L. Prater, who promised me I could write another book. Even when I was completely convinced I'd never be able to finish this one, or any other. You were right. I did it.

My undying gratitude goes to Rebekah and Roxie, who beta read this book when my anxicty level was at one thousand percent and provided valuable insight. Thank you also for not hating this book and promising me that everything would be okay.

Additional thanks to Amber T for assisting with last-minute image requests and cover adjustments, and Rebekah for deciding that "we could do better" with our chapter images. Fortunately, no authors were slapped in the making of this book.

This book would not be possible without the assistance of my French authenticity readers, Laurent and Laura. Thank you both so much for your insight into French culture and dirty talk. I'll never be able to look you in the eye again.

Thank you also to my architecture authenticity readers, Jim and Bonnie. You were extraordinarily helpful for me during this process and I'll be forever grateful for your corrections and confirmations.

Thank you to Aliyah at Forever Star Cover Designs for

coming up with this knockout for me. I'm thoroughly obsessed!

And finally, thank *you*, dear reader. Thank you for being here and reading Maggie and Ethan's story. Thank you for supporting this dream of mine. I wouldn't be here without you.

ABOUT THE AUTHOR

Veronica Wynne is a writer managing her anxiety one romance novel at a time.

She enjoys writing about strong heroines because she believes with her whole chest that women are capable of absolutely anything and that any hero worth his salt will love them for being strong.

When she's not writing, she's reading, knitting, thinking about writing, forgetting to water her plants, and talking about kissing books with her bestie on The Chick Lit Book Club Podcast. She lives in northern Ohio with her husband, highly energetic child, and rescue dog who is probably digging flower bulbs out of the garden at this very moment.

Find more at www.veronicawynne.com.

facebook.com/veronicawynneauthor

instagram.com/veronicaiswriting

tiktok.com/@veronicaiswriting

threads.net/@veronicaiswriting

ALSO BY VERONICA WYNNE

Meet Me at Home

Meet Me Book 3 (Coming 2025)

www.ingramcontent.com/pod-product-compliance
Lightning Source LLC
Chambersburg PA
CBHW060607300726
48975CB00005B/1479